The Making of Ha

Chris Pears

THE MAKING OF HARRY MANNING

First edition. May 12, 2021.

Written by Chris Pearsall.

Prologue

Friday, 17 June 2016

Maggie's hair tickles my forehead as I kiss her cheek. 'Give me a shout when it's tea break,' I say, rolling my neck and stretching my shoulders, preparing for battle. I only make it to the kitchen door before she fires a warning shot.

'H!'

I stop and turn. Her head is still in the paperwork for the house sale.

Without looking up, she taps the terracotta pig with her pen. 'Be brutal up there.'

I assess my position and consider the options, deciding on a tactical withdrawal. I raise my fist.

'Brutal,' I confirm to the top of her head.

The sound of Radio 2 fades as I head upstairs, pausing on the landing. Emily's door is open. She's still fast asleep, training for student life. Teddy Pickering looks at me from a chair in the corner of her room, a piece of skimpy underwear on his lap.

'Typical,' Pickering tuts.

'You're going to enjoy it at Cambridge,' I tell him.

Pickering looks down at the thong on his lap. 'Can't I come sailing with you two instead?'

'That decision is way above my pay grade, and you know it.'

'They might do things to me,' he says, desperation in his voice. 'I thought you were . . . uncouth . . . but . . .' He looks back at the thong.

1

'Thanks.'

'Come on, H. I don't take up much room.'

'I'll mention it to the boss when she's in a good mood.'

His eyes widen. 'I can't wait that long!' he says, immediately realising his error.

I glance down the stairs. 'Lucky for you, she didn't hear that.'

'I did . . .' Maggie says, just loud enough for me to hear.

'Looks like it's every man, and bear, for himself,' I tell Pickering.

'No change there then, eh?'

Rex is stretched out on the landing. He lifts his head from his paws and looks around to see who I'm talking to. He glances into Em's room and cocks his head.

The Alsatian yawns as I scratch him behind his ear.

He's easily the best dog I ever worked with. I'm glad we retired together.

'Take care of her, won't you?' I ask Pickering.

'Like I did you?'

I nod and we share a moment.

Rex licks his chops and settles his head back on his paws, his eyes still on me.

I step on the loft ladder and climb. The creaking of the steps competes with the noise from my knees: a lifetime of action has taken its toll. Turning away from the bare light bulb, I make my way towards the pile of boxes. My shadow throws crazy shapes around the loft as I move forwards. Squeezing past the water tank, I bang my head on the rafters. I reach up to rub the lump already forming, putting my hand through a spider's web.

I shudder. 'Bloody spiders.'

I can already taste the dust that I've disturbed and regret not bringing a mug of tea with me. I kneel on the chipboard floor. Downsizing seemed such a good idea six months ago.

The next box to be sorted has 'Produce of Kent' stencilled on the side, which dates it to when I was around ten. Grandad, in a moment of typical seventies anti-PC logic, decided that the way to cheer Dad up was to start mass-producing a home-made depressant, so we made our own beer. Dad came home one day with a recipe from a 'hippy' he worked with and asked Gran if she had any nutmeg, which he'd been told would make the brew hallucinogenic. Thankfully, Gran lied and said she hadn't got any on account of the fact it wasn't Christmas. Grandad always insisted 'we do things properly', so he'd bought all the ingredients separately, not the prepacked 'rubbish' everyone else was brewing. It made no difference; the project came to an end the following year.

I look at all the remaining boxes and think of my promise. I was trying to be brutal but dithered over the daftest items. Things came to a head yesterday with the 'terracotta pig incident'. Before Maggie and me had Emily and Joe, we'd taken a year off and sailed our first boat to the Med. In Portugal, we'd had a grand night out at a restaurant, where each table had a small terracotta pig as its centrepiece. The pig's back was cut away, creating a small grill, where a tiny charcoal fire glowed in its belly. We spent the evening cooking sausage and meat that came with each round of drinks. It was a great idea. A few days later, we found the pig-grills for sale in a local market and bought one.

When I put the pig grill on the 'must keep' pile, Maggie had reacted badly. She'd pointed out that we'd never used it. I reminded her what a good idea the pig-grill was. She reminded me that 'That was thirty bloody years ago, Harry!' We'd agreed to disagree, which meant that the pig-grill was going to Oxfam, where it would fool some other poor sod into thinking it was a good idea and continue its life of useless admiration.

Maggie's profanities are still ringing in my ears. The box feels light as I give it an experimental shake, almost like it's empty. I think of how to explain to Maggie why we've been moving empty boxes from posting to posting for thirty years. I'll tackle that problem when I have to, by not mentioning it.

At the mere threat of being cut, the tape sealing the box disintegrates. I open it and a cloud of dust rises into my face, making me sneeze. It's full of straw. When I was a young, the team on the kids' TV programme *Blue Peter* had had a tortoise. Each year, they'd pack it away in a box full of straw for winter hibernation.

'Oh, Christ,' I croak.

They always made holes in the box for ventilation while the tortoise crawled around the TV studio. I checked my box for ventilation holes.

None.

What would a forty-year-old tortoise corpse be like? Did the poor creature suffer as it tried to escape its cardboard prison, its nails breaking off in its futile effort to claw its way to freedom? It's like a scene from that Vincent Price horror film I can't remember the name of.

I check the lid for evidence of an attempted escape.

Nothing.

The relief at the lack of tortoise nails embedded in the lid is replaced by a depressing thought: I'm old enough to have packed a box with straw once . . . I sweep this thought away as I remember I never *owned* a tortoise. How could I have forgotten I never owned a tortoise? On balance, I feel this is still a better outcome than being the owner of a mummified tortoise corpse with matching cardboard coffin.

I push aside what I now realise isn't straw but dried hops used in brewing and the first thing I see is red, white and blue circles on a camouflaged wing. I pick up the plastic aeroplane and turn it over to examine the duck-egg blue underside. The wheels are retracted – it's airborne. I rummage deeper, looking for its nemesis, and there it is, the Messerschmitt Bf 109.

THE MESSERSCHMITT TEARS past me on the starboard side and climbs.

The dog fight begins.

The joystick quivers as I apply full throttle and take the Spitfire into a vertical climb through the clear blue sky, rotating as I gain altitude to get an overview of the battle – the Battle of Britain.

'Watch out, Red Leader, he's coming out of the sun,' the radio crackles in my ear.

I bank to the left and dive. The Spitfire's superior power and handling give me the edge. I loop round and head straight at the enemy, releasing cannon fire across the cockpit and starboard wing, shredding both the pilot and the controls. The 109 is dead in the air, smoke and flames trailing behind it as I watch it spiralling down into the English Channel.

'That's the end of Jerry. Let's head back, boys. Last one home buys the Scotch,' I tell the lads.

'Roger that, Red Leader.'

Looking out of the cockpit, I can see children playing in the fields, squinting up as we fly low over the white cliffs of Dover to our base at Biggin Hill.

PRODUCE OF KENT, INDEED.

More! I need more . . .

Further down, I find the shadow of an aircraft, a Lancaster. The matt black and dark camouflage tells me it's a night bomber. I hum

The Dam Busters theme tune. The Lancaster's undercarriage is down, coming in to land after another successful mission.

There's something else further down. I shift the straw, red paint, antifouling. I know what it is. Strange. Despite the significance, I have no recollection of packing it away. I lift it up and with one hand on the stern, one on the bow, I turn the ship to face me.

'She was a good-looking ship, wasn't she, Harry?'

Grandad's voice is soft, close behind me, and I can tell he's smiling. I wait a moment and realise I'm holding my breath. I don't doubt my sanity – it's not the first time I've heard his voice since . . . I breathe out.

'It's been a long time,' I remember. 'Why now?'

'It's just . . . you know . . . when you opened that box.'

I hold the battleship I'd built and built again.

'It's a battlecruiser,' he corrects me.

I look at HMS *Hood* and see it all at once – not just the ship, but my childhood.

Chapter 1

Monday, 17 March 1975

The first bullet passed through my jacket sleeve and the plate glass window of the hotel turned opaque as it fractured into a million pieces. Time slowed. I looked at my arm. A puff of vaporised fabric disappeared in a vortex as the bullet shattered the mirrored backdrop of the bar. The weight of Gran's disappointment at ruining my new suit glued me to the spot, the thought of her disapproval far scarier than any bullet. I tried to speak, but my mouth was dry, my tongue uncooperative.

The second bullet passed through the window and the glass fell in a neat pile on the marble floor. I followed its path through Grandad's shoulder, flinching as it ricocheted off the perfect varnished bar in a spray of splintered wood. That was going to take a lot of sanding out.

I looked at my damaged sleeve, the broken glass and ruined bar top. My heart sank as the familiar feeling of dread swept over me, cold and disabling. It ate at my stomach as I realised the task before me. This was going to take a lifetime to fix. But I knew it was a job I had to do.

A muzzle flash caught my eye and I crouched beside Grandad as the villains emptied their machine guns in our direction. Glass and alcohol showered down on us. I took the knife from my boot and cut the blood-soaked material away from Grandad's wound, gauging the damage.

'Careful, yeh clumsy bugger.'

I ignored him and continued to chop my way through his shirt. The bullet had gone in just under his collarbone, missing his shoulder joint

7

by a fraction. Blood pulsed out of the hole and dribbled down his front, coagulating in his grey chest hair.

'It's only a flesh wound,' I assured him.

'They're all bloody flesh wounds!' He glared at me. 'They're the worst kind.' His voice was a mixture of shock and sarcasm. 'The trouble with this particular flesh wound is that it's in my bloody flesh.'

His teeth ground as I packed a dressing into the hole to stem the bleeding. He tried to inspect the wound.

'How bad is it?' he asked.

'I've seen worse,' I told him as I wrapped the bandage around.

'Wh-where?' he grimaced as I tied it off.

'Er, on the telly. Don't you remember? In that John Wayne film where he was a—'

'This isn't the telly though, is it?'

'No, bu . . .'

We turned to stare at a young woman running across the hotel lobby towards us, her high heels clip-clopping on the polished tiles. Her short dress was made of kitchen foil or some other space-age material. I recognised her from the Grattan *catalogue.*

'Oh, Jack, Jack, are you okay?' She threw herself at Grandad and hugged him, her dress riding up her thighs.

He looked at me over her shoulder and winked as he stroked her long blonde hair.

'The doctor says I'll live, but I'm not sure he knows what he's doing. I'm lucky you're here, nurse,' he said, staring into her eyes like he were in a trance.

'Nurse!' I scoffed. 'Are you sure she knows what she's doing?'

'Oh, she definitely does, H,' he smiled. 'Now, why don't you bugger off and catch the baddies? There's a good lad.'

I didn't want to leave them alone, but he was right.

'Don't go anywhere. I'll be back,' I said.

The model snogged Grandad ferociously, her face buried in his beard. His hand emerged from somewhere inside her dress, waving me away. I looked on as his fingers walked across her shoulders and slipped down her back, fondling her backside. His thumbnail broke through the delicate material and ran up her spine, splitting the foil dress in two, exposing her perfect tanned skin.

Gathering my disapproval, I ran across the lobby, stopping to wait for the automatic doors to open instead of climbing through the shattered window. People in evening gowns and suits were strolling around the fountain, oblivious to the danger. I skidded to a stop on the gravel as I reached my car. Climbing into the driver's seat, I took a moment to admire the workmanship of the Aston Martin's interior. My smile turned to a frown when the passenger door opened and an arm appeared, holding a pistol. It was no surprise when Watson climbed in and stuck a gun into my ribs.

'Is there no trick you're not too dim to fall for, Manning?'

I tried to untangle his words. Of course there were some tricks I wasn't too dim . . . I ignored him and concentrated on not needing the loo.

He waved the tip of the pistol in my face. 'Drive.'

The Aston lurched forwards. Gravel flew into the air and landed in the fountain as we sped away.

'You know that's going to block up the water pump, don't you?' I told him.

'Don't concern yourself with the pump, Manning. What you need to worry about is the gun in your side.' He jabbed the pistol to emphasise his point. 'And what I'm going to do to you when we get to my secret headquarters.'

'Where are we going, damn you?' I snarled.

'To my secret headquarters, like I just said, you moron.'

I glanced at the gun. A Luger – bloody typical. The Luger was the pistol of choice for the evil and demented.

'Don't call me a mor . . . Ouch!'

He pushed the barrel into my side again.

As we drove in silence, I formulated a plan. We were approaching his base. The castle was lit against a black sky. Guards stood around the entrance. It was time to make a move.

'I don't know what your game is, Watson, but your plan will never work.'

'How do you know? You've not asked what my plan is. How do you know it won't work?'

'People like you never win, Watson.'

'Are you sure?' he asked. His cold blue eyes showed no emotion.

'Er . . . yes . . . very sure.'

A smirk blossomed into a grin on his ugly face.

'It's just that when I look around the world, it seems to me that evil is thriving. You might say it's a Boom! industry.'

I flinched and my foot slipped off the accelerator pedal. I took a fresh approach.

'You shot my grandad, you coward.'

'No,' he yawned. 'I paid somebody else to shoot him, so I could get you on your own and do this . . .'

I yelped as the pistol connected with the already tenderised patch of rib.

'You'd better stop that or else.'

'Or else what?'

My thumb flicked the top of the gear lever and I grinned.

'I've just done it three times,' he continued, 'and you've done nothi—'

I turned away from the explosion as the ejector seat shot most of him out through the roof. Something splashed on my face. Watson's hand still held the gun as his severed arm fell into the footwell. I dropped a gear and hit the accelerator, flicking switches on the central console as I sped towards the guards. The headlights dropped to reveal the machine guns and I pulled hard on the handbrake. Tyres squealed and guns roared into life, leaving an arc of destruction as the car spun round. Sparks burst in my mirrors as the guards' shots ricocheted off the bulletproof shield.

As I accelerated away from the castle, headlights appeared in my mirrors – two cars were following. One must have had some kind of supercharger, because he was soon alongside. I looked at my options within the special features of the car's console.

'That'll do.' I pressed the button.

A faint whirring sound came from the wheels, followed by a satisfying clunk as the devices locked in place. I pulled hard on the wheel and sent the Aston into the side of Watson's henchmen. The driver lost control as their tyres shredded. A fireball lit up the road as their car smashed into a refuse lorry.

'More rubbish off the street.'

The last car in pursuit was catching up with me. Not to worry. I still had a few tricks up my sleeve.

I tapped on the console once more. Smoke and oil shot out of the exhaust pipe and moments later, their car emerged from the cloud, flying off the cliff. I shifted into top gear and raced back to Grandad.

As I pulled up outside the hotel, I noticed its similarity to my school; although it definitely was a hotel, because my school didn't have a bar. Grandad was perched on a stool having a drink with my new sexy stepgrandma.

I adjusted my trousers. I still needed to find the loo – I was bursting.

I scanned the signs in the lobby. What kind of hotel doesn't have toilets? I looked for someone to complain to, but there wasn't anyone at the reception desk. I went to the bar and sat next to Grandad.

'All done, Harry?'

I nodded.

'Is Watson dead?' he asked.

'Well,' I said, putting the severed arm on the bar. 'I can't say for certain, but he's definitely armless.'

Our chuckles reflected off the glass shelving. Grandad gestured to the barman and ordered me a drink.

'How do like your tea, Mr Manning?' he asked.

'Milk and four sugars.'

'Shaken or stirred?'

Grandad joined in the punchline.

'Don't stir it; he doesn't like it sweet.'

I folded my arms on the bar and rested my head, suddenly exhausted. The barman placed the tea in front of me. The image of the Aston Martin DB5 was reflected on the side of the mug, its doors open, machine guns ready.

'Don't go to sleep, Harry.'

I needed the loo, now!

'Harry, don't go back to sleep.'

I FELT A WET PATCH grow near my hip.

'Harry,' Gran shouted through the door, 'don't go back to sleep, you're going to be late for school.'

The red leather and silver paintwork of the DB5 were reflected in the white glaze of the mug on my bedside table. The plastic figure of James Bond looked straight ahead. I tried to hang on to the image of the foil-wrapped beauty, but the memory was lost. It left me with a desperate urge for the loo, and the barrel of Watson's gun stuck in my side.

'Okay,' I croaked.

I viewed the world through teenage eyes for the first time, held my breath and waited. They'd made such a big deal of it that I was sure when it happened, something spectacular would occur. But my room looked like it had the night before. Dust still clung to the cotton holding the model planes overhead, my dressing gown hung behind the door, ships and tanks decorated every available surface. The alarm clock, a swish 'travel' type that folded into the case to become the stand, sat on my bedside table next to my toy cars. The *Grattan* catalogue was still on the floor, open at the lingerie section. Alice Cooper's mad stare leered at me from the poster as he screamed into his microphone, a severed doll's head dripping with blood held up in triumph. Teddy Pickering sat with his head tilted to one side.

Could a teenager be friends with a teddy?

I looked at the ladies in their lingerie.

Maybe being a teenager *was* going to be different, after all. Teddy Pickering's brown eyes judged me. Gran's footsteps faded as I reached under the covers and pulled out the bright red water pistol, its filler cap loose, the contents lost. The red Luger dangled in my hand as I moved around the bed, spinning at the last moment to face the mirror, the gun held in a double-handed grip. The one-armed figure raised his pistol. I fired until the magazine was empty. Watson's body slumped to the floor. I lifted the gun and blew the smoke clear of the barrel.

'The name's Manning, Harry Manning.'

I threw my damp pyjama bottoms over Pickering's head and got dressed; he didn't need to see everything.

'I'll talk to you later,' I told him as I left.

'Can't wait,' was his muffled reply.

I went downstairs to the bathroom, pausing on the halfway landing at the first turn of the twisting staircase to look out of the window. The gentle hum of the milk float's electric motor was interspersed with the rattle of bottles as it made its frequent stops down the street.

I splashed some water on my face and wetted down the more eccentric sections of my long hair. It was a constant battle with Gran to be allowed to grow it longer, but at least it was one I was winning. They were so infrequent, even minor victories had to be relished. I crossed the hall to the kitchen and pushed back the sliding door.

Gran was at the stove. I looked around. 'Where's Grandad?'

She turned the heat off and poured the contents of the saucepan into a mug.

'He's having a lie-in, love.'

I looked at her, bemused. Grandad never had lie-ins.

'He's not feeling so good,' she added.

That was even stranger. He was never poorly – neither of them was. Some families on the estate lived at the doctors, but we were never ill. Although, we did have a habit of dying young, which I suppose balanced things out. Both Gran and Grandad were in their seventies, so it shouldn't be a surprise that they might suffer the odd illness.

I pushed the thought of death aside and scanned the room for presents. There were two small, soft packages on the kitchen table, one each from our two neighbours, Aunty Joyce and Aunty Silvia. They'd credited the husbands on the gift cards, but I knew from bitter experience that they wouldn't have had anything to do with the purchase, more's the pity. Ron, Sylvia's husband, had parachuted into France and then fought his way across Europe in the war. Les, Joyce's husband, had been crushed in a mining accident and had lost both of his legs. Given a chance, they might have had a better idea of what a thirteen-year-old boy would want.

I gave the packages an experimental prod. Bloody typical – it was underwear or socks again.

The worst example of unwanted present-giving was from Aunty Joyce. A few of Christmases ago she'd bought me a chocolate snowman. It sat and watched me open my other parcels, teasing me. Breakfast wasn't being provided as promptly as my stomach required, and it was too early to go across to Gran and Grandad's, so I'd felt justified in making a start on the chocolate offering.

I'd weighed him in my hand. Great. It was solid. Not the thin shell I'd been expecting. I'd started gnawing at its head while opening the next present. Something wasn't right, but it took too long to register. The snowman wasn't chocolate. It was soap! Soap! For a boy! What kind of present was that? I'd spat out the frothy mess into the wrapping paper and washed my mouth out with the most flavoursome drink I could find – milk.

It was a long time before I could eat white chocolate with any confidence. When would these people learn? We don't want things like that and never have.

I looked at the two presents again. I'd open them later. I switched my attention to the cards, giving each a gentle shake as I opened them; none of them contained any money. I wondered what Mark and Keith would have waiting for me at school. It couldn't be any worse. Or could it?

Gran handed me a cup of milky coffee. 'Happy birthday, Harry.'

At the table, Tony the Tiger watched me from the side of the box as I munched my way through a bowl of Frosties. Gran and I had widely differing views on which cereal we should buy. My choice was the one that included the best toy. Gran would make her purchase based on 'nutritional value' – a fancy *Tomorrow's World* idea that would never catch on, at least not until Mr Kellogg stopped coating corn in increasingly thick layers of sugar and giving away helicopters.

'Don't forget to come home for your lunch,' she reminded me.

Within fifteen minutes of waking, I was on my way to school. My mind was full of anticipation at what the new teenage world offered me. I'd kept the fact that it was my birthday a secret from all but my closest friends. Although I could see the benefit of girls knowing, birthday kisses a tantalising possibility, it was essential that Watson and his cronies didn't get to know. I shivered at the thought. The best

I could hope for was my homework being flushed down the bog. The worst was . . . well, best not to think about that.

The tide of kids increased and tributaries became streams, emptying into the torrent that swept past the shops and across the main road. The lollypop lady was doing her best to control the deluge. Reaching the point of no return, I joined Mark and Keith sat on the wall by the main gates, broad grins on their faces. Mark jumped down and reached into his bag.

'I've got something for you, Harry.'

Oh no! Do *not* give me a card here . . . I looked around in panic to see who was watching.

'This is for you.' He pulled out his hand.

His V-sign was a welcome insult.

'I got you some chocolate,' said Keith, 'but I ate it on the way.'

'That's why you're a fat git,' I told him.

'Sod off,' he said, climbing down, straining to slow his descent.

'How'd you get up there, anyway?' I looked around. 'I can't see a crane.'

Keith held the lapels of his blazer and puffed out his chest. 'I refer my honourable friend to my previous answer.'

'He's been watching the news again,' said Mark. 'I've told him no good will come of it, but he will insist on trying to educate himself.'

We pushed and shoved each other as we made our way down the path. At least someone was interested in his education. I'd not seen any evidence that the teachers in the ugly building ahead of us were. Keith acted as a shield as Mark slipped a chocolate bar into my pocket.

'Happy birthday,' he whispered.

Despite their efforts at secrecy, I still glanced around.

'Yeah, happy birthday, yeh ugly bugger,' Keith added.

Miss Cutts called the register under my lustful gaze. Her skirt rode up over her knees.

'Do you know why I've given you a detention, Harry?'
My hand slid up her leg, under the tartan fabric.
'Harry Manning? Harry Manning!'

Dragged back to reality, I had to accept that I was, in fact, 'Here, miss.'

I made my way to history – a subject I hated almost as much as I hated every other. As always, I was in the bottom stream. Mark and Keith both found the work easier, so most of the time we were in separate classes, only meeting up at break time. It was my misfortune that Watson was also thick, so I spent much of my time, literally, within striking distance of him. I weaved my way down the crowded corridor, wondering why everybody was always going the other way.

A group of girls was heading towards me, Jane Fellowes among them. She was one of the few girls I could talk to without appearing like an idiot. As we got closer, she looked straight at me, her eyes wide. Was she looking at me? Her gaze intensified. She was definitely looking at me now.

I composed myself, not wanting to mess it up. I smiled, but her smile faded and she winced. Feeling stupid for paying her attention, I stepped to the side, my leg collapsing as I received a kick to the back of my thigh. I hit the floor in a crumpled heap. Annoyed at my mates for being so heavy-handed – Keith could be such a clumsy bugger – I got to one knee, ready to give him a bollocking, just as Watson barged into me, knocking me into the radiator.

Watson was laughing, no doubt telling the other lads the reason for singling me out. They were all the same, misfits like him, just as likely to fight each other as anyone else. They swaggered on down the corridor as I tried to get up, but my dead leg wouldn't let me. I put my hand on the radiator for support. The heat built and I focused my mind on the hot metal, feeling stupid enough to deserve the pain it brought. When I couldn't bear it any longer, I let go and opened my eyes. Jane was next to me.

'I tried to warn you,' she said.

'Thanks.' I put some weight on my leg; it was already improving.

'Do you want to put your arm around me and I'll take you to see the nurse?'

Like an idiot, I declined the offer. She leaned close to me, her cheek brushing against mine. I could feel her breath on my ear.

'Happy birthday, Harry.'

My face glowed with embarrassment and regret as I mumbled more thanks and hobbled off to find additional misery in the three-field crop rotation system.

At last, it was lunchtime. Keen to escape as quickly as possible, as soon as I'd crossed the main road, I ran. Away from the teachers and the bullies. I ran towards presents, freedom and birthday cake. My pace increased the nearer to home I got. The smell of baking wafted down the drive, pulling me home. I was the Starship Enterprise caught in a tractor beam, powerless to resist. I slowed, out of breath, panting as I approached the back door.

'Yay! I'm a teenager!' I yelled.

My enthusiasm evaporated as I looked into the crowded kitchen. The visitors weren't here to see me.

'Shush.' Ron from next door raised his finger to his lips. 'Your grandad's not well.'

I looked at Gran for confirmation.

'He's got a migraine,' she said, although without the certainty I expected from her; she was always in command of the house and the kitchen was her HQ.

Aunty Joyce was there, too.

'Let me know if you need any help, Lily,' she said, retreating.

'Thanks, Joyce. I will, love.'

I thought back to my parents' funerals. Joyce had been a constant visitor, helping Gran with washing and the shopping. They'd been neighbours since the estate had been built.

She squeezed past me, almost whispering as an afterthought, 'Happy birthday, Harry.'

'I'll get out yer way,' Ron said, his usual gruff manner softening just a fraction as he left through the back door, leaving a void I couldn't fill.

Gran put a cheese sandwich on the table. 'Sorry, love, I've not . . .' Her voice trailed off.

My enthusiasm for presents had disappeared, along with my appetite.

'It's okay, Gran.'

'I'm baking you a cake,' she said.

The smell of warm chocolate had already registered in my subconscious.

'I'll have some later with Grandad.'

I didn't need to include Gran, because although she baked the best cakes in the world, she never ate any herself. Her tiny figure reflected her tiny appetite. In times of stress, she stopped eating altogether. I took after her. Grandad went the other way, eating his way through piles of biscuits and cakes whenever he was doing a job in the workshop. Stress didn't seem to play a part; it was only availability that slowed down his consumption. His Father Christmas belly now matched his white hair and beard.

I sat on the back step with my sandwich. Shielded from the breeze, the heat of the sun did little to lift my mood. The greenhouse at the bottom of the garden was alive with trays of seedlings. It wouldn't be long before Grandad needed help down at the allotment, preparing the ground for planting. The rose bushes were ringed by a generous dressing of horse muck, the prickly stems sharply backlit by the spring sunshine. The borders were full of, daffodils and crocuses, all readying themselves for a big show in a few weeks. I chewed at a corner of the bread, taking several gulps to get the dry morsel down, feeling every inch of its movement down my gullet.

Returning to the kitchen, I put the plate on the table, the sandwich hardly touched, and looked at the ceiling.

'He'll be up later,' Gran reassured. 'I'm doing a lamb shoulder for your tea.' She patted a slab of meat.

It was Grandad's favourite. He'd soon be out of bed when the whiff of that cooking made its way upstairs.

Thankful to be out in the fresh air, it was almost a relief to be going back to school. A couple of older lads from our estate walked the opposite way, two Jack Russells running beside them, air rifles over their shoulders. One of them cuddled a ferret. Its furry body wriggled through his grip as he swapped hands to create an infinite tunnel. As I drew close, one of them winked.

'What you got this aft', young 'un?'

'Double maths.'

'We've got double rabbiting,' his mate said, grinning at his own joke.

His rotten teeth looked like tombstones covered in moss. He held the ferret up as evidence. I smiled as we went our separate ways. How bad would things have to be before I had the guts to bunk off school? I thought of Gran's face as the school bobby brought me home. I knew I'd never do it.

The afternoon dragged as only double maths can.

When I got home, the kitchen was empty. The radio played to itself on the cupboard in the alcove beside the chimney breast.

'Grandad, I'm home!'

The house was never empty.

'Hello?' I said, expecting to get more response from my whisper.

My sandwich sat on the draining board, the sink still full of dirty cups.

I put my head round the door into the hall.

'Gran?'

No reply.

I'd just put my first foot on the stairs, when I heard the front door open. Gran looked flustered.

'What's up, Gran?'

'I've just been round to Joyce's. Your grandad's no better. I've phoned the doctor. He's on his way.'

Joyce and Les were one of the few families on the estate with a phone. My mind went back to a Sunday night in February three years earlier. As usual, Dad was out drinking at the British Legion, the working men's club up the street. Gran had been over to our house to check on me at about eight o'clock and I'd gone to bed around ten. Dad was out drinking a lot more since Mum had died. When she was alive, he'd just go out on a Friday night and a Sunday lunchtime on his own or with Grandad. On Saturday nights, the four of them would go out together and watch the entertainment at the Legion. But since Mum had gone, Dad was in the club every night he wasn't working. At least he'd still got a job. The coking plant had closed, but a mate of his had got him a job at another plant in Rotherham. It was that job that would be the death of him.

After Mum died, I slept in their bed with him. And that night, I remember waking when I heard him stumbling around, getting undressed. He huffed and cursed before flopping back on the pillow, snoring within seconds. I fell back to sleep. The next time I woke, he was sitting on the edge of the bed, swearing.

'What's the matter?' I asked but got no answer.

I sat up, trying to make out the shapes in the dark. The smell of stale beer and sweat hung around him.

'What's up, Dad?' I was nearly in tears.

'My bloody arm!' His voice was strained and angry.

I got up and switched on the light. He was sat on the bed clutching his left arm, rocking backwards and forwards, his pyjama top stuck to his skin with sweat.

'Dad, what's up?'

I wiped the snot and tears away with my sleeve. Then I sat next to him, repulsed by his cold, clammy skin. Something was seriously wrong.

'Let me fetch Grandad.'

'No.'

'Let me go to Aunty Joyce's, then.'

'There's no need.'

'I can ask her to phone the doctor.'

'No, I'll lose my job,' he said, gasping as another spasm shot through him.

'You won't. Why would you?'

'I've only just passed the medical. If they find out . . .' But another spasm cut him off. 'I could just chop the bloody thing off,' he screamed, making me jump.

Even at ten years old, I knew I had to do something. I didn't ask again. I ran from the room.

'I'm going to call the doctor.'

I flew down the stairs and put on my shoes. Feeling guilty at the relief of leaving him, I unlocked the door and ran across to Aunty Joyce's. Banging on the door and rattling the letter box, I peered through the slit, shouting at the top of my lungs into the hall.

'Aunty Joyce! Aunty Joyce!'

After what seemed an eternity, I heard a voice. Joyce's head was at the landing window. I waved and it opened.

'Who is it?' she asked, a hint of fear in her voice.

'It's Harry. Can you call the doctor?'

'Harry? What's up, love?'

'Can you ring the doctor? Dad's not well.'

The window closed and lights came on as she made her way to the front door. I fidgeted in anxious frustration as the bolts and locks rattled open. At last, the door opened. Joyce gripped the collar of her dressing gown, squinting into the dark.

'Come in, love,' she said, waving me past her like a traffic bobby.

I hesitated; I needed to tell Gran and Grandad.

'Can we just call the doctor, please.' I rushed the words, knowing I didn't have long to wait for more tears to follow.

'Come here, Harry, love.' She reached out, trying to bring me in under her motherly wing.

'I've got to tell Gran and Grandad,' I sobbed, turning away and running to the adjoining semi.

Banging on the door, I went through the same routine. Grandad went to see Dad with Joyce while I stayed with Gran. She opened the fire grate, throwing on a few pieces of coal to try to rekindle the ashes. I sat and watched the coal smoulder as we waited for the doctor to come. Gran stood at the door, looking into the street. The cold air crept past her, chilling the house.

After a while, I heard Gran speaking as someone approached. Grandad came into the kitchen and held her hand. I looked past them, expecting Dad to follow. But he didn't. I looked at Grandad and knew.

'He's dead, isn't he?'

Grandad said nothing. I could see words were beyond him. He just picked me up and squeezed the tears from me. My head whirled with fear and uncertainty until a single clear thought gripped me.

'They're not going to put me in a home, are they?'

'No.'

Grandad's voice was certain. I knew everything would be alright. He'd make sure it was, like he always did.

The doctor arrived much too late. After the funeral director had taken Dad away, I went back across to fetch my school uniform. It didn't feel like home. I was an intruder.

Sitting in his chair, I jumped up from the wet cushion. I realised immediately, this was where he'd died. He'd lost control of his bladder as the heart attack took him. I lifted the cushion, turned it over and sat down again. This house wasn't my home and hadn't been for a long time. When I left that night, I never went back.

Now, I worried the doctor would be too late to help Grandad.

'Is he still in bed?'

'Yeah,' Gran said, glancing upstairs.

'What's wrong with him?'

'I don't know, love. The headaches have got a lot worse and he keeps . . .' She sniffled into her hanky.

I bit my lip in frustration at my inability to help. But then, like the cavalry, Joyce arrived and swept Gran into the kitchen, whispering words of comfort. I fumbled around self-consciously as the two women embraced, Gran sobbing into Joyce's shoulder.

'Can I go up and see him?' I asked.

Gran hesitated. She looked at Joyce.

'He can pop up for five, can't he, Lily?' Joyce's eyes darted between us.

Gran nodded.

'Just come back down when the doctor arrives, Harry,' Joyce said.

The bright sunlight streaming through the landing window failed to ease the sense of doom as I put my foot on the first tread. The house seemed smaller than it ever had. The banister I'd climbed over and dangled from with Keith and Mark, paratroopers dropping into enemy territory, now seemed inadequate to entertain me as it once had.

Out on the street, a group of kids sped past on their bikes, heads ducked, the sound of lollipop sticks rattling on the spokes adding to their motorbike fantasy. The world looked normal.

I stood in the doorway. A thin sunbeam shone through a gap in the drawn curtains. Reluctant to switch on the light, I stood for a moment to let my eyes adjust to the dimness of the room. Muffled voices came from the kitchen, distorted murmurs of concern.

Grandad's outline emerged, propped high on a stack of pillows. His bushy white beard seemed bigger than usual, as if his face had shrunk. His wiry white hair, usually swept back with hair cream, was a chaotic mess, sticking out in all directions. As I approached, his eyes opened.

'Howdy, partner.' The words were thick and sluggish. 'Happy birthday.'

My eyes pricked as I used my smile to hold back the tears, fumbling with the corner of the bedspread. His hand enclosed mine. A swallow tattoo swooped between his thumb and forefinger, distorted by the wrinkled, dry skin. I traced my finger over the compass rose tattooed around his wrist where a watch should have been, as I'd done a thousand times before. Out of sight on his forearms were an anchor bound with chain and a tea clipper under full sail. On his upper left arm, a lighthouse was battered by waves, on the right, a ship's wheel was lashed by a rope to his bicep. Across his left shoulder was a banner with the name of a ship, HMS *Hood*.

'Are you going to be okay?' I asked.

'I'd better be, it's your birthday and we've got to get your present, haven't we?'

'It doesn't matter,' I lied.

He sniffed the air. 'Smells like Gran's made me a cake. If you're a good lad, I'll let you have a bit,' he winced, 'seeing as it's your birthday.' He let out a small groan.

Relieved to hear the muffled voice of Dr Crowther, I backed away, pulling my hand from his loose grip.

I did my best to force a smile.

The doctor paused as we crossed paths halfway up the stairs on the middle landing.

'You're growing up, aren't you, Harry?' he said, tousling my hair.

'I'm a teenager.'

'I know. It doesn't seem two minutes since you were born.'

Dr Crowther glanced up to Grandad's bedroom. 'Now, let me see what's wrong with Grandad, mmm?'

I looked up from the bottom step, the moment burned into my mind. The doctor's big overcoat hung on his thin shoulders, his trilby still on his head and his medical bag gripped in his right hand

Gran fussed around doing bits of nothing while Joyce took over her role and switched on the kettle. I watched TV, waiting for the verdict. Just as *Blue Peter* was starting, Dr Crowther came down. I followed him into the kitchen.

'I'm going to get him admitted to hospital, Lily. His blood pressure's low and there are other tests that we need to perform.'

'When are you going to take him in?' she asked.

'Oh, sorry.' He realised his error, glancing at Aunty Joyce. 'I'm going to call an ambulance immediately.'

Joyce gave Gran the hug I wished I could have before leading the doctor away so he could use their phone. I looked at Gran, unsure what to say.

'He's as tough as old boots, Harry. He'll be right as rain in no time.'

She didn't convince me, and I don't think she convinced herself.

Although I could hear Gran getting ready for bed later that evening, the house seemed empty without Grandad. I moved around my room, rearranging my models. I positioned the planes in different ways, my smile fading as my forehead furrowed, settling on the nose cones, which were all in line. The tanks were troublesome. I placed them with their bodies lined up, but the gun barrels were different lengths and I was annoyed I couldn't make them look neater.

'It doesn't matter,' Pickering said quietly.

I knew that, but I still fretted that I hadn't got it right.

Chapter 2

Tuesday, 18 March 1975

The tide had turned and the secondary modern schooling system spewed us out. The crowds thinned and I rounded the final corner alone. To get all the misery out of the way, as soon as I got in, I opened some of what I knew would be unwanted presents. It was as I'd suspected: underwear, gloves, socks and slippers. Despite the certainty I'd felt about the contents, I was still disappointed, but then I noticed a large package on the table that I couldn't fathom out. It was from Gran and Grandad. I poked it.

Hmm, soft like the other rubbish. Perhaps it was another dressing gown . . .

I wasn't in the mood for any more nonsense and put it to one side. Grandad would be home soon. I'd open it then, so he'd be able to share the burden of my dissatisfaction.

I turned my mind to more pressing matters. If my joke was going to work, I needed to get the whole thing just right.

'Did you get everything, Gran?'

'It's all in here.' She patted her shopping basket and shook her head. 'He's made you as daft as he is.'

'Dafter,' I claimed, standing up straight and sticking out my chest as if ready to receive a medal.

She looked at me with pity. 'If only it were a competition, Harry.'

My shoulders slumped. She didn't understand at all. 'But it *is*, Grandma.' That's exactly what it was.

The evening was dark and cold. Rain threatened. We huddled in the concrete bus shelter, avoiding the puddle in the corner. I looked at it and remembered Grandad's comments: 'Doesn't the council teach them how to use a spirit level?' I tutted on his behalf and stuck my head round the corner when I heard an engine.

'It's here, Gran.'

We got on the double-decker and sat downstairs. My nose wrinkled at the smell of cigarettes and damp dogs. Wiping the condensation on the inside of the window turned the outside world into an oil painting as the grubby detail of life disappeared in a blur of coloured light.

The stink of damp dog persisted, despite there not being any dogs on board. Were dogs even allowed on buses? I looked around for a sign but couldn't see one. And when precisely did a damp dog become a wet dog? Who decided these things? There was probably a mathematical formula to calculate how long it would take to dry a dog. There were many things to consider: length of fur, size of dog, air temperature. And how would one stop it from shaking the excess water off before the experiment started? That would be a problem. It wasn't as simple as I first thought; it could take ages to sort everything out. I bet I'd even get invited on the telly to talk about the results. Most likely, John Craven's *Newsround*.

My plan faltered when I realised the equations would involve algebra, which was something I couldn't even spell, let alone do. I'd have to take a more casual, less scientific approach and settle for an appearance on *Magpie*.

Water puddled at the bottom of the window where we were sat. The rubber seal was mouldy and rotting, perfect for picking. I wasn't the first; there were nail marks all along the bottom. More than likely it was other kids, but this kind of thing could be irresistible, even to grown men. It didn't occur to me that a lady might have done it – as I was sure women's lib wasn't that advanced in Yorkshire. I remembered how Dad used to fight with me about who would get the honour of picking the dead skin off my feet. I had the advantage that they were my feet. But he pointed out that he had a better angle of attack. We usually shared.

The bus was filling as we got closer to town. The conductress was only young, maybe still a teenager. It seemed a pleasant way to earn a living. I watched her as she strode with confidence up and down the bus; her ability not to fall over was impressive. She was pretty, and I wondered what the rules were about Yorkshire Traction staff and passengers going out together.

LIKE ONE OF THOSE SMOOTH guys off the telly, I winked at her. Her eyebrows flicked towards the ceiling. Message received and understood.

I followed her up the steps, her backside swinging only inches from my face. Reaching out, I touched the taught material and felt her muscles work as she climbed to the top deck. Turning, she smiled and took my hand from her bum before leading me to the back seats.

'This is where the bad boys sit, Harry,' she said as we slid along the red vinyl seat.

Out of sight of the other passengers, we kissed. My fingers pulled at the leather straps holding the ticket machine to her body. I reached around her back to find the buckles. The rough material of her tunic was like a school blazer, the fluffy kind that the poor kids had to wear. I yanked it up, but the money pouch's straps held it down. She fumbled with me, trying to free herself from the restrictions. I pulled hard at her jacket, but the straps held firm. We continued to snog as the bus came to a stop.

Stomping feet of authority made their way towards us . . . The ticket inspector had spoiled our first date. I adjusted my trousers as she straightened her uniform and scurried back to work.

He rocked on his heels and looked down at me past his Hitler moustache.

'You're a bit too young for her, aren't you?'

'We're both teenagers,' I said, my voice cracking under the interrogation.

I thought about repeating myself in a gruff voice.

The inspector sniffed the air, narrowed his eyes and looked at me. 'Did you bring a dog on the bus, lad?'

'ARE THEY ALLOWED?' I said.

'What did you say, love?'

'Nothing, Gran.' I shrank into my seat while still trying to glimpse the bus conductress.

The town centre was quiet, but as we walked past the town hall, the few people around drew together, all heading for the same place – the main entrance of the hospital. We bumbled around along endless corridors until we found ward twelve. The staff nurse told us to wait; nobody was of a mind to argue with the formidable figure as she marched up and down, issuing orders to terrified juniors.

We felt ridiculously overdressed in the stifling heat. People were stripping off, having difficulty holding on to their discarded layers as well as the flowers and gifts for their loved ones as they mopped their sweaty brows. I breathed in the distinct aroma of hospitals. Like the universal smell of old people, it was immediately recognisable but difficult to pin down. It had a base of antiseptic, a hint of boiled cabbage, a dash of toilet juice and a pinch of something unidentifiably dreadful. Whatever it was, it made me feel uneasy.

The ward sister nodded to two nurses. It was time.

The doors opened and the crowd poured in. It was just like a scene from a comedy film. I expected to see a junior doctor come flying towards us, dragged along by an industrial floor polisher. It was a long ward and it was surprising how similar that men wearing pyjamas looked. Fortunately, they didn't all have bushy white beards, so Grandad was easy to spot.

We found him at the far end of the ward, sat up straight, covers folded down, hands together in his lap. He was smiling and looked a lot better than he had yesterday, but I suppose that's the point of being in hospital. Gran put her bag down, took her coat off, threw it on the chair back and gave Grandad a hug. I stood back as they whispered greetings at each other. Grandad's hands slid from her back to her arms. Then he squeezed her hands before finally releasing her from his grip.

'Crikey, Jack, it's boiling in here,' she said, taking off her cardigan and unwinding her scarf.

'It's not when you're sat in your jim-jams, Lily.'

She sat heavily in the only chair available and pulled at the collar of her dress, blowing air from the corner of her mouth onto her face. I'd always found that odd – it generally made me feel hotter. She pulled a magazine from her bag and settled down, fanning herself. I looked around for another chair.

'Only one chair per patient, H. Come and sit up here.' Grandad patted the bed.

Holding the bag close to me so he couldn't peek, I asked, 'we've brought you something. Would you like to see?'

'Oh, I love surprises,' he said, rubbing his hands together and straightening his beard.

We'll see about that . . .

David Attenborough had given me some useful advice in a recent nature documentary, so I knew that wild animals, which could include grandads, were at their most dangerous when wounded. Proceeding with caution, I pulled out a small bunch of daffodils and handed them to him. His smile vanished.

He looked me straight in the eye. 'What are *they*?'

'Daffodils.' I loved pointing out the obvious, especially to Grandad.

'I can see they're daffodils, but what *are* they?' He said it slowly, like he were talking to an idiot.

'*They* are a present.' I matched his tone.

'It's spring, Jack,' said Gran.

She enjoyed spelling out the obvious, too; it was one of our family's favourite subjects.

Grandad looked at her. 'I know it's spring.' Then back to me. 'And I know they're daffodils. But what the hell have you got me those for?'

I moved my face closer to his, so there was no doubt who I was talking to, while my robotic voice laid out the facts. 'Well, we thought they might cheer you up.'

He leaned forwards. So we were nose to nose. 'Well, they're doing a bloody rubbish job so far!'

'Maybe,' said Gran, 'it'll turn out like one of them things you told him about. You know the ones.'

'What things?'

I loved to see Gran flummox him.

'One of them delayed reactions, silly.'

She was right, but there was a big question mark on Grandad's face.

'A *what*?'

'You'll see. An hour after we've gone, you'll be wetting yourself laughing.'

'Well, I hope you're right, Lily, because it sure doesn't look like I'm going to be laughing while you're here, that's for certain.'

She shook her head and turned back to her magazine.

'And don't set it about that I've been wetting myself, either,' Grandad added.

'Have you?' I asked.

'Of course not.' He looked around again and lowered his voice. 'It's not my bladder that's the problem.'

'What is it, then?'

'I've no idea. They're doing tests.' He sat back. 'They haven't told me the results yet. To be honest, I'm not sure they know what they're doing.'

This was both a surprise and a disappointment. There again, I'd never been in a hospital before; I'd only been to the doctors once with chickenpox, nearly interrupting our annual holiday to Cornwall. Fortunately, the spots cleared up and I didn't have to spend time in 'quarantine'. But for months after, every time Grandad saw me he asked in his best attempt at a pirate voice, 'Are the pox still on yeh, lad?' Anyway, the hospital was one of those places I'd hoped people actually did know what they were doing. But maybe the world was stranger than I'd thought and *Carry On Doctor* was a documentary. I looked in the bag.

His eyebrows lifted. 'Is there something else in there, lad?'

'Course there is. How daft do you think I am, Grandad?'

'I'd rather not say until after I've received all of my presents, if that's all the same to you.'

That sounded like an insult, but he said it in such a friendly way that it got past me before I could decipher the code. This was exactly the kind of cunning behaviour that Attenborough had warned me about.

'We've watched enough films together to know that you don't just bring flowers when you visit somebody in hospital.' With that, I reached in and pulled out a brown paper bag before handing it over.

Suspicious, he weighed it, taking a peep.

'Grapes?' he said, his sense of humour still absent.

I nodded. Everything was going to plan.

'Are they seedless?'

I shook my head. 'Sold out.'

'Yeh know the pips get stuck in my teeth, don't yeh?'

'Oh yeah,' I said. 'It's one of my favourite Lonnie Donegan songs.' I didn't even try to keep a straight face.

'Pleased with that one, are you?' He asked.

Nodding even more vigorously, I made myself dizzy. As my vision cleared, I was keen to explain my grape strategy.

'It's like what you were telling me; it's a distraction.'

He looked at me for further clarification; I think. I offered it anyway.

'It's like what you told me. When you hurt yourself and you rub it, it distracts you from the pain.' Although I was happy with the explanation, I could see Grandad wasn't. 'If you eat the grapes when you're in pain, the pips in your teeth will distract you.'

'But I'm not in pain.'

'But you might be.'

'I've come into hospital to stop the pain, not to start it.'

'But if it comes back, these will help.' I rustled the bag.

'So, let me get this clear. Your answer to me being in pain is to make me eat something that's going to hurt? Pain on top of more pain. Is that right?'

'Yeah. You told me that one pain cancels out the other.'

'When the bloody hell did I tell you that?' he said, louder than necessary.

'Shush,' said Gran.

'When did I bloody tell you that?' he whispered.

'And stop swearing,' she said without looking up from her magazine.

Grandad looked at her for a moment. I could see he was confused. No doubt he'd be wondering if he stopped swearing, was he allowed to start shouting again.

'When did I tell you that?' he said in a loud whisper – a sensible compromise, I thought.

'Er . . .' I was beginning to doubt what had until very recently seemed like perfect sense, then I remembered. 'It's like what you told me – two wrongs don't make a right.' That would help him to understand.

He tilted his head.

It hadn't.

'Same thing,' I offered.

'Oh,' he nodded, finally getting it. 'So two wrongs *don't* make a right, but two pains *do* make a *not* a pain. Is that it?'

I nodded, but with much less enthusiasm. This must be how the Gestapo got you to talk. I wouldn't crack under the pressure; he was only going to get my name, rank and serial number. Although he already knew my name, I wasn't sure of my rank and if I'd ever had one, I'd forgotten my serial number. I realised this was why soldiers had dog tags, so they didn't have to remember this stuff. What do dogs wear? People tags?

'Is there anything else in there?' Grandad nodded towards the bag, all signs of happiness having disappeared from his face.

I tried to look serious as I handed over a small bottle of Lucozade. It seemed like every patient had a bottle of the sickly, sweet fizzy drink on their bedside cabinet. The firm must be making a fortune. The yellow cellophane wrapper crunched under his grip.

'Oh, it just gets worse.' He slumped back on his pillow, rolling from side to side, moaning. 'Nurse, nurse, make it stop.'

Gran tutted at his amateur dramatics.

'It'll make you better,' I said, sitting upright and sending him a winning smile.

He closed one eye and opened the other wide. 'Better than what?'

I had to think fast. 'Better than before.'

He took a long, deep breath and bit his bottom lip, like a bad actor trying to control his temper. 'I was alright before. But now I need something to make me feel better than right now.' He looked at the bottle in his hand. 'It's not even a big bottle,' he grumbled.

I leaned in closer. 'Its *special* Lucozade.'

'And what's special about it?' he asked as he undid the twist tie on the cellophane I'd carefully replaced.

'Trust me,' I said.

'Trust you? It'll be a long time before I can trust anybody after tonight's performance!'

The bottle opened without its usual fizz. It can only have taken a tenth of a second for him to realise. His shoulders came up as he grinned. I could see his neck muscles tighten.

'Is it . . .?'

'Yes, it's *special* Lucozade,' Gran declared to the ward from behind her magazine.

He sniffed the contents before taking a sip. 'Ah, now that *is* special.' He patted my hand. 'I knew you wouldn't let me down.'

I beamed, pleased that the plan had worked. The buzzer went – it was time to go. Activity erupted around the ward as people said their goodbyes.

'Give your grandad a kiss, Harry,' said Gran. 'Give me a minute and I'll see you out there.' She pointed towards the far end of the ward.

I leaned over and hugged him.

'I'll be home soon, H,' he said as he kissed my forehead.

I joined the river of people and waited in the corridor. I looked around self-consciously, but no one paid me any attention. I watched

the nurses preparing to serve tea and biscuits. The confection on offer was only Rich Tea, so I wasn't disappointed to be missing out.

Gran was the last to leave. She smiled at me as she fastened her
coat.

'What did he say about the cake?'

'Oh, sorry, love, I completely forgot.' She continued buttoning,
the shopping basket on the floor.

Picking up the bag, I held it like a rugby ball and glanced at the
nurses' station.

*MATRON'S EYES MET MINE and narrowed. I scowled back at her.
We both looked at the ward doors.*

*'Stop that boy!' she screeched as I ran, my shoulder charging the
doors open.*

*Sturdy legs drove comfortable shoes heavily into the floor as Matron
gave chase. All eyes turned my way as I burst into the room. The long
passage between the beds seemed to narrow and extend.*

*A couple of nurses broke off from their tasks, disturbed by the com-
motion. Another continued to pump the blood pressure cuff wrapped
around her patient's arm. His spectacles trembled as the pressure built
up, the inevitable explosion from the cuff blowing off his wig. We all
watched as the toupee flew across the floor like a scalded rat. The nurse
threw down the blood pressure pump, gritted her teeth and moved to in-
tercept me.*

*I ran as fast as I could, but she was going to get me. She leapt
in slow motion, flying through the air in an impressive arc, her arms
outstretched, ready to tackle me to the ground. At the last moment, I
jumped and grabbed at the mechanism holding a man's leg in traction,
leaving her grasping at thin air as I hauled the man high in the air by
his broken leg. She tripped and sprawled onto the floor, her momentum*

taking her under the bed. There was a loud metal clang as her head connected with a bedpan. She slid out and thudded into the wall, unconscious and covered in pee.

One of the nurses started towards me. I looked at the man on whose bed I now stood. His eyes smiled at me from a full-body plaster cast as his thumb, the only bit of his body he could move, flicked up in support. After bounding from bed to bed, high above the nurse's flailing grasp, I landed on the floor and did a forward roll before kneeling to catch my breath.

Anticipating my next move, another nurse stood between Grandad and me. She scowled and spread her legs, spitting on her palm. She rubbed her hands together, crouching in preparation for a scrum. Her feet shuffled as I ran towards her. At the last moment, I lobbed the shopping bag over her head. As she reached high to grab it, I slid between her legs, pulling down her frilly knickers as I went under. She shrieked as she attended to her disrupted underwear.

A man with big ears and a face like a walnut cackled as I caught the bag. Like the man in the advert delivering a box of Black Magic chocolates, I handed the birthday cake to Grandad. Silently turning to face the army of staff who had followed me in, I realised I had to escape before Matron rallied her troops.

Walnut Face leapt out of bed, his eye patch adding menace as he kicked off the brakes and pushed his bed towards me.

'Jump on here, young 'un. I'll give you a push.' His good eye sparkled with mischief.

Grabbing a tray and a sweeping brush, I held them like a charging knight and we quickly picked up speed, cheered on by the other patients. Halfway down the ward, he let go with one final heave. I watched in horror as Matron stepped through the door, crossed her arms and barred my way.

Unable to stop, I hurtled towards her. I looked around in desperation for a way out. Just then, the doors behind her burst open and *a porter pushed a tea trolley into her. Distracted, she turned round to see what was happening. My bed scooped her up and she rolled on board, knocking me off. The tea trolley was bashed aside as Matron flew through the double doors, across the corridor and towards the lift. The doors pinged open and she piled into a group of junior doctors. The consultant's arrival was perfectly timed, his whiskers twitching irritably as he took in the chaotic scene. Matron's chubby legs flailed helplessly as the doors of the lift slammed shut.*

AS I LEFT THE WARD, the door bumped into a porter's tea trolley.

'Watch where you're going, you clumsy bugger,' he said out of the corner of his mouth.

The other half of his face was preoccupied with keeping hold of his Woodbine. The ash hung precariously, ready to drop into some poor sod's brew.

'Sorry,' I said.

Gran stared at his retreating back and I looked at the nurses' station. A young nurse smiled at me. Matron put down her pen.

'What the hell do you think you're doing?' Matron yelled in our direction.

'Oh, you're in bother now,' said the porter, smirking out of the vacant side of his gob as he turned back.

Matron headed our way. I hid behind Gran.

'I'm sorry about this,' she said to us. 'What have I told you about smoking on my ward?' she hissed at the hapless porter, snatching the cigarette from his mouth and offering it up for examination.

The porter looked at it in surprise, as if someone had planted it to set him up.

'This is a hospital, not a taproom.'

'I, err . . .' His feeble reply faltered at the first hurdle.

'I've just about had enough . . .' She stopped, glancing at us before turning her attention back to the porter. 'I'll see you in my office when you're finished.'

The porter disappeared into the ward. Matron looked at Gran and shook her head.

'Men!' she declared before turning back to her duties.

'Can we get going now?' asked Gran.

Walking up the drive to the house, I paused to pick another daffodil from the border. The yellow flower heads seem to glow in the orange street light. Inside, I took the empty rum bottle, its contents safely smuggled into hospital for Grandad, and half filled it with water. I placed the daffodil inside the neck and popped it on Gran's dressing table. The daffodil's head bowed in recognition of my performance in the hospital.

I lay awake for a long time, smiling into the darkness and thinking about the trick I'd played on Grandad.

Chapter 3

Wednesday, 19 March 1975

The hall hummed with chatter as we took our seats in assembly. Keith was telling Mark and me about a news programme he'd seen where he claimed to have watched an Arab getting shot in the head, but it all sounded a bit too gruesome for us to believe. My laughter at the outrageous claim was stifled by a sharp pain at the back of my head. It was so extreme it took a moment to realise someone was pulling my hair. The short ones, just above my collar. The only way to fight it was to lean back in an attempt to lessen the pressure. My back arched and my feet scrambled for purchase. The chair flexed a little but was fastened to the others beside me.

'What the hell are you doing, boy?' The head teacher's voice boomed around the room, drawing everyone's attention to my acrobatics.

My head was so far back I was able to see Watson's upside-down face grinning at me. He let go and I flopped into my seat, but in my haste to get away, I half slid off the plastic chair and finished up in sort of limbo stance, my arms flailing, trying to regain my seat.

'Get off the floor, you stupid boy.'

The head teacher took two steps towards me before realising he had another scuffle to quell at the other side of the room.

I sat down, leaning forwards in a vain attempt to stay out of Watson's reach, flattening my hair to disguise my effort to rub the painful patch. It didn't work.

The head teacher moved around the stage, swapping his attention from one side of the room to the other. Every time Watson had the chance, he leaned forwards and pulled again. Short, vicious tugs that yanked my head back. His mates giggled each time.

I stood at the first opportunity to leave, turning to scowl at him.

'His grandad asked me to look after him.' Watson nudged the lad next to him.

My heart sank at the thought. Grandad was a mate of Watson's dad. I could imagine Grandad seeing the size of Watson and thinking he'd act as my bodyguard. Instead, all he'd done was single me out as a prime target. I resigned myself to another three years of torment.

When I got home from school, Grandad was standing in front of the fire, leaning on his new walking stick. I dropped my bag and hugged him, hiding a letter from school behind the clock, fulfilling my responsibility to bring it home as instructed by Mr Fisher, our year tutor, and also complying with my agenda to make it disappear. He'd applied his cologne. Although I never witnessed it, he sprayed it on every morning and once again smelled of engine oil, burnt metal and mints. I breathed it in and relaxed in its healing power. At last, things were back to normal.

'You got any homework, H?' he asked, pointing at the satchel.

'No, but I've got a present to open.' I pointed at the parcel on the table.

'Hmm. I see I've taught you well, Grasshopper,' said Grandad, his inscrutable narrow eyes evaluating me. 'Go on, then. Get changed.'

Pickering sat and watched me. He seemed happy that Grandad was home, too.

'Don't you think he's going to notice the letter you tried to hide?'

I looked at him, disappointed that he thought my plan wouldn't work.

'Of course not. He's only just got out of hospital and—'

'Remember what Attenborough said,' he warned.

When I returned, Grandad was lounging in his chair, a 'guilty' sign flashing over his head. I looked down at the landslide of cake crumbs littering his jumper. I picked up a fragment and offered it as evidence. His cheeks bulged with his last greedy mouthful.

'Happy birthday, H,' he mumbled, forcing more crumbs to cascade from his mouth, gathering in an unsightly pile between his legs.

He tried to cross them to conceal the evidence, but after several attempts gave up. Struggling out of the chair, emitting a series of involuntary grunts, he stood up and brushed the cake bits onto the rug just as Gran came in.

'It's good to be home,' he said, smacking his tongue around his dentures and grinning.

We all looked at the mess he'd made.

'Hmm,' said Gran as she went to the pantry for the dustpan and brush.

'Come on, then. Let's see what you've got.' He rubbed his hands together. 'Hee-hee, I love opening presents,' he chuckled.

Gran shook her head. 'It's his present, Jack.'

'I know, Lily, but it might be chocolate. He might want to share.'

I held up the large, soft package and raised my eyebrows. 'How could this be chocolate?'

He shrugged but leaned closer, just in case he was right.

Gran stood fidgeting with her apron as I tore at the wrapping paper. A parka! And it wasn't one of the cheap nylon imposters that some lads had to tolerate. This was the real thing: cotton, fishtail, rabbit fur trim around the hood and a paisley lining.

'Is it the right sort?' Gran asked.

We'd been through all the versions that were 'not right', several times, as I'd witnessed numerous disappointed kids who had been conned into wearing a knock-off cheapo version at school and suffered endless teasing by those who knew the difference.

'It's fantastic,' I beamed. 'I'll be able to wear this when I get a scooter.'

The colour drained from Gran's face and she snapped, 'You're not getting a motorbike!'

She rarely lost her temper. A little deflated, I tried to explain.

'It's not a motorbike, Gran, it's a scooter.'

'Has it got two wheels and a motor?' she asked in exasperation.

'Well, yeah, bu—'

'Then it's a motorbike!' She turned to Grandad for support. 'Tell him, Jack.'

I knew Grandad would see reason.

'Grandad says it's the rider that's dangerous, not the machine, didn't you, Grandad?'

Gran's stony gaze held Grandad in her spell. I sympathised – it had locked onto me often enough.

He turned away with difficulty. 'Gran doesn't want you to get hurt, Harry, that's all.'

'I know, but you said . . .'

Grandad held up a finger to shush me. 'It's four years before you can ride a bike.'

'He's *not* having a bike,' said Gran.

'Four years,' he repeated, holding up four fingers for the slow-witted before suggesting, 'Isn't there something else we could argue about in the meantime?'

We all had a little think. I scratched my chin, just to be sure they knew I was thinking. For the moment, we were stumped.

Gran broke the silence.

'I'll let you know as soon as I think of something.'

He put his arm around her. 'That's the spirit, Lily.' He turned back to me. 'Anyway, when you get a job, you'll be able to afford a car.' He lowered himself into the chair on his stick, making it look like hard work.

A car would be even better, although the parka would look a lot better if I had a scooter.

'You can help me fix it, can't you, Grandad? When it breaks down.'

Gran even seemed upset at the thought of me getting a car. She held her handkerchief to her face and went upstairs.

'Of course I will. Anyhow,' Grandad winked, 'it's a long time until you'll have the money to buy a bike or a car. You've got lots of school time first.'

'Grandad! You're supposed to be cheering me up! It's my birthday. Well . . . it was.'

'I know, and me being poorly spoilt it, didn't it?' He put his hand on my shoulder.

'A bit,' I conceded.

'Come here.' He pulled me into his arms and became serious. 'You're not bothered about school, are you?'

I shrugged.

'You know it's important to do well though, don't you?'

I shrugged again.

'What's wrong, H?' he persisted, putting his hands on my shoulders and turning me to face him.

The world closed in around me.

'It's just . . . I . . .' My eyes prickled as I fought back the tears.

'Is somebody picking on you? Do you want me to come and sort 'em out?' He held up his fists. 'Put 'em up, put 'em up. I'll hit 'em with a left, then a right.'

I think that was the lion from *The Wizard of Oz*.

'It's not just the bullies, Grandad, it's everything.'

'You're not going to like it, H.'

He was right. I knew what was coming and I didn't like it.

'You know you need to hit them back, don't you?'

'I know. You've told me before. But ... '

'The bigger they come—' he started.

'The harder they fall,' I finished with a lack of conviction that was nothing short of world-class.

He ruffled my hair. 'Go and get some coal, H, there's a good lad.'

I waddled in, straining with the short handled shovel, and waited at his back as he raked the embers. I threw the coal on and put the shovel back in the workshop. When I returned, he was reading the letter I'd hidden.

'You forgot to mention this, H.' He waved the paper at me like Prime Minister Chamberlain returning from his negotiations with Hitler. 'You probably got side-tracked in the excitement of my return,' he said sarcastically.

I confirmed that that was indeed what had happened.

'So, which subjects are you going to drop?'

'Err . . . English, maths, chemistry, biology, physics, geography and history.' I counted on my fingers. 'Oh! and domestic science, RE and music . . . and metalwork.'

'What does that leave you with?'

'Woodwork and games.'

'And Spanish and art,' he reminded me.

'Oh, I forgot. I'm dropping them, too.'

'Hilarious.' He pointed at the settee. 'Sit.' He flopped back into his chair. 'Have you read this letter?' he asked, holding it up like a 'wanted' poster.

'Are you going to give me a test?'

'No.'

'Then yes, I have read it.'

'What does it say?'

'I thought you said you weren't going to test me.'

He raised his eyebrows and called me an idiot for believing him.

'You can't drop maths or English for a start. And you've got to take at least one science and—'

'I know, Grandad. I don't like anything. I'm no good at any of it.'
I could feel the tears building, hating myself for crying.

'Come on, H, you must like something.'

I had to think hard.

'Well . . .' I sniffed, 'I like outdoor pursuits.'

Outdoor pursuits was the occasional outing with Mr Gibson.
We'd go rock climbing or canoeing or off on some other adventure.

'I know you do, but the rest of it?' Grandad looked at me over
his glasses.

'I just can't do it, Grandad.' The tears were back again as I struggled to express my lack of academic ability.

'Don't worry, Harry. One day you'll find something that you can
do really well, then work will be easy. You know what they say.'

I'd heard a few things that 'they' had to say and in my experience,
it was always cobblers. Would this be any different?

'Find a job you love and you'll never have to work another day in
your life.'

Mmm . . . no, it was the same old nonsense, but with a twist.
Cobblers and a puzzle. A new combination 'they' must have been
holding back until I was a teenager; although I still felt ill-prepared
to deal with the dual onslaught. My lack of understanding dripped
from my eyes.

'What that means is if you find a job you enjoy, it doesn't seem
like work at all.'

Work that you enjoy? It had never occurred to me that some people had jobs they liked. All of our neighbours worked in factories or
down the pit – they didn't look like people who enjoyed their work.
Most took every opportunity available not to bother going at all.

'Tell me,' Grandad said, 'does everybody like outdoor pursuits?'

'Fatty Foster doesn't!'

'I bet he doesn't.' Grandad's laughter turned into a cough, his
hand trembled on the handle of his stick.

'But, Grandad, you can't do outdoor pursuits as a job.'

'Mr Gibson does.'

Grandad made a good point, which was annoying. It was 'the obvious' rearing its ugly head again.

'And what about that fella on the telly you were talking about the other week? The one on *Blue Peter*. That Chris Bonington.'

I remembered how the mountaineer Chris Bonington had been on *Blue Peter* talking about his latest expedition to Mount Everest. It didn't seem possible, but I asked him anyway.

'So is his job being a mountaineer?'

'Well, that's how he makes a living. It's the same thing. He gets people to give him money or equipment, then he goes on adventures and writes a book about it. He gets money for that. Then he goes on telly and talks about it. He gets money for that, too. Then—'

'You get paid for being on *Blue Peter*?' I'd clearly misunderstood what Grandad was saying – the answer couldn't possibly be yes.

'Yes,' said Grandad.

Imagine that! Getting paid for being on the telly.

'Grandad? The money and gear people give him to go on these adventures with . . .'

'Yes, love.'

'Does he have to pay them back?' Of course he did.

'No!'

Damn, you'd think I'd get one right just by chance . . . Nonetheless, I had to admit, the new teenage world just got a little bit better.

He continued, 'It's called sponsorship. It's the same when cigarette firms put their name on a racing car, like that Scalextric car you've got, the John Player Special. They pay a lot of money for that.'

BONINGTON PAUSED ON the summit and looked around. In a rash move, he took off his gloves and scarf. His cavalier attitude to frostbite could only end in tears, or icicles. He reached into his rucksack. The black packet of the John Player cigarettes glistened in the Himalayan sun, the perfect contrast to the snowy peaks surrounding him. He shielded the match from the wind and inhaled deeply. The nicotine coursed through his body and he leaned on his ice axe. He turned towards me and winked, exhaling the toxic fumes into the clear air.

'They pay me to smoke these, Harry!' His chuckle turned into a rasping coughing fit, which concluded with him gobbing out a ball of green phlegm.

I SHOOK MY HEAD TO remove the image of the irresponsible Bonington. This was a day when the world wouldn't be the same. Bonington had said summiting Everest was one of the best moments in his life.

'What was the best time in your life, Grandad?'

He looked over my head. I could almost hear the film clicking through sprockets. I turned to where he was looking, half expecting to see the movie of his memories projected onto the wall from his eyes.

A half-smile on his face, he said, 'You know, I like it now. I enjoy being retired and spending time with your gran.'

I waited.

'Oh, and you.'

Thank you.

'And I like taking it easy.'

I could see the appeal, pottering in the garage, making stuff, eating Gran's cake and drinking tea.

'But,' he added, 'I don't like being old, with all the aches and pains, and I didn't like being in hospital.' He turned serious. 'It may seem strange, Harry, but my time on the *Hood* during the war was the best time for me.'

It didn't seem strange at all. War looked great.

'I was young and fit. And when you're in the navy, you don't have to worry about money or food or anything except getting hit by a torpedo!'

Ah yes, there's always a downside.

'You should give some thought to joining the navy. The marines – that's like doing outdoor pursuits all the time. You just need to pick something and stick at it. You can be anything you want to be. Once you find the thing you want to do, working hard to be successful at it is dead easy because you're enjoy it.'

Grandad made these decisions sound so simple, but my mind was a fuzz of confusion. I couldn't seem to keep anything in focus. Just thinking about anything annoyed and frustrated me.

'Life was simpler for me back then. We were the goodies, the Germans were the baddies. We had to fight, so that's what we did. But those days with those lads on that ship, that was the best time for me. It was like . . .'

Uncomfortable in the silence that followed, I filled it up.

'Keith's mum says school days are the best days of your life.' It had been on my mind ever since she'd said it. It couldn't be true, could it? I hated it. The thought that this was the best that life had to offer was depressing. 'Is it true?' I asked. 'Is it going to get worse as I grow up?'

'Probably not.'

That wasn't the reassurance I was hoping for.

'Different people find their place at different times, H. For some, it's their school days. Others, it's when they go out dancing and boozing. Some people love it when they have kids. Some even like it when they have grandkids,' he said, raising his arms as if the idea were preposterous. 'Nobody feels they're at their best all the time and if they say they are, they're lying.'

He seemed very certain about all this.

'People handle life in different ways. Some fight to get what they want. Some give up, some just keep trying. Some people are determined and shape their life the way they want it to be, some are prepared to accept a compromise and some don't give a shit.'

Instinct made me looked round to see if Gran was in ear-shot, but the coast was clear. I wasn't sure what it all meant, but the fact he was so sure gave me confidence that it would sort itself out.

'How about we save Gran the bother of cooking and have fish and chips instead?' He pushed himself back in the chair, trying to straighten his body as he fumbled in his pocket for some cash. 'You could go in your new . . .'

My hands were already deep in my parka pockets when he looked up.

A short while later, I held Gran's raffia shopping bag inside my parka, squashing the lump down as much as possible. The streets were empty as I made my way to the chip shop. Gran was struggling to keep up with all the housework, particularly now Grandad was home, throwing crumbs everywhere. She still had to do her cleaning job at the bookies each evening and I didn't mind helping, especially if it meant fish and chips. Today was one of those evenings. And it wasn't even Friday!

Rounding the last corner, I stopped dead. It was Watson. I reversed out of sight and peeped over the hedge. Watson and some older lads were standing outside the chippy. There was no way I was going to go in there while they were around. I dithered, hoping they would clear off. But five minutes later, they were still there, and I was getting cold.

I went to Dale's at the top of the estate instead. Whatever the distance, I didn't care. There was no way I was going anywhere near him out of school. Most kids stayed on their own estate – whatever your age, you were at risk if you strayed too far. Watson was one of the few confident enough to stray onto enemy territory.

Vague dark shapes moved in and out of focus as people shifted around behind Dale's steamed-up window. Some sat on the windowsill, their coats sticking to the wet glass. The atmosphere was thick with greasy warmth as I stepped inside to the bell's chime. Everyone looked around to see who the newcomer was. I pushed the door shut but met resistance as Mrs Kershaw, one of the dinner ladies from my junior school, followed me in.

The slim woman looked like a barrel, apparently wearing every item of clothing she possessed. Despite that, she shivered next to me. I moved forwards to separate us, but she moved forwards, too. The old man in front of me smelt of something unpleasant and I immediately regretted my tactics.

'Can you put me a haddock in, please?' I asked as Mr Dale banged the wire scoop on the stainless steel of the chip hopper. The cabinet had pies, sausages and fishcakes waiting, but it seemed the requests for fish had taken the owners by surprise, as none were ready.

He leaned back as he poured in another bucketful of chips, sending up a cloud of steam. Or was it smoke? The sizzling fat quietened as he shut the lid.

Unsure if I'd been heard I shouted, 'can you put a haddock in for my gran?' just as the noise died down.

I withdrew my reddening face into my parka like a tortoise. Annoyed with myself, I touched the hot glass of the cabinet, increasing the time I held it there until I was certain I'd blistered my finger. Closer examination showed no sign of any damage.

Somebody prodded my back. I looked round, but the voice came from behind the counter.

'I said, what else can I get you, love?'

I gave the woman the rest of Gran's order and hid my foolishness by drawing lines in the spilt salt on the counter.

A fat woman ahead of me took out her purse, caught off guard by the request for payment. She rummaged and chuntered about the price, receiving a cold stare from the flushed face of Mr Dale. Mrs Dale wrapped the woman's order in clean white paper, which apparently wasn't the way she liked them wrapped. She looked down and pursed her lips, wrinkled from a lifetime of sucking on cigs, and lemons. The sour-faced old crow.

'I prefer them wrapped in newspaper; I think it's more authentic,' she announced to the crowded shop. 'Like they do at Shaw's.'

'Well, missus,' said Mr Dale, holding the chip scoop like an axe, 'not so long ago, we used to take old newspapers, tear them into pieces, thread them on a string and hang them up to use in the loo.'

The woman looked perplexed, wondering as we all were where this story would lead.

'What's your point?' she said.

I knew a trap when I saw one, having fallen into many of Grandad's.

'Well, we don't do that anymore, so here's what I think. If newspaper isn't good enough to wipe your arse on, I don't think it's good enough to eat your tea off!'

The woman flinched, gathered her order and scarpered.

Mr Dale took his annoyance out on Gran's haddock. I recoiled as he flung it into the display cabinet towards my face. I shuffled forwards, producing my shopping bag at the last moment for fear of further ridicule. But as usual, nobody was paying attention.

To compensate for the prolonged walk, I ran home, keeping a watchful eye for Watson and other hazards.

Fumes from the salt and vinegar rose into my face and despite my best efforts, a stifled coughing fit escaped through my nose. How could such a toxic smell be so delicious?

'Take it easy, H,' Grandad warned as he pinched one of my chips. 'Maybe you *should* keep chemistry when you select your subjects next year.' He closed his eyes and inhaled. 'Ahh, nothing says "eat me" like hydrogen chloride.'

I was never sure when he was joking. I looked at Gran for guidance. She put a plate of buttered bread on the table.

'He does know some rubbish, Harry.'

That wasn't any help.

He looked offended but conceded, 'It's true, Lily, I do.'

I briefly considered the possibility that there was *some* science worth learning.

'Your mate Frank called while you were in hospital,' said Gran.

I paused, my fork hovering short of its target, the fish and chips forgotten. Watson's dad, Frank, was a committeeman over at the Legion, one of the hard men on the neighbouring estate.

'Did he drop that cash off?' Grandad asked.

She sat and joined us, always the last to sit and the first up after we'd eaten.

'He did. It's behind the radio.'

I glanced over at the silent set. For some reason, Gran always put her fish and chips on a plate, discarding the paper. Pointlessly, she forced plates under our wrappings, as a token gesture to civilisation.

'I don't like him, Jack.'

'Not many do, Lily.' He paused and shrugged. 'But he's always been alright with me.'

But she wasn't done with him yet.

'He was asking if you wanted to take him and some of his cronies to Cheltenham this year.'

Grandad often got invited to take the local bad lads to the races. The blokes he took sold tips to gullible racegoers or Frank Watson did the three-card trick, using Bill Donleavy's back as a table, disappearing in a flash at the first sight of the bobbies. They always made sure the driver was well looked after and he'd return home with pockets full of coins. Sometimes I was allowed to join them when there was a spare seat.

'I'll see him at the club on Sunday.'

'He gives me the willies.' She continued her attack. 'When he talks to you, he just looks straight through you. It's creepy. If half the stories I hear about him in the bookies are true, I'd steer clear of him if I were you.'

Grandad stopped eating, his knife and fork sticking up like he was about to start banging the table top. My eyes pinged between them – it was like watching tennis.

'If you take notice of half the stuff you hear at the bookies, then you're only a quarter of the woman I thought you were.'

Fractions bounced around my skull until the boggling was complete.

The kettle boiled and she was up again.

'I hear some good stuff.' She wiped her hands on her pinny as she made the tea.

'You never tell me the good stuff,' Grandad winked at me.

'If I did, Jack, then you'd know as much as me, wouldn't you?' The spoon rattled around the cups. She set them down. 'And that wouldn't be right, would it?' she said into his ear, pecking him on the cheek.

Grandad raised his eyebrows and conceded, 'No, Lily, that would never do.'

She turned to get the teapot. He made a grimace at her back.

'And don't pull faces,' she said.

Grandad threw his arms out and looked around, protesting his innocence as I hoovered up the last of his chips. He shook his fist. I used my last big chip as a gum shield and showed him the result. He recoiled in disgust, which was exactly the effect I was looking for.

'Has Bill dropped his bets off?' Grandad asked.

'He did. It's been a busy day, even without looking after you two.'

Bill Lambert had to pass our house to get to the bookies. Depending on what shift he was working, he'd either collect Gran's bets and take them for her, or more often he'd drop his bets off for Gran to take for him. If he wasn't working, he'd call in half a dozen times throughout the day, checking and reporting on his progress as he gradually handed his wage over the counter.

I wiped my greasy hands unsuccessfully on the paper wrapping. As I left the table, I rubbed my fingers together, testing the thickness of the gloop.

'Go and wash your hands properly, please,' Gran said over her shoulder.

Grandad smirked at me from his perch at the table.

After we'd eaten, they sent me across to the Legion.

'Do you want me to write it down?' Asked Gran.

'No, I'll remember.' I took the coins and stuffed them deep in my pocket.

In the porch, I rolled up the hood of my parka and drew the zip up to my nose. The wet handle slipped out of my grip twice before I closed the outer door. Another of Grandad's sayings – more haste, less speed – echoed in my empty head as I made my way down the drive and across the street. The smoke from a thousand coal fires struggled into the damp air before falling back to earth, creating a swirling halo around each street light. A couple of younger kids had set up a ramp in the club's floodlit car park, but they'd set the bricks up the wrong way, so every time they did a jump, the board collapsed and they had to rebuild it.

The periscope view through my parka hood nearly cost me a black eye as I climbed the steps to the club's entrance. My attention was still on the infant daredevils as a man strode through the door, which luckily hit the end of my toe before my nose.

'Ay-up, young 'un.' He looked around before retreating into the no man's land between the two sets of double doors.

We shared the space as I unfastened my parka and slid back the hood. He lit a cigarette, sending up clouds of smoke, which filled the confined space. A loud belch followed, echoing around us. Too late, I realised the expression that passed across his ruddy features was the sign that he'd farted. The smell hit me and I moved to get past him.

'How's your grandad?' the stinkpot asked.

I looked at his features through the cigarette smoke which at least had the effect of masking the rancid fart fumes. I recognised him but didn't know his name. Just another one of the old blokes in three-piece suits who sat in the club for a living once they'd retired.

'He's just got back home,' I offered, willing him to lose interest.

'Have they said what's up with him?'

I shrugged, embarrassed that I didn't know the answer.

There appeared to be a general disregard for medical science among the old folk, as he told me, 'Huh, bloody doctors, they don't know what they're on about.'

I resisted the urge to defend them. Instead, I held my breath to avoid inhaling any more of the poisonous gases than was necessary. What would the doctors make of my admission if I was overcome by the foul air?

THE LIGHTS OF THE CORRIDOR whizzed overhead as they pushed me towards theatre.

'What's wrong with him, nurse?'

'We don't know, Doctor. They found him slumped in the entrance to a working men's club.'

'Get the stomach pump, plenty of hot water and some towels.'

I tried to explain that I wasn't drunk or pregnant, but my words were lost as they clamped a mask over my face. Voices drifted into my groggy brain as the anaesthetic took effect.

'Is it his left or right leg we're going to amputate?'

'ANYWAY,' SAID THE OLD man, still prattling on, 'that's why he's only got one leg, but his adenoids are still causing him grief.'

Mercifully, before my lungs collapsed or exploded, somebody else came in, bringing a welcome breeze to clear the air.

'Ay-up, Col,' he said to the stinkpot. 'How-do, Harry.' He paused briefly, sniffed the air and gave me a filthy look.

A car tooted outside and the stink bomb mumbled something as he left. Sheepishly, I opened the door and let the man go first, following him into the club.

The taproom was the only bar of three open in the week; they only used the much bigger concert room and the snug Friday to Sunday or for special occasions like weddings or the Easter bonnet parade. The lino tiles on the well-trodden route to the bar had worn through to the colourless core. It made the dull cream-and-orange of the other tiles look even dingier. Despite there being an ashtray on every table, the floor was covered with cig butts and the air was now just pure smoke. Winnie Graham, one of Gran's mates from the bookies, was firing pennies into a one-armed bandit as fast as the machine would allow. Her entertainment was occasionally interrupted by a pathetic digital tune that extravagantly announced a win before grudgingly spitting back one in ten coins in compensation for her effort.

I stood at the bar, unsure if I still needed to perch on the brass footrest now I was a teenager. I looked at the other men stood near me and copied them, putting one foot on. Resting my chin on my hands, I lifted my head on my thumbs. Spotting a straw in an empty bottle, I clamped it between my top lip and my nose while sliding the sodden beer mats around on the glossy varnish of the bar. Catching my reflection in the mirrored backdrop, I pulled faces and wiggled the straw like a circus strongman's moustache.

'I hear your grandad's back home, Harry.' The landlady leaned forwards, tapping cigarette ash into the heavy glass dish and presenting her significant bosom.

I jerked upright, unwilling to get too close to the fleshy valley of her cleavage.

'Yeah, he came home this afternoon.' The forgotten straw fell to the floor.

'Tell him there's a few lads ready to buy him a pint when he's next in,' she said.

Murmured confirmation came from both ends of the bar, one man lifting his glass in salute.

'What can I get you, love?' she asked.

'Two bottles of Mackeson Stout, a bottle of fizzy orange and a Babycham, please.'

I heard Grandad's name mentioned in a hushed conversation across the bar. I looked at them, trying to hear what they were saying, when the man next to me gave me a nudge.

'Looks like you're celebrating, Harry.'

I looked at Bill Donleavy, but he was glaring at the two whisperers. His gaze softened as he looked at me.

'Has your Gran had a win on the horses?'

'No, Grandad's back home.'

'I know, yeh daft bugger.' He touched my arm. 'Tell him we've missed him, won't yeh?'

I smiled back and told him I would as the landlady plonked the bottles on the bar.

'Oh, and a packet of cheese and onion crisps, please.'

She disappeared out of sight, rummaging in a box in the store-room.

I tapped the footrest as I waited, looking down and counting the dog-ends on the floor and seeing how many cigarette brands I could identify. An enormous pair of black boots stepped beside me, the hobnails grinding on the brass as he took up the traditional stance. My eyes traced a path over his filthy jeans, black leather jacket, long greasy hair and dandruff-flecked beard. I jumped as his helmet dropped onto the bar top. I stared into the black visor as he rolled a cigarette with his greasy fingers. He opened his jacket to reveal a Black Sabbath T-shirt straining to contain his fat gut. The cigarette almost disappeared as he lit it with a lighter that had the intensity of a flamethrower, before blowing the smoke into my face.

'Are you a mod, then?' The giant growled at me.

I'd seen the mods and rockers battling on the seafront in Brighton on the news last summer. I'd joked with Mark and Keith about which gang we were in. It was a question thrown around the playground. The answer had never seemed so important or, bearing in mind my parka, so obvious. I gulped but stayed silent.

'Because I bloody hate mods,' he said, confirming my worst fears.

'Oi! Leave him alone,' said Bill Donleavy. 'He's only a kid.'

'Keep your nose out, you old fart,' the biker said, casually dismissing Bill's suggestion.

The landlady returned with my crisps. Instinctively sensing the tension, she looked around for the cause of the friction. My hand trembled as I put the coins in her palm.

'Pint of mild,' the biker barked.

She didn't acknowledge him but gave me a friendly wink as she dropped the money into the cash register, still trying to decipher exactly what was going on as she pulled his pint.

The biker glared around the room until his stare was met at the far end of the bar. I hadn't noticed Frank Watson until then.

'What the hell are you looking at?' the biker unwisely asked.

Frank said nothing; he just stared back.

'I said, what you staring—'

'Have you had a bad day?' Frank said, his voice giving no clue to his mood.

'Eh?'

Frank finished his pint and set the empty glass down with deliberate precision.

'I said, have you had a bad day?' Frank clarified, still not giving anything away.

The biker chewed on his lip as he thought of his next move.

'Why?'

Frank explained, like a teacher delivering a maths formula to class.

'Well, you see, it's like this. If you continue to pick on kids and pensioners, your bad day is going to get a lot worse before it gets any better.' Frank pushed his mouth into a shape that had many of the features of a smile but fooled no one.

My eyes shot around the bar. Everyone's attention was on the biker. Only Winnie continued her mission, regardless. The barrels of the one-armed bandit tumbled, falling into place – one, two, three . . .

THE GUNSLINGER'S GLOVED fingers flexed, hovering above his six-shooter as the loudmouth cowboy made his choice. The piano player faltered to a stop.

. . . FOUR.

The final tumbler dropped into place and the machine chirped its distorted tune, delivering more disappointment in the shape of a single coin that rattled into the metal hopper.

THE LOUDMOUTH SWALLOWED his pride and took his drink to the far corner of the saloon. The piano player struck up a nervous tune as murmured conversation resumed.

FRANK'S GAZE DROPPED back to his empty glass.

'Same again, please, Bet,' he said.

The barmaid shook her head and let out a sigh, thankful that the drama was over.

The bottles hung heavily in the parka pockets like two Colt revolvers. I understood why gunslingers tied the bottom of their holsters to their legs as the bottles swung around and banged into my thighs.

Before bed, I practiced quick-draw with my water pistol, to see if I could beat my reflection. Letting out an enormous burp, I turned and smiled at Pickering as smaller, less impressive aftershocks followed.

'Charmed, I'm sure,' he said, pursing his lips and shuddering.

Chapter 4

Saturday, 22 March 1975

Grandad's hand steered me down the hall, giving me an extra shove through the porch. The letter box rattled as the door shut and I stumbled down the drive, getting authentically close to falling. I recovered just in time and rocked from side to side as I straightened my coat. Grandad's gaze held firm as he walked around the car, disappearing as he climbed in. Drops of water shivered on the roof as the car rocked, joining forces to create rivulets that trickled off in all directions. I had to knock on the window to remind him to unlock my door.

'Oh, it's you. I forgot you were coming with me,' he claimed as I climbed into the passenger seat and onto a carrier full of books.

Somehow, my leg became tangled with his new walking stick. Already flustered, I put the bag of books and the stick on the back seat as the starter motor struggled, firing up the engine on the third attempt. He released the handbrake and gravity dragged the turquoise Morris Marina down the short, steep drive, *The Sweeney*'s theme tune played in my head. The chase was on.

Gritty images of the London streets in *The Sweeney*'s opening sequence bore little resemblance to the semi-detached council housing we drove through.

'Is this the best car you've ever had, Grandad?'

The Marina's plastic interior showed the battle scars inflicted by previous owners.

'Of course not,' he exclaimed as we drove past the shops at the bottom of the estate. 'When I first joined up, I had a sky-blue E-Type Jag.'

'Like the Corgi one I've got?'

'Yeah. That's why I got that one as a present when you lost your front teeth.'

I remember him taking me to John Burton's toy shop on the way home from the dentist, still groggy from the anaesthetic and dreaming of helicopters landing on top of the Legion. The Jag sat on my bedside table between James Bond's Aston Martin and the Batmobile.

'What happened to it?' I asked, as we pulled up at the T-junction with the main road. I looked both ways for traffic. 'All clear,' I confirmed.

But he stayed put.

I was just about to repeat myself, when I spotted some kids in their football kits trying to cross the road from the school gates opposite, walking blindly into the space we were just about to pull into.

'Well,' he continued, 'when I was young and daft like you'—Grandad's finger tapped on the steering wheel as he patiently waited for them to clear the way—'I used to drive a bit too fast. One day, I lost control in the wet and wrapped it around a tree. That's how I lost my front teeth'—he bared his dentures—'and I've had falsies ever since.' He flipped his lower set halfway out to show me.

I shrank away from him as we pulled out and accelerated down the empty road towards town.

'So when you lost your teeth,' he continued, 'it reminded me of the time I was an idiot and I got you the same car.'

Sometimes he made it difficult to tell where the insults were, but I always knew they were never far away.

'Was it fast?'

'Was it fast? It went like shit off a shovel! And don't tell your gran I've been swearing.'

It was a warning that was pointless, as he knew full well I'd tell her at the earliest opportunity.

'It cornered like a dream,' he shouted above the increasing noise.

HE CHANGED DOWN A GEAR and the V12 engine roared as we raced into the countryside. I wound down the window and stuck my head out. The wind whipped my hair around my ears and drove the moisture from my eyes as my cheeks flapped in the increased airflow. Grandad took the Jag's tyres to the limit. We screeched around the lanes, waving at people who stopped to admire the classic design.

'Make it go faster,' I shrieked into the wind.

The words got swept up and shredded as they left my mouth. Grandad raced to the edge of town, only easing off when the busy Saturday morning traffic slowed us to a crawl.

I BEAMED AT HIM.

'You've got a splattered fly stuck in your teeth,' he claimed.

I curled my top lip, drawing my nail across the enamel to dislodge any hitchhikers but finding nothing. I offered them for inspection.

'All clear,' he said. 'You must have eaten it.'

I swallowed, trying to sense the insect descending my gullet. I thought I could feel its futile attempts to stay afloat in my stomach, but after inducing a little burp, the sensation vanished.

We stopped with a modest skid as Grandad applied the handbrake a bit too early. The engine stalled and the vehicle lurched beyond the marked lines and into a clump of stinging nettles. My raised eyebrows asked him to confirm my suspicion.

'I meant to do that,' he said.

We made slow progress across the compacted dirt, stepping around the puddles as we headed towards the beacon of the town hall. We passed through arcades as shoppers and workers traipsed to the bus station. Grandad had a rest on Regent Street to catch his breath before we made the last push onto Shambles Street.

Our first port of call was William K. Bollocks and Sons, or something equally dull, which we just called the clock shop. I looked at the window display, if that's what you could call it. They'd draped faded yellow fabric over a series of obstacles that looked suspiciously like bricks. Rusty staples held the material on an ancient pegboard, brown stains giving away their position along the back edge. The pegboard's paint was losing its fight to stay stuck on the rotting wood. A darker patch of colour – the shadow of a long-removed clock – capped each peak. Thick dust covered the scene. A single wooden clock sat in the desolate landscape.

I looked across at the town hall clock. Then back at the display. This is what the town would look like after a nuclear explosion.

The doorbell pinged in bright contrast as Grandad pushed his way in. A man in his fifties was talking to a young couple about the carriage clock they'd had repaired. They were trapped under his spell, eyes glazed and unblinking as they were told the history of the ugly device. The shop owner went on and on about God knows what until eventually getting the message. He stopped talking mid-sentence, took their money and stuffed it in the till. He cranked a brass handle on the side of the old wooden box and a receipt emerged from the top like a tongue poking out. A final insult to all of the customers. The young couple escaped and he turned his attention to us, his pale, waxy complexion exaggerating his disappointment at the couple's lack of appreciation of their inheritance.

'It'll be back within six months,' he said. 'Young 'uns haven't got a bloody clue how to look after stuff.'

He glared at me, judging my ability to take care of things I didn't give a toss about. I couldn't offer him much hope.

Grandad stared at him, a false half-smile on his face. The man shuffled, feeling the pressure, breathing shallow breaths as Grandad's willpower pushed down on him. The smoke from the tab in the ashtray flickered as he exhaled from the corner of his mouth. He straightened his back and pushed out his chest, but neither was up to the task. He realised it was a battle he couldn't win. Both his will and his back broke, and he slumped into his natural stoop.

'What can I do for you today?' he asked, defeated.

'Make this work again,' Grandad said, his tone at the edge of his patience as he handed over his wristwatch.

The shopkeeper took the watch and turned it over in his hands, instantly engaged. He swung the magnifier attached to his specs into action as he scrutinised the watch from all angles.

'I've only seen one of these before,' he said to the watch before remembering we were there. He looked up and blinked. 'An officer had one in Bandung.' He put his fist to his mouth and bit into his knuckles to stop the words from spilling out.

Grandad stepped forwards and reached out as if to take the watch back. But to my surprise, he took the man's hand in his, helping to support the weight of the watch and the memory. The shopkeeper fought to control his emotions, anger and fear only just contained inside a barbed wire cage of frustration.

'Until the Japs took it off him.' He spat the words out, glad to be rid of them, before clamping his jaw shut.

The ticking clocks that covered the walls counted out seconds that seemed like a lifetime as the shopkeeper silently relived the memory of the Japanese prisoner-of-war camp.

The moment between them passed and the man regained his composure.

'The malaria flares up every now and then,' he said by way of explanation. 'Can you give me a couple of weeks to sort it out?'

'Take all the time you need,' Grandad said. 'Harry will come and pick it up.' He cast his eyes over the display. 'We want it to be right, don't we?' he said, turning to include me.

I smiled at him.

'Aye, we do,' the shopkeeper said to himself.

Glad to be outside, Grandad folded the receipt into his wallet and we made our way further up Shambles Street.

Grandad unwound his scarf and undid buttons as we waited in the tiled lobby of the toy shop for the lift to descend. The scene was straight out of a gangster movie. The boss was waiting behind a stack of cash for the gang to assemble. I couldn't believe that there wasn't a major fault with the lift mechanism, as the noise it made was horrendous. But after much crashing and clanging, the lift arrived with a gentle 'ping'. Grandad hauled the metal grill open, the scissor action more than capable of slicing through a carelessly positioned finger.

I looked at the gap between the lift floor and the lobby tiles. I was sure I could see a pile of severed digits among the cobwebs. Before Grandad could seal us off, two men in suits stepped in, each with a briefcase. There was little doubt in my mind that they concealed machine guns. The door shut with a thud and I pressed number one, feeling the snap of the relay switch as the light came on to confirm our destination. The lift jerked into motion, the smell of burning grease and overworked electric motors filling the small space. Grandad seemed relaxed despite the noise, the smell and the hitmen. It always felt like a risky journey and if I ever came alone, I used the stairs. The gangsters dragged open the gates to reveal the wonderland that was John Burton's toy shop.

THE SUITCASES FELL open and their machine guns roared into life. Staff and customers fell in the hail of bullets. Train sets and Lego buildings disintegrated as they stepped forwards, hunting out their target. A giant owl tried to hide behind a pile of Barbies. The mobsters swept the dolls aside and emptied their guns into the bird, his head exploding in a mess of kapok and feathers.

'NOT SUCH A WISE GUY now, huh!' I chuckled.

One of the assassins turned to look at me before heading in the direction of the office, probably to blow the safe.

Grandad looked straight ahead. 'You know you said that out loud, don't you?'

'Yeah. I'm like you; I meant to do it.'

We approached the counter and the owner, an old man in a three-piece suit, greeted us, smiling and shaking Grandad's hand. He was always polite, but when I came shopping with Keith and Mark, he'd follow us round, making sure we didn't nick anything. The suit always made me suspicious, as the only time Grandad or his mates wore a suit was when they went to the club. I wondered if this guy had a drink problem.

Grandad started chatting to the owner and within seconds knew about his shrapnel wound, which he'd picked up in the war. Gran's brother, Uncle Arthur, had picked up an SS dagger, which seemed like a much more sensible memento. He'd mounted it above the mantelpiece, looking a little out of place against the flock wallpaper of his living room. On the odd occasions we'd visited, he'd allowed me to hold it and I was able to make a few experimental thrusts before some spoilsport took it off me 'before somebody got hurt'.

I broke away from Grandad and disappeared into the labyrinth of displays and shelving, the train sets and Scalextric cars whizzing past my ears. Despite knowing how much was there, I checked the coins in my pocket again and wandered around waiting for Grandad to catch up, which he did about two hours later.

'Have you picked something, H?'

'No, I was waiting for you.'

He looked around the shop. 'Give me a clue, then.'

'There's not much I can afford.' I offered the coins up for inspection.

'No,' he confirmed, 'that's not going to buy much, is it?' He scratched his whiskers. 'What you could do with is a relative with a bit of cash in their pocket.'

I smiled and pointed a pistoled finger at him.

'No, it would have to be somebody who likes you.' He clutched his tummy like an out-of-season Santa.

'Very funny.'

'Oh, sorry,' he said with a serious face, 'did you think that was a joke? Have I upset you?'

My bottom lip quivered as I built up the pressure to force out some tears.

'Are you okay, H? Do you need the loo?'

I couldn't give in too soon, so I continued to screw my eyes tightly shut, finally opening them to find him gone. I looked around and found him tucked behind a display of Meccano, looking at the Airfix models.

'Oh, there you are,' he said, pretending to be innocent.

We stood side by side perusing the selection; the fact was, I'd got most of the good ones already. I cast a glance towards the Hornby trains – the working model village was a tempting distraction, but I was getting too old for train sets. Anyway, we didn't have anywhere to leave the track permanently set up, so I never got the chance to make all the extra bits like trees and bushes. I needed to get some-thing more grown-up. The galleons were out of my price range. In any case, I'd already got HMS *Victory*, the *Golden Hind* and the *Cutty Sark*. That only left the *Royal Sovereign*, which didn't really offer anything different.

'What about one of these, then?' He pointed to the Second World War ships.

'I've not got enough money for a battleship,' I said.

He chuntered something and picked one up. I glanced over but could only see the bottom of the box.

'What about this one?'

I lifted it from his hand.

'I told you. I haven't got enough for a battleship,' I said, handing it back and walking away.

'It's not a battleship,' he claimed, continuing to look at the box.

I tried to ignore him, but he didn't make it easy.

Back at his side again, I looked at the ship: HMS *Hood*.

'It looks like a battleship.' My finger tapped at the guns shooting out flames and smoke.

'That's because you don't know what you're on about.'

This was a regular semi-insult he threw around when we got to the limits of my knowledge and although mildly offensive, it was mainly true.

'What's the difference?'

He didn't answer. I watched his eyes flicking around the image on the box, the light playing tricks on me as the water appeared to ripple past the speeding ship in the reflection off his glasses.

'Only four of us survived when she sank.'

His words fell out like a confession. But I was always wary of his traps. If this was an act, it was a good one. He'd told me hundreds of stories, but the ones from his time in the war had been bits of daft-ness, like the ship's monkey that would wait for the cat to pass by, jumping on its back and riding it around the deck like a jockey. Or the sailor who went ashore in full dress uniform, only to return the next morning in a dress, with no recollection of the night's events.

'You never told me you were on the *Hood* when it sank.'

He bowed his head and the seriousness lifted.

'I think it's about time I did, don't you?'

I smiled and put my hand in my pocket then handed him my money in what I hoped would only be a symbolic gesture. He saved me.

'It's okay, H. I'll buy this for you; you keep saving for that car.' He nudged me. 'Or a motorbike,' he winked, bringing his hand up to conceal his grin.

Instinct kicked in and despite knowing she was at home, we both looked around to make sure Gran hadn't overheard. He handed me the box and greedily took in the scene: the stormy sea, the guns firing, spouts of water shooting into the air as the German shells landed short of their target. I nibbled at my bottom lip, already anticipating the challenge ahead.

'Happy?' he asked.

My broad smile confirmed I was.

The moment was tainted by the inevitable 'but'.

'But,' he said, 'if we're going to build the *Hood* together, H, we've got to do it right.'

This was always his way: 'do the job right', 'measure twice, cut once', 'if a job's worth doing, it's worth doing well' were the chants trotted out whenever I helped him in the workshop. Other nonsensical ones, like 'many a mickle makes a muckle', were thrown in at random to keep me on my toes.

He counted off on his fingers. 'We're going to need paint, glue, some brushes.'

'And thinners,' I pointed out, 'for cleaning them.'

'Good lad.'

'Sandpaper?' I suggested. 'For rubbing the burs off.'

'I've got loads in the workshop. Good.' He clapped his hands together. 'Sounds like we've got a plan.'

Grandad sat on a bench across from the town hall while I returned his library books. I placed them side by side on the returns counter. The covers looked the same, the lone gunslinger standing in a dusty street, a distant enemy about to draw, the scene witnessed by a woman watching from a shop doorway, a handkerchief held to her face. I'd tried to read one of them once but found the slow build-up to the killing tedious. I'd never read a book all the way through since the bedtime story of *The Travels of Little Red Squirrel*. From my experience with his cowboy book, I didn't think I was missing much. The TV seemed a much more convenient way to waste my time.

When I rejoined him, he was deep in conversation with a woman and her daughter. I hung around trying to look impatient, without success. In the end, it was only their appointment at the hairdressers that forced them to leave. They walked away clutching each other's arms and laughing, the older woman casting a quick look over her shoulder. Grandad winked, encouraging more giggles. A half-smile hung around his face as we slowly made our way back to the car, only disappearing when the engine stalled four more times as he manoeuvred out of the car park.

When we got home, Gran was sat at the kitchen table, her head buried in the sports pages of the *Daily Mirror*, her betting slips lined up on the table. The writing wobbled over the two-part dockets in unsteady capitals. She sat back and nibbled the end on her specs, eyeing my carrier bag.

'Grandad's bought me an Airfix model of the *Hood*,' I told her.

'The *Hood*?' she said, swivelling round to look at Grandad.

'Yeah. I thought it would be nice for us to build it together,' he said, biting the inside of his cheek.

She held him for a moment in the power of her stare before releasing him.

'Good,' she said. 'It'll keep the pair of you out of my way.' She put her specs back on and returned to the runners and riders. 'Hopefully,' she added, under her breath.

'I'm going to do some potting in the greenhouse,' Grandad said, placing the car keys on the table next to her, giving her arm a squeeze.

She scooped them up and dropped them into her apron pocket without looking up.

'Don't overdo it, Jack,' she said, absorbed in her options.

He confirmed he'd behave himself and I went upstairs with my bag of goodies. I put everything on the dressing table, arranging and rearranging their order.

Hunger drew us back to the kitchen. As a training exercise, Gran had left us the components of a sandwich – a bit of practice before we built the *Hood*. She'd taken her tea and a piece of fruit cake and retired to the lounge to watch the racing. Grandad took charge of sandwich assembly, hacking up the ham and cheese before realising he'd forgotten the piccalilli. He took them apart to smear the luminous yellow mixture over the ham and the plate. He handed me the bodge-up with a shrug, but neither of us was in a position to be fussy.

As we tucked in, the television announced that the first race at Kempton Park was 'under starter's orders'. He winked at me as the commentator confirmed, 'And they're off.'

We silently stalked into the hall, peeped through the gap of the open door into the living room and watched her. She sat back in the settee, her eyes glued to the action, hands holding reins, bouncing in the chair as her horse took each jump. We never knew which horse she backed, but it was always Willie Carson and Jonjo O'Neill over the jumps, or Lester Piggott in a 'flat' race.

As they rounded the last bend, the commentary got increasingly frantic. The race was close and the commentator's voice rose in pitch then turned into an unfathomable babble of jockey and horse names. Gran clutched her betting slip in her fist and moved forwards in her seat, her fist pumping, her left hand tapping her thigh as if she were applying the whip.

Her lips fluttered. 'Come on!' she growled, moving even closer, her bum only just perched on the cushion. 'Come on, yeh beauty,' she cried, now louder and with more conviction.

The race reached its climax and Blue Midnight made a last lunge for the line. Gran threw her betting slip on the floor and slumped back in the chair. We reversed into the kitchen, giggling.

Her voice drifted down the hall, 'Yeh useless bloody thing.'

A few minutes later, she joined us.

Grandad bravely asked, 'How did you get on, Lil?'

'It came in second. Jonjo was robbed.' She showed no signs of the drama as she dropped her cup in the bowl and turned towards our grinning mugs. 'What's up with you two?'

We tried, unsuccessfully, to straighten our faces.

'You're not right in your heads,' she said as she took her frustration out on the cups and plates.

Bill Lambert's cough announced his arrival long before he walked in. Like many men on the estate, Bill had worked down the pit since he left school. Now, close to retirement, the forty-odd years of breathing in coal dust were taking their toll. I'd seen it before with Nige Parkinson's uncle, Andy. Nige was one of the older lads we'd occasionally knock around with.

His uncle Andy lived with them a few doors down from Keith. We'd often see him getting whatever fresh air his lungs still had the capacity to use, leaning heavily on the gateposts between the privet hedges. His string vest and pyjama bottoms stained brown, all thoughts of his presentation gone, his head would be bowed, his tangled hair hanging around his unshaven face. And he'd cough. A miner's cough. Once you've heard it, it's easy to identify from a cold or flu. A miner's cough rasps from the core and rolls out in green-yellow gobs onto the pavement. Sometimes we'd go to Nige's house to play a board game when rain interrupted play and Andy would be asleep on the settee, a plastic cup on the carpet beside him, half full of phlegm.

Bill was going the same way. The manhole cover on the drive rattled and he paused, letting loose a final cannon of mucus onto the drive before coming in. Like all other visitors, there was no knocking. He took up his usual position in the doorway between the kitchen and the hall, leaning against the frame. His nicotine-stained teeth grinned as he told of yesterday's success on the horses. I don't know why he bothered. His winnings were on the mantelpiece. Gran had known of his success while he was still riding the conveyor to the coal face. The afternoon shift was no barrier to his dedication.

'How did you do? Did you put that treble on?' he asked, gulping for air, the steep driveway having taken its toll.

'Aye, but the last one let me down.' Gran made her excuses for Lester Piggott and told Bill of her tactics for today.

'Oh, I've got a couple of them marked up 'n' all.' He handed over today's slips and the exact money required as Gran passed yesterday's slips and winnings into his other hand.

'Check it, Bill. Make sure they've got it right.'

Bill looked at the pile of change in his fist and smiled at the payout.

'Right, I'd best be off. See you later.'

'See yeh, Bill.' Gran waved the racing pages at him as he left, turning her attention back to the paper to make her final choices.

It was only then that I realised Bill never called her by her name – any name. Not Lily or Mrs Manning or anything. Thinking about it, the only people to call her Lily were family. Everyone on the estate called her Mrs Manning, but they all called Grandad, Jack.

'Come on, Harry. Let's get started,' Grandad shouted.

His voice competed with the opening music of the soppy film Gran always watched when the racing had finished. Sometimes I'd be able to persuade her to watch the wrestling with me instead, but if it was a musical, I had no chance. Unable to stomach any of that rubbish, I'd retreat to my room to play the few records I'd accumulated. Sometimes I'd listen to Grandad's war movie themes album, *The Dam Busters* or *633 Squadron*, adding drama to my Airfix dogfights.

'Coming,' I shouted, bounding downstairs.

Howard Keel was already warbling on the telly as Gran put a crumble in the oven. She brushed the flour from her hands and threw the tea towel onto the draining board before rushing past me. Grandad was waiting for me in the workshop, which was just a garage attached to the side of the house. I closed the sliding door and severed the connection to the outside world. The ancient angle lamp cast its light over the bench like an alien invader.

I jumped as Gran's voice boomed from the other side of the door.

'Put the heater on, Jack. You'll catch your d—' There was a stifled cry as she dropped something. 'And make sure you put your togs on before you start; you know that glue's a bugger to get off.'

We looked towards the kitchen.

'Better do as she says, H. We don't want to upset her.' He sniffed the air. 'Smells like apple crumble.' He rubbed his hands together and smacked his lips. 'I'll sort him out, Lily,' he said croakily, clearing his throat into the top of his fist. 'Better put your ovies on, H.'

Our overalls hung on hooks like two deflated scarecrows, our work boots beneath them, mine a perfect miniature of his. I pulled them over my jeans, wriggling into the top half. It wouldn't be long before I'd outgrow them.

Tools were suspended on brackets and rusty nails around the walls of the workshop. Shelves were stacked with jam jars full of screws and bolts, while tin cans held screwdrivers and chisels. He had a hammer collection ready to hit anything and everything. Because of his engineering skills, there was always somebody bringing their lawnmower, trailer or car to be fixed, sharpened or welded. He could mend anything. I don't know how much money changed hands, but there was always a visitor with a selection of veg from their allotment or, when it became a craze, a few bottles of home-made wine. Grandad once had a go at home brewing beer. Not satisfied with the local ingredients, he'd bought the hops from an old navy mate in Kent, but the project had stopped when Dad died. The gear sat unused in the corner. Now, he just had his visits to the British Legion club.

'And your boots.' Grandad pointed at my feet.

I slid them on, kneeling to tie the laces.

'Did you check for spiders?' He looked down at my 'sea boots'.

Damn, I always forgot to check for spiders. I wiggled my toes and stamped my feet.

'Dead now,' I smiled, happy with my anti-spider tactics.

But then I thought about the possibility of one being in the toe end of the 'generous-fitting' boots, as Grandad had described the oversized clodhoppers. The spider could have pushed itself back with its hairy legs as my toes wriggled just in front of its nose. I decided not to take any chances, so I kicked the bare brickwork, sending my toes to the end of the boot. Got yeh! That turned out to be a mistake, as kicking a wall can often be, and I'm speaking as someone who has extensive experience of kicking a wide selection of solid objects. My toes throbbed gently as Grandad looked at me.

'That spider could have had babies and now they're all orphans.'

'Mummy spider will look after them.'

'That *was* mummy spider. She ate her husband after the babies hatched.'

'Why?' I asked.

'No use for him now,' he shrugged. 'That's why you should always do the washing-up and a bit of hoovering, so there's always a reason for them to keep you alive.'

I gulped.

'Come on,' he said. 'Let's get on with it.'

I switched the radio on and turned the dial to Radio 1.

'What you putting that rubbish on for?'

'It's not rubbish,' I exclaimed. '*And* Alice Cooper's got a new single out.'

'I can't stand her,' he said, scrunching his face up to hide his smirk. 'Come on, H, put Radio 2 on.'

Johnny Cash was Grandad's favourite and was a regular on the old folks' station. I didn't react, hoping he'd forget. He pretended to clear the workbench before reaching past me and trying to get to the tuning dial, jostling me out of the way.

'Watch where you're going, H,' he said as he pushed into me.

I jostled back, surprised at my adolescent strength. He wasn't a man who could easily be jostled. But now he was puffing and panting, and it was closer to an even fight. After a short, determined struggle, he let me win.

'Be a good lad and bring me a stool over, will yeh?'

The legs of the heavy wooden stool slid with ease over the oily floor. It was one of two, 'salvaged' from the British Legion club when the snug had had a 'refit'. From what I could tell, a refit comprised new stools and repainting the room the same colour as before: nicotine cream.

The temperamental paraffin heater cooperated for once and lit the first time. I turned it up to full blast, dragged the other stool into place and climbed up. My work boots dangled from my spindly legs. They were just a pair of black wellies chopped down to work boot size. Grandad had cut a slit down the front, glued in a tongue made from a piece of welly top, then he'd punched holes so they had laces like his, although my laces were string.

'Ready?' he asked.

'Ready,' I confirmed.

'Okay, let's see what we've got.'

He opened the box, laid the parts out on the bench and unfolded the instructions.

'What's first, Grandad?'

'Just a sec.'

'Do we glue the bottom together?'

He looked at me over his glasses. 'It's called the hull.'

'Do we glue the hull together?'

'Just a sec.'

I could see he was looking at the parts in what seemed to be unnecessary detail. Chuntering to himself, he put down his glasses and rubbed his eyes.

'They must have designed it just before the refit; there are still loads of things wrong with it.'

This was news: they refitted ships as well as working men's clubs. I gripped the stool with my legs.

THE TABLES WERE PACKED with the hungry crew. Despite the storm and the decorators, work in the mess hall continued around us. I attempted to stop my stool from sliding around on the pitching deck by digging my fork into the table; others noticed and copied the tactic. Despite the grimacing of those doing their best to anchor themselves, we were still washed from one side of the room to the other with each passing wave. The sound of hundreds of fork prongs being dragged across the metal table tops reverberated around the confines of the room. My

spine acted as a conductor for the dreadful din, and my face distorted as I cringed and shuddered.

Cream paint and spilt food washed across the floor, the decorators sliding around on their ladders, brush strokes tracing their movement on the walls as they tried in vain to apply the paint. Exasperated, the cook threw down his ladle in frustration, helpless to stop the pots of soup from slopping over the stove and extinguishing the burners.

'H!'

'Urgh?'

'The heater's gone out.' Grandad pointed at the troublesome contraption.

I relit it and sat back at the bench.

'Have we got to take it back?' I asked.

'They won't give me a refund; I've had it for thirty-odd years.'

'Not the hea—' Damn! He'd got me again.

He made a half-hearted attempt to keep the smirk off his face and continued, 'No, she's just not the way I remember her.'

The question mark on my forehead prompted him.

'When I was in the navy.'

'I know you were in the navy, but you called it . . . her.'

I looked at the box lid, the mean-looking ship tearing through the stormy sea, all guns blazing. Surely the *Hood* was male.

'All ships and boats are female.'

'No mister ships?'

'Always ladies, Harry. I can't explain, but when we get aboard, you'll see. 'Come here . . .'

He leaned over, put his arm around me and pulled me close. He smoothed the instructions out on the bench and I could feel his whiskers tickling my neck. I closed my eyes and held his hand.

'After they'd designed the *Hood*, the Germans invented armour-piercing shells. So the top brass had to make changes to the plans, making the armour thicker on the sides. No one gave any thought to the possibility that shells might fall on the deck, idiots. The *Hood* was supposed to be the first of three ships of the same design. But the *Hood* was the only one that got built.'

'Where did they build it?' I said quietly.

'In Scotland, Glasgow, on the River Clyde.'

RAIN FELL STEADILY and the wet cobbles were like miniature islands separated by water flowing between them. Tall buildings lined both sides of the street, four and five stories high. Decades of exposure to the Industrial Revolution had turned the stone black – a revolution that was still in full swing in Glasgow, the beating heart of the nation's industrial body.

Grandad pointed his stick at the buildings. 'These are the offices where the Hood *was designed.'*

I was surprised to find the wet cobbles weren't slippery as we walked between the two buildings. On each side was a metal spiral staircase leading to the upper floors. We walked to the building on our right, stopping at the bottom of the steps.

'Are you sure we're allowed, Grandad?'

'Course we are; they're expecting us.'

The steel handrail was cold and I shivered as I led the way, shrinking self-consciously at the noisy reverberation of our steps on the metal. At the top, I grabbed Grandad's sleeve and paused again in front of the door. He looked at me, winked and reached past for the handle.

The office was dimly lit and there were four large desks spaced equally down its length. A couple of men were working under a pool of light at the desk farthest away, their backs to us. Pinned to the walls all around the room were the plans, all marked 'HOOD CLASS'. Each showed a different view of the ship.

'Are these the instructions, Grandad?' I whispered.

Despite my hushed tone, the two men turned round. They could have been father and son. The older man had a small moustache. He looked like a professor with his round glasses and tweed suit. The other man was much younger, maybe in his mid-twenties, clean-shaven. His shirtsleeves were rolled up and his green tank top was the only colourful garment worn by either man. They both had short hair, held flat with Brylcreem. The older one was smoking a pipe, the younger, a cigarette. Thick smoke lay in a layer just above our heads, like the room had its own weather system. The older man was the first to speak.

'Glad you could make it, Jack.'

They both smiled at us.

'You've come to have a look at 460, haven't you?'

I looked up at Grandad.

'Design number 460,' said the younger man. 'That's what we call the Hood *class in the office.'*

'That's right, sir,' Grandad said in a clipped voice.

The older man glanced at the large wooden clock on the wall.

'Well, gentlemen, I apologise, but I'm going to have to dash. I've got a bit of business to attend to at the Admiralty.' He tapped his nose with his forefinger. 'Hush-hush, don't yeh know.'

We both followed suit, tapping our noses, too.

'We understand, sir. Thanks for allowing us to visit,' Grandad said in a strange posh accent.

I looked at him and he just shrugged.

'Nice to almost meet you, Harry,' the man said as he put on his overcoat and hat. 'I'll leave you in the capable hands of Mr Brown.' He tapped the shoulder of his young colleague.

With a small wave, he turned and disappeared through the doors at the far end of the room, letting in a draught that rippled its way through the office. I always thought it odd that Grandad changed how he spoke, depending on whom he was talking to. It was just as well we didn't know any foreigners, or it could have got embarrassing.

'So,' said Mr Brown, 'you've got your own ship to build, eh, Harry?' Mr Brown spoke with a Scottish twang. 'You can call me John now the boss has gone.'

It wasn't a harsh accent, but there was no doubt where he was from.

'Yeah, but it's only . . . small.' I looked again at the plans on the wall. 'Are these the instructions?'

'That's right,' said Brown, smiling, 'but we call them blueprints. Do you know why that is?'

'No,' I shrugged.

'Well, it's because they're prints . . . and . . . they're blue.'

Brown and Grandad both seemed to think this was hilarious.

'Just our little joke,' said Brown.

Yeah, very little.

'Although,' he added, 'that really is *why they're called blueprints.'*

Grandad looked at Brown. 'Funny and factual.'

They both started laughing again.

'Why is some of it in red, then?' I asked. 'Are they red-prints?'

'Don't be daft, Harry,' said Brown.

I looked at Grandad.

'Can he call me daft?'

'Oh yes,' he confirmed.

'What's the first job you've got to do, Jack?' asked Brown.

'We've got to glue the bottom together,' I told him.

Grandad raised his eyebrows.

'Bond the hull together,' I corrected.

'You'd best see how the lads do it in the yard.' Brown pointed to a door on the other side of the office.

We thanked him and headed off. I took the metal steps two at a time, pausing halfway down to let Grandad catch up, but he instantly pushed me in the back.

'Get a move on, H.'

I jumped the last two steps onto the rough concrete yard. The door at the top of the steps opened, the light spilling out into the murky afternoon. Brown stood on the landing.

'You forgot something,' he shouted down.

Grandad's hand fell on my shoulder as I set off to retrieve his walking stick.

'I don't think I'm going to need that here, H.'

Brown smiled and disappeared inside. We looked at Grandad's legs. He held the left one out and shook it. I was disappointed not to hear a bell jangle. I followed suit, then we shook our right legs. Caught up in the moment, we linked arms and skipped across the cobbles. I hummed the theme tune from The Wizard of Oz. *As we got closer to the* Hood, *I pushed Grandad away from me, certain that skipping would be frowned upon in the shipyard but only succeeding in throwing myself off balance as he was unaffected by my effort.*

The outline of the Hood *loomed above us across the yard and men were working along the full length of the ship. Scaffolding surrounded the* Hood*'s skeleton and some steel plate was already fixed at the front, but wherever there was space, there was activity. The noise grew louder as we got closer.*

Then silence.

The workers stopped and turned towards us. The scene dimmed and a spotlight illuminated a lone figure. He hit the scaffolding with his giant spanner. Bang. Then again. Bang. We slowed to a stop and stared. The lone figure started beating out a rhythm: bang-thump-clang-crash, bang-thump-clang-crash. The pace increased as others joined in.

Grandad looked at me.

'This is all your fault, isn't it?'

'I don't even like musicals,' I claimed as the lights played across the workers on the scaffolding.

My jaw hung loose as one group broke into a tap-dancing routine, their hobnailed boots reverberating around the yard as they jumped from one platform to another, swinging on the uprights. They moved around the structure, stamping out the rhythm.

Others sang. 'He doesn't like our mus-i-cal, he doesn't like our mus-i-cal,' as they got faster and faster, repeating the same line over and over, while others filled in the harmony. 'Noo, he doesn't liiike, oh . . . he doesn't like.'

Most of the workforce was now on the ground, coming towards us in neat rows, moving left and right, clicking their heels at each change of direction, still singing, 'He doesn't like our mus-i-cal.' The pace slowed and they clicked their fingers in time with the slow spanner beat, then it picked up quickly. One man came to the fore, getting closer and closer as the noise swelled in crescendo of bangs, stomps and singing . . . And stopped.

The frontman broke off and came over to us, the others instantly back at work.

'I hope this isn't going to happen often,' Grandad sighed, looking at me.

I had nothing to say.

The man jogged up to us, 'That you, Jack?'

'It is. And this is Harry.'

'Alright, Harry? Good to see yeh both. I'm Stewart, but you can call me Mr Donnelly.' He leaned close and frowned. 'Yer hairs very long, son. Are you one o' them—'

'Glam rocker,' said Grandad.

'Glam rocker, is it?' Mr Donnelly said, his thick Scottish accent stressing his apparent dim view of such a thing.

He shook his head and sighed. I shrank into Grandad. Donnelly burst out laughing.

'Come on, daft lad.' He reached down and cupped his hand around my head then led me forwards. 'Do yeh wanna come 'n' have a look at what we're up to?'

As we walked across the yard, I wondered if everyone we met was going to call me daft. I glanced at Grandad and realised they probably were.

The noise got louder.

'Yer bonding yer hull just now, is that right?' Donnelly shouted at Grandad.

'Aye,' Grandad shouted back, 'but I wanted to show him how the big lads do it,' he said in his own version of a Scottish accent.

'Och, there's nae many big lads here, Jack. We let the cranes do all the work.'

Both men were shouting to be heard above the din.

'Follow me, lads. And watch yer step; there's nae many places you can fall over here and you don't want to go getting yourself' a serious injury.'

I could hear the pleasure in Donnelly's voice as he told the story of a tea boy who had tripped over a pipe and lost his hand in some unfathomable machine. We climbed onto one of the platforms where the men were working. Grandad followed me up the ladder, banging his head into my backside as we climbed up.

'Grandad, give up.'

'Och, bairns!' he growled.

Donnelly shouted to a group of men. One of them broke off and came over. He was about twenty and a mass of curly ginger hair stuck out in all directions.

'I'm Andrew,' he said in an even broader Scottish accent than Donnelly's. 'Andrew Campbell. Andy, if yeh like. Yeh can leave 'em wi' me, Stewart, if yeh like.'

Donnelly nodded and climbed up to one of the higher levels.

'It's Jack 'n' Harry, right?' said Andy.

'Aye,' said Grandad; his accent was getting stronger, too. 'Can we show Harry how yeh fix the plates together?'

'Course we can. If you like, there's one just coming in now.' He pointed over our heads.

A crane was holding a small piece of metal suspended by chains, but as it got closer, I realised it was huge – as tall as a man but five times longer. The crane slowed, hand signals guiding it in. After a lot of adjustments, the plate finally came to a stop. Steel bars, like giant screws, held the plate in position. The men worked quickly but methodically, unfastening the chains. Then the driver swung them out of the way as soon as it was clear, returning for another load before quickly moving on to the next.

Each finished section was covered with chalk marks: squares, circles, triangles and other odd shapes, with lines drawn through them. The finished rivets were marked with a big blob of coloured paint. It was like an Egyptian graffiti artist had gone berserk. I asked Andrew what it meant and he told me that each of the symbols identified a different riveting gang. The coloured markers were where the timekeeper had counted each rivet to work out how much money the gang had earned that day. This ensured they paid for all the work completed, but as Andrew added with a smile, 'None of it twice.'

They were ready to start.

The riveting gang moved in, working quickly and methodically. The 'heater' threw white-hot rivets from the brazier as casually as tossing a tennis ball to the 'holder'. The 'riveters' stood on each side of the plate.

'Yeh might wanna stand further back, lads,' Andrew said. 'It might be a wee bit—'

I could see his mouth move, but we didn't hear the last word, as the jack-hammer fired up. We both jumped but pretended that we hadn't.

Bang! Bang! Bang!

Despite the cold, the lads were dripping with sweat.

Bang! Bang! Bang!

I STOPPED HAMMERING the rivet and looked at the two pieces of metal held loosely together.

Grandad shrugged. 'Not bad for a first go, H.'

I gave them a gentle tug and they fell apart. Cobblers! I threw the pieces into the 'they might come in handy one day' box under the bench.

Once the two halves of the *Hood*'s hull were fixed, we secured the main deck. I followed Grandad's instructions and cut short lengths of masking tape, sticking them to the back of my hand until needed. The pleasantly toxic smell of glue filled the workshop. Grandad used the pieces of tape to draw the hull together, clamping the deck securely in position.

'Looks like that's done the job, H.' He gave an approving nod. 'Not much we can do until the glue dries.'

'Tea's ready!' Gran shouted.

We fought each other through the doorway, Grandad letting me win again.

'What's all the banging about?' she asked.

'I'm just showing him how to do a bit of riveting, Lil.'

She served us each a steaming bowl of stew.

'I'm going to leave you two to it,' she said. 'Crumble's in the oven and the custard's in the pan. I'm off to watch the rest of the film. You can wash up, Harry.'

Grandad chuckled.

'And you can dry, Jack.'

His grin faded.

Grandad's slow pace made me wonder if he was ever going to finish his crumble. I held up my spoon distractedly, eyeing up his bowl and letting out a small yelp as hot custard dripped on my hand. Grandad shook his head as I wiped it on my overalls. I scraped up the last of the custard, making sure I got every morsel. When I looked up, Grandad was staring at me.

'Leave the pattern on the bowl, H.'

'Have you finished?' I asked hopefully.

'I bloody haven't, no.' He pulled the bowl closer, curling his arm around it for protection.

My mind wandered while I visited the loo, returning to see that Grandad had now finished. I plonked myself down and leaned back.

Waving my spoon around to conduct the conversation, I asked him, 'You know you said all boats and ships were female?'

He folded his arms and rested them on the table in anticipation of me saying something moronic.

'What about cars?' I asked.

He pursed his lips. 'Why do you ask?' He let out a small burp.

'One of my mates at school says they have a car called Fred.'

'And you thought about that while you were having a wee, did you?' He looked at my hands.

'I was going to wash them in here.' I pointed at the sink.

'Go on then, yeh muck tub.'

I could feel his eyes on my back, making sure I did a proper job. I couldn't understand grown-ups' obsession with hand-washing after a toilet visit. It's not like I'd had a poo . . .

'So, has our car got a name?'

'Course it hasn't,' he said.

He seemed very certain.

'A boat or a ship has a soul, a character. They're put together by men who are artists. They put love into it. Each man does his part and when it's finished, they've created something that has a life of its own.'

'Like Frankenstein?' I suggested.

'Like Frankenstein, but a lot prettier.'

'Like the bride of Frankenstein?' I asked, warming to the subject I knew something about.

'I'm not sure she had a soul,' he said, laughing and moving forwards to sit on the edge of his chair. 'Anyway,' he said, 'I can tell you for sure, cars don't have souls.' He reached out and pulled me to him. 'But,' he whispered, 'if you promise not to tell your gran, I'll tell you a secret.'

I nodded, eager to be involved in any kind of lads-only conspiracy.

'Well, they don't have souls, but'—he checked over his shoulder to make sure Gran hadn't sneaked back in—'they do have arseholes! Usually driving 'em!'

'Grandad!'

'Shush! You don't want to get into trouble with your Gran, do you?'

'Me? It's you who's been swearing.' The laughter leaked out of me. I'm glad I went for a wee when I did, otherwise I may have had an accident.

He lifted his shoulders and tucked his head down like he was trying to avoid chuckle bullets. He held me close and his scent filled my head.

'Are you still hungry?' he whispered, enjoying the secrecy.

I nodded eagerly.

'In that case,' he said, still whispering but tightening his hold on me, 'what about a bit of chin pie?'

He rubbed his whiskery chin all over my face and neck while I squirmed and giggled until he unexpectedly released his grip and I fell between his legs onto the floor. He stood up, brushed some bits off his overalls onto me and looked down.

'Come on, H. Stop mucking about,' he said as he walked away, leaving me satisfied and crumpled on the rug in front of the fire.

I looked at the embers, bending them to my will, watching the images of red-hot rivets flying through the air and guns firing flames across a stormy seascape.

The evening passed in a haze of fizzy pop, screeching tyres and gun smoke as Bond battled with Goldfinger on ITV.

Chapter 5

Sunday, 23 March 1975

On Sunday morning, I watched Gran march across the street to do her cleaning job at the bookies. On weekdays she had to do the work in the evening, but on weekends she broke up the routine, leaving Saturday's mess to stew overnight, returning home mid-morning to take control of the kitchen and prepare Sunday dinner. It was always ready for when Grandad got back from the club just after two o'clock. On a good day, we'd all retire to slouch in the living room and watch a film, preferably a western. Gran would help us to count the Indians who copped it. Sometimes she'd stay in the kitchen listening to the lonely easy listening on Radio 2, enjoying the peace it offered.

I mooched aimlessly around the house, watching what meagre offerings the TV had for me, *Farming Outlook* the miserable highlight. I munched on a piece of toast in the kitchen, the oven building up the familiar aroma as the meat joint cooked. I stood still for too long. Grandad spotted me and called me to the greenhouse. Trays full of seedlings filled the top shelf on both sides.

'Do me a favour, H. Take these down to Joe Sefton's allotment, will you?' He pointed to a tray, 'spring cabbage' neatly printed on the lollypop stick label.

I looked around at all the other sticks and realised there were a lot more sticks than I'd seen lollypops. Maybe he'd got a secret lollypop habit. It was something I needed to talk to him about, but best to wait until he wasn't expecting it.

My new teenage brain was working well, so despite having bugger all to do, I quickly thought of an excuse not to go.

'How do you know he'll be there?'

As a teenager, I felt it was my duty to resist doing anything to help without at least putting up a fight. He was ready for me, counting off the 'facts' on his fingers.

'It's Sunday morning, the weather's nice but it's going to rain later, it's a busy time.' His hand waved across the trays and pots before him. 'He hates his missus and we're talking about Joe Sefton. The pubs aren't open – where else is he going to be?'

The cabbage seedlings wobbled in the tray as I made my way through the estate, revealing every imperfection in my movement. They'd still need protecting, but in a few weeks, after the threat of a late frost had passed, they could be planted out. I gave them a sniff. They didn't smell like cabbages. Presumably, sometime soon, that would change. Big fluffy clouds with grey centres drifted across the sky like Zeppelin airships, ready to drop their payload.

Joe Sefton was leaning on his hoe as I came through the gate; weeds were sticking their heads above ground for the first time this year. Beads of sweat bubbled on his forehead despite the cool breeze, but Joe Sefton was a big bloke – even standing still looked like hard work.

'Ay-up, Harry,' he said, taking my intrusion as his cue to have a cigarette break.

The pile of pallets creaked as he sat down. I set the seedlings on the ground and sat beside him. Stained with nicotine and mud, his fat fingers did an expert job of rolling the thinnest cigarette I'd ever seen. He sucked the smoke deep into his lungs and coughed, his simple brain unable to see the connection. He pulled a bag of mint imperials from his jacket and offered them up. I dipped my hand in and pulled one out.

'Take a couple,' he encouraged, shaking the bag.

Although I wasn't that bothered about mints, I took his advice and dropped the spares into my parka pocket.

'How's your grandad?'

The words hung around us, insisting on an answer.

'He's not been well.'

'Aye.' He coughed again, spitting a piece of his lung onto the earth. 'I heard.'

It hadn't occurred to me that other people would be thinking about him. Of course they were – he had loads of mates.

'Tell him I've got some sweet peas in the greenhouse. I'll see him . . . err . . . later.'

He picked up the seedlings with difficulty and put them in his cold frame, the dog-end of the cig dangling from his lips, the smoke curling into his eye with no ill effect. That takes practice.

I looked over at Grandad's allotment next door. The prepared soil was still fallow, a few shoots starting to show. Last winter's cabbage and sprouts were now brown and yellow, canes already in position for the unplanted runner beans.

'I've done a bit of weeding, but . . .'

Joe Sefton's voice trailed off as we both looked at the vegetable patch, the lack of attention since Grandad had been in hospital already visible. My pulse quickened as I thought about how big the task was – a job that could never be finished.

'There's always somebody who'd be willing to take it over,' he coughed, 'if it ever gets too much for him.'

How many more seasons did Joe have in him? He looked ready to drop at any moment.

I left him fumbling with another cigarette paper and roamed the allotment's interweaving paths. It wouldn't be long before Grandad

was back down here. My teenage status would give me even more excuses not to help. But my adolescent strength would come in handy
when the ground needed digging in the winter. It would be even better than previous years – I'd have more to complain about, but I'd be
more useful to him when I inevitably gave in.

Drifting around the maze, I reached the boundary with the next
housing estate. A tall hawthorn hedge did its best to keep the two
separate. I walked along looking for nests, although I knew they'd
be last year's, the thin foliage not giving enough cover for this year's
brood. I peeped through the hedge into the neighbouring gardens,
pausing when I saw movement. He didn't know anybody was watching.

I looked at the boy and dog with envy. The boy was on his knees
holding a chunk of old rope, throwing it into the garden and patting
the ground like a drum kit, encouraging the dog to bring it back. It
was a Border collie cross, just another mongrel on a housing estate
with a thousand like him. But despite its lowly ancestry, even at a distance I could tell this dog had character. We'd never had a dog. I'd
never seen the point until now. What would it be like to have a friend
who didn't fall out with you, one who wanted nothing from you other than food and company?

The boy was teasing his pet. Whipping the rope from side to side,
the dog followed each movement, bouncing left and right, its back
legs making slight adjustments for balance. The boy thrust the rope
into the dog's face. The dog bit it and shook it vigorously, trying to
drag it out of the boy's hand but stopping when it succeeded, only to
start again when the boy tried to take it off him. I wanted to join in;
but it was impossible.

The boy grinned and growled at his best mate. It was something
you couldn't share. Any intrusion would shatter the moment and the
magic would be lost.

I backed away from the hedge, envious of their friendship.

Gran came home just after me. She did a quick tour of the house, finding me in the workshop.

'Where's your Grandad?'

I shrugged. 'Upstairs?'

She frowned and left, leaving the door to the workshop open.

'Jack!' she shouted into the hall.

A muffled reply came from the bathroom.

'Are you alright, Jack?

I couldn't hear anything Grandad said. She hung up her coat, then came into the kitchen chuntering, but turned back into the hall and opened the bathroom door.

'Are you having me on?' she asked in a sharp tone.

'No, why?' Grandad didn't seem to expect conflict.

'Why? Because you've only just got out of hospital and . . .' She slammed the door as hard as she could, the air trapped in the small room preventing the dramatic exit she was looking for.

She marched past me without a word, my curiosity drawing me into the kitchen. At the sink, she took it out on the dirty pots and pans that were still there from breakfast.

Grandad emerged from the bathroom, his grey wiry chest hair sticking through his vest, still towelling down his face and neck.

'I'm only going across for a couple of pints,' he said, leaning on the handrail as he made his way upstairs.

I sat with Gran in the kitchen and as she pretended to read the paper, I pretended to read my comic. The muffled wrenching sound of wood and glass smashing made us both jump. We automatically looked at the ceiling together. Gran started to move, but I put my hand on her arm.

'I'll go and see what's wrong.'

As I stepped into the hall, his voice rang out. I peered up at the landing to find him looking down over the handrail dressed only in his shirt and underpants.

'Come and give me a hand, will you?'

Gran looked at the ceiling then at me before returning her gaze to the paper.

Grandad sat on the bed, his suit laid out beside him. The mirror of their dressing table was shattered on the floor, the wooden frame smashed beyond repair.

'Just get me started with my trousers, will you, H?' He pointed to his feet.

Offering them up, I knelt in front of him, lifting each foot and dropping it into the leg hole. After gathering up the material to get his feet through, I wriggled the waistband past his knees and up into his hands, staying close as we stood up, just in case he lost his balance. He fumbled for a long time with his belt and buttons, then put on his shoes. He was already wiping beads of sweat from his brow. I remained by his side as we made painful progress down the stairs. He put on his jacket and waddled through the hall, leaning heavily on his stick as he opened the front door.

'See you later,' he said without looking back.

I watched him struggle across the street, his suit jacket flapping as the wind buffeted him.

An hour later, a commotion dragged us away from the goggle-box. Frank Watson and Bill Donleavy stood in the hall, Grandad hanging between them. They all looked up as we emerged from the living room.

'Jack's not feeling so good, missus.' Frank took most of Grandad's weight in the confined space.

'Oh, Jack,' said Gran. 'Can you help me get him upstairs?'

'Come on, Jack,' said Frank. 'Let's get you to bed.'

Gran followed them as they made their way up the stairs, leaving Bill and me in the hall.

'Is he drunk?' I asked.

'No,' he said, chuckling. 'He didn't even finish his first pint. I know he's taking some tablets; they might have reacted with the booze.' He looked uncomfortable. 'I'm going to get back, Harry. Tell him I'll see him later.'

I closed the door behind him. As I got to the top of the stairs, Frank Watson emerged. Rather than pass him on the narrow landing, I went into my room.

'Let me know if you need any help,' he said, without waiting for a reply.

When I was sure he'd gone, I went to see what was up.

Gran removed Grandad's jacket.

'Come on, Jack. Let's get you in bed.'

She struggled with his sleeves, pulling them down his arms. Grandad didn't seem able to help.

'Harry,' she said, 'go round to Joyce's and ask her to ring Dr Crowther.'

'No!' Grandad said before I had time to move.

'Jack, you're not well.'

'I'm fine. It was just a bad pint or—'

'Harry, go to Joyce's,' she repeated.

'I said no!' he yelled, his shoulders slumped. 'You can ring him in the morning if I'm no better.' His anger spent, he said weakly, 'Just help me into bed, Lily.'

'It's okay, Harry.' She cocked her head towards the door. 'I'll get your grandad to bed, then I'll be down. Put the kettle on, please, love. Fill it up and I'll make a hot-water bottle for Grandad.'

I walked away as they argued, their hissed conversation hiding none of the anger. Their clash concluded with a sharp, 'I know,' from Grandad. Gran filled the hot-water bottle in silence, returning to prepare the veg for the spoilt meal.

Gran and I ate Sunday lunch in silence. When we'd finished I went back to the *Hood*, smoothing out the instructions. Sluggish after our meal, I did some of the boring bits, fixing the driveshafts, propellers and the rudder to the hull. Then I secured the boat deck in position, built the conning tower and attached the funnels. My stomach turned when I looked at all the small pieces that remained. This was usually the part I enjoyed the most. It just wasn't the same without Grandad. My heart wasn't in it. Suddenly aware I was alone, the workshop seemed cold, damp and unwelcoming, and I was glad to escape.

Gran was finishing the washing-up.

'Take the fire into the room please, love.'

I went to get the short-handled shovel from the workshop.

'You'll have to clean the grate out first.'

I set the shovel down. After moving the grate aside, I hooked the ash pan with its handle and emptied it into the dustbin. Then readied myself for the tricky bit. I wriggled the leading edge of the shovel into the flaming coals of the kitchen fire, scooping up as many as possible. Then I tapped the shovel while it was still in the fireplace to dislodge any coals that might otherwise fall off. The disturbed fire was already showing its displeasure at the interruption by spilling smoke into the room and crackling menacingly. The heat on my hand was building, so I had to hurry.

Gripping the shovel with both hands, I carefully lifted it. Moving swiftly, I made my way through the hall and into the living room. The heat and smoke wafted into my face and I leaned back to minimise the discomfort. But when you're carrying a fire on a shovel, there's a limit to how far away you can get.

I avoided spilling any of the red-hot coals onto the carpet – historic scars showed the evidence of previous failures, not all of them mine – and tipped it into the grate. Then I threw on a few bits of coal, but not so much that I smothered it; it needed time to settle into its new home.

We followed the fire and set up camp in the living room. This routine was always dictated by what was on the telly. Weekdays it was the six o'clock news, weekends it was Bruce Forsythe or a movie that lured us in.

Sunday afternoons were a drag. The TV couldn't be relied upon. It was just as likely to throw up a love story as it was a western or a comedy. Today was another let-down. Rock Hudson, an unreliable movie star at best, was falling in love with Doris Day, again. I left Gran to it.

'Don't disturb your grandad, Harry, he needs some rest.'

I slunk upstairs, lingering at the landing window to watch the rain, which had moved in to complete the misery. Gran had removed the *Grattan* catalogue, so I lay there looking up at the aeroplanes dangling from my ceiling, flicking through the pages of the Airfix price list. Pickering watched me. He cleared his throat.

'Haven't you got some homework to do?'

I looked at my school bag, knowing full well the horror that lay inside. History. It was high on the list of subjects to be dropped. How was it possible for Hollywood to create an endless stream of entertaining historical epics and yet the best they could come up with at school was Jethro Tull and his sodding seed drill? Why didn't we do something about war? Or Jason and the Argonauts. As was obvious from the TV, there was plenty to go at.

The rain pecked at the window, driven by gusts of wind as the weather deteriorated. The *Golden Hind* sat on my windowsill, weathering the storm. I focused on my alarm clock, the movement of the fingers slowing as I observed them.

ROPES CREAKED AS THE swell passed under the ship. The sails hung from the spars, lifeless in the still air. Men sat around in the blaz-

ing heat, following the shade around the deck, determined not to do anything that wasn't essential. Drake stood next to the wheel, watching, willing the wind to appear after weeks of waiting.

   'What day is it, bosun?'

   'Sunday, sir.'

   'Sunday!' Drake tutted. 'I should have bloody known.'

ALL THAT PLASTIC ON the ship gave me a brainwave. I rushed downstairs and into the workshop, where I snapped off all the *Hood*'s remaining components, placing them in the box bottom. I took the plastic frame they'd been attached to, along with the box lid, and settled in front of the kitchen fire. The hearth still radiated the warmth built up in the bricks and ash, but there weren't any flames. I put the *Hood*'s box in the grate and I reached up for the matches on the mantelpiece. The plastic frames were entangled, like the steel rings magicians separate. I tried their technique, jiggling them to dislodge the pieces. To my surprise, it worked.

   I lit a match and held it under the plastic frame that the components of the *Hood* had been fixed to. As the end of the thin plastic sizzled and boiled, I held it as high as I could over the *Hood*'s box. The heat built quickly and the molten tip grew, then it started to drip. Miniature firebombs fell, leaving a trail of black smoke as they zipped through the air.

WE ALL LOOKED UP AT the rumbling sky. A flaming missile ripped through the air, tearing a hole in the grey clouds. Flames boiled and rippled on its surface as the flaming bomb tore its way through the atmosphere, a trail of black smoke marking its path. The meteorite

streaked towards the Hood as we stood on the deck, helpless, the red-hot molten surface of the bomb visible as it flew towards us. It splashed into the sea and exploded, blistering-hot bombs boiling the surrounding water. The unmistakable smell of burning plastic drifted towards the ship as we tried to outrun the attack. But the invisible tormentor had us in its sights.

The bombs were getting closer until the inevitable happened and the first one struck the deck just forward of the big guns. The bomb exploded, sending fragments of molten plastic in all directions. Men ran screaming, their clothes scorched and smouldering and jumped into the sea, as more missiles found their target. We looked skywards, desperate to take action but helpless under the onslaught. Everyone ran for cover as the bombardment continued, missiles hitting the conning tower and boat deck, setting fire to the wooden boats and their canvas covers.

I pulled Grandad with me and ran towards the pom-pom gun on the starboard side. I took up my position behind the gun, calling out instructions to Grandad as he wound the handles that swung the platform round. As the bombs continued to fall, I traced their path into the cloud, estimating the position of the alien ship.

Grandad made the final adjustments and I opened fire. The eight gun barrels of the pom-pom roared into life, recoiling into the gun's housing. Magazines full of ammo dropped into the auto-feed hoppers. I yelled at Grandad to load more, desperate to keep up the attack. The pom-pom's barrels were almost vertical as I aimed through the crude sight. The barrage was relentless, bombs exploding all around us. A fire had taken hold and was sweeping aft, towards the rear of the ship. I continued to fire at the invisible target until the ammunition ran out.

We stared into the sky as an explosion like distant thunder growled from the clouds. The crew cheered as the frame of the alien spaceship fell through the sky. But the ship was going to hit us. I grabbed Grandad and dragged him aft, diving into the sea as the spaceship hit the Hood.

We surfaced and watched the giant burning ship sizzle as it cartwheeled into the ocean, smashing the Hood *to pieces.*

BLUE-AND-GREEN FLAMES engulfed the *Hood*'s image as the last bit of the plastic frame fell from my fingers and crashed into the burning box. The brittle ash shattered and fell around the molten plastic.

Blowing on my fingertips to cool them, I looked at the clock on the mantelpiece above me. It was almost six o'clock.

After flicking on the radio, I cleaned up the mess I'd made in the hearth and endured the last few easy-listening tunes as the presenter said a prolonged goodbye. Then BBC Radio 2 joined forces with Radio 1 to present Sunday's highlight: the top 20 countdown. I took the radio with me. The music was loud in the echo chamber of the bathroom as I listened in vain for Alice Cooper's latest offering to be played. Why didn't more people like him? Tony Blackburn ran down the top 20 as I put my head under the cooling bathwater to see how long I could hold my breath. The test was interrupted by a loud banging.

'Harry? Are you done yet?' Gran's voice forced me to the surface. 'Don't forget to wash your hair.'

'Yes, Gran.'

I shook the water from my ears, only to have my worst fears confirmed. I looked into the depths. Drowning myself seemed an appealing option as Blackburn continued to pour misery on my day by announcing the Bay City Rollers were still at number one.

Feeling out of sorts, I stuck my head into the living room. Gran was watching *Songs of Praise* – the programme that made people go to church and pretend to sing, just so they could be on the telly. I retreated upstairs. I'd be glad when Sunday was over. But the worst bit was still to come. Things were always worse in the dark.

Mum and Dad had both died on a Sunday night, and now Grandad was poorly next door. I glanced continually at the wall separating us, waiting for a call or noise that would give me the excuse to go and see him. I went onto the landing and crept up to their bedroom, pressing my ear to the door. Relieved at the sound of his gentle snores, I withdrew into my room. In the absence of any distraction, my mind was drawn to another miserable Sunday night four years earlier.

Mum had suffered a stroke at the end of a long, hot summer. It happened when I was at school. She made a slow recovery and we visited every day. After three weeks, they took her out of intensive care and put her on a general ward. That was where she contracted pneumonia. They took her back to intensive care and we waited. A knock from Aunty Joyce woke us just after midnight. The hospital had rung her and Dad was to ring them back. He took me to Gran and Grandad's, where I sat on the floor in the kitchen, my back against the washing machine, waiting.

When Dad returned, he looked at the floor and said, 'You don't have to worry about visiting her tomorrow.'

Gran cried. Grandad whispered comforting words as he held her. Dad didn't know what to do. I didn't go to him. I waited. Grandad beckoned me over and they gathered me up. I buried my head between them as we all thought about my mum, their only child.

I never understood or forgave Dad for his pathetic, insensitive announcement.

I held Pickering's hand as I drifted off to sleep and the day came to a fitful end.

Chapter 6

Monday, 24 March 1975

If I stared at my bedroom wall long enough and relaxed, it was impossible to tell how far away it was. The swirling patterns pulsated like the start of *Dr Who*, but I had to concentrate – any distraction dragged me back to reality, allowing me to focus on the shadows cast by the bumps created by the tiny pieces of wood trapped inside the wallpaper. Trapped, that is, until I liberated them.

It was a delicate, addictive operation; I had to ration myself for fear of dismantling the entire wall. It needed skill, too; you had to get your fingernail in at just the right spot – lift the paper, catch the chip of wood with your fingernail and drag it out. If you could master this, then it was possible to extract the tiny bits of wood and smooth the paper back down, leaving no trace of your activity. The best place to do this was along the edge of the bed, just under the level of the mattress – easy enough to get at, but impossible for adults to detect.

The dogged determination of the men in *Colditz* TV series had inspired me. They'd shovelled away in terrible conditions for years, creating a tunnel under the castle walls to escape from the German prison. They completed it the week the war ended. Likewise, I'd been extracting the woodchips one by one along the length of my bed. Now, I needed to find another patch of wallpaper where they'd never think of searching. The strip down the side of the wardrobe was the favourite, but behind the dressing table was safest. Unfortunately, I wouldn't be able to do either while lying in bed.

Voices filtered through the wall into my room. I lay still, trying to make out what they were saying but really not wanting to know. A sense of dread hung around the house as it had after Mum's death. Dad hadn't taken it well – none of us had, but at least we'd carried on. Dad just stopped. He didn't bother about the house, himself or me. Grandad and Gran tried their best, but he wasn't interested, not in anything. Although nobody said it, when he died the following year, there was a sense of relief. I came to live with my grandparents, which was no big deal – I hadn't thought of the house across the street as home for a long time. When I asked Grandad if I could change my name from Busfield to Manning, no one seemed surprised or disappointed.

All was quiet and I crept downstairs. Gran wasn't there. I made myself a jam sandwich and felt like a rebel as I left for school, having not bothered to brush my teeth. Gran emerged from Joyce's just as I was passing.

'Harry.' She called me back. 'Sorry, love, I just popped round to Joyce's. I've had to call the doctor again. Have you had something to eat?'

I held up the crust still in my hand.

'Oh, Harry, that's not a proper breakfast. Are you going to be alright?'

I nodded.

'Stay at school for your lunch, will you? Give me some time to catch up with things.'

I didn't ask about the doctor. The truth was, I didn't want to know. As long as he made Grandad better, that's all I was bothered about. Before Gran could dive in for our usual kiss, I backed away.

'I'll see you later,' I said.

'Harry!' she shouted. 'Have you had a wash and cleaned your teeth?'

I nodded and rushed away, looking around to make sure nobody had overheard. Running my tongue around my teeth as I walked, I scraped the front ones clean with my fingernail, examining the results, curious as to why it didn't resemble any of the food I'd eaten. It was addictive and I had to force myself to stop as I got closer to school for fear of ridicule.

Our first lesson was physics, which was a favourite. Not because I understood it – I wasn't even interested in it – but it was one of the few lessons where Mark and Keith had also failed to reach the required grade for the advanced group, so at least we were in it together. We all paid a heavy price for our lack of ability. Watson's company. He was always the one behind whatever was making the teacher's, and our lives, a misery. Mr Reeds was soft; he had no control over the kids. Even when I failed to hand in my homework, a frown and light tutting was the worst punishment he could dish out.

It must have taken him fifteen minutes to get everyone sat down and paying attention. He could only do this by distributing Bunsen burners and the promise of fire. Fire, as any kid will tell you, is the best thing to attract attention. You could start a fire in a field with no one in sight and within five minutes there would be a gang of lads, all poking it and commenting on how it should be managed. The advice came in a comment like, 'Get another tyre on,' or some similar encouragement to make it bigger and therefore better.

Today, Watson surpassed himself. Because the inventive destruction went unnoticed. Mr Reeds made the fatal error of leaving us alone after issuing the burners. Even Mr Reeds wasn't dim enough to leave us to play with fire. But that didn't stop Watson. He disconnected the burner's rubber pipe from the gas tap and connected it to the water tap. I couldn't believe no one had thought of it before. Genius thinking and a spectacular effect.

The water pressure wasn't that fierce, but when it was forced through the tiny jet meant for the gas, it became a serious weapon.

This is why I'm not an evil genius. He dismissed the obvious thing to do, which was to douse everyone in the class, and instead aimed the jet of water at the suspended ceiling. The tiles were soft – at least, soft enough. The water jet cut through them with ease. It was very impressive. Watson used his water laser to cut a series of shapes in the tiles and then once again, he showed his genius. He didn't cut any shapes out completely – none of the cuts joined up to cause pieces to fall – he just made enough cuts to bring the tile to the edge of collapse, but no further.

The next time the caretaker had to work on the electrics or whatever else lurked behind the panels, he'd no doubt find the tiles disintegrating at the slightest touch. Even the water didn't come back down. I discussed this with Mark and Keith at length, and we concluded that the dust up there must have soaked it up. Whatever it was, when Mr Reeds came back in, he was oblivious to the damage. Watson received our grudging admiration. Which made our lunchtime encounter even more annoying.

'What are you three poofs doing?' said Watson.

We weren't doing anything, as usual. Just hanging around outside the form room, keen to get back inside to soak up more interesting facts. We backed up, the rough timber cladding digging into my back, my hands feeling around, hoping to find a trapdoor. You'd have thought we'd have been used to it by now, but his attention always caught us off guard. We stood like three deserters facing a firing squad.

Keith was first to cop it. Watson grabbed the lapels of his blazer and pulled him forwards.

'Say you're a poof.'

Keith's shirt rode up as Watson's grip tightened, Keith's white belly poking out. My stomach turned in sympathy. Watson towered above him. Keith complied without protest.

'I'm a poof.'

His sincerity was impressive. Maybe he should try to get a part in the school play. Maybe he wasn't acting, maybe he really thought he was a poof.

I was next. I faked an attempt at resistance, but a knee to my thigh, another dead leg, soon made me admit I was in fact a poof.

Mark must have used the time, unwisely, as it turned out, to come up with a witty reply.

'Say you're a poof,' said Watson.

'You're a poof,' said Mark.

I closed my eyes, willing him not to continue but knowing it was already too late.

'What?' Watson's hands rested on Mark's shoulders like he was giving him fatherly advice.

'You told me to say you're a poof, so I did.'

My heart sank when I realised he was going to say it again.

'You're a poof.'

I don't know how he generated such force over such a short distance, but Watson's hand moved from Mark's shoulder to the side of his face hard enough to knock him over. Only Watson's single-handed grip stopped him from falling. A small noise – what someone who wasn't a friend might call a whimper – left Mark's throat. Watson allowed Mark to slump forwards, then he banged him back against the wooden building. The loud thud as his head hit the cladding drew attention from passers-by. I swear Mark passed out for a second, his eyes pointing in opposite directions, focused on nothing. Watson held him in place and continued. Mark got a dead leg, too.

Watson didn't allow him to correct the error of fighting back, not yet. He took hold of Mark's tie as if to straighten it and instead carried on tightening it until Mark's cheeks were purple.

Watson put his forehead to Mark's and forced his head back again. 'What did you say?'

Mark had had enough. We'd all had enough.

'I'm a poof,' he confessed.

'I know,' said Watson as he walked away.

It took Mark a while to come round and regain his usual pasty complexion.

'We should start doing karate or judo,' Keith suggested.

It was one of our better ideas, which just shows you what a bunch of pillocks we were.

When I got home, I was relieved to see the workshop light was on. Grandad was tinkering and things were back to normal. I crept in, hoping to surprise him.

'Hiya, love,' he said as I made my final approach.

I ignored the fact that he'd spoilt my plan and stood next to him at the bench. He'd done some work on the *Hood*. There were patches of brown on the sides. I ran my finger over them, searching for imperfections. There weren't any. I examined my fingertips for clues, but they were clean.

'What have you been doing, Grandad?'

'Some overtime while you were getting an education.'

'I haven't been getting an education, Grandad, I've been to school.' Pleased with myself, I allowed the audience time to applaud. When none came, I pressed on. 'Anyway, I thought we were supposed to be doing this together.'

'Sorry, H, I just got carried away.'

His apology seemed genuine, but just to be certain, I put my hands on my hips, in a manner the TV had taught me was the best stance to show disappointment. It didn't seem to work very well.

Instead of bowing his head in shame, he just smiled and said, 'The armour belt was missing and the torpedo tubes weren't right. I've used some filler to add more flare to the hull and I did a bit of work on the gun barrels as well. Err . . . oh, and I made the forward breakwater more realistic and I sanded the planking out of the shelter deck, cos that was just painted steel. And, err . . .' He bit his lip and looked at the ceiling. 'That's it.'

Blimey, Charlie! The new pieces he'd fitted were just as good as the plastic kit – better, in fact. I looked at him with undisguised admiration. Then I spotted the knife. What would Gran say if she knew he'd been using her best knife to make the guns better? He winked at me and held his forefinger to his lips, putting his other arm around my shoulder.

'We want it to be right, H, don't we?'

His secret was safe with me, for the moment. The things I had on him were piling up. One day I might need the ammo.

'Paint?' I asked.

He nodded and his mouth opened, but it was Gran's voice that came from the kitchen.

'Harry.'

His shrug told me he couldn't help. I stuck my head around the door. She was putting on her coat.

'I need you to come and help me clean up over the road.'

I looked back at the grey ship.

'Don't worry,' said Grandad, 'I won't start it until you get back.' He seemed to regret the commitment. 'I'll just do a bit of preparation.'

I glanced between him, the *Hood* and Gran. I weighed my options, as if I had a choice.

'Go and get changed, love. I need to get cracking,' Gran said as she tied her scarf under her chin.

This is always a show of intent in a Gran.

Upstairs, I found Pickering propped up on the neatly made bed, resting against a pile of pillows, his legs tucked under the covers.

'I hope you didn't tell Gran any of my secrets,' I said, dropping my school uniform in a pile on the floor.

'Course not. My lips are sealed.'

I cast him a glance as my head popped out of my old jumper.

'Look, they're actually sealed.' He strained the stitching around his mouth.

'You are a very funny bear.'

'You know you should hang your uniform up, don't you?' said Pickering.

'It—'

'And don't tell me it's one of your favourite Lonnie Donegan songs; you've used that gag already.'

'I'll do it later,' I said, stepping over the pile of clothes.

'Don't forget to hang your uniform up,' Gran shouted.

'Don't say a word,' I warned him as I hung my clothes on the back of the door.

I could hear him chortling as I left the room.

The anonymous concrete building was out of bounds to kids and the cream exterior gave no clue to its function. It stood on waste ground sandwiched between a group of dilapidated garages and well-tended allotments on the edge of the club car park. After the kids' TV had finished and we'd said goodbye to *Pugwash* or *Rhubarb*, when the last of the pudding and biscuits had been scoffed, for the kids on the estate, this became our playground.

The club doors had only just opened, but men were already drinking, settled as if they'd been there all day. I walked beside Gran to the badly painted black steel door. The only sign the building might have a purpose at all was the array of telephone cables that snaked down to the windowless cube. A loose metal sheet creaked in the breeze. Gran held the door key from the moment we left the house. The lights of the club car park were only switched on when it was busy at weekends and when we left the pool of light coming through the club doors, it was pitch-black.

The door opened to reveal a void. Despite the possibility of were-wolves and vampires, she stepped inside with confidence and disappeared behind the door. Moments later, the fluorescent lights flickered into life, exposing the most miserable of scenes. It was Gran's job to clean it. She dragged the mop and bucket from the store cupboard.

'I'll start in the office, Harry. Can you sweep up, love?' She passed me the long-handled brush and turned as she made her way into the caged office.

Her face showed grim determination. This wasn't a job to enjoy.

I'd helped often enough to know what I had to do. Screwed up betting slips littered the place. Even though there were ashtrays, there were still hundreds of dog-ends and a thick layer of fag ash on the green-painted concrete floor. The walls were covered with today's edition of the *Racing Post*. The pages pinned to corkboards around the room detailed the runners and riders of every race in Britain that day. Large blackboards listed the prices for the next race, constantly updated as the odds changed. The speakers, now silent in the corner, resting before delivering another day's worth of disappointment, were the mouthpiece of 'the wire' – the system that connected every bookmaker to every racecourse.

A shelf that ran the length of the wall was just wide enough to write out a betting slip and pens hung on string every few feet. I ran my hand along it, sending the pens swinging as Gran filled her bucket. Starting in the far corner, the brush slid over the floor with ease. Gathering the discarded slips into a neat pile in the centre of the room was oddly rewarding. It felt good to be doing a job I could complete within my attention span. The disturbed cigarette ash clogged my nostrils and throat. It was easy to see why smokers spat a lot. I experimented, trying to spit like a cowboy, but only succeeded in dribbling down my chin. I wiped my mouth on my sleeve. Gran had made me put my overalls on, so the trail of saliva was of little concern.

'Harry! What are you doing?'

'I've got something in my mouth,' I bleated.

'Come on, love. We don't want to be here all night, do we.'

I wouldn't have minded. It would have been like spending a night in a haunted castle or a mad scientist's dungeon. I got back to my sweeping.

THE PILE OF BETTING slips rustled. I looked at the professor for an explanation.

'It's obvious now! How could I have been so stupid? The missing ingredient necessary to create new life spontaneously had to contain a genetic compound that matched the primitive nature of the simple life form. Spittle was the perfect match. Anything more advanced than the most rudimentary DNA wouldn't work – it would be too complex, too sophisticated.'

The simple creature dragged itself out of the pile of betting slips and slithered across the floor towards me. I backed into the corner, holding the dumb creature at bay with the broom.

'Harry, don't you understand, the first life form it has seen is you. You are connected by a genetic code as long as eternity.' A lightbulb glowed above his head. 'Maybe longer!'

The creature reached out, its wide eyes pleading for attention. I shook my head and retreated, my back against the wall.

The professor clasped his hands together in glee. 'Harry, this is a new beginning for us all. My lifetime's work has come to fruition. They laughed at me when I first proposed my ideas, but now, now they'll have to listen.'

Drool spilt from the creature's distended jaw as its deformed arm reached out. The tongue, too big for its mouth, sloshed around between its sharp, vicious teeth. It was trying to speak! It gurgled as the professor looked on. The first word of a new life form: 'Dadda!'

'HARRY! WHAT *are* you doing?' Gran's voice pierced the scene and the creature withdrew into the pile of debris.

'Sweeping up,' I said, pointing at the pile of litter.

'Well hurry up. I'm ready to run the mop around.'

My mouth opened to explain, but the noise stayed in my head. I pushed the pile into the corner and scooped it up with a small shovel, struggling to get the last of the fag ash up. The imperfections of the leading edge of the shovel let the ash slide underneath, only getting a fraction with each attempt.

'Leave that, love. I'll get it with the mop.'

She leaned over to counterbalance the bucket of soapy water she carried, dropping it in the centre of the room. Gran worked around the edges first, leaving herself a thin corridor to retreat through. Then she worked backwards until we stood in the same corner near the office entrance. She stopped to admire her work, the glossy wet floor reflecting the cold neon tubes.

'Bugger, I've forgotten to take the papers down.' She looked around at the walls and let out a small sob, pulling her hanky from her pinny pocket, the cheerful lilac flowers clashing with her sudden sadness.

'It's okay, Gran, I'll get them.'

'The floor . . .' She stopped, unable to speak without crying.

I touched her hand that still gripped the mop handle. Her inflamed, arthritic knuckles looked like roots wrapped around a stem. She dabbed her eyes and composed herself.

'It's not . . . oh, I don't know.' She sniffled and shook her head. 'Oh, Harry . . .'

'I'll tiptoe,' I assured her and set off to take down the obsolete papers, taking care not to spoil the clean floor.

She chuntered to herself, but I couldn't tell what she was saying.

When I returned, she was washing the coffee mugs in the sink. I folded the papers and put them in the black bin bag she'd used, then I stepped up onto the bare wood planks of the office floor and sat on the stool behind the counter, the adding machine and till in front of me. Long metal spikes stuck out of timber blocks. It was where the bookie kept their copy of the betting slips. The timber blocks had once been different colours, but now they were bare wood and grime. Only flecks of the once vibrant paint remained.

I put my palm on the spike and relaxed, letting gravity do what I didn't have the guts to. My hand closed as the pressure increased to the point I couldn't stand it anymore. The wooden base lifted before clattering on the desk. I glanced at Gran, but the running water had drowned out the noise. I examined my palm. Perhaps I was tougher than I thought.

In the centre was a small dome of blood surrounded by reddened skin. I stretched my fingers as far back as possible. The blob fractured and ran down the valley of a crease. I clenched my fist, held it high and tried to squeeze the blood out, but nothing emerged. When I opened my hand, the blood had smeared onto my fingertips and the flow had stopped. Still, I was proud of having deliberately inflicted a wound on myself that bled. It felt like I'd achieved more here than in a full day of schooling.

'Come on,' Gran said, drying her hands on her pinny. 'Let's get back home and see what Grandad's doing, eh?'

I jumped down from the stool, scooped up the bin bag and followed her.

When we got home, Grandad was snoozing in the chair next to the fire. He didn't wake until Gran shook his shoulder.

'Jack!'

'Ooo,' he yawned, 'I must have nodded off.'

He looked at us. His eyes were red like he'd been crying.

'All done, Lil?'

'It is,' she said, flicking on the gas ring under the chip pan.

'Was he any use?' He nodded in my direction and raised his eyebrows, winking at me when he was sure Gran wasn't looking.

'Course he was. Weren't you, love?' She looked over her shoulder at me.

Grandad looked doubtful. I pulled a face at him and we called a truce.

After dinner, we went back to the workshop to work on the *Hood*. He sat on a stool scratching his beard. Next to the red paint was an empty pot of grey.

'Grandad! I thought you said you were just going to do some preparation?'

'Come on, H, you should know by now. You can't believe a word I say.' He smiled and nudged me. 'I only did the topsides. I've saved the best bit. Now then, listen up.' He explained how the antifouling paint stopped barnacles and seaweed from growing on the bottom. 'Come on, let's get cracking.'

He dipped his brush in the red paint and pretended to flick it at me. Flinching, I lost my balance.

'Steady on, H,' he said, grabbing my arm. 'This is no place to fall.'

THE CONCRETE FLOOR of the dock pulsated as I stared down, teetering on the edge of the thin plank, my arms flailing. The plank was suspended from the deck by ropes. I regained my composure and turned to face the ship's side. Something splashed on the back of my neck. When I looked up, Grandad pretended to be painting. He was on another plank, above me and to the left.

'I think a seagull just pooed on you,' he shouted.

I looked up to find the culprit, but the sky was clear and empty. I could feel the heat of the sun, or maybe it was toxic seagull poo on my neck. Other men on planks were painting all around us.

I watched in horror as he swung from rope to rope like a chimp, paintbrush clamped in his mouth, before sliding down to join me. The plank rocked wildly and I dropped to my knees, screaming. 'What are you doing, Grandad?'

The timber scraped and banged into the side of the ship.

'Mind your fingers,' he warned. 'Don't get them between the plank and the hull or you'll lose 'em.'

I stayed low until the plank was steady again, focusing on his right boot, which started tapping the wood.

'Come on, H. Get up! We've got work to do.'

I raised myself on wobbly legs, trying not to look beyond the thin wooden platform, using Grandad and the hull to steady myself, realising too late the paint was still wet. We both looked at my red palm.

'I should have mentioned that before,' he said, unconcerned about the 60-foot drop just one step away.

I bent down and dipped my brush into the paint.

'What are you doing?' he asked.

'Painting?'

'This bit's done now.'

I scraped the paint off my brush on the rim of the pot and looked at the hull. It was, except for the hand-shaped bit in the middle. With a quick flourish of my brush, the handprint disappeared.

'What now?' I asked.

'We've got to release the ropes to get to the next section below us.'

That at least had the advantage of putting us closer to the ground, but I couldn't see how we could do it.

'How do we do that?'

'We?' he questioned.

But I had no answer.

'Well, what we'd normally do is that you'd unfasten the rope on your end, I'd do the same at mine and together we'd lower ourselves to the next section. But because you don't know what you're doing'—I conceded the insult—*'I'm going to do both ends.'*

The plank was 10-feet long, so I couldn't see how he was going to do that, but then I found out. Without warning, he lowered his end 2 foot.

My feet slipped out from under me and I grabbed the rope, keeping hold of my brush but not the paint pot. I watched helplessly as it slid towards Grandad. Just before it disappeared over the edge, he stood on it and brought it to a halt. Then walked casually to my end of the plank. Before I'd got to my feet, he reached over my head, grabbed the block and tackle, and lowered my end by 4 feet. I fell backwards. My legs shot up as my body went down. Grandad's grinning face watched as the paint pot slid between my legs, only stopping when it hit my balls.

'Good catch, H,' he chuckled. 'We'll make a painter of you yet.'

After we'd done a few sections, I could accept the adjustments of the plank without screaming, and by the time we'd finished, my balls had stopped aching.

'Is it tea break yet, Grandad?'

He looked at his watch-less wrist. 'I think it is.'

GRANDAD RUFFLED MY hair, leaning on the bench.

'We've done a good job there, H.'

We stood side by side, admiring our work, the light from the angle lamp isolating us from the rest of the world in an island of happiness.

'I'll tidy up, you get the kettle on.'

Gran was making herself a cuppa as I stepped into the kitchen. She turned, still stirring her tea.

'Is it going well?' She dropped her spoon and put her hand to her mouth.

'What's up, Gran?'

She took my face in her hands and rubbed my cheek, offering her thumb as evidence: red paint. I twisted from her grip to look back at the workshop door, Grandad's silent laughter was deafening.

'Here.' She rummaged under the sink and thrust a crusty cloth and a bottle of white spirit into my chest. 'I don't want any of that stuff on my towels,' she warned, forcing me towards the bathroom.

My mottled reflection smiled back at me as I dealt with the damage. I worked the spirit into my skin with the nail brush, finishing off with carbolic soap. I scoured off the tops of my spots, which, after rinsing, gave me the appearance of someone just out of skin graft surgery. Happy with my radiated look, I left to seek Gran's approval, half blinded from the effects of 'white spirit eye' and already regretting my casual approach to rinsing.

I bumped into Grandad. He was stood outside the bathroom door, hiding in full sight as he'd later claim. I conceded the effectiveness of the ambush as I looked up at him, squinting through my watery eyes, my face glowing from the scrubbing.

'You look redder now than when I painted you,' he said, laughing like a loony.

His unreasonable happiness at my misfortune forced me to wind up my fist and threaten him.

'Why, I oughta . . .'

The only effect was to make him switch his walking stick to the other hand. I continued my attack.

'I suppose you think you're funny, do you?'

'Oh yeah, very funny, indeed.'

'With all that paint splattered on me, Gran thought I'd got measles.'

'German measles, *ja?*'

His accent slipped as he tried to control his mirth and his right arm shot into the air in a Nazi salute, but his heel click failed because he was only wearing slippers.

'Flaming Germans,' I chuntered as I made the tea.

Chapter 7

Tuesday, 25 March 1975

Another boring day at school was over. Gangs of kids hung around the main gates, waiting for buses to ship them off to the outlying villages. Outside the shops, groups of them were doing a terrible job of hiding their illicit cigarettes as smoke billowed from the scrummages.

I spotted one lonely soul – a kid in the year below me. He wandered through the crowds as oblivious to them as they were to him. He moved like a ghost, ignored by everyone, in his own world, kicking a stone up the street. I wondered what the future held for him. Would he end up shuffling through the estate for the rest of his life?

Some older girls passed me, giggling about the latest boy they fancied and planning their weekend. Their short skirts danced around, their loose interpretation of school uniform rules a constant delight. Entranced, my eyes were glued to their backsides. I stumbled sideways as Keith barged into me.

'Which one do you fancy?' he said, loud enough for one girl to turn just as I was pointing at her.

She smiled over her shoulder before telling her mates, who turned round to see, dissolving into a giggling clump of gorgeousness. I whacked him with my bag and we twirled up the street, swinging our bags at each other in the middle of the road, the girls forgotten in our dizzy battle. Keith's garden gate creaked and slammed shut. As soon as I was alone, the reality of home life pushed aside my fantasies of future girlfriends.

The car wasn't on the drive, so Grandad must be out somewhere. Gran was gathering the washing from the line in the back garden.

THE SAILS CRACKED LIKE a whip in the rising gale. The captain shouted orders. I balanced on the rope as I clung on to the yard arm, edging my way towards her, struggling to gather up the stiff canvas.

'DON'T LET THEM FALL on the ground, Harry,' Gran said as I dropped the bed sheet into the wicker basket. 'And make sure all the pegs are off.'

I collected the pegs as best I could, holding them in my fist, repeatedly dropping them, not knowing why I was reluctant to put them in her apron pocket as she was doing. It was a relief when she told me to leave her to it.

Although the car had gone, I found Grandad dozing in the kitchen as I passed through, but when I returned from my room, he was in the workshop looking at the *Hood*. I stood beside him. His elbow dug into my ribs.

'I think we should get this ship in the water, don't you?'

'What about all this?' I pointed at all the components still to be fitted.

'We'll sort that lot out when the tugs have dragged her into the fitting-out basin.' He put his walking stick on the bench and looked at his watch-less wrist.

'*OOPS, IT'S NEARLY TIME. Try to keep up, H, we don't want to be late.*' Grandad ran down the slipway towards the stern. '*Come on, H.*'

I scurried after him, squinting as explosions of sunlight reflected off the giant bronze propeller blades.

'These are what the Hood *is going to slide down.*'

Grandad dipped his forefinger into the thick yellow grease that covered the steel rails supporting the ship, then rubbed it between his fingers and sniffed. It seemed to meet his approval. He scraped most of it off on a timber strut and scanned the yard, looking for something, his hand held out in front of him. I joined the search, although I didn't know what I was looking for.

Whatever it was, we didn't find it. His brow furrowed in frustration and he wiped his fingers on my overalls. Sighing I shook my head in disappointment. He shrugged, smiling. I decided not to say anything, as I was already looking forward to bringing it up later.

'*You see all this chain, H?*'

I nodded. '*Course I can; it's massive.*'

'*Alright, alright, don't get cocky. They're fastened to the hull so she doesn't slide too fast into the river.*'

I craned my neck and looked at the ship. Never mind fast – how on earth could something that big slide anywhere? The sound of the brass band didn't seem out of place among the metalwork of the yard. Grandad drew my attention to a platform at the bow of the ship.

'*That's where Lady Hood is going to smash the bottle of bubbly.*'

The music stopped, replaced by a muffled voice: '*. . . and all who sail in her.*'

As she spoke, there was an explosion. It must have been a hell of a big champagne bottle to make a noise like that.

'*That's the charge that releases the bolt holding her in place.*'

Relieved at not having said anything daft, I was still unsure how a single bolt could hold a ship in place. Reality overrode my lack of imagination as the Hood *began to move.*

'Should we get out of the way, Grandad?'

'Oh yeah, we should for sure,' he said, distracted by some technical detail.

Huge timbers that had been holding her in place toppled, crashing onto the ground beside us. The giant chain links rumbled like thunder. I jogged clear of the danger.

'Come on, Grandad,' I shouted above the din, 'run!'

Grandad was jumping over the chains like a kid skipping in a giant's playground. He was so engrossed that he didn't hear my warning or see the chain that connected with the back of his legs, sweeping him on his backside. He laughed at himself as he struggled to stand. But his smile soon faded as he got dragged down the slipway, his foot trapped in the chain. He looked at me, his mouth moving, but the words were overwhelmed by the thunderous noise.

His efforts to free himself became more frantic as he got closer to the water. I ran down the slipway, hurling myself onto the chain and riding it like a bucking bronco, the steel grinding on the concrete, shuddering through my spine as it gained momentum. His boot was wedged inside one of the links, but I knew what to do.

My body shook, blurring my vision as I fought to untie his lace. I pulled his leg with all of my might, dragging his foot out of the boot. At the last second, we rolled to the side as the ship rushed past us, creating a whirlwind, throwing rust and muck into the air. I turned my back and shielded my face from the flying debris as the vortex tugged at my clothes.

We sat on the filthy slipway as the Hood hit the water, sending up an enormous surge, which rebounded back and forth across the River Clyde. The dust settled around us as we sat, hypnotised by the pattern of interlacing waves. A few minutes later, the tugs moved in to shove her into the fitting-out basin.

I retrieved Grandad's boot from the water's edge and found his glasses, both lenses smashed. I handed him his boot and watched in awe

as he balanced on one leg, bringing the other up to refit the lost footwear.
He looked up as he tied the lace.

'That was good, wasn't it?'

I was just about to point out that yes, it was, except for the obvious
mistake we made by standing under a ship as it was being launched,
when a voice rang out in the distance.

'Jack! Harry!'

An arm waved among a group of people watching the ceremony
from the metal staircases on the side of the office building. I shielded my
eyes, trying to see who it was.

'It's John Brown,' Grandad said, waving back at the distant figure.

I offered him his smashed spectacles. He took them, folding them
with care before throwing them into the Clyde.

'Why the bloody hell didn't we watch from up there, Grandad?'

'I thought this would be more exciting,' he said, slapping me hard
on the back.

AS SCRIPTED, I STUMBLED into the workbench. Clouds of
dust rose into my face as Grandad brushed off the muck from his
overalls. He pushed his specs up his nose.

'We'd better get you cleaned up. Here, let me sort you out.'

I surrendered, putting my hands in the air and rotating as he
brushed me with unnecessary vigour. He looked me up and down,
not satisfied.

'Your face is filthy,' he said, offering me an old mirror.

Water had seeped behind the glass, causing the silvered surface to
peel off. Large brown patches made the thing next to useless.

'Where?' I asked. The distorted reflection offered few clues.

He held my shoulder and touched my face.

'Here, here and here,' said Grandad in his clipped RAF voice.

I realised I'd fallen for another trick. He looked for something to wipe off the greasy smears. Like a kidnapper with chloroform, he advanced towards me with an oily rag. I turned and ran into the kitchen, bumping into Gran.

'Watch where you're going, love.'

I tried to break free, but she held on, cleaning her floury hands in my hair.

'Have either of you seen my best peeling knife?'

I stayed close to Gran as Grandad hobbled from the workshop, pretending to be innocent. He rested in the doorway, leaning on the frame, and pointed his stick at me.

'He's got himself filthy, Lily, and . . . and he's been swearing.'

'Grandad!'

She turned me round and held me at arm's length.

'Have you been swearing, Harry?' Her eyes scanned the muck on my face.

'I only said bloody'

'Oh my Gawd,' said Grandad behind me, 'he's at it again!'

'Honestly,' said Gran, pulling her handkerchief from her sleeve, examining my face and the pristine white cotton, then changing her mind. 'You two are too daft to laugh at.'

Her grip loosened and I wriggled free.

'Shall we have a cuppa?' Grandad said.

'By all means. Help yourselves,' she said as she walked away. 'There's a sandwich on the side. I'm going to change the bedding.'

'I'll make it,' I said.

'That's a good idea,' he said, slumping in his chair. 'Put four sugars in mine, but don't stir it; I don't like it sweet.'

I handed Grandad his mug.

'Where's my biscuit?' he asked in a tone that suggested there was already skulduggery on my part.

I pointed out to him that we didn't have any. Biscuitlessness, like scurvy, sounds hilarious but is deadly serious.

He wiped his hands over his face, his fingers drawing down his cheeks, pulling his eyes open and turning his mouth into an exaggerated frown.

'OK,' he said, his voice full of regret, 'I suppose you're old enough to know.' He paused, building the tension before confessing, the words tumbling out. 'I've got a secret stash in the workshop.'

My mouth gaped in silent condemnation of his treachery. He tried to brush it aside.

'If you fetch the tin, I'll share with you.'

'What did your last slave die of?' I asked.

'Well, it wasn't bloody idleness.' He paused, biting his lip. 'I think the last one died from being beaten with a spanner until his brains fell out all over the workshop floor. It made a right mess. But to be honest, I've killed that many I've forgotten.'

I examined the garage floor. It was covered in stains, any of which could have been brains, but the thought of splattered brains only seemed to stimulate my appetite.

'Where do you hide the virtuals, then?' I shouted at him.

'Victuals, not virtuals, yeh great nana. In a biscuit tin under the bench.'

I drew back the curtain that hid 'the things that will come in handy one day' storage area. It was the perfect hiding place. Buried among the old biscuit tins full of odd screws and nails was one full of odd biscuits. I admired the old sea dog's cunning. We'd seen a film where somebody had used similar tactics to hide a bomb in a warehouse. I stopped rummaging and listened.

THE TICKING WAS FAINT. I shuffled the tins around and listened again. I picked up the Cadbury tin and eased the lid open, mindful of booby traps. The red glow of the timer's digits winked at me. The counting down continued: 25, 24, 23. Time was running out. Blue or red?

The decision was harder than I thought. Sweat dripped from my nose onto the detonator. I froze.

Blue or red?

I made my choice, to hell with the consequences.

It was red.

The timer stopped, two seconds left.

Mission accomplished, I put the lid back on and replaced the tin among the others. Nobody would ever know how close the world had come to disaster.

GRANDAD REMOVED THE red paper sleeve off the KitKat and ran his thumb down the silver foil, dividing the spoils. I was always happy with the division of KitKats. It was easy to be accurate and left no option for him to keep the 'big half'.

'That's four pence you owe me,' he said, handing me my share.

'Put it on the tab,' I said with a wave as I returned to the *Hood*. 'My valet will settle my account.'

I spent the rest of the evening fixing the remaining bits while Grandad rested, reading the newspaper and snoozing. The rough burs on each piece where it attached to the plastic frame needed rubbing away and sanding. Using a pair of tweezers and Grandad's magnifier, I dipped the tiny components into a blob of glue and set them in place. Searchlights and aerials, radars and rangefinders were all fixed to the conning tower. Pom-poms and high-angle guns, the derricks for the lifeboats and a dozen small boats were also glued into position. I fastened all the remaining pieces on my own, but I wanted Grandad to be there when we fitted the four big 15-inch guns as they were hoisted into place.

Grandad stood beside me and we looked at the *Hood*. It sat under the spotlight of his angle lamp, the four-gun turrets lined up beside it.

'How did they get these on board, Grandad?'

'THIS MONSTER.' GRANDAD pointed at the structure in front of us.

My eyes followed the ladder that ran up the outside of the steel tower of the crane, my neck joints clicking as I reached the limit of my flexibility.

'Titan.' He banged his fist on the metal rail. 'It can lift 160 tonnes,' he said, absently rubbing his knuckles. 'Can you manage to climb up on your own?'

'Eh?'

'You'll be fine; I'll keep an eye on you.'

I inhaled the workshop atmosphere, trying to draw strength from it.

'Come on, H, let's get cracking. Up you get,' he said, pointing his thumb.

'Are you having me on?'

'You know I never joke, H.'

'You're always—'

'About cranes,' he interrupted.

Maybe he was right, as I couldn't think of any crane-related jokes he'd told me.

The rungs of the ladder were like ice and I shivered as the cold crept up my arms. The air at the bottom was motionless, but as we climbed, the wind increased. At the top, it was howling.

Grandad struggled up the last of the steps. I reached down and helped him onto the platform. My overalls filled with air, making me look like the Michelin . . . boy. The wind whipped them as I struggled forwards. Reaching past him to open the sliding door, we stepped inside. I deflated as he closed the door.

Sitting in the driver's seat, I scanned the controls. Interlocking my fingers, I pushed my hands out in front of me, cracking my knuckles.

'Right, let's get on with it,' Grandad encouraged.

We were looking down on the Hood, *the giant guns lined up along the dockside. Barrel by barrel, gun by gun, I loaded them into position. Grandad stood by my shoulder, guiding me, pointing out which was the right order and generally slowing down the entire process.*

'That's X turret, the one nearest the middle on the stern,' he said.

I swivelled the chair round.

'I know,' I told him in a drawn-out, exasperated voice.

He grinned and gave me the thumbs up.

Finally, they were all in place.

'IT WAS THE LARGEST crane in the world when it was first built.' Grandad held the *Hood* close to look at my work. 'You've done a good job there, H, well done.' He turned the model to face us. 'Those guns made a hell of a noise when they went off.' His finger touched the tip of the big gun barrels. 'Each of the shells weighed about the same as you.' He paused, staring at the ship. 'All that money, all that effort and expectation . . .' His expression hardened. 'Nobody could have anticipated how we'd feel the first time those guns were fired in anger.'

FROM THE FOREDECK, we watched a sailor step out onto the starboard signal yard and raise a new set of flags on the halyard. The guns of other ships nearby immediately roared into life.

Grandad started to speak. 'That's the signal to—'

I fell to the floor as the noise of the explosion reverberated inside my skull, deafening me and distorting my vision. The wood planking of the deck rippled as my eyes regained their shape.

Boom! The Hood's *guns fired again.*

I shook my head and looked up at Grandad. His mouth was moving, but there was no noise.

'What?' I shouted.

'I said, that was the signal to open fire.' His voice sounded like it was in a tunnel and his face screwed up in anticipation of the next salvo. 'We really should have ear defenders on,' he said.

'Is it too late?' I asked.

'Oh yeah, the damage is done now,' he said cheerfully. 'I said the da—'

Boom! Boom!

A turret let loose its shells.

'There's no need to shout,' I told him.

'Very funny.'

'Aren't you frightened that the Germans are going to start firing back at us?'

'No, are you?'

I shrugged.

'We're not firing the guns at the Germans, H, we're shooting at the French.'

'Aren't the French on our side?' I asked.

'Oh yes, definitely.'

'Then why are we shooting at them?'

'That's a good question.' He pointed at the blur of land. 'That's North Africa, Algeria, a place called Mers-el-Kébir. It's a French naval

base. The French have just signed an agreement with Germany. Churchill doesn't want the French ships to fall into German hands. He's given the French commanders four options: join up with our navy and fight, sail the ships to the safety of a British port and leave them there, sail them to the French-controlled Caribbean, or sink the ships where they are.'

'Which one did the French pick?'

'None, and that's why we've just launched the attack. We're going to sink the ships for them.'

The big guns fired again. Small plumes of smoke rose from the port, the sound of the explosions arriving a few seconds after.

'This is the first time the Hood has fired her guns at a real target.' He looked at me. 'And we're firing at our allies.'

GRANDAD SET THE *Hood* in its stand and wiped his hands on his jumper, trying to cleanse himself of his part in a shameful episode.

We joined Gran in the living room in time to see the opening sequence of *The World at War* documentary. The German advance into Poland complete, people waited on railway platforms, their fate no longer in their own hands.

In my room later, I looked at Pickering for answers.

'Sometimes it's easy to see who the enemy is, Harry, but not always.'

Drifting off, I realised I'd forgotten to ask Grandad where our car was.

Chapter 8

Wednesday, 26 March 1975

After committing to another grim day at school, we made our way to woodwork. Because there was only one workshop, there was no streaming, so we were all in it together. It was the only class where I was with my mates, and also better than them. I had to hold on to any triumph, no matter how minor.

We tried our best to shelter under the inadequate canopy outside the workshops, but the driving rain blew in sideways, reducing the protected area by half, which meant there was only space for a quarter of the class. There was a system that decided who was in and who was out. It worked like this: tough kids stood in the rain without coats to show how hard they were and the more saturated you got, the higher your status. Weaklings were squeezed out and accepted their fate with no attempt to fight. They stood apart from all other groups and each other, all hope beaten out of them.

They reminded me of Jews being herded by SS officers on the railway platform, having watched in silent horror the previous night's episode of *The World at War*, where a German officer had raised the chin of an old woman with the tip of his whip. She was a grandmother like mine. I swallowed the bitter truth.

'Resistance is futile.'

'You can say that again,' Mark said as we fought to stake our claim on the damp edges.

The three of us worked together against the softer individuals, whose chief concern was not getting their hair wet.

After a long wait, the door opened and the diminutive figure of Mr Potts appeared as he stuck his bearded face out. His spectacles were rendered useless as a squall of rain swept in, splattering the lenses. He took them off and wiped them on a grubby handkerchief as we filed past, the wiser ones keeping their distance. His nickname, Death Breath, was well deserved.

We put on our brown aprons and collected our projects. I looked around at the different levels of skill. They'd limited the choices of task to three options: a stool, a letter rack or a sculpture. The sculpture was open to interpretation – abstract was a popular style. Some took the concept to the limit and presented a block of wood on a stick. Keith and Mark had to choose between making a bad stool or a good letter rack. I was aiming for a good stool. I was at the sanding stage, which was always the most tedious bit and seemed to go on for weeks.

Once we were occupied, old Death Breath started on his own project. It had nothing to do with anything that was going on in school and the story was that he was building a coffin for his ageing mother who he lived with; although the panel clamped in the vice looked more like a cupboard door. His speed and skill impressed me as he eyed the length of wood, measuring the angles with an ancient set square.

Calloused fingers ran along the edge of the timber, gauging the work required. He picked up a plane, removing the blade for sharpening, rotating the metal on the whetstone in a steady, hypnotic circular movement before cleaning and resetting it. His plane hissed over the wood, creating neat curls of teak that floated to the ground. He saw me watching and stopped work, wiping his hands on his apron as he approached.

'How are you getting on, Harry?'

I recoiled from his foul breath. Potts' eyes saddened at my reaction. He looked me in the eye.

'Nobody's perfect, Harry.'

I looked down, embarrassed.

'You're doing a good job,' he said. 'Look . . .' He took the sandpaper from me. 'Don't just use your hands.' He took up a stance like a boxer. 'Put your body behind it. Use all of your weight.'

He slid the paper over the front of the stool seat, creating in one stroke the same as fifteen minutes of toil from me.

'If you put a little more effort into it, Harry, we could make a carpenter of you yet.'

He handed me the sandpaper and went off to break up a fight between two kids who'd found the pile of shavings and were lobbing them across the workshop at each other.

Later that afternoon, elated at being free of school, my heart sank as I watched the coal truck brake to a stop on the street, wincing as the driver struggled to find reverse gear, the cogs grinding before meshing together. I rushed up the drive ahead of the reversing wagon.

'The coal man's here,' I told Gran as I ran through the kitchen and into the garage to open the doors.

I had to be quick, as a delay might mean the driver dropped the load at the bottom of the drive, which would turn a job I didn't like into a chore I hated. The driver was still sorting out the paperwork as I wedged the doors open with a pair of bricks we kept for the purpose. I waved him back with a confidence I didn't often feel.

The air brakes exhaled as the truck stopped on the slope. Despite his bulk, the driver jumped from his cab and handed me the bill before releasing the bolts that held the tailgate in place. His blue overalls stretched to breaking point across his fat arse as he climbed onto the mudguard and into the back to unfasten the pins holding the dividing boards that separated the 4 tons of coal. Ours was the last on the wagon. The driver jumped down, weighing up the available space.

'I'll back up a bit,' he said, returning to the cab.

Although I knew he'd use the brakes again, I still jumped at the loud escape of air. The tail lights glowed briefly in the confined space of the workshop doorway. He pulled levers and the hydraulic ram lifted the bed of the coal truck. Pieces of coal fell down the face of the load as the hinged gates swung up. As it reached the critical point, the load slid down, flattening as it spread out. Rumbling and rattling down the metal floor, it pushed the tailgate aside before settling in a neat pile, half inside and half outside the workshop doorway. The driver climbed over the pile to get my signature on the delivery ticket.

'You're earning your pocket money this week, eh?' he said, turning to check the load was out. A small pile still clung in the top corner. 'I'll give it a shake,' he said, climbing back into the cab.

The truck lurched forwards and stopped. The tailgate dragged over the top of the coal and a couple of bucketfuls bounced and rattled onto the drive, the tailgate slamming against the back of the wagon. Climbing over the coal as the bed of the truck fell back, I secured the bolts of the tailgate and gave the driver a wave as he pulled away.

When I went inside, Gran was preparing dinner.

'Your grandad's having a nap, Harry.'

I gave her a hug and went to get changed. A new walking frame stood in the hall. I ran my hands over the plastic hand grips. I didn't think it was something that Grandad needed, but I supposed it was better to have it around, just in case. I thought about where these things came from. Dr Crowther, I guessed. The feeling of unease about Grandad was replaced by one of unease about shifting the coal. I quickly changed out of my uniform and went back down.

Back in the workshop, I leaned on the shovel. A sense of fore-boding gripped me as I looked at the black mountain. The uneasy feeling from my dream returned. I looked at the impossible task. I felt it could never be finished, but I knew I had no option but to face it. A wave of despair almost overwhelmed me before subsiding and leaving me drained. My shoulders slumped and I was on the verge of tears.

'One shovelful at a time, H.' Grandad's voice rasped over my shoulder, making me jump. 'Remember what I said?'

I did. This was the actual story that had inspired a hundred others. How do you paint a wall? How do you build a ship? How do you dig over a plot of land? How do you get fit? How do you get through anything that's in your way? The answer was always: one shovelful at a time. His stories often lacked a connection to reality as I saw it. Not this one. This was the answer to everything, according to Grandad. He shuffled in, his slippers scraping over the dusty floor.

'Pass me a bit.'

He pointed at the pile and I passed a lump over. He held it in his hand, his elbows resting on his walking frame, turning the piece over and over.

'Give me a subject you don't like at school.'

'Geography,' I said without hesitation.

'Ancient forests dropped leaves and branches and tree trunks, layer after layer, each adding to the pile. Over tens of thousands of years it collected. Then the Earth's crust moved and it got drawn down, squashed, then pushed back to the surface millions of years later, but only in a few places. Yorkshire was one.' He looked up. 'Give me another.'

'History.'

'It connects every family in Yorkshire.' He held the lump of coal higher. 'It's why there's a town here. We've been digging up this stuff since the Romans were here a thousand years ago.'

I knew I'd have to think hard to catch him out. 'What about games?'

'You only get time to play games if you've earned enough money to have some time off. Coal gives us money and time to enjoy it.'

'Art?'

'Colliery brass bands.'

'Chemistry?'

'Coal gas.'

'Physics?'

'Coke, carbon, steel.'

'Religious education?'

'Don't be so blooming daft, H. You know there isn't a God.' He tossed the piece of coal into the store. 'That's all the help you're going to get from me,' he winked and shuffled back into the kitchen. 'Don't forget, one shovelful at a time.'

I watched the door slide shut and looked again at the daunting pile before turning my attention to the coal store. They'd built the brick coal bunker into the corner of the workshop and the front was open. I wedged a series of boards inside the door frame. The technique was to build the retaining boards as you filled the bunker. But you didn't build them too early, because that meant you'd have to throw the coal higher. And, if you hit a newly positioned board with a shovelful of coal, it would knock the board backwards, meaning you'd have to stop and reposition it. I removed two boards that had fallen back on top of the coal as the level had dropped and turned back to the pile.

To begin with, it was easy. The coal was close to the store and the boards were low, so I started shovelling from the inside. All I had to do was scoop up the coal and rotate, using the momentum to launch the coal into the large opening. But as the boards got higher, the target got smaller and I had to throw the coal further. Grandad was an expert. Even when there was just a thin slit, he could still throw the coal from the far end of the pile and the mound would stay the same shape it had been on the shovel as it sailed through the air. He never missed the target. I had 100 per cent record, too – I never hit it.

It wasn't long before I had to shovel up the coal and walk four or five steps before swinging the load higher than my head. I was lucky to get half on target. The rest clattered into the boards or against the door to the kitchen, creating more mess and dust that I'd have to clean up. Towards the end, I only half filled the shovel, taking my time not to add to the clean-up job. It was dusk before I started the final sweep-up.

I leaned on the brush and looked out into the murky night. Fog swirled in a vortex at the top of the drive. There was always a pile of empty crisp and fag packets, collected by the wind and dropped at our front door by a quirk of aerodynamics. The occasional lone figure passed unidentified under the street lamp across the road.

I STOOD ON FO'C'SLE deck at the front of the ship under the shadow of the big guns, gazing at the flat sea. This far forwards, there was no disturbance from the engines. The Hood *was just an unfeeling machine moving through a grey world. The only noise was the steady hiss of the bow wave as we sliced through the water. I tried to find something to focus on – something else, anything else. There was a faint whoosh in the distance, repeating and growing closer. I scanned the horizon, trying to identify the source of the noise.*

For a moment, the fog thinned and I could see. An enormous whale launched itself into the air, its body almost leaving the water. It hung there, defying gravity and time, water cascading down its body, before turning and falling sideways back into the sea, splitting the water and sending spray high into the air. The fog closed in again but the noise continued, as though the whale knew I was too fragile to be left alone.

I CLOSED THE GARAGE doors, trapping wisps of fog that disappeared like the ghostly spouts of long-dead whales.

Under the umbrella of light from the rusty desktop lamp, I traced my finger over the gouges in the workbench, like the scarred face of an ageing prize fighter. Its sturdy presence reassured me I could rely on some things to last. I left the familiar old tools and comforting smells and returned to the brightness of the kitchen.

'Are you going to wash your hands before you get in the bath?' Gran asked as if there were alternatives.

I'd fallen for this one before. They lulled you into a false sense of power, making you believe for a moment that there were options for you to choose. I tried to think through the choices but got distracted by the illogical pointlessness of washing my hands before I got in the bath. It's like tidying up before visitors come round and make a mess. Although this kind of argument would at least receive congratulations from Grandad for trying, Gran's sense of humour was a thin veneer covering her practical core.

'Yeah,' I confirmed, slinking into the bathroom.

I did a double take in the mirror. Sweat had created tide marks in the coal dust from my forehead to my neck.

My feet ground grit into the enamel as I stepped from the bath a while later. I stared into the grey water. Gran may have a point. The last of it gurgled away, leaving a ring of scum around bath and residue in the bottom that looked like someone had been panning for gold. I suppose that's why they had showers at the pit. But why did footballers all share the same bath? Maybe Grandad was right and they were all a bunch of poofs.

'Harry!' I jumped at Gran's voice, just the other side of the door, covering myself self-consciously. 'Dinner's ready.'

That evening I sat on the settee in my pyjamas with Grandad and we watched TV with Gran until the chimes of Big Ben punctuated the headlines. The newsreader's sombre tones listed the disasters of the day. Everyone in the world either seemed to be fighting, on strike or fighting for the right to strike. I watched bemused as the reporters tried to explain who was killing whom and why, but none of it made any sense. Gran was asleep in her chair by the end. Grandad nodded his head towards the door and followed me into the hall.

'Come on, I'll tuck you in,' he said.

Did teenagers need to be tucked in? I made a mild protest.

'Don't you think I'm a bit too old for that?'

He shook his head. Pleased at being overruled, I made my way upstairs.

'You're not too old for this, either.' He started the once familiar bedtime rhyme:

> To bed, to bed, said Sleepyhead.
> There's time enough, said Slow.
> Put on the pan, said Greedy guts.
> Let's eat before we go.

When I was little, Mum would start the rhyme as a whisper and chase me up the stairs, increasing in volume and speed as we ran to my room and I tumbled into bed, pulling the covers over my head 'before she got me'.

She'd always finish with, 'Sleep tight, don't let the bed bugs bite.' And she always left the door to my room ajar, allowing the light from the landing to filter in.

But there was no running tonight. Grandad shuffled behind me. I looked out of the landing window and let him catch up. Men were pouring out of the Legion on unsteady legs, waving and shouting at their mates as they made their way home.

Grandad's beard was rough as he gave me a cuddle.

'I used to say that rhyme to your mum and one day you'll be able to say it to your kids.' He tucked the sheets under me, pinning me in a tight cocoon. 'Oh, I wish she was still here to see you. She'd be proud of you, like me and your gran are.'

I shrank down into the bedding, embarrassed at his words and not knowing what to say. It took him a long time to get back downstairs. The muffled noise of them talking drifted up the stairs, like a foreign language, the rhythm familiar but the words unknown.

I woke to the unusual sound of raised voices. Opening the door, I closed my eyes and listened. Still unable to make out what was being said, I knew I needed to get closer. Treading on the outer edge of the stairs to minimise creaks, I made my way down, looking into the street, hoping to see someone quarrelling.

I sat on the stairs and waited until the argument resumed, knowing if I feigned a stomach ache, it would make it stop. I wanted it to stop. But I wanted to know what they were saying even more. They started again. Muffled through the door, only the occasional words made sense. They were trying to keep the volume down, but emotions drove it up.

'Not everything's a joke, Jack. I think we should tell him.'

'What difference will it make?'

'It's only right that he should understand before it's too late.'

'It's already too late, Lily. We can only do our best.'

'Our best? That won't be good enough this time, will it?'

'It'll have to be, because that's all we've got.'

'I hope you know what you're doing, Jack.'

'Let me handle this my way, Lily, please.'

'Do what you like, but don't forget, it's me who's got to pick up the pieces and put it back together . . . after.'

The door to the living room opened and Gran came out.

'You've done it before, Lily.' Grandad's voice was still a loud whisper.

She walked through the hall to the kitchen, unaware I was there.

'I know I have,' she said to herself, 'too many times.'

I retreated to my room, thinking of a way to interpret what had been said that had a happy ending but failing. I looked through the darkness to where Pickering sat.

'Why don't you have a chat to Gran in the morning?' he said.

It was good advice.

'You could ask about the car at the same time,' he added.

I lay awake for a long time before falling asleep.

Chapter 9

Thursday, 27 March 1975

Determined not to get distracted with chores, as soon as I got home the next afternoon, I got changed and finished off the *Hood*, painting the boats and decks. Grandad was in bed and Gran was doing her cleaning job. The newspaper covering the workbench stuck to my hands and left grey smudges of ink.

Reluctantly, I tackled my geography homework, my half-hearted efforts let down further by the inky smears. How did other kids find enthusiasm for this stuff? I was certain it was a complete waste of time. It wasn't just geography and physics – I couldn't see the point in any subject. There seemed no connection between what people did for a job and the things school tried to stuff into my head. I closed the book, knowing I'd done what I could but that somehow there was more I could have done. It all seemed pointless.

Gran returned home, bringing life into the house and rousing me, setting me to work preparing the fire in the living room and running the hoover round. I watched Grandad struggle down the stairs, each step taking all of his effort and concentration. Only when he got to the bottom did he look and acknowledge me, winking at me as he wearily shuffled into the kitchen.

I ran the hoover towards the front door, the dust and grit rattling up the pipe. After removing the head, I ran the steel pipe around the skirting board like Gran had shown me. I opened the door to the porch and knelt to get the muck that had collected at the base of the door frame. Then I put the end of the pipe onto the carpet near the door and dragged it, pushing down hard. Annoyingly, it revealed another layer of hidden dirt. I lifted the pipe and dug it in harder each time, stabbing it down and drawing it back, frustrated that each time I did it, more dirt could be found. When would it be clean? Faster and faster I jabbed at the carpet until tears rolled down my face. I stopped and hugged the plastic tube. The only consolation was that the noise of the hoover drowned my sobbing.

We sat at the table and I chased my peas around a piece of gammon. Using the mashed potato as glue on the back of my fork, I systematically mopped them up.

'What did you do today, love?' Gran asked.

'Rural studies.'

'Rural studies?' Grandad launched his attack. 'What? Leaves and that?'

Gran chuckled, despite the fact she didn't usually want to encourage him.

'It's all sorts. We were talking about options today and about careers advice.'

Grandad perked up. 'What did they advise, then?'

'Do you think I should go down the pit?' I asked, ignoring his question and answering it at the same time.

'The money's good,' he said.

'You can do better than that, can't you, love?' Gran said, but she didn't seem convinced.

Neither was I.

The alternative career bombs they threw at me all missed their target and my mind drifted to the top of a snowy peak with Bonington.

After we'd eaten, Grandad joined me in the workshop to see the finished ship.

'We've done a good job there, H,' he said, transferring his weight onto my shoulder. His bony finger reached out towards the model, its tip quivering close to the ship's bridge. 'It was a hell of a view from up there, H.' He looked longingly at the ship. 'I went up with another lad,' he chuckled, 'but I could probably get you up there as well, as long as you do as I tell you.'

GRANDAD'S FIRM HAND *pushed my back into the stone wall as the workers passed us. He peeped round the corner. It was all clear. A truck rolled across the yard, its low gears grinding as it trundled past. This was our chance.*

As it drew level with us, he waved me to follow and we jogged alongside the truck, the green canvas juddering as it made its way across the rough ground. When we got close to a pile of wooden boxes on the queue side, we left the cover of the truck and crouched beside the crates. Grandad did a series of hand gestures. I shrugged. Unless he was giving me instructions on how to kill and pluck a chicken, I had no idea what the nonsense meant.

It was soon clear, as he jumped up and ran to the next refuge, a pile of sacks. I dropped by his side, panting. We worked our way alongside the cargo. Grandad looked round the corner, so I did, too, my head level with his knees. It was all clear; the Hood *was in sight, three bridges connecting it to the dock. Guards patrolled the yard. We waited for a chance to climb on board.*

Neither of us heard the man approach.

'Morning, lads.'

Startled, I turned and looked down at his footwear. Who would have thought brogues were good for sneaking around.

John Brown looked past us. 'She's a beauty, isn't she?'

We followed his gaze and both nodded in agreement. The Hood's *painted steelwork absorbed the feeble light released by the dull sky.*

'I was just going to have a nosy about. Do you want to join me?'

'Are we allowed?' I asked.

'What's the plan, John?' said Grandad, ignoring me.

Brown relaxed, basking in his role as the mastermind. He leaned against the hessian bags and reached inside his tank top, retrieving a pack of Park Drive cigarettes from his shirt pocket. He eased a few out and offered one to Grandad, who accepted. Brown shielded the lit match and offered it up in cupped hands before lighting his own. Both men took deep draws, the tips glowing in the dull light, before tilting back their heads and exhaling. If ever there was a way to give the game away, I thought, that's it. Grandad tried to hide the fag when he realised I was watching him.

'I thought you said it was a disgusting habit.' I pointed at the coffin nail.

Brown looked at the cigarette. 'Is it?' he asked, unsure if it was the cigarette we were talking about.

'You said it was a stupid waste of money.'

'Oh, it is,' Grandad confirmed as he took another deep draw.

'Is it?' repeated Brown.

'You said it was bad for health and it would ruin your lungs,' I continued.

'Does it?' Brown asked. 'It's not done me any harm,' he said, stifling a cough without blushing. 'Anyway'—he returned to the plan—'I've been watching the guards all morning.' He pointed the cigarette.

We both turned.

'Don't look, whatever you do.'

We snapped our heads back.

'Why not?' I asked.

My eyes flicked round to see whatever it was I shouldn't be looking at.

'Dunno, but that's what they always say in the movies, isn't it?' Brown shrugged.

'I'll be subtle,' said Grandad, scratching his head and turning towards the Hood.

I followed his move. Sure enough, the guards were walking away from their station.

Brown continued, 'They patrol the yard in the same pattern when they leave that post. They don't return for fifteen minutes, which gives us just enough time to have a peek before they return.'

'Are we allowed?' I asked again. My stomach fluttered in anticipation.

'Yes, no problem,' said Brown, 'as long as they don't catch us.'

They both dropped the tab ends on the floor, twisting them out with their feet in a tuneless dance.

'We're in,' said Grandad, spitting out a piece of tobacco. 'Lead the way.'

Brown strode forwards. 'If we're spotted,' he said, 'try to look official.'

I feared my welly work boots might be about to let me down.

We paused at the bottom of the gangway and stared at the sign.

'It's just a question of interpretation,' said Brown.

I read out loud: 'Entry forbidden.'

Brown smiled and unhooking the chain.

We came aboard on the starboard side of the quarterdeck. Grandad was in his element as we explored.

'This way, H,' he said running towards the superstructure.

We climbed up an external staircase and inside the Hood. After a few twists and turns and more steps, we came out on deck again.

'This is the boat deck,' said Grandad.

Brown looked around. 'I forgot, Jack. You know more about the ship than me.'

'It's your tour, John,' he claimed but carried on leading the way.

'These are the 4-inch Mk V high-angle guns,' Brown said as we rushed past. Panting, he added, 'These rooms are storage for ammo, wet-weather gear and some of the marines' kit. That's the night defence control station.' We ran past the ship's boats. 'That . . .' he said breathlessly, but then gave up.

Grandad turned and waved. 'Come on. We need to get going. I want to get to the bridge.'

Brown was firing whatever snippets he could between breaths.

We followed Grandad up and up, staircase after staircase, until we came to a large open room with windows around three sides. Brown stumbled in behind us.

'This is where it all happens, Harry,' Grandad said, pointing at the wiring and piping that emerged from the bowels of the ship.

'Come on,' said Grandad, urging us on. 'We've got this far. I'm feeling lucky. Let's carry on.'

I'd lost count of how many levels we'd gone up, but now we had to climb a steel ladder on the outside of the conning tower.

Grandad hung on one arm and turned to us. 'It's a lot easier to do this in the dock than it is at sea in a force nine.'

'I'm glad I'm leaving that to you lads,' Brown replied.

I shivered as the cool breeze found the sweat patches on my back. We continued up the external ladders. The spotting top was the highest platform on the ship. Windows surrounded the structure, allowing men to see the telltale smoke plumes of enemy ships. I took deep breaths and took in the scene around the yard. There were ships under construction and others were tied up, waiting to be fitted out. But Grandad only let us pause for a moment.

'Best not push our luck, H. Come on, let's get going.'

Brown only had time to step onto the deck before turning and following us out. As we descended, Grandad picked up the pace, taking the steps two or three at a time, his legs a blur as he pulled ahead. He *stopped at the top of a narrow staircase, grinning over his shoulder as I caught up.*

'Watch this, H. This is how we used to do it . . .' He put his forearms on the steel rails, his hands gripping the bars, and lifted his feet off the deck. Then he stuck his legs straight out in front of him like a gymnast and let go, arms still resting on the handrails.

He slid down the rails, picking up speed, landing with a thud on the steel deck. The bar was set, the competition was on. Brown was next. Controlling his speed by gripping the bar, he landed gently next to Grandad. Now it was my turn.

Grandad's mouth was moving, but all I could hear was the blood rushing through my head as I gathered speed. When I hit the deck, my legs collapsed and I fell forwards. Grandad and Brown grabbed me, bringing me to a stop, my nose an inch from the steel wall.

We spilt outside and jogged along the boat deck, Grandad turning and side-stepping along like a boxer in training, chuckling at my attempt to copy him. We ran at full pelt down the gangway. Grandad jumped over the chain and I got ready to do the same. But Brown refused the hurdle. I had no time to stop. The collision knocked Brown over the chain and me on my backside. Grandad tutted at the fiasco.

'Get up, yeh daft buggers. You're going to get us locked up.' Grandad held out a hand and pulled Brown to his feet. 'Are you okay?' he said, chuckling as Brown brushed himself down, keen to gain respectability.

'Sorry, lads, but I need to get back to work,' he said.

We shook hands and he limped off towards his office.

Taking a deep breath, Grandad extended his arms out, stretching his chest. He wiped the sweat from his face onto his thick black beard.

GRANDAD RAN HIS FINGERS through his Father Christmas whiskers, wincing when he tried to move.

'I must have twisted my knee as I came down the steps,' Grandad said, leaning on the bench and clutching his leg. His energetic story-telling had got the better of him. Sweat dripped from the tip of his nose and splattered in the dust. 'Give me a hand, H.'

He abandoned his walking frame and put his arm across my shoulders. I put my arm around his thin waist and we hobbled into the kitchen. Gran caught us, like bank robbers fleeing the scene of the crime.

'What's up, Jack? What have you done?'

'Grandad was just showing me . . .' Grandad glared at me and I stuttered to a halt. 'He's hurt his leg.'

'Aww, Jack,' Gran said, stroking his face.

He took her hand and held it against his chest. Hovering uselessly, I could neither leave nor help. Gran broke away.

'I'll make a cuppa,' she said, turning away from us.

Grandad looked pale and tired. He reached out and held my hand, drawing me closer. I perched on the chair arm with my arm around him.

'Better make it a special tea I think, H,' he said, patting my leg.

Gran looked over her shoulder and gave her approval. I left them whispering as I rummaged in the sideboard in the hall for the rum bottle. The new bottle had already been started, its contents down to its shoulder.

We both helped Grandad back upstairs to bed. After Gran was satisfied he was comfortable, she left us alone. A few minutes later I heard the front door closed.

I sat on the bed watching him sip his special tea, the aroma of the rum exotic and sweet.

'There's nothing to be recommended about getting old, H.' His breath came in shallow gasps. He closed his eyes, breathing through his nose. He opened them. 'Sorry, H.'

'It's okay,' I told him.

'I never thought I'd get like this when I was your age.' He shook his head. 'Don't get so caught up in life, Harry, that you forget it's going to end one day. Make the most of your time; it won't last forever.'

Although I'd thought a lot about death, it was only at that moment I realised I'd never thought about my own. I tried to imagine what it would be like, not being able to move or think. As he often did, he read my mind.

'It's nothing to be frightened of. It wouldn't make any difference, anyway. We're all alive, and that means we're going to die. But I wish somebody had said that to me at your age.' He stared into his palm, flexing his fingers. 'I don't think I started thinking properly until your mum got married.' He held my gaze. 'You'll understand what I'm talking about when you get older. At least I hope you will.' He squeezed my hand. 'It took me a long time to realise who I was, what kind of person I was. I wasn't that pleased with what I discovered. But you've got something I didn't have.'

The more my brow furrowed, the more his smile broadened, but I still didn't see it coming.

'You see, H, I didn't have a fantastic grandad like you've got.'

I nudged into him.

'Careful. Don't spill my tea.' He took a loud slurp. 'By the time I understood how the world worked, it was too late. I'd lost my nerve. Don't let that happen to you. If you get an opportunity to do something, do it. Take chances. When you're young, there's always time to recover, to get over it and have another go,' he paused. 'But not when you get old. Then it really is . . .' His smile faded. 'Don't leave it too late, Harry. It's not a nice feeling.'

I sat with him, silently working through what he'd said. I don't know how long I stayed there, but when Gran came home, Grandad was asleep. She ushered me off the bed and I reluctantly left them alone.

Chapter 10

Friday, 28 March 1975

'I'll do it while I'm here, if you like.'

The unfamiliar voice filled the house and made me sit up.

'Are you sure you don't mind?' Gran asked the visitor.

'It's no trouble. Can I get what I need from Jack's bench?'

The voice sounded confident. It had a practical approach. Like Grandad's, it was a voice that got things done.

'Of course you can. I'll put the kettle on.'

'I'll have it sorted by the time the doctor's done.'

It was only then I noticed the muffled voices coming from their bedroom. Annoyed that I might already have missed something interesting, I quickly got dressed and went to investigate. Gran was in the kitchen. The visitor was rummaging around in the workshop.

'What's up, Gran?'

'We're going to bring the bed down and put it in the front room; Grandad's struggling with the stairs.'

I looked towards the workshop. My curiosity vanished when Frank Watson's head appeared.

'Do you know where he keeps his spanners?'

Now I had a face to match the sound, it had a different feel. His low, rough voice wasn't confident – it sounded annoyed.

'Show Mr Watson where the tools are please, love.'

My body tensed as I brushed past Watson's dad. Fumbling around under the bench, I could feel his brooding mass behind me, making the simple job into a much bigger task. I found the spanners and stood up, not wanting to look him in the eye. He took the canvas roll without a word. I watched his back as he walked away. He had some kind of aura about him. You couldn't identify it. I don't think science would have helped. Perhaps an exorcist could. I hung around the kitchen, trying to find a purpose and failing.

Watson's dad brought the bed down in pieces and I looked on from the doorway as he set it up. Gran touched my shoulder as she squeezed past, placing a mug of tea on the windowsill.

'Harry's in the same class as your lad, Frank,' she said, trying to neutralise the silent thunder that surrounded him.

He looked up, glancing at me. 'Is he?'

His words hung between us until Gran's discomfort forced her to retreat.

'I'll go and see what the doctor's got to say,' she said, although she only got as far as the kitchen.

I watched Frank working. He looked normal, happily slurping his tea while putting the bed together. But something was wrong deep inside and nothing could stop it from spilling out and contaminating everything nearby.

Dr Crowther shouted down.

'Excuse me. Could you give me a hand, please?'

I moved towards the stairs, but just as I put my foot on the first step, Frank's hand fell on my shoulder, stopping me dead.

They emerged from the bedroom. Grandad hung around Frank's neck like a wounded soldier being rescued from the battlefield. I stood in the hall with Gran. Dr Crowther brought up the rear guard. Frank didn't flinch as Grandad's feet missed their target and slipped on the stairs, his dressing gown belt unfastening as they progressed. At the bottom, Grandad straightened himself, insisting he could manage the short walk to the kitchen without help. Frank hovered close by as a precaution. Grandad made it to the table, lowering himself onto the chair.

'Are you stopping for another, Frank?' Grandad asked, still wheezing from the strain.

Gran glanced at the kettle, no doubt willing it to break.

'No, I'm going to get off, Jack,' he said, impersonating someone cheerful. 'I'll drop the cash in for the car early next week.'

'Cheers, Frank, I'll see you . . .' We all watched Grandad as he fought to control a coughing fit. '. . . later on.'

'Aye.' Frank was looking at Grandad with sad eyes. 'Don't forget. Send the lad down if you need anything.'

Without waiting for a reply, he left.

We all looked at the space where he'd stood. Even the air seemed reluctant to fill the void until it was certain he'd left. Gran breathed a sigh of relief.

'I'm grateful for the help, Jack, but I'm glad he's gone.'

'He's alright, Lily.'

'I'm going to make up the bed,' she said as she scurried away.

'Make me a brew, H, will you? There's a good lad.'

So that's where the car had gone. I hated the idea that Watson and his dad would be sitting in our car. But I suppose that meant Grandad would be getting a newer one, once he was better.

We'd brought the *Hood* in from the workshop and it took pride of place on the kitchen table. I put down his mug and joined him. An old metal cash box had appeared from its usual home in the bottom of my grandparents' wardrobe, its lid wedged open by the paperwork spilling out. I pulled the heavy box towards me, dragging the tablecloth with it, the material scrunching up and distorting around the ship, forming waves across its surface, the bleached timber of the exposed tabletop standing in for a shoreline. I looked at him, expecting a jibe at my sloppiness, but Grandad was engrossed in the pages of an old photo album I'd not seen before.

The tattoos on his arms were misshapen by his wrinkled skin. The weight he'd lost exposed his shrunken muscles and they twitched out of synch with his movement. He'd perked up after the doctor's visit, but the whites of his eyes were creamy and I felt Grandad was a long way behind them.

As I lifted the lid, the paperwork rose like a pile of towels pressed down in a washing powder advert. I looked at an old passport. Dad's name was on the front, but when I opened it, Mum's photo was on the inside, too, just getting a mention as a side note. A wad of old rent books was held together with a rubber band, the pastel covers a different colour for each year. There was a pile of notes from Gran's church when she was younger – thank-yous for the contributions she'd made in the fifties and sixties. Dad's identity book from his time in the merchant navy sat among bright red wax seals stamped onto the Prudential insurance policies.

'This was on the *Hood*,' he said, noisily salvaging bits of KitKat from his false teeth with his tongue.

He pointed at a picture of him with three mates. They sat on a vent or a bollard, arms folded. All wore caps except Grandad. He was in the middle, his hair flopping into his face.

'That's Connie on my right.' His finger tapped the man on the left.

'That's your left.' I pointed out his error.

'He's on my right in the photo.'

'He's not; he's on your left.'

'Which is my right hand in the picture?' he said, a note of irritation in his voice.

I looked again – there was trap round here somewhere.

'Oh, I see.'

'Said the blind man,' he mocked.

Connie was wearing overalls, his belt done up too tight, his hat pushed high on his head. It made him look like he had a massive forehead; either that or he had a massive forehead.

'That's Digger on *my* right.'

'I know. Okay, I get it.'

Digger was leaning against the superstructure, his cap at a racy angle. A fag hung from his right hand.

'And that's Jonesy.'

He was standing behind Grandad, his shirt undone. All four wore broad smiles.

'This was the last time we were all together on the *Hood*. A couple of weeks later, they got transferred to other ships.'

I turned the page. A set of small square pictures showed the *Hood* in port, their crinkle-cut edges setting them apart.

'Where was this?'

'Gibraltar. It was always a favourite spot for the lads. A bit of time to relax,' he said, putting his hands behind his head and closing his eyes to demonstrate relaxing.

'Sunbathing?' I asked.

His arms flopped back on the table with a thud. 'When I say relax, what I mean is drinking and fighting.'

I nodded, adding it to the other code words he used, like 'we'll see', which really meant 'no', or 'I had a win on the horses', which in fact meant 'one of my horses won, but the other nine lost'.

'We had plenty of fun there, I can tell you.' His eyes sparkled. 'And plenty of fun that I can't tell you about, ha ha.' He nudged me.

I didn't understand what that was code for.

The comforting rhythm of Gran's veg chopping faltered as I waited for an explanation. Gran looked at him.

He cleared his throat and looked a little sheepish before asking me, 'Did I ever tell you about when I got my medal for swimming?'

'What was that for?'

'Swimming.' He coughed again and we both watched a bit of KitKat fly across the table like a missile, landing in the tablecloth ocean, just short of the *Hood*.

'I know, but what kind?'

'The kind you do in the water.'

'You know what I mean. Breaststroke, crawl, butterfly . . .' I acted each one out, much to his amusement.

'Backstroke, doggy-paddle'—he completed the list—'we didn't care about that stuff,' he said, excitement in his voice. 'Just get there first, that's all I was bothered about.'

Sitting up straight, I took a deep breath and puffed out my chest, glad that the conversation had moved on to a subject I could speak about with authority. As casually as I could, I told him.

'I always do the front crawl when I want to swim fast.' I stretched my arms out as if preparing for the Olympic final. 'Like Tarzan.' I held my arms up and flexed my muscles.

The moment was marred as a small burp escaped unchecked.

'Tarzan?' he exclaimed, squeezing my puny biceps. 'More like Tarzan Tin Ribs.'

My arms flopped down and I waited for the next insult.

'Your dad told me you set off like Johnny Weissmuller after that pedalo capsized in Falmouth.'

This was a very famous incident; well, it was in our house. Almost as famous as the time I rocked the rocking chair too far with my mate Keith in it. Trapped underneath, the only thing that made sense to my junior brain was the need for leg protection and therefore I shouted, 'Get my wellies, get my wellies.' I'm not sure how I thought that would help, but it made perfect sense to the six-year-old me.

The 'pedalo incident', as nobody called it, happened early in a two-week holiday in Cornwall. I was there with Mum and Dad. We left Mum sunbathing and hired a pedalo. I don't know how, but a passing speed boat sent waves towards us big enough to cause our capsize. A month earlier I'd got my 'ten lengths' swimming badge at school, but I hadn't had the chance to show off my new skills, until now.

As soon as I hit the water, I was off, just like Johnny Weissmuller, as Dad would later recount. Johnny Weissmuller was *Dad's* Tarzan. He was an ex-Olympic swimming champion. He was good, but not as good as Ron Ely. He was *my* Tarzan and far superior, mainly because he was in colour, which is always better, or so I thought.

I was nine when the wonders of the colour telly swept into my life. I'd just got to the height where I didn't fit between the arms of our two-seater settee and three-seaters hadn't been invented yet. It was a Friday night and I was watching Van Helsing, the vampire hunter, chase Dracula around Transylvania. Dad came home from work, opened the living room door and leaned in.

'Hey, Harry. Derek Hargreaves had an accident at work; I had to take him home.'

'Is he dead?' I asked, still concentrating on the undead.

Dracula had just scored a direct hit on a busty maiden.

'Don't be daft; he's got a new telly.'

'Oh yeah.'

Van Helsing had him cornered.

'A colour telly,' Dad added.

Dracula looked up from the moaning woman. A colour telly?

We didn't know anybody with a colour telly. I sat up and looked at him for the first time, then back at Dracula, blood dripping from his fangs.

'*On the Buses* was on,' he said.

But I was watching the pool of crimson blood spread across the black-and-white screen.

'Guess what colour the buses are?'

It was a daft question. Yorkshire Traction buses were red. The only other buses I'd seen were Corgi and Dinky toys. They made London transport buses, red buses. This must be one of his lame jokes, like how many ferrets can you get in a bag?

'Thirteen,' he'd claim. 'It's a big bag!' he'd say as he grabbed me for a double kidney tickle. 'Unlucky for some!' he'd shout as I collapsed in a heap on the floor.

I played along this time, confident I knew my subject.

'Red,' I said with conviction.

'No.'

'What?'

'They're green.'

'What!'

'Green buses,' he chuckled and went off to make himself a cuppa, leaving me floundering in my new reality.

Grandad's bony elbow weakly prodded me in the ribs. 'Oi, are you paying attention?' he said, tapping the album.

I rubbed my side.

'This is where I got my medal.' He bent his elbows and flexed his arms. 'It was the swimming final, where the top two men from each heat would swim for the championship of the *Hood*. I'd come second in the last heat. At the halfway point I was in the lead, but I slowed down, saving my energy for the big race.'

WE STOOD ON A FLOATING platform, one of several fixed between the ship and quay wall. The races were held between two of them, tethered about 50 yards apart. Officers and ratings lined the Hood's *deck. Everyone wanted to get a look at the action. The crews of the other ships filled the quayside, the uniformed crowd speckled between the drab overalls of dock workers. The competitors were in their trunks, milling*

around on the floating platforms. I looked among the fit, tanned bodies for Grandad, then I realised one of them belonged to him. His beer belly had gone, replaced by defined stomach muscles. An officer used a loudhailer to call the crowd to order. A buzz of anticipation wriggled through the audience.

Everyone was enjoying a few hours of distraction from the mundane maintenance of dockside life. The platform rocked as men moved around, sending small pulsating wavelets across the flat surface. The Mediterranean sun reflected on the side of the Hood, the dull grey paint giving nothing back. Shoals of fish were hanging around in the platform's shade, the brave ones darting out to nibble on an apple core or stray peanut shell. Anything in the water was examined with sharp nibbles before being torn to shreds or allowed to sink. The less intelligent fish gave the inedible pieces a second try, not trusting the initial assessment.

After a bit of arguing over their positions, the swimmers were ready. Grandad was nearest the ship. They lined up, their toes hooked over the edge of the platform to give them maximum purchase when they launched. I flinched as the starting pistol fired. Grandad did a gigantic leap and took the lead. The water boiled around them. It was impossible to distinguish them; only their position gave away who was who.

There were three out in front. At the halfway point, Grandad was second but still in the race. They must all be Tarzan fans, because everyone was doing the crawl. As they approached the finish line, I was shouting for Grandad, but he was only in third place. He needed to make his move soon or he'd lose the medal. I realised he wouldn't make it. He kept looking up to see where he was. Everyone was shouting and cheering.

The first hand touched the platform, but it wasn't Grandad's. He was going to be seco . . .

Hold on.

As Grandad approached the platform, he dived and swam underneath us. What was he up to? This was a disaster. Second and third place touched to finish. Grandad surfaced on the opposite side and swam *on. The men were jeering and laughing, congratulating the winner, but Grandad just kept going. Now everyone was looking at him, wondering what the hell he was doing.*

There was a small group of officers on the Hood *pointing into the water, their voices lost in the celebrations. Grandad lifted his head, then dived. There was still no clue why.*

The crowd was quiet. The longer he stayed down, the quieter it got. Everyone was spellbound by his performance.

We all stared at the patch of water where he'd disappeared. Time stood still.

Then Grandad broke the surface. He turned on his back and swam with one hand towards the platform. It was only then that we could see the white uniform of the young officer who had fallen over the side. No doubt under the influence of too much rum. He'd hit his head as he fell and was unconscious by the time he landed in the water. His mates had seen him go in but were unable to raise the alarm above the din of the cheering crowd. None were brave or daft enough to jump in from the Hood's *deck 30 feet above the water.*

Helping hands reached down to pull the officer from the water. Grandad lifted himself onto the platform and someone passed him a lit cigarette. He sat with his legs dangling and stared into the distance, sucking the smoke deep into his lungs. I watched the ash fall into the water and dissolve. Snapping out of his trance, he swapped the cigarette to his other hand, hiding it behind his leg. He raised his forefinger to his lips and winked.

A WRY SMILE SPREAD from Grandad's mouth to the rest of his face as he peered over his specs.

My eyes narrowed. 'You said you got the medal for winning the swimming race?' I was still proud of him, but he'd always said details were important.

'No, I didn't. I said I got a medal for swimming.'

'But—'

'Hold on a sec . . .' He delved into the green metal cash box and lifted out some papers. The Prudential's trilby-wearing salesman strode confidently across the documents. He pulled out a small wooden box, flipped the clasp and handed me the medal. 'Here, have a shufti at that.'

It was heavier than I'd expected. I traced my finger over the gold embossed anchor, the blue background matching the blue-and-white ribbon. I rotated the medal as I read: For Gallantry in Saving Lives at Sea.

'There you are. I told you. That's my swimming medal.'

My mouth flapped around, but I had nothing to say.

'And that's what I got it for, 'swimming' over to the lad, 'swimming' down to grab the drunken idiot and 'swimming' back to the platform. It was a full-on swimming caper, start to finish.'

The smile on my face was so big it hurt.

'Take swimming out of it and, well, it's not such a happy ending, is it, H?'

He'd tricked me again. In the meantime, I figured I might as well join in.

'If you were to take away the swimming'—I put my hand to my chin, to exaggerate the pondering—'what you've got left is your basic "man falls in water and drowns" story.'

'Exactly,' he exclaimed, banging his hand on the table and making me jump. 'And nobody wants to listen to a story like that, do they?'

He was right, they didn't.

The stories continued to the background sound of a bubbling stew pot.

In another photo, Grandad was on a horse. The strange thing was, it didn't seem that strange to see him dressed as a cowboy.

'Where was that one taken?' I asked.

'Uruguay, near the end of the war. We were on leave and visited a ranch. I had to catch that horse before I could climb on it to have my picture taken.'

'Do you know how to throw a lasso?'

'Of course I do.' He took the belt from his dressing gown. 'Any sailor worth his salt needs to know about rope-work. Here, I'll show you.'

THE TIMBER FENCE FLEXED as I leaned back, pulling myself up to straddle the top rail. I adjusted my position to get the round pole fixed between my bum cheeks. Grandad climbed over the fence and into the corral. I passed him the rope. The stallion trotted up and down at the far side of the enclosure, full of nervous energy. Other cowboys came over to watch. One of them, dressed all in black, wore a two-gun rig, the pearl handles of the six-shooters reflected the bright Montevideo sun. The leather of his gloves creaked as his fingers flexed. A stalk of grass quivered as he chewed it in the corner of his mouth, taking in the scene with cold blue eyes.

As Grandad approached the horse, it ran round the edge of the corral, sending up clouds of dust as it kicked its back legs high into the air. Grandad rotated in the centre, focusing all of his attention on its every move, swinging the loop in his right hand, his left holding the rest of the coils.

One cowboy shouted, 'Hey, Ringo, he can handle a rope better than you.'

I looked around to see who he was talking to. The man in black turned and his hand dropped towards his gun.

'What did you say?'

The crowd separated, leaving the cowboy alone.

He swallowed. 'I didn't mean nothin'. I's just foolin'.'

Ringo turned away and spat into the dirt.

The loop of rope shot out from Grandad's grip, tightening around the horse's neck. Muscle and veins rippled under its skin as it picked up speed. Grandad took a turn around his arm and sat back as the rope tightened, the heels of his boots digging into the dusty ground as the horse pulled him forwards. Grandad walked his hands up the rope, getting closer to the horse. As he did so, he started talking to it, soothing words I couldn't hear, but the horse calmed and stopped fighting.

Grandad walked the stallion over to me. I reached out to touch his nose, but the horse pulled away, its eyes wild and dangerous. Grandad continued to stroke and pat the horse's neck, calming him once more. As Grandad left the corral and passed through the gate, Ringo approached him, his hat tipped low over his eyes. Grandad handed me the rope.

'Here, give it to me,' said Ringo.

'Is it yours?' asked Grandad.

I wound the rope loosely around the top rail of the fence like the cowboys did in the movies.

'It is now,' Ringo said, pushing his hat back to reveal his deadly stare.

Ringo's hand moved towards his pistol, but Grandad stepped forwards. As Ringo drew his gun, Grandad pulled it from his grip. Whipping it back in one smooth movement, hitting Ringo across the cheek with the butt.

'Now, why don't you piss off before I lose my temper,' snarled Grandad as Ringo wiped his cheek with the back of his glove, examining the blood that had rolled down his face.

Ringo stood still for a moment before turning and walking away.

We tied the horse up outside the photographer's shop and the man came out and set his camera up. Grandad climbed onto the horse and struck a pose, sliding onto the ground when the photographer was done. We were just admiring the result, when a shout came from across the street.

'Watch out!'

Grandad turned and dropped to one knee, pulling the revolver from his belt, fanning the hammer and emptying the chamber. Ringo hit the ground hard, sending up a plume of red dust. His still body lay in the dirt across the street. Grandad swivelled the gun around his finger, forwards then backwards, slipping it straight into his holster.

GRANDAD WINKED AT ME, flicking the terry towel belt off the teapot and rethreading it around his waist.

'Is that true?' I beamed.

'Sure thing, partner.'

Gran glanced over at us, shaking her head as she turned back to the sink and the dirty dishes. 'Why don't you go into the other room? I've lit the fire.'

We took the *Hood* and the album and left the hard seats of the kitchen for the sofa in the cramped front room, the bed now taking up all the spare space.

'This was one of my favourite places, H. Malta.'

Grandad's nail scraped across the page several times before he caught the postcard's edge. Prising it from its corner fastenings, he offered it to me.

'Where's Malta?' I asked.

The photo showed a curved wall with a promenade below it. The sea was alive with small boats. An ancient fort protected the town, the open sea laying beyond the breakwater.

'At the bottom of Italy and Sicily, near North Africa. It's a beautiful place. It took a real pounding during the war. I was there in 1937, under Captain Pridham. Now that man *did* know how to handle a ship.'

Words washed over me. Like a grain of sand on the beach, I was part of something big but powerless to resist the force of Grandad's energy. The water rippled, sending sparkles of sunlight onto my face and around the room. The boats moved, light, colours and noise spreading around us as they swept us into the picture.

'LOOK!' GRANDAD POINTED towards the land. 'You can just make out the entrance.'

I looked in the direction he was pointing but couldn't make out any detail, just a strip of rock with buildings on it.

'I can't see it, Grandad.'

'It'll get clearer as we get nearer to shore. Some harbours are difficult to see until you're close in.'

The sun was blistering. We were on the Hood's *starboard lookout platform, jutting out over the deck at the side of the bridge. Fishing boats were heading home after an early start. The island was getting bigger every minute.*

'Now look, H. You can see Valletta in the middle there. That's Marsamxett Harbour on the right and that's Grand Harbour on the left. We're going in that one.' He pointed to the left.

He was pulling my leg again.

'They'll never get the Hood *in there, Grandad.' I laughed at the preposterous idea – the harbour entrance was way too small.*

'I told you the captain knew what he was doing, didn't I?'

We stepped aside and the captain and other officers joined us out on the platform, binoculars glued to their faces, pointing ahead and plan-

ning the final approach. I was expecting the captain to go back inside and take the wheel, but when I looked, there was no wheel. All around the room were brass funnels.

'These are the voice pipes,' said Grandad, 'so the captain can talk to the helmsman above us and the engine room below.'

The captain approached the pipes and gave the command.

'Slow!'

The captain's confident voice clashed with my own misgivings as we passed the outer harbour wall.

'That doesn't just mean go slower. It means the slowest speed the ship can do and still be under control.'

Back on the platform, the chatter and excitement of the crowds could be heard above the gentle hum of the engines. The walls of the harbour were covered with people. What a sight this must be. We were heading straight for Valletta town.

As we reached the centre of the harbour, men on deck prepared the lines. There was activity everywhere. The captain was cool-headed, giving instructions to the engine room and his helmsman.

'What's happening, Grandad? Are we going to anchor?'

'No, there's not enough space for that. We're going to pick up a mooring. That's like an anchor that's already been put down for visiting ships. One will be secured on the bow and another on the stern, but first we've got to turn round. Just watch this.'

It was obvious to me that there wasn't anywhere near enough space to turn the ship inside the port. I waited in anticipation of the big crunch, the bow and stern knocking both stone and spectators into the water as the Hood wedged itself between the ancient harbour walls. No doubt the officers would be walking around after this one, scratching their heads and hitting each other with their caps. Another fine mess!

The ship came to a stop.

'The captain's going to put the left engines in reverse and the right-hand engines forward.' Grandad cocked his head. 'Listen.'

Captain Pridham's crisp voice issued the order. 'Full revs ahead starboard, full revs aft port.'

The ship vibrated through my loose grasp on the rail and as it increased, I tightened my grip. The reverberations rose from my knuckles to my arm and into my head, rattling my teeth. It increased until I feared she might shake herself to pieces. The power of the engines working against each other seemed nonsense to me. But then we slowly began to rotate on the spot. Now facing out to sea, the men on deck got busy with the cables to fasten us to the moorings. As the engines came to a stop, Grandad pointed to the ship's clock.

'I timed it,' he said, delight on his face. 'From passing the breakwater to engines stop, fifteen minutes flat.'

THE *Hood* rotated in Grandad's hand. 'Impressive, eh?' He pointed at the postcard. 'Valletta's a great place. I loved going into town and hiring one of the little sailing skiffs to go fishing.'

'Do you know how to sail a boat, Grandad? Without using an engine? With . . . just with . . . just using the . . . er . . .'

'Sails?' Grandad looked over his glasses. 'Course I do. I was off every chance I could get, sailing, swimming, fishing—'

'What was the biggest fish you ever caught?'

'Well, I didn't have a tape measure on me, but when I hooked it, it was that mad it shot off and towed me all the way around the island, backwards! I finally got it aboard and hit it on the head with my boot. When I took it back to the ship to cut it up, I had to do it in the bath.'

The blood bath! It was no surprise that the expression came from the old sailors. The guts and innards would block up the plughole for sure. I wrinkled my nose at the thought of the horrible stink.

'What's up with you?'

I snapped out of my fishy nightmare. 'Er . . . nothing.'

He looked at me suspiciously.

Gran stuck her head round the door. 'I'm going to put some fish and chips on in half an hour. I'm just going to pop to the shop. Harry? Keep an eye on the fire in here. Don't bother with the one in the kitchen; I'll sort it out when I get back. And set the table please, love.'

'I'll keep him busy, Lil, don't you worry.'

'Make sure he gets a wash, Jack,' she added. 'I'll see you in a bit.'

'Do yeh fancy learning how to sail, H?'

'Will they teach me how to sail if I go in the marines?'

'Possibly.' He scratched his beard. 'But I can show you some of the basics, if you like. It'll give you a head start on the other lads.'

I nodded, eager to start my training.

WE STOOD ON THE QUAYSIDE in Valletta, fishing gear piled around us. Dozens of little boats bobbed in the sunshine, their warps straining in the to and fro of the gentle swell, excited and keen to get to sea. Old fishermen sat on the quay side, chatting and smoking as they fixed their nets and sorted lines, their brown weather-beaten hands moving with swift precision. This looked like work you could enjoy. The smell of stale fish rose in waves as the nets were disturbed.

Grandad pointed out the pros and cons of the different boat designs as we walked along, but they all looked the same to me. Ahead of us was a group of five old men, smoking and spitting. They must have been professionals, because they seemed pretty good at it. Grandad walked over to them. I stayed back, fearing a coating of spittle and ash – a washable version of tar and feathers. Grandad handed over some notes as the ancient walls of the old town loomed above, unchanged since the days of Drake. I ran along the harbour walls, jumping from bales to barrels, fighting off the pirates with cutlass and pistols. 'Take that, yeh scurvy dog.'

Long John Silver looked at me and narrowed his eyes.

Grandad didn't have a peg leg or a parrot, but his pirate act was none the less authentic.

'You're not planning a mutineer, are yeh, lad? We'll have none o' that skulduggery on my ship, squab, and you can lay to that.'

Silver's expression from Treasure Island *snapped me to attention. 'Yes, sir,' I saluted.*

'Yes?'

'No. I mean no, sir!'

'Right, then, let's get this skiff shipshape and cast off. Untie the for'd line, squab.'

After pushing the boat away from the quay, Grandad fixed the oars, rowing out into some space to sort out the sail and catch the breeze.

'You take the tiller, lad. I'll hoist the mainsail and we'll see what lies beyond the breakwater of damnation as we make our way into the ocean of doom, ha haar.'

I shielded my eyes and squinted into the sun as he hoisted the sail.

'Twenty degrees to port, squab!'

I pulled the tiller to starboard and the sail filled, the boat leaning under the pressure of the wind. Grandad pulled on ropes and the speed increased. We were off.

The Hood *dominated the harbour.*

'We'll aim for her stern, H.'

Grandad must have got fed up with Long John Silver, as his voice returned to normal.

'We call this a starboard tack because the wind is coming over the starboard side. When we get well past the stern, but before we hit the rocks, we'll tack. That means we're going to turn to the right and the boat will lean over the other way. You'll have to change sides and sit over there. I'll sort the sail out.'

I was glad to hear that whatever he'd just said we were going to do, we were going to do it before we hit the rocks.

The little boat had just one sail.

'It's called a lateen rig. Easy to sail and good to windward,' he explained.

We sailed under the stern of the Hood *and waved at the sailors on deck. As we approached the rocky shore, he gave the command.*

'Helms-a-lee.'

That was my queue to push the tiller and move over to the port bench.

I JUMPED FROM ONE SIDE of the bed to the other.

'Careful, H,' he warned from the settee. 'Wait till the wind fills the sail, then we'll pick up speed. There she goes.'

I leaned over the side of the bed and looked at the swirling blue of the carpet.

GRANDAD ADJUSTED THE ropes and we sailed on port tack, along the side of the Hood *and across her bow. After a couple more tacks, we were in the open sea.*

Grandad stood at the side of the mast. He sucked his finger and held it in the air. 'Wind's about 5 knots, H.' Then he dipped it in the water. 'Current's heading south-west, about 2 knots. Now, let's get this line overboard, or it'll be hard rations for you, lad.' Long John was back. 'Luckily for me, I packed some sandwiches, an apple and a small bottle a pop – rum-flavoured. It's m' favourite, so it is, ha haar.'

The fishing line was wrapped around a piece of battered bleached wood and a silver lure about 5 inches long glistened on the end. He dropped the lure over the side and let the pressure of it dragging through the water pull the line, the rough wood spinning in his hands.

When most of the line had unspooled, he clenched his fists and the wood stopped spinning. He tied the line off to a cleat.

'Keep checking it, Harry.'

I gave it an experimental tug.

'If you hold it in your hand, you'll be able to tell when we get a bite.'

'Why, what'll happen?'

'The line'll get snatched out of your hand and if it's a big 'un, you might lose a finger or two. But it's a price I'm prepared to pay for a good feed.'

The line twanged as I let go. I looked at my hand, trying to make two fingers fold to simulate severing, but I could only get one finger to bend; the rest seemed to be linked together.

'Mind the helm, lad,' came a shout from Long John.

I got us back on track. 'Steady as she goes, Cap'n,' I yelled into the breeze.

The water tickled my palm and rushed between my fingers as my spare hand trailed in the water, the other gripping the tiller. The boat responded to any gusts, heeling over and increasing in speed, lifting my hand clear of the water as the angle increased. Grandad moved around the boat, tweaking the lines that controlled the sail. I couldn't see what difference he was making, but I could see he was in his element, and so was I.

'Shall we stop for a swim? There's a little cove over there.' He pointed to an opening on the left. 'Let's get that line wound in so we don't get tangled up when we anchor.'

The line bit deep into my fingers as I tested the strain.

'I think it's caught on something, Grandad.'

'It is, H.' He pointed off the stern. 'It's caught on that fish!'

I couldn't see anything. My brow furrowed as I scanned the surface. When it jumped clear of the water, it was much further away than I'd expected, thrashing around in the air. Blue, green and yellow flashes of colour caught the sun before it dived again. I watched for a while, the jumping and diving holding me in a spell.

'Harry? Harry?'

I looked across at Grandad.

'Let's reel it in, shipmate. Quick sticks or we'll lose it!'

'What sort is it, Grandad?'

'It's a dorado! It's going to take some getting in; it's a big 'un alright. Here, H, you take the tiller. I'll get it started and you can take over when I've tired him out.'

We swapped places. Grandad grabbed the main sheet.

'I'm gonna spill some wind from the sail; it'll slow us down a bit.' He released the rope and let it run through his fingers. 'I don't want to go too slow, though. We need to keep the pressure on the line, or it'll shake the lure free and get away.'

I could feel the speed decrease and the sail flapped around.

'Don't worry about that; it's just a bit of noise, that's all.'

My attention switched from steering to Grandad, then the fish and the sail. He picked up the wooden spool and undid the figure-of-eight loops around the cleat. But before he'd finished the last one, the line sprang off and pulled him forwards.

'Bloody hell!' He wedged his feet on the transom and pulled. 'Come on, yeh bugger.'

Even Grandad struggled to pull the line in. He looked at me and puffed out his cheeks, resting before returning to the task.

Well, if the fish was getting tired, it was doing a good job of hiding it. As it got closer to the boat, it seemed to get angrier, fighting harder all the time, jumping and thrashing around in the air. But yard by yard, the line was drawn in. The leaps got less frantic. The battle was won.

'There,' Grandad huffed. 'It's knackered and so am I,' he said, mopping his brow. 'You do the last bit and get him aboard. Let me get hold of the tiller; you'll need both hands free for this.'

We shuffled around and swapped places. I turned the makeshift reel as I'd seen him do it, half a turn with the left hand, then half a turn with the right, until the fish was right at the back of the boat.

'This is the tricky bit, H. You've got to be quick. Keep it close in and tight with your left hand, then reach down and put your hand into its gills and drag it in!

I looked at him. Really?

'Come on, shipmate! Be quick or we're going to lose it.'

I fumbled with the improvised spool as butterflies turned somersaults in my stomach. Flustered, I shifted position, twitching and twisting my body to get myself into the best spot. Settling with my right hip wedged against the transom and my left legs stuck out as a counterbalance, I reached down. It lay still as it was dragged through the water.

The silver lure reflected the sun onto the tired paintwork of the boat's stern. I could see the hook was embedded deep in its mouth, its silver tip poking out of its cheek. Vibrant yellows and greens of its skin clashed with the deep blue of the sea. I hooked my toe under the bench and reached further as my hand slid under its chin. I scrabbled around to find its gills. Closing my eyes, I shuddered as I slid my fingers into the smooth inner workings of the fish. I needed this to end.

Thrilled at our success, I held the fish high in triumph, striking the perfect pose, and beamed at Grandad. If only we'd brought a camera.

My moment of glory was short-lived, as the fish exploded into life. Caught off guard, I lost my balance and fell backwards into the bilges, the fish thrashing around on top of me, its head flailing in front of my face, the hooks of the lure close to my nose. Its tail slapped against my bare legs as I struggled to free myself. One whack caught me in the balls.

'What yeh doing, yeh silly bugger? Wrestling with it?'

I FOUGHT WITH THE PILLOW on the floor as Grandad shouted encouragement. God knows how, but I managed to hit myself between my legs. Still wincing, I said, 'Grandad?'

'What's up?'

'Are you sure this is what it's like when you catch a fish?'

'Course I'm sure. Come on, let's get on with it; Gran'll be back soon.'

I WAS STILL CATCHING my breath from the ball-bashing as I wriggled out from underneath the crazed fish. I watched in horror as its body spasmed and shuddered in the bottom of the boat before lying still again. But was it another false ending?

'Is it dead now?' I asked.

'Probably not,' Grandad said cheerfully. 'Here, hit it on the head with that.' He handed one of the spare wooden pins that held the sail ropes in place; it was like a small truncheon. 'Hold it still with your left hand and give it a good whack, right on top of its nut!'

I gritted my teeth and crouched. The fish was about 2 feet long, the blue, green and yellow markings blending across its body. I watched in dismay as it started thrashing around again, cutting its head open on the underside of the seat. The lure clattered against the wood like a baby gone mad with a rattle, blood splattering over both us and the boat. Alice Cooper would have been proud.

'Come on, H, put it out of its misery.'

What about my misery? I reckoned I'd make a better helmsman than a fish killer. I reached down and grabbed it around the back of the neck with my left hand, swiftly bringing the club down onto its head. Blood spurted in all directions. Still, the damn thing was thrashing about. I hit it again and again and again.

'H!'

I looked at Grandad.

'He's had enough,' he said.

As I looked down at the bloody mess, I felt its heart stutter to a stop. I watched the colours that were so vibrant a few seconds ago fade to a dull grey. When it really was dead, there was no doubt. A few moments later, it was difficult to believe it had ever been alive at all. I was excited and appalled in equal measure. My stomach recovered from the slaughter and rumbled.

'Can we eat it, Grandad?'

'Spoken like a true sailor,' he said. 'I think it's too late to throw it back, don't you?'

I looked again at the blood covered corps.

'Are we going to take it back to the ship?'

'We're not! I'm not sharing this with that lot. You're lucky I'm sharing it with you. Come on, let's get this boat sorted out.'

'Where's the cove gone?'

Mild panic displaced the excitement as I looked around; the entrance had vanished.

'It's back there.' He pointed over my shoulder. 'We've overrun, but that's no bother. Here, take the helm again and when I say, pull it towards you. We can spin it round, easy-peasy. Just give me a second to get the sail sheeted back in, then we'll have enough speed to tack.'

Grandad pulled on the main sheet and the boat picked up speed and heeled over.

'Now!'

I pulled the tiller and we spun round, Grandad sorting the sail out while I steered for shore. We entered the narrow cove ten minutes later.

'Now, H, when we get closer to the beach, we're going to drop the sail. The speed we've got should carry us in. If you steer over to that corner'—he pointed to a still patch of water near the beach—'it'll be nice and calm. If you see, that rocky outcrop is protecting that end of the beach from the waves.'

I looked at the features he'd pointed out. It's funny how something that appeared mysterious could seem so logical when you knew how it worked.

'Get ready, H. Lots of noise for a few secs.'

As we approached the beach, Grandad gave the order to push the tiller and I turned the boat into the wind. He let the mainsheet run free before releasing another line that held the timber spar at the top of the mast. The sail cracked like a whip before it fell in an untidy mess across the boat. Grandad pushed it aside as it fell to keep it out of the puddles of blood before he moved forwards to deal with the anchor.

He dropped the anchor and let the warp run through his hands as the boat drifted towards the beach.

'I'm going to let the rope out until the water is shallow enough to wade in. Use the boat hook to test the depth and let me know when you can think we can stand.'

The breeze ruffled my shirt as I stabbed the boat hook down. I struggled to hold it vertically, surprised by how buoyant the heavy wooden staff was. At last, I struck the seabed.

'Okay, Grandad.'

The anchor rope creaked on the Samson post as we settled to the breeze.

'Right,' he said, 'let's get ashore. You first, H.'

I jumped into the shallow water. Owing to my poor calculations of depths-to-height ratio, the water I jumped into was about 6 inches deeper than I was tall. I came up spurting water from my mouth.

'Tell me you meant to do that, H.'

'I . . . meant . . . to . . . d-do . . . that,' I said between coughing fits.

'I knew you did. Swim to the beach and I'll meet you there.'

Grandad walked to the bow and let out more line. The boat drifted back as I swam alongside. He whistled a tuneless tune and watched me. Swimming breaststroke, I concentrated on my technique, as he had the perfect view to comment on my performance. My hands pushed into the soft sand and I stood up. Securing the line again, Grandad walked to the stern, rolled his trousers up and stepped into knee-deep water. Then he took another line up the beach and tied it to a tree.

He looked around. 'Right!' He clapped his hands. 'Let's get sorted. I'll clean the boat and gut the fish, you collect firewood. Don't forget to pick up some little sticks to get it going.' Then in his RAF voice, he added, 'We'll rendezvous back here in fifteen minutes. No need to synchronise watches. Now, chop-chop and keep an eye out for pirates.'

I snapped to attention. 'Aye-aye, Cap'n.' My feet sank through the hot surface of the sand into the cooler depths beneath as I ran off on my mission.

The small beach was backed by a pine forest. Clouds of flies flew up from the seaweed that lay in a lazy line between the wet and dry sand as I made two piles of wood near the boat, one of small sticks, one of larger stuff. There were a few huge pieces that I tried to lift but couldn't even move. I spotted a large clump of rope – the fluffy ends would be ideal to start the fire with. Grandad stood with the fish dangling from his fist, judging my efforts.

'Well done, H.'

'Look, Grandad, I got this . . .' I held up the rope. 'We could use it to start the fire with.'

He looked critically at my contribution.

'Afraid not, H.'

I was disappointed. I thought that was a good idea. I turned to throw it back where I'd found it.

'Where yeh going?'

'You said we couldn't use it.'

'I didn't. I said it was "a frayed knot"!' He winked.

'Grandad! Your jokes are getting worse.'

'My jokes are the same, it's just that everything else is getting better. That just makes them seem worse, relatively speaking. It's like when

you're sat on a train and the train next to you starts moving and you think you're rolling backwards.'

'What are *you on about?'*

'Relativity. Haven't you studied Albert Einstein at school?'

I shook my head.

'What about space-time?' he asked.

I shook my head again. 'I know a bit about dinner time,' I offered.

'That's ma boy,' said Grandad. He pulled a box of matches from his pocket and knelt on the sand. 'What I need now,' he said, 'is that big untidy bundle'—I held up the rope—'to pass me that piece of rope.' He held his belly so his sides didn't split.

I chucked the rope towards his head and he grabbed it before it hit him, but sand flew off and stuck to the beads of sweat on his face and chest.

I covered my mouth with my hand. 'Oops.'

'Oh, that's it now. You're not having either the eyes or the head. You'll just have to have the meat and that's final.'

I folded my arms, stamped my foot into the sand and looked glum.

He held out his hand. 'Don't sulk. Nobody likes a cry baby.'

'Mums do!' I pointed out.

'They don't. They just pretend to, because they don't want the bad publicity.'

He got to work on the fire and I watched him closely to make sure he did it right.

'Light that bit, Grandad . . .' I pointed out a particularly frayed bit of rope.

'Leave it to me,' he chuntered. 'There's nothing worse than a backseat arsonist.'

He lit the right bit anyway. Then some small sticks went on. I added a few choice twigs, which crackled as the fire took hold. Soon, we were putting the bigger pieces on.

'GOOD LAD,' GRANDAD said, looking approvingly at the banked-up fire. 'Go and set the table now, H.'

I laid out knives and forks in the kitchen. Picking them up, I pretended to use them, just to make sure I'd got them the right way round. I rushed back to join him in the living room.

GRANDAD FETCHED A PLANK from the far side of the beach, rinsing it in the sea on his way back.

'We'll use this as a plate to cook it on.'

He sat it next to the fire to dry and set to preparing the fish while I went for a swim and lost myself in the world of ships and boats. I looked down to see if there was any treasure on the seabed, my legs frantically treading water, but the reflection and ripples got in the way. All noise stopped as I ducked my head below the surface.

'DON'T FORGET TO GET a wash, H,' Grandad reminded me.

I filled the sink to the overflow and splashed water on my face. The front door banged – Gran was back. I dipped my head into the cool water.

THE UNDERSEA WORLD was just a big blue blur that stung my eyes. I swam down as far as I could, the pain in my ears forcing me to turn back before I got anywhere near the bottom. When I came up, Grandad was waving.

The fire had burned low. The fish rested on the wooden plank on the embers, the edges of the improvised plate smouldered, occasionally doused by rivulets of fish juice that dripped and sizzled onto the hot coals.

'Look at that, H! Cooked to perfection, if I say so myself.'

He used the knife to tease out the fins and scrape away the skin, then he slid it down the lateral line to roll back pieces of perfectly cooked bone-free fish.

He handed me a large piece. I juggled the hot meat from hand to hand before taking a bite, rolling it around my mouth and inhaling in short gasps to cool it. It tasted gorgeous.

GRAN LIFTED THE PLATES, Grandad's fish untouched.

'Sorry, Lil,' he said, 'I thought—'

'It's okay, love, I've done a pan of stew,' she said, scraping the fish into the bin.

The world really was changing shape into something unrecognisable when we threw away food like that.

'You can help yourself whenever you feel up to it.'

The hot water tank grumbled as Gran filled the washing up bowl, her head bowed over the sink. I watched the soap suds pour down the plates in slow motion as she leaned them on the draining board. Then she dried her hands and went on a cleaning mission upstairs. I looked at the ceiling, like a terrier under a ferret's cage, trying to follow her movements, odd noises occasionally giving me a clue to her whereabouts. Pickering had better keep his mouth shut.

We left Gran to her chores and settled down on the settee, Grandad's bony hip rubbing against mine, the photo album on our laps.

AFTER WE'D STUFFED ourselves full, we lay on the sand, soaking up the sun, Grandad quietly singing:

> *Fifteen men on the dead man's chest—*
> *. . . Yo-ho-ho, and a bottle of rum!*
> *Drink and the devil had done for the rest—*
> *. . . Yo-ho-ho, and a bottle of rum!*

While Grandad nodded off, I swung onto the deck of the Portuguese merchant ship, firing my pistol and holding my cutlass in my mouth, the metallic taste setting my teeth on edge. I held the blade against the captain's throat. He released his sword and it clattered on the deck. Spitting out the metallic aftertaste, I only managed to send it dribbling down my chin.

Grandad called me over after his nap.

'Come on, Harry. We need to get back before the sea breeze drops.'

I sat up and looked around, wiping the drool off my chin. The sun was low in the sky and its power had faded.

'I don't fancy having to row all the way home,' Grandad said as we waded out and climbed aboard.

He pulled up the anchor and rowed us out of the bay against the falling breeze. We turned to starboard and set the sail. We weren't going as fast as before, but that didn't matter.

'Here, H, what about this?' He pulled a black cloth from his pocket and let it fly in the breeze to reveal the white skull and crossbones of the Jolly Roger. 'Let's get this hoisted and give the lads on the Hood *something to think about.'*

As we sailed into Grand Harbour, the wind picked up, stronger than ever.

'Last blow before sunset!' Grandad shouted.

The wind was behind us and we raced along, the waves getting bigger and breaking their white frothy tops. Grandad waved at the Hood *as we passed, but I was too busy steering to pay them attention.*

'Don't let her gybe!' yelled Grandad as the biggest wave of the day picked us up and we surfed at full speed down its front.

Our bow wave sent spray high into the air on both sides as we hurtled along.

'Ye-ha,' he yelled like a cowboy. 'Not bad for an old man.'

The breeze dropped and our speed slowed as we sailed into the shadow of Valletta. Approaching the quay wall, Grandad gave the order.

'Helm to starboard.'

I pushed the tiller away from me and the boat turned to port. He stepped forwards and dropped the sail. We came to rest on the quay wall so gently that, as Grandad said, 'We wouldn't have cracked an egg!' A few old sea dogs were watching as we tied up, enjoying the shade and a glass of wine. They gave Grandad a nod of approval as we walked past.

HE RAN HIS FINGER ACROSS a postcard. The picture must have been taken from a plane. Valletta sat on top of cliffs, the honey-coloured stone bathed in the last rays of the setting sun. Bright little carriages could be seen at the head of the main road into town.

'I love it here, H.' Grandad caressed the image. 'We'd catch a karozzin into town, strolling around like we owned the place,' he chuckled. 'The amount of money we spent there, we probably could have bought the whole bloody island.'

I was sure I could hear the faint clip-clopping of horses' hooves on the cobbled stones of the ancient streets. Grandad's smile broadened.

'Is it that funny?' I asked.

'What?'

'Whatever it is you're thinking about.'

'Oh yes,' he nodded, smiling. 'I was just thinking, if banging two halves of a coconut together makes the sound of horses' hooves.'

I was keen to see where he was going with this one.

'I wonder . . . if you chop a horse in half and bang the pieces together, do you think it would make the sound of a coconut?'

All of my effort went into keeping a blank expression.

'Good one, eh?'

'Yeah,' I conceded, 'not bad for an old bloke.'

Winding his fist up, he replied, 'Why, I oughta . . .'

GRANDAD CHASED ME TOWARDS town. I put on a burst of speed, expecting a hand on my shoulder at any second. But when I looked back, he'd flagged down a carriage and hopped in. The reins snapped behind the horse's ear as they pulled away from the curb. I put out a hitch-hiker's thumb, closed one eye and compared its size to the horse as they approached.

Grandad's hand waved royally as they trotted past. A little further along, they slowed down, allowing me to catch up. Ignoring Grandad's outstretched hand, I jumped onto the step, hanging off the side of the carriage and leaning out as it picked up speed, happy to let the breeze take away the last bits of moisture from my damp clothes.

The karozzin was like a Victorian carriage that had been squashed, like it had been hit from behind. There were curtains, gathered on each corner like a four-poster bed. We gained height as we approached the city centre and I looked down at the harbour to see the Hood's conning tower being engulfed by the shadow of the city as the sun set.

The ride ended at a large stone fountain in an open square where the carriages could turn. The cafes and bars were full, the best seats already taken. Everyone looked smart at the end of a working day, drink-

ing coffee or beer. My focus switched from the finery on sale in the shops to our scruffy, salt-encrusted reflections.

One shop in particular grabbed our attention. It must have been a relic from the island's time used as a pirate's hideout, because the window was full of knives – not the kitchen type, the fighting type. Grandad wanted to go in and see them close up. The shop's walls were lined with swords, shields, spears and bayonets. Under a glass-topped counter, an impressive selection of knuckledusters and knives lay tantalisingly out of reach.

As we scanned the display, the shop owner's chubby hand reached in and selected a bone-handled flick knife. His fingers were full of gold rings and a chunky bracelet was revealed as his shirtsleeve slid up his wrist. He licked his lips in anticipation of a sale as Grandad held the weapon and turned over the price tag.

'What do you want one of them for, Grandad?' I asked.

'So Gran can have her peeling knife back.' He flicked the blade out repeatedly, admiring the action. 'You can't get these in England.' It seemed like a poor reason. 'Besides, if we get into bother, I'd rather have a knife in my pocket that I don't need than not have one and wish I had.'

'Why don't you just carry a gun, then?'

He folded the blade away. 'Don't be daft, H.' He looked around the shop for confirmation before whispering, 'they don't sell guns.'

Grandad paused in the doorway and slipped his new toy into his pocket. We stepped back into the street.

'Here, H.' Grandad pointed at a bar. 'Let's stop for a drink.'

I thought about the mixture of sailors on leave and affordable deadly weapons. Alcohol – the final ingredient in the disaster cocktail.

We sat down at the only free table and I looked at the sign over the door: The Gut. Maybe they should have considered some of the more obvious options, like The Red Lion or The King's Arms, before settling on that name. The waitress brought out our drinks and I sipped on my lemonade as we watched the world go by.

*A smartly dressed middle-aged man, presumably the owner, came
out.*

'Jack Manning! Good to see you again, my friend,' he said.

'Harry, meet Charlie.'

*Charlie looked like an accountant, not somebody who would work
in a pub. They chatted for a while until Charlie spotted somebody else he
knew. He shook hands with us and wandered over to greet them.*

'Charlie's been here for years,' said Grandad.

'Does he own the joint?' I tried out my Humphrey Bogart.

*Grandad looked at me with admiration, or pity. He shook his head.
I wasn't sure if he was dismayed at my impersonation or answering my
question. I pressed on.*

'Is he a waiter?'

'No. He, er, he's an entertainer.'

'A comic?'

'No, er, an impersonator.'

'Who does he do?'

'Anybody . . . everybody.'

'When's he on, could we come and see him later?'

'No, H, it'll be too late . . . past your bedtime.'

*We strolled through the streets to the old fort, my finger tracing the
mortar lines as we passed through an arch, the honey-coloured stone
warmer as we stepped onto the open terrace. The* Hood *dominated the
harbour below. We perched on the barrel of an ancient cannon and
watched the sky turn orange. Grandad told me about the fort and the
countries that had ruled the island.*

*'The nation that controls Malta also controls the shipping through
the Strait of Sicily, so no ships can go east or west through the gap without the approval of whoever holds this little island. That's why Malta
has always been fought over, which is why it's still so important to the
navy.' He pointed out the picket boats from the* Hood *that were used to*

run the liberty men ashore. 'There'll be some headaches on board in the morning,' Grandad warned, but nobody in the boats heard him.

Darkness arrived quickly as we walked down the street and into a different world. The gentle hum of polite conversation was gone. Music spilt out into the night from the bars, where sailors and girls were drinking and dancing. We weaved our way through the crowded narrow lanes into a small piazza.

'Jack! Jack!'

A group of sailors shouted us over. They were all either drunk or well on their way there.

'Come an' have a drink, Jack.' Before he got an answer, the sailor called out, 'Tessa, same again and one for Jack.'

They all lifted their glasses and emptied them in one gulp, banging the empties on the table as they whooped and stomped their feet.

One of the others shouted, 'And a gimlet for the youngster.'

I watched our plan to get back to the ship evaporate into the night.

'Sit down, sit down,' they insisted.

One lad jumped up and grabbed some spare chairs from the neighbouring table as another pulled at Grandad's sleeve.

'Here, Jack, we've just had a few down in Floriana. There are some smart-looking lasses down there.'

Like his mates, he was dressed in his best 'shore' kit, his hair flattened in place with Brylcreem. He wore a huge grin, which was unfortunate, as it exposed a mouthful of rotten teeth. The S's slid through the gaps in an exaggerated lisp.

'They're not interested in ratings, Giddy,' Grandad explained as if he were talking to a kid who had made an unrealistic request for a Christmas present. 'They're looking for an officer to take 'em home.'

Giddy ignored him.

'There was one lass in particular.' He held out his hands to cup an enormous pair of breasts. 'She took a bit of a fancy to me.'

'What was his name again?' asked one of his mates.

'Sod off,' said Giddy.

The sailors all started jeering. He shushed them and turned to me.

'They don't like it when I come out with 'em. It's because I'm irresistible to women.' His hand flicked out and hit my knee as he winked. 'They don't stand a chance with the lasses when I'm on the prowl.' He sat back in his chair. 'I'm telling yeh, I'm in there for sure.'

He was tapping his feet and rubbing his hands together. He looked like he was ready to explode.

Grandad looked at him. 'Remind me, Giddy, how did you get your nickname?'

Giddy made a move to explain, then realised Grandad was pulling his leg.

'Bugger off! You're only bloody jealous.' He leaned in close and I recoiled from his foul breath. 'They're only bloody jealous, young 'un.'

The spray of saliva was unavoidable. I nodded and leaned back as far as gravity would allow without toppling over.

Grandad spoke to their leader. 'Jim, did you go to the Forty-Three?'

'Course we did.' Jim was offended at the suggestion they might not have. 'We're off to The Gut next,' he said, as if this proved his capability of organising a night out.

'I thought you said we were going to The Empire,' a sailor with a cut above his eye complained before turning to me. 'Thought we'd watch the women boxing. You ever seen ladies boxing, young 'un?'

I shook my head.

'They only wear swimming costumes,' he whispered, as if this explained everything.

I wondered whether it was a female boxer who had given him his injury.

One of the others dismissed the idea.

'I'm going up to Sliema Creek with the destroyer men.'

'Well, if you're looking for a good hiding,' said Grandad, 'that's a good place to start.'

'Are you two coming?' Jim asked.

'You must think I'm bloody daft.'

They all looked at Grandad and nodded. He shrugged off the abuse.

'Not a chance. I'm not taking him in there with you lot.' Grandad flicked his thumb in my direction.

They looked around at each other.

'Why, what's wrong with him?' asked Jim.

'It's not Harry, you silly sod, it's you lot.' He singled out Giddy. 'Look at him.'

Giddy looked around, offended.

I couldn't miss the chance to show off my local knowledge.

'I'll be alright, Grandad,' I chipped in. 'We could go back to The Gut and watch Charlie do his act.'

Everyone stopped talking and stared.

'Is he older than he looks, Jack?' asked one.

'You been in The Gut before, young 'un?' said another.

'Yeah. We called on the way to the fort and had a drink with Charlie.'

They all started cheering. Nudging elbows rocked me as heavy hands slapped me on the back. I smirked in happy ignorance under the pummelling.

'Hey, Jack, we could take him up to Strait Street later, let him empty his kit bag,' Jim suggested.

Before Grandad answered, the drinks arrived to a rowdy cheer.

'Come on, young 'un, have a taste of that.' Giddy handed me a glass from the tray.

'What's in it?' I asked.

'Lime 'n' things,' Giddy said with a smile. 'Do you like lime?'

'I like lemonade.'

'Lemons, limes, same thing.' He waved the detail away with his hand. 'This is like limeade, for grown-ups.'

I took a swig. My body couldn't decide what to disapprove of first. The gin seared my lungs as my face contorted at the sourness of the lime juice. I coughed and spat most of it over the table. The rest spilled down my shirt. Each breath brought on another coughing fit as I tried to focus on the laughing crew through a teary fog.

Grandad just shook his head. 'They must pay you lot too much if you've got cash spare to buy him drinks to spit out.'

He ordered me a proper lemonade as the jokes continued. In a natural lull, he nudged me.

'Come on. Let's get going, shall we?'

Resisting their half-hearted effort to make us stay, we wandered off down the street. As we reached The Gut, a woman with massive boobs was snogging a sailor. We drew level and I looked up at her . . . him. It was! Blimey . . . Charlie. She looked at me and pouted.

'Come up and see me sometime.'

Her hips thrusted forwards provocatively with each word that slid past her glossed lips. I clung to Grandad as we went on our way. Glancing over my shoulder, Charlie was adjusting her, I mean his . . . It wasn't clear what was being adjusted.

The flow of human traffic was still heading into town. There was an occasional shout from somebody who Grandad knew. I looked down at the ancient cobbles and thought about the pirates and cut-throats who had walked the same route. When we got down to the harbour, one of the boats was just pulling away, empty. Another full of sailors moved into its place. They jumped ashore, scampering up the steps, and strode off into the night.

We stepped aboard the motorboat. The engine's solid beat increased and the choppy waves slapped on the hull as we picked up speed. We rocked in unison as we passed through the wake of another picket shuttling the men ashore. As we approached the Hood, men were climbing down a rope ladder suspended from a crane. The sailors wobbled across a plank that stuck out of the side of the ship to reach the wavering ladder. I looked at Grandad doubtfully.

'Come on. You'll be fine. I'll keep an eye on you.'

We circled round while the other boat loaded up, taking its place as it pulled away.

'Let me go first,' Grandad said, manoeuvring me out of the way.

His technique was the one he'd told me about years ago – place his feet on the opposite sides of the ladder, heels in. I wasn't bad at climbing, and I'd impressed my mates and Mr Gibson in PE with my inside knowledge of the sailor's technique.

As I climbed, another picket boat came alongside. The sailors inside it were unconscious – they must have made an early start. We leaned over the rail as the lads on the deck used one of the cranes to winch down a cargo net. They rolled the sailors into it and hoisted them aboard, their faces squashed against the rope mesh, arms and legs stuck out at odd angles. Like a gruesome 3D jigsaw, the jumble of bodies was dumped on the deck. One head puked. Moans turned to shrieks of protest as they turned the hosepipe on them.

'To bring them round,' the sailor said to me with a wink.

It didn't work. They just lay there in a filthy, wet drunken pile. It was hard to imagine they'd think of this as a good night out when they woke in the morning.

The Hood was quiet now most of the men were ashore. We made our way up to the boat deck. Grandad 'liberated' two camp beds from a store and we lay side by side. The lights of the waterfront bars shimmered on the still water, where a bright flashing light high above town stood out.

'Is that a lighthouse, Grandad?' I pointed a lazy finger in the general direction.

'No, H, that's the signal station. They're sending messages in Morse code to the ships.'

I slumped back on the rough canvas, scanning the sky, making a wish after each shooting star. The air was so still and the temperature so aligned with my own that I couldn't sense where I stopped and the world began. I listened for a long time to Grandad's breathing, steady and re-assuring, before drifting off to sleep.

GRAN LOOKED FROM THE TV to me and smiled – a weak smile forced to the surface by willpower alone. She looked weary, her resources no doubt on the brink of failure. But I'd seen her like this before and I knew she wouldn't fail. She was the foundation that our home was built on. I knew it was solid and I knew that whatever else life might throw at her, she'd always pull through, always be there for us. For me.

I put my hand on hers and kissed her forehead. 'Night night, Gran.'

'Night night, love,' she said as I left.

Chapter 11

Saturday, 29 March 1975

Lying in bed, I tried to make smoke rings with my breath in the icy air before reluctantly getting up and pulling on my cold clothes, shivering and rubbing my arms to generate some warmth. I opened the curtains and turned to leave, but was drawn back. Unable to resist the temptation of a blank canvas, I drew the outline of a sailing boat in the condensation on the window. The cold droplets ran down my arm, wetting my sleeve and puddling at the bottom of the window frame. The wood, soft from years of neglect, yielded to my poking finger. They'd been painted while shut, sealing them forever. Only the small one at the top still opened.

As the first up, I took on my responsibility and fetched some sticks from the workshop, using one to rake through the cinders in the grate. With care, I lifted out the pan of cold ash, unlocked the back door and cursed as the pan caught on the door frame, sending a mini avalanche of grey powder onto the lino. The lid of the dustbin jammed and more ash spilt as I rattled it off in frustration.

I used the lid to shield my face from the column of dust that rose as the ash hit the bottom of the bin with a satisfying whump. Replacing the lid to contain the dust cloud, I wandered back inside. After placing scrunched-up balls from pages of the *Daily Mirror* in the grate, I made a lattice of sticks on top before placing a few bits of coal on the wooden raft. The first match fractured and fizzed like a shooting star, burning out in the hearth, the acrid smoke drawn up the chimney by the draught. A wood pigeon cooed on the roof and I could hear its claws struggle to gain purchase on the chimney pot rim.

My second match caught and I held it for a moment to make sure the wood of the matchstick was well lit before lighting the paper in three places. The flames changed colour as the fire burnt off the ink and the sticks crackled as the fire took hold. I snatched at a piece of coal that rolled off the pyre, already too hot to hold, and tried to re-place it several times, merely succeeding in flicking it from one side of the grate to the other before resorting to the tongs to set it back in place.

I turned my attention to making tea. Cold air hit my legs as I opened the pantry door. No milk. Outside, I could hear the faint whir of an electric motor. Glass bottles rattled as the milk float stopped. I looked at the wall, following the footsteps on the path outside. The milk bottles clinked on the step just as the kettle boiled. The blue tits didn't waste any time and two flew away from the bottle tops as I opened the door.

My thumb rested on the bottle rim and I rolled it forwards to push the silver cap inside before hooking my forefinger nail under the foil to lift it off, so as not to distort it any more than necessary for reuse. The cream was thick and claggy as I took a swig before adding some to my brew. I threw more coal on to the fire and pushed the fret up to the grate to reduce the air flow before snuggling down with my mug in front of the fire. The heat built quickly and I sat staring into the flames while sipping my tea.

'Oh, good lad,' Gran said, looking at the fire, but her smile faded as she lifted her gaze to the mantelpiece. 'My clock must have stopped. Dr Crowther will be here any minute.'

She scurried off to their improvised bedroom, returning a few minutes later, just in time for Dr Crowther's arrival, interrupting her cuppa. It sat ignored next to the clock as she intercepted him in the hall.

'Would you like a cup of tea, Doctor?'

'I'm fine, thanks. You make this young fella his breakfast.'

She hovered, unable to help or rest.

'Why's he come again?' I asked.

'He's just come to make sure Grandad's comfortable.'

'Why did they let him out if he's still not well?'

'Your grandad wanted to be at home, with you and me. You know he hated it in hospital.' Her brow furrowed. 'Dr Crowther's going to come every day now, to give him an injection for the pain and make sure he's okay.'

'Aren't they going to take him back to hospital?'

Gran looked down. 'No, love, he's staying at home now, until . . .'

Backing into the hall, the full understanding of what was happening dawned on me. I grabbed my parka and left the door open behind me as I fled.

I ran across the playing fields, away from the houses, ignoring the puddles and mud. I ran until my breath was a rasping strain, until it was all I could think about as bent over, gasping, at the side of the canal. Like the dorado, I was in an alien world, unable to adapt.

I picked up a stick and slashed at the undergrowth, cutting down anything I could reach, slashing and crashing until the stick broke. I threw the remnant at a crow on the opposite bank, missing it by miles. I walked into the morning, avoiding people, ducking into the undergrowth when anyone approached, hiding but desperate for company.

After hours of wandering, as it often did, hunger drove me home.

'Dr Crowther's gone, love,' Gran said as soon as I walked in.

I already knew; his Rover stood out among the battered old cars on the street.

'Grandad's feeling a lot better. He wants to see you.'

I wanted to see him, too.

'Here, love, take him this.' She sloshed a generous slug of rum into his tea. 'I'll bring you something to eat. Grandad's already given me my instructions.' She raised her eyebrows and smiled.

Light streamed in through the open curtains onto him as he sat in bed, sharply defining every crumple in the bedding and his pyjamas. The photo album lay open on his lap. I handed him his tea and sat beside him. His skin looked old and dry, the tendons on his arm trembling despite his stillness. He looked at me through misty eyes, but Grandad was still here. He pointed to a photo, the foredeck of the *Hood* buried deep in a wave.

'The navy's biggest submarine,' he claimed in a low, croaking voice.

It was good to hear him still joking. The mug trembled as he lifted it to his lips. His eyes closed as he sipped.

'I thought her nickname was *The Mighty Hood*?' I asked.

Phlegm crackled as he cleared his throat. 'It was, but she sometimes looked more like a sub. All that additional armour they put on when they realised she was vulnerable weighed her down. She was what we called "a wet ship".' His breathing faltered.

'Aren't all ships wet? At least on the bottom.'

'Yeh nutcase. It means she sat low in the water. A lot of water came over the bow.' He had to pause to catch his breath. 'She was a handful when she was heading into a big sea.' His eyelids drooped. 'Don't forget, H, when you're at sea, keep one hand for yourself and one for the ship.'

'What does that mean?'

'It means hold with one hand all the time when you're in a big seaway.' He dipped his bony finger into his tea and flicked it at me.

I wiped my hand over my face.

I RECEIVED ANOTHER drenching as the Hood *split the next wave open, the wind ripping it to shreds.*

'*Hold on,*' *Grandad shouted.* '*Whoo-hoo! It's gonna be a stormy night.*'

Grandad held onto the inner rail, his waterproof jacket done up to his chin, the hood flapping in the wind. Freezing rain stung my cheeks and hands. Water ran along the deck, tormented by the wind, creating a miniature version of the raging sea. I clung to a post supporting a steel staircase, the cold metal numbing my fingers. The icy water found the weaknesses in my waterproof and I shivered as I wiped the rain and spray from my face. The salt stung my eyes and my lips tingled.

The sea was a white mess. It was a battle between the wind and rain, the wind building the waves, driving them forwards before they broke into a white turmoil as the rain smashed down, flattening the surface. There was no separation between the sky and sea, just a cauldron of grey.

My boots struggled to keep a grip on the wet deck as the gusts tried to pull me free.

'*Is it like this a lot?*' *I shouted, trying to make myself heard above the howling wind.*

'*No, it's not always this mild,*' *Grandad beamed.* '*Wish I'd brought my brolly!*'

As the bow plunged into another wave, the front of the ship and much of the fo'c'sle deck disappeared underwater. The wave rolled over the deck, shooting into the air as the guns blocked its path. It hung motionless at its apex before the wind grabbed it, smashing it into the conning tower. We were the only ones on deck.

Grandad pointed towards a door. We had to get our timing right, or we'd be letting loads of water into the ship. The Hood *hit another wave and we waited for the water to disperse. I watched Grandad as he counted down with his fingers: three, two,* one! *He ran over to me, grabbed my coat, pulled me out from behind the steps and dragged me forwards.*

He opened the door with difficulty, fighting the weight of the steel being pushed by the wind.

As the ship rolled, rain trapped in the life rafts fixed above the doorway fell onto Grandad. But as he'd pointed out to me when I'd helped in the allotment one rainy day, you can only get so wet, then it doesn't matter. We stumbled over the threshold and the wind slammed the door shut. Seconds later, we could hear the sound of water rushing along the deck on the other side of the door. Grandad's beard glistened and he blew a water droplet from the end of his nose.

'Come on, H. Let's see if we can get a brew.' He set a fast pace, striding off down the corridor. 'Oh! and a slice of toast . . . I mean two slices . . . I mean two slices . . . each.'

A trail of smoke snaked down the corridor, like a cartoon scent. I expected the smell of baking and took a deep breath, coughing as I inhaled solder fumes instead. A sailor fixing the radio watched me as I strode past his workshop.

The kitchen was a hive of activity. Grandad went over to the cook and returned a few minutes later with two cups of cocoa and a plate of toast. He led the way into the room next to the bakery.

'This'll do us, H. Sit yourself down there.'

The smell of warm bread filled the room, loaves stacked neatly on stainless racking.

'It's the bread cooling room; it's where they put the bread to—'

'Cool?' I suggested.

'Good,' he said, 'I can see you've been paying attention.'

GRAN SERVED OUR ORDER of toast and cocoa, setting the tray between us on the bed.

'Cocoa at this time of day? The world's gone mad, Jack.' She kissed him on the head. 'Are you two alright for a bit while I do a bit of baking?'

We confirmed that we'd manage without her until the next meal.

'Take it easy, Jack,' she said as she was leaving.

'This was always a favourite of mine.' Grandad held up a slice of toast and his mug. Butter dripped off the corner of the bread and dropped inside his pyjama sleeve, but he didn't notice. 'I'd get myself tucked away in that cooling room whenever I could. Most of the time you were with your mates and that was great, but the opportunities to have some time to yourself were few and far between, so you had to grab the chances whenever you could.'

Butter glistened on his lips and a rivulet ran from the corner of his mouth into his beard. Despite the state of his own face, he was still keen to point out the mess I was making.

'You'd best get that butter wiped off your chin or you're going to be in trouble with your gran again.'

I drew my sleeve across my face as he dabbed his mouth delicately with his hanky.

'You mucky pup,' he said, pursing his lips.

I put my mug down and wriggled off the bed, careful not to disturb the tray.

'Where are you going?' he asked.

'I need the loo.'

'The loo? Oh! crikey. Have I ever told you about the bogs on the *Hood*?'

I shook my head.

'Well, the best way to describe a visit to the carzey on the ship is that it was an adventure. Now, if you wanted a wee, that was easy. They had urinals just like the ones at the Legion.' He took off his specs. 'It is a wee that you need, isn't it?'

I shook my head.

'Mmm, well, in that case, you had to have your wits about you. Particularly if there was a big sea running and you needed to go for a . . .' He searched for the right phrase. 'Let's call it a more substantial visit, shall we?'

I didn't care what he called it. The cocoa and toast churned in my guts as I anticipated the gory detail his stories often included.

'Before you started, you had to take your trousers and underpants off and hang them up.'

'Why did you have to do that?'

'I'm coming to that bit, aren't I?'

I hoped so, but I wished he'd hurry up.

'The problem was, the pipe that took the muck away went straight into the sea.'

His finger pointed down into his cocoa and my guts grumbled at the image he'd implanted.

'That's all well and good, but, the non-return valves got jammed open with sh . . . with muck. So that meant that the sea could come up the pipe, as well. Now . . .' His bony finger pointed at me. 'Because the *Hood* sat so low in the water, if there was a big sea, as the bow of the ship went down, the sea came up. If you got your timing wrong, it came right up and smacked you!' His finger swirled round, drawing a circle, then he pierced the loop with a quick upwards motion. 'Right up yer jacksy.'

I flinched at the final thrust, shifting uncomfortably as my stomach turned again. 'I need to go,' I pleaded.

He shrugged, smirking. 'Don't let me stop you!'

When I returned, he pointed at another photo. 'Here, H, look at this one.'

I climbed back on the bed. He waited for me to get comfy before asking me to take the tray back to Gran. I grumbled but did as asked, bringing the aroma of chocolate cake back with me. He closed his eyes and inhaled as I settled beside him.

'Look at these two, H.' He pointed to two young sailors, their arms around each other's shoulders. 'That's young Jon Pertwee, next to Cookie.'

I looked closely. He was right – it was Jon Pertwee, the actor that played Dr Who.

'I didn't know you were mates with Dr Who.'

'We weren't really mates, but I knew him,' he chuckled. 'The first time I met him, he came stumbling out of the bogs covered in sh . . . covered in muck.' His nose wrinkled. 'Oh, H, he stunk. He was in a right mess. He came out with his trousers round his ankles and slipped on the wet floor as the ship rolled.' He laughed. 'Oh, it was horrible, the poor bugger.' His smile faded for a moment. 'Did you wash your hands, by the way?'

I offered them up to his nose.

'Give up, you scruff. You could have just nodded.'

I grinned at him then looked at the photo again.

The other bloke was in overalls. He'd removed the top half and tied them round his waist. He was covered in grease or some other filth.

'He doesn't look like a cook.' I pointed at the other man with Dr Who.

'He's not *a* cook.' Grandad exaggerated the A. 'He's F. Cook.'

'What kind of effin cook?' I asked, baffled.

'Fred Cook,' he said with a straight face.

I blushed and kicked myself for falling into another trap.

'You wouldn't want him anywhere near the kitchen, but if you had an engine problem, he was genius. The best mechanic I ever worked with.'

'Talking of which, we need to get this ship into dock, H, to repair the damage.'

'What damage?'

Grandad pointed to the photos of the *Hood* in dry dock, carpenters at work on the deck.

'It was what they call an incident. Sometimes they call it an accident or a misunderstanding. It's what posh folk call something that was their fault when they don't want to get into trouble for it. They prefer to blame God or some other poor bugger.'

WE LOOKED OVER THE starboard rail.

'I thought you didn't believe in God,' I said.

'I don't. That's what makes Him the perfect scapegoat.' Grandad pointed out to sea. 'That's HMS Renown.' *He picked out the ship closest to us. 'And these others'—his arm swept over the convoy in our wake—'have just taken part in an exercise off the coast of northern Spain.' His thumb flicked over his shoulder. 'A place called Arosa Bay.'*

I turned to see land partly concealed by haze. The sea was calm and the sun was out. It was difficult to see how anything could go wrong on a day like this. Grandad read my mind.

'Never underestimate people's ability to balls it up, H, even on a nice day.'

We had the perfect view from the quarterdeck, at the stern of the Hood, *the guns of Y turret towering above us.*

'The exercise has just finished. Captain Sawbridge on the Renown *has just received a message from Rear Admiral Bailey to fall in line with the* Hood *and then turn to port, but he thinks the* Hood *is going to turn to port before he falls in line behind her. Captain Tower on the* Hood *thinks he's going to fall in behind the* Hood *and then they're going to turn to port together. Nobody's sure what Admiral Bailey is expecting, which is why it's going to turn into a shitstorm.' He beamed a big, false grin. 'Watch.'*

'Shouldn't we warn them?'

'Nah, let's leave 'em to it,' he said, happy to let the toffs look like idiots.

The Renown *was on our starboard side and slowly, she made the turn, putting her on a collision course with the* Hood. *Nobody but us was paying attention to the approaching* Renown. *It seemed inconceivable that the two captains were going to let a collision occur. Grandad looked at his watch-less wrist.*

'Any minute now.'

Realisation spread through the Hood *and the tannoy announced,* 'Close all watertight doors. All hands clear the starboard side.'

I looked up at Grandad.

'Don't worry, H, I know how this turns out. We're safe here.'

The crew knew the code. That call meant there was something to see over there. Officers tried in vain to stop the younger sailors, who ran to the starboard side to get the best view of the action. But the draw was too strong. The Renown *was close now.*

'They've passed the point where they can do anything to stop this, H. Captain Tower is going to . . . There she goes.'

The Hood *turned to the right, causing her stern to swing out to the left in an attempt to lessen the impact.*

One officer ran into the group of sailors in front of us and shouted, 'Bugger off! The Renown's coming aboard!'

A moment later, as the sailors scattered, the Renown *hit us. The ship shook from stem to stern. I fell to my knees as the deck shook under me. The bow of the* Renown *smashed into the side of the* Hood *and scraped down the deck, planks splintering. The inner and outer rails were torn out and dropped back onto the deck. The two ships stayed together for a few moments until the* Renown *was put into reverse. Like a scolded dog withdrawing from its owner's leg, they separated.*

We walked over to get a better look at the mess.

'Let this be a lesson, H. Just because somebody is in charge, it doesn't mean they know what they're doing.'

GRANDAD TAPPED HIS finger on the photo. 'So that's another load of work to sort out in Portsmouth.'

'What other jobs need doing?' I asked.

'Well . . .' He counted the jobs off on his fingers. 'The Admiralty knows that the anti-aircraft guns aren't up to the job, so they need replacing. There's always rust to be dealt with and plenty of painting to do. The damage the *Renown* did is a lot worse than it looks. Both starboard props and shafts are smashed.'

'How long is that going to take to fix?'

'Months. There's going to be a lot of scrapping before she's back in action.'

It hadn't occurred to me they'd have loads of scrap metal to get rid of, but it was obvious now I thought about it. A couple of times a year the rag-and-bone man would come round our estate on his horse and cart, collecting anything of value. The balloons he hand-ed out in payment for the old clothes and scrap metal were rapidly abused to destruction, ideally popped just behind a mate's ear. They must get hundreds of balloons for an anti-aircraft gun. The sailors would have a hell of a job controlling them if it was a windy day.

'Who do they sell the scrap to, then?'

'Not that kind of scrapping. Fighting. There was a lot of bother aboard while we were there, a lot of scrapping.' He held his fist up close to his chin, his elbows tucked in to protect his ribs, and threw out a few experimental jabs and hooks.

'Why? What? Who were you fighting with?'

He rubbed his muscles after his workout.

'The top brass employed some local contractors to speed the job up. The Ministry of Defence gave them some of the work our lads should have been doing and we didn't get on with them. They weren't navy lads and we didn't like them. Some of their so-called engineers didn't know one end of a spanner from the other.'

'To be fair, they do look quite similar,' I pointed out before I had a chance to think.

'Quite similar?' said Grandad, looking me up and down. 'Just whose side are you on, young fella m' lad?'

'Your side,' I confirmed.

'Mmm . . . that *is* the correct answer,' he said, but his voice was full of suspicion. 'There was one bloke in particular I didn't like, a feller called Sullivan. I couldn't stand him. He was one of the foremen and always causing trouble, throwing his weight around.' Grandad's fists clenched and the muscles in his face tightened as he spoke. 'Sometimes people don't give you a choice but to fight back, H.' A smile crept onto his lips. 'And sometimes they just make it too easy.'

'How do you mean?'

'There were some people I looked for an excuse to have a punch up with. Sullivan was one of them. It all started with a brew.'

'You had a fight over a mug of tea?'

'Don't say it like that, H. You make it sound like I was being unreasonable.' He leaned into me and we bumped shoulders. 'It wasn't over tea as such. Me and Jonesy were just going to get some tea.' He lowered his voice to a determined whisper. 'Never stand between a grown man and the kettle, H.'

WE WALKED THROUGH THE docks under a grey sky, weaving around the puddles from a recent downpour, their surfaces glistening with the multi-coloured swirls of spilt oil. The place smelt like Grandad's workshop. Distorted metal rods protruded from lumps of fractured concrete that fringed the bomb craters that peppered the site. Colour was

in short supply. Every piece of metal was grey, the buildings were black with soot, and the men wore dark suits and flat caps. The only bright spots were the flags flying from the ships. It reminded me of Mum and Dad's wedding photo, the black-and-white image livened by the roses of her bouquet, hand-tinted in red.

There were dozens of ships inside the protective walls of the port, others at anchor, waiting to enter or preparing to leave. From where we were, it was difficult to tell where one ship finished and another started. As we got closer to the Hood, *its outline became more distinct. She sat in a dry dock, her main deck level with the surrounding yard, the damage to the propellers from its collision with the* Renown *obvious even from a distance.*

Teams of men were working all over the ship, the repairs to the quarterdeck well under way. The ship sat on large stone pillars, to allow work to be carried out under the hull. The ship was held in place by timber posts suspended from ropes fastened to the ship's rail at one end. The other end sat on a stone shelf built into the dry dock. There were four bridges from the dockside to the ship. We used the one nearest the stern.

Carpenters prepared the new planks. Wood shavings littered the deck, the breeze gathering them up, swirling them around as it made its way between obstacles and deposited them in drifts against the base of the big guns. Dark patches on the bare steel showed where the rail had been welded. Grandad was talking to another sailor and they were laughing at something or somebody. The sailor looked over at me. Grandad turned and beckoned me over.

'Here, H.'

I ran over to them.

'Harry, this is Jonesy.'

We shook hands, which always made me feel like a grown-up. Jonesy smiled and slapped Grandad's shoulder, blushing and looking at the floor when Grandad introduced him as his best mate.

'Come on,' said Jonesy. 'Let's see if we can scrounge a brew.'

'Good thinking,' said Grandad.

'I'll just get my tools together.' Jonesy threw his gear into a canvas bag. 'Come on, it's this—'

'The nearest canteen is this way,' I told them, running ahead, pausing at the doorway to make sure they were following me before turning and running full pelt into a group of men. The lead man was solid and I was knocked flat on my backside. 'Sorry,' I squeaked, embarrassed more than hurt.

The man I'd run into leaned forwards and I held out my hand. Instead of helping me, he grabbed the front of my coat just under my chin and pulled me up towards him, his face close to mine.

'What the hell are you doing here?'

I could smell the booze on his breath.

Grandad and Jonesy's distant laughter echoed as they stepped inside the ship. I turned my head towards them, restricted by the man's grip.

'Grandad,' I croaked, tears prickling my eyes.

Jonesy stopped. Grandad didn't.

He didn't break his stride. The man's grip on me relaxed, but he didn't let go. The crack reverberated around the steel walls as Grandad delivered a vicious slap to the side of the man's head. I was dropped, forgotten. Without pause, Grandad shoved the man's face and propelled him back into his mates.

'Touch him again, Sullivan, and I'll bloody kill yeh,' Grandad snarled, his right hand drawn back, fist clenched.

'Alright, Grandad, keep yer hair on. He walked in to me. I was just helping the little fella up.' He turned and smirked at his mates, who were all laughing.

'Get out of my way,' Grandad hissed.

'Or what? You two gonna sort us out, are yeh?'

Grandad stayed put.

'Two navy lads against seven of you lot? Doesn't seem fair, does it, Sullivan? Why don't you piss off and get another half-dozen of you to even it up?'

'Big talk from an old man and the ship's monkey. Come on, lads, let's teach these two—'

'Three.' Jonesy stepped forwards. 'Teach these three a lesson, you innumerate prick!' He looked down at the large spanner in his hand. He seemed surprised to see it there. 'Let's call it three and a half, shall we?' He seemed happy with the maths.

'What's it got to do with you?' Sullivan snapped.

'It's got bugger all to do with me. I've just got a compulsion to stick my nose into other people's business. It's just the way I am.' Jonesy stepped forwards. 'It's one of my many flaws. Another is my uncontrollable temper when I get wound up by arseholes like you.'

Sullivan looked at Jonesy, Grandad, then the spanner.

'I'm not done with you, Manning.' Sullivan pointed his finger in Grandad's face. 'Not by a long shot.'

The men circled around us, keeping their distance. Grandad and Jonesy turned, facing them all the way.

'Ready when you are, ladies,' Jonesy said, twirling the spanner round his finger like a six-shooter as they passed.

Grandad left a trail of dissipating anger in his wake as we made our way in search of tea.

The queue shuffled forwards as we scanned the packed canteen, willing space to appear. I'd seen Grandad try the same technique when he was gardening, staring at the spade, willing it to dig a trench for his spuds. This time it worked. I made a mental note to consider it a future tactic.

A couple of men among a group waved for us to join them. As we approached the crowded table, three of the men got up and left. I recognised Connie and Digger from the photo. It turned out that Connie did have a big forehead, after all.

Grandad was talking to them excitedly about the altercation, re-living the glory. Jonesy spotted me looking around. He put a supportive hand on my arm.

'Don't worry, Harry, they don't come in here,' he assured.

I relaxed a little, but my tea still showed evidence of my nerves as its surface juddered. I concentrated, trying to make it stop. The chatter of the room faded to an indistinct hum. But the noise of a tin mug banging down on the tables made me jump out of my trance.

'ARE YOU ALRIGHT, JACK?' Gran asked.

A fresh mug of tea sat on the windowsill, its surface rippling.

Grandad looked up. 'We are, Lil. We're just getting to the good bit.'

She smiled as she left. 'Don't let him overdo it, Harry.'

I promised I'd look after him and we turned our attention back to the album. Grandad's hand turned the page and he rested his palm on the photo, shielding it from view.

'Do you enjoy fighting with your mates, H? A bit of rough and tumble?'

He put his fists up and shadow-boxed in front of my face, smiling, his face animated, teasing and playful. All I could do was flinch when he got too close to my nose.

I shrugged.

He put down his fists, disappointed with my response. Even play-fighting made me uncomfortable. It just wasn't in me.

'Don't you find it exciting?'

I didn't answer.

Twisting slowly, he turned towards me.

'Have you ever had a fight?'

I shook my head.

He took my hand and rubbed my knuckles with his thumb. Nobody had ever hit me, not really. Mum and Dad hadn't, Gran and Grandad hadn't – they'd never even got cross. There had been a few scuffles at school, but nothing like the scraps I'd witnessed in the playground, where kids got broken noses and burst lips. I'd always backed down or run off or talked my way out of bother. I didn't want to tell Grandad that, but I couldn't bring myself to lie.

'It's OK, H. That's why I asked Frank Watson's lad to look after you.'

I didn't tell him it was that that had made me a target.

'How come you're mates with Watson's dad? Everybody else hates him.'

He thought for a moment. 'I don't know if they hate him . . .' He paused. 'Well, they probably do hate him, but the reason they hate him is that they're frightened of him. People can tell he's not bothered, he's not scared. A man who doesn't care about the consequences is dangerous. People can sense it.'

He went quiet. His breathing was slow and I could hear the air moving through his airways.

'I've got a bit of that in me too, H. Maybe Frank can sense it. I've said it before, but he's always been alright with me. We always have a laugh in the Legion; he's been a good mate.' Pausing again, his eyes narrowed. 'I think he looks at me like a father figure. He's never talked to me about it, but I don't think he had much of a childhood.' He patted my leg. 'Sometimes people become like their parents, repeating the same patterns, good or bad. And sometimes they go completely the other way. Kids with parents who drink too much often never touch the stuff, yet other times they become alcoholics.'

I didn't know if I was the same as Dad or not.

'Who do I take after?' I asked him, unsure if I wanted to know the answer.

'You're like your mum,' he said. 'She got on with everybody.' He smiled at her photo on the mantelpiece. 'Getting on with people is like fighting. It's something you learn how to do, H. If you get a crack from your dad'—he leaned closer—'or your grandad,' he laughed, 'you're going to be less scared in a fight. On the other hand, if your parents chat to everyone they meet'—he glanced at Mum's picture—'you're not going to be intimidated when you meet new people.'

He turned the page of the album.

'Everything people do, they learned how to do it. You can do the same.' He flattened the new page of the album. 'Fighting is just like anything else. Some don't like it, some people fight because they've got no choice and . . .' His hand rested on the page, covering the photo. His eyes came to life and a sly grin grew into the broad smile of a younger man. He lifted his hand to reveal the scene and shrugged. 'Others fight because they like it.'

MEN PACKED THE QUARTERDECK, except for an area under the barrels of the Y turret. It took a moment to realise what was going on. But as I stood on the rail to get a better view, it was clear. They'd set up a boxing ring and there was a fight in progress.

The ropes that defined the ring were hung from timber uprights in each corner and covered in padding. The posts were held in place by ropes leading off in all directions, tied to bollards, vents and even the gun barrels. One thing you can be sure of on a ship is that there's always plenty of rope and blokes who know how to use it.

'Come on, Grandad.' I climbed down from the rail. 'Let's get down . . .' I said to the spot where he'd stood, his head disappearing down the steps.

I sprinted after him, grabbed the handrail and watched him taking the steps three at a time before disappearing round the corner. He must be confident that I could keep up with him, because he never looked back. When Grandad reached the top of an open staircase, he jumped without pausing and sat on the rail, sliding down swiftly. His shirt billowed as his speed increased before he hit the deck running. Despite using the steps conventionally, I was still agile enough to keep pace with him. I caught up with him as we reached the outer edges of the crowd.

I tugged at the back of his sweat-sodden shirt. He turned and a look of surprise passed across his face before he smiled and grabbed my hand, pulling me behind as he pushed into the crowd. Some pushed back, annoyed elbows trying to stop our progress, unhappy at the disruption. But Grandad just forced our way through, stopping to stand on tiptoes, making sure we were going in the right direction. He stopped again and turned to me, shouting to make himself heard above the din.

'Jonesy's over in the red corner.'

The crowd was becoming louder and denser, the smell of stale sweat and cigarette smoke having their own battle in my nostrils. As we neared the corner, we could see Jonesy sat on a stool, just inside the ring. He was patching up a fighter between rounds. The ref rang the bell and Jonesy bobbed between the ropes, leaning on the corner post, watching his man. Grandad put a hand on his shoulder. Jonesy twisted round, a pair of scissors in his hand.

Grandad backed off and held up his hands. Jonesy's battered face softened and he lowered the scissors. His left eye was closed, swollen and bruised, his other eye black. He had a plaster over his broken nose and a fat lip.

'What the bloody hell happened to you?' Grandad asked. 'Have you been in the ring without me to look after you?'

Jonesy dropped the scissors into a wooden box containing his 'corner kit'.

'I got caught on my own in the bogs. Sullivan and his cronies. I did my best, Jack, but . . . there were at least five of them. They're over there.' He pointed to the opposite corner.

I recognised Sullivan and three of the men we'd encountered earlier. They were so engrossed in the fight, they didn't notice us.

'What round is this, Jonesy?'

'Six. Last round.' His good eye narrowed. 'I know that look, Jack.' The rough skin of his hands rasped as he rubbed them together. 'What's on your mind?'

Connie and Digger pushed through to join us.

'I've got an idea.'

Grandad put his arms around Jonesy and me, and we all huddled together to hear the plan.

I stayed with Jonesy, while Connie and Digger disappeared into the throng with Grandad, working their way through the crowd behind Sullivan and his crew. The final bell rang, Jonesy's man the victor.

I watched Digger and Connie's progress through the crowd until they were in position. The referee looked at his clipboard to see who was up next. That was their queue.

They both stepped onto the bottom rope, one on each side of Sullivan, and pushed the top rope up. Sullivan looked at them, confusion on his face. Grandad ran from the crowd and shoulder-charged Sullivan, sending him flying into the ring, stepping in after him. They released the ropes.

Boos rang out from the crowd, but Grandad stepped into the centre of the ring and shouted, 'Bonus bout, lads, lay your bets.'

Everyone cheered.

Sullivan wasn't fazed. He looked around, spotted his gang and directed them to his corner. To be fair to him, he showed no hesitation. He was as keen to fight as Grandad was. The ref spoke to both of them and seemed happy to let the fight go ahead. Grandad approached our corner. He had his back to me, facing the ring. He took off his shirt and vest. All *traces of the cuddly old man who told me daft jokes and bedtime stories had vanished. There was a small scar on his side I'd not noticed before – I think it was a stab wound. He stretched his shoulders, bringing his arms together across the front of his body. The muscles of his back, neck and arms rippled under the skin as he clenched his fists.*

Jonesy got into the ring. Grandad's hands were rock steady as Jonesy applied tape to his knuckles and laced up his gloves.

'Watch him, Jack, he's a dirty bastard.'

Grandad stared ahead. He rolled his neck and thumped his gloves together.

'So am I,' he hissed.

Jonesy smiled as the bell went and ducked between the ropes, leaving Grandad alone with Sullivan.

Round 1.

The two fighters moved towards each other. This was nothing like the heavyweight fights I'd seen on the telly – two big, lumbering giants sussing each other out for three rounds before landing a punch. Within seconds, they were at it. It looked like Grandad had met his match. Sullivan was as fit as him and maybe even bigger.

There were jabs and hooks thrown from both of them, but Sullivan was the first to land a big one. He swung his left hand into Grandad's ribs. We heard the rush of air leaving Grandad's lungs and saw him wince. So did Sullivan. He didn't give Grandad a moment to recover, but in his haste to finish it, he got careless.

He swung wildly at Grandad, hoping to land the knockout blow. But Grandad's defence was strong. He held his gloves up to his face, arms close to his body to shield his ribs. Sullivan's onslaught continued, but Grandad's arms took most of the blows. He pushed Grandad against the ropes. We'd watched Muhammad Ali do the same trick with George Foreman in Zaire, the rumble in the jungle. Even Gran had been throwing mock punches as we'd sat on the edge of our seats watching Ali win after seven rounds of soaking up the punishment.

Sure enough, when Sullivan paused for a second to catch his breath, Grandad sent out a perfect jab, straight into Sullivan's chin. He rocked back, but the bell went before Grandad could follow it up.

I called that round a draw.

Neither man seemed tired as Grandad came back to the corner. Jonesy handed him a drink of water. Grandad closed his eyes and poured it over his head before taking a swig. Jonesy wiped Grandad's face as the bell rang.

Round 2.

There was no let-up in the pace, both men coming out fast, throwing punches as soon and as hard as they could. Sullivan was giving as good as he got. He had Grandad pinned in a corner and was raining a salvo of body shots. One landed below the belt. I could see Grandad's face screw up – that must have hurt. The crowd jeered.

Another hook from Sullivan left a cut above Grandad's right eye. The ref stepped in to give Grandad the chance to recover from the foul blow. After a few seconds, the ref stepped aside and the fight continued.

Although he'd had time to recover, it was obvious the low blow had hurt Grandad. Sullivan didn't let the advantage go to waste. He hit Grandad with a quick combination, right, left, right. Grandad was in trouble.

Sullivan took a step back, feeling he'd done enough to give himself a breather before going back in to finish him off.

But Grandad still had plenty left in him. As Sullivan stepped back, Grandad came forwards again, taking Sullivan by surprise. Grandad wasn't that badly hurt. He jabbed with his left as he pushed Sullivan back. Then he stepped through and landed an enormous right uppercut. I could hear Sullivan's teeth cracking together.

'Go on, Grandad!' I shouted at the top of my voice. 'Kill him!'

Now it was Sullivan who was struggling.

Lucky for him, the bell rang again.

It was only then that I realised nobody else was shouting and every-one was looking at me! Some older sailors were shaking their heads, the younger ones giggling.

'What's up?' I looked at Jonesy.

'Well, the rules are that we only cheer the lads between rounds.'

'Why didn't you tell me?'

'I forgot,' Jonesy said as he stepped into the ring, giving Grandad a drink before turning his attention to the cut eye.

He used a small iron to push the swelling down around the cut, then smeared some Vaseline onto the wound to stop it from bleeding into Grandad's eye and to prevent the leather of Sullivan's gloves from tear-ing it open again.

Round 3.

Grandad came out more cautious this time. Left foot forwards, jab-bing with his left, then switching stance and leading with his right, keeping Sullivan guessing. He manoeuvred Sullivan towards his own corner. Connie and Digger stood behind Sullivan's men. Grandad stepped up the jabs and pushed Sullivan back, swinging a big right-han-der, which Sullivan easily dodged, but only by throwing himself against the ropes. Digger and Connie grabbed his arms – the trap set.

The crowd roared into life, jeering, thinking Grandad was cheating. As expected, Sullivan's mates stepped in to help, trying to wrench Con-nie and Digger off their man.

Grandad rushed forwards. Bang-bang – a left and a right jab, ei-ther side of Sullivan's head, breaking the noses of Sullivan's cronies. They fell back, blood pouring from their faces. Connie and Digger released Sullivan, who took a quick glance behind to see what had happened.

'That's for Jonesy,' Grandad shouted into his face.

Cheers echoed around the ring.

'I thought they weren't supposed to cheer during the fight,' I yelled to Jonesy, barely able to make myself heard above the racket.

He looked down at me. 'Well I'm not bloody telling 'em.'

When the bell went at the end of the round, the noise continued. The word had got out that something was happening and the crowd had doubled in size.

Round 4.

Wound up by Grandad's trick, Sullivan was taking chances from the start. He swung big arcing hooks, determined to end it. But they weren't landing. Grandad could easily duck or sway back. Sullivan was tiring.

Grandad was biding his time, waiting until Sullivan was out of steam and for his chance to end it. It was a risky strategy. If one of those big punches landed, Grandad was a goner.

The fighters parted momentarily, then Grandad was moving forwards again, jabbing with his left, then feigning a right uppercut, landing a left hook instead, followed by a big swinging right that came down on Sullivan's temple. Sullivan dropped to the floor, flat on his belly. He came to and looked around the ring. He pushed himself up onto his knees, his hands still supporting his body. Grandad bent down towards him. He cocked his head, trying to hear what Sullivan was saying.

'I've had enough,' Sullivan croaked.

Grandad moved his head closer to reply. 'You've had enough when I bloody say so.' And with that, Grandad stood up and looked at him.

Before the ref could jump in, he swung a vicious right hand into the side of Sullivan's head. The crowd were going berserk, throwing whatever they could lay their hands on into the ring. The contractors in the crowd were booing, angry at Grandad's flouting of the rules by hitting their man while he was down. But the majority were crew and they didn't seem to care about boxing etiquette. They just wanted blood and Grandad had given it to them.

He stood in the ring and looked around at the crowd, his arm held up like a true champ. Sullivan lay on the deck, unmoving. I was sure he was dead.

Some medics came in and took him out on a stretcher. The crowd pushed and celebrated, some waving their winnings and throwing their caps in the air. Grandad came over to us.

'Well,' said Jonesy, 'that seems to have sorted that out.'

Grandad cocked his head. 'It was a close one.'

He breathed heavily, his chest glistening with sweat as Jonesy removed Grandad's gloves and bindings. Grandad's torso was solid, each muscle visible in his stomach, shoulders and chest, huge biceps connected to the sinew of his forearms. I was proud of him, and a little scared at the same time.

The crowd dispersed and we went to find a sink where Grandad could have a rinse. A few other sailors clapped Grandad on the back, 'Well done, Jack,' ringing out as we walked through the ship.

In the shower room, Grandad flopped onto a stool, exhausted. The ruthless fighter slowly faded. The adrenalin dissipated and his body softened as Jonesy fixed his eye. By the time the repair was complete, the grandad I knew had returned, laughing and joking as usual.

THE FIGHT HAD TAKEN it out of Grandad. His eyes drooped and his head fell to the side, a gentle rumbling snore escaping through his nose. I sat and watched him. His breaths came in short, erratic bursts. Like an anxious parent watching a newborn, afraid to leave its side, I wanted to be there in case of emergency. But he wasn't that fragile. He was a fighter. Hadn't he just shown that? I trudged upstairs to my room. Pickering was waiting for me.

'How is he?'

'You should have seen the boxing match. It was brilliant. Grandad gave *Sullivan* a proper good hiding.' I sent my fists in a flurry of jabs and hooks.

He glanced down. 'I hope his footwork was better than yours,' he said.

I stopped. 'I was just showing you.'

'Good,' said Pickering, 'because if you tackle Watson like that, you'll be coming second.'

'If you know so much about it, why don't you show me how?'

'What, with *my* knees? And I haven't got any elbows . . . and my shoulders only do this . . .' His shoulder joint rotated. 'I bet I could still give you a thrashing, though.'

'Oh yeah?'

'Yeah.'

'Come on, then.' I picked him up and watched his feet as he wriggled around.

'It's not a fair fight. You'd be in a higher weight category. I'm more of a super bantamweight.' His feet did a passable imitation of the Ali shuffle. 'Put 'em up, put 'em up.'

His arm rotated five times and he landed the perfect uppercut on my chin. I fell back on the bed. He stood on my chest and lifted his arms in victory, rotating slowly, taking in the applause from the crowd. Then he fell back, sitting on my stomach.

'Ouch, yeh great oaf. You're not as much of a lightweight as you think.'

'Yeah, I know. I'm what they call "compact".'

'I think you mean dense.'

'I have a great "mass" – it's not the same as being dense. It's the same as being big-boned, except I haven't got any bones. I've got "big mass", instead.'

He demonstrated by jumping up and down on my guts until I rolled over, taking him with me.

'How did you lose your ear?'

'The word "lose" doesn't really convey the full picture and implies that I'm careless with my body parts. Anyway, it's a painful memory.'

'Is it?'

'Yeah. And it's a painful memory because it was a painful incident, as you well know.'

'Me?'

'Yeah. You ripped it off during one of your regular tantrums when you were a toddler.'

'Are you sure it was me? I can't remember doing it.'

'Well, the alternative is that it was a grown-up who ripped it off in a tantrum, and I know where I'm placing my bet.' He almost put his paws on his hips, defying me to contradict him.

'You're probably right.'

'Yeah, I usually, probably, always am.'

'Do you think there's going to be any more "scrapping"?' He sniggered at my earlier misunderstanding.

'Well, its Saturday night, so there's a good chance.'

We lay together looking at the model planes suspended from the ceiling. I pointed out the differences between the bombers and the fighters. We'd been mates a long time and I enjoyed having him around, most of the time.

I could sense his unease – he had something to say. Rolling over, I turned my back on him. But of course, once a bear's got something on his mind, he can't keep his gob shut.

'How much time has he got left?'

'Grandad?'

'Er, yeah.'

'I don't know.'

'I think you need to think about—'

'I'll see you later. Grandad's going to finish off the story.'

His sigh tried to hold me back, but I pulled away.

Grandad was sitting up, eyes closed. His thin shoulders drooped, so it wasn't clear where his arms started. I approached the bed and sat beside him. The album was open on his lap, showing a photo of him holding aloft the trophy for winning the boxing tournament. Beside it was the clipping from the *Hood*'s on-board newspaper, *The Chough*. I'd laughed with him and we'd joked about the name. It was a kind of crow, like a fat blackbird, but chuff was also slang replacement for any swear word, when swearing wasn't aloud.

His eyes opened and he yawned, smacking his lips. 'I wouldn't mind a drink, H.'

'Gran's making tea. Do you want a sip of water?' I reached for the glass.

'Mmm . . . I was thinking of something a bit stronger.' He wrung his hands together.

IT WAS DUSK AS GRANDAD, Jonesy and I walked out of the docks.
  '*I need a drink,' said Grandad.*
  We walked across the street to The King's Arms. It stood alone in a sea of rubble, buildings on both sides, demolished by German night bombing. The elaborate green tiles were perfect, despite the bombed-out buildings that surrounded it. Cream inlaid panels had scenes of ancient naval battles painted in a pale blue, like the finest porcelain. High green doors welcomed us.
  '*Leave it open, fellas; the rush is due anytime,' shouted the landlord.*
  Jonesy was the last through and he kicked a wooden wedge under the door.
  '*Cheers, lads. What can I get you?'*
  '*Three pints,' said Grandad.*
  The landlord looked down at me. 'Three?'
  '*Aye, two pints of bitter and a pint of lemonade.'*

'Lemonade?' I whinged.

'Okay, make it a shandy,' said Grandad.

That was better. At least it looked like beer. Having experience of sailor's humour, I could imagine the endless jokes if I sat with a pint of pop. A paper brolly is the only thing that could have made it worse.

'Coming up.' The landlord leaned back on the pump handle. 'They're saying there's been some fisticuffs in the yard today. The lads are talking about nothing else.'

There were a dozen contractors on the other side of the pub, huddled together, pointing at the three of us.

'Yeah, we heard about that. Sounded like a good scrap,' Grandad said with a straight but battle-scarred face.

'I don't know about that,' said the barman. 'Some of the lads think it was an unfair fight.' He looked at Grandad with a sly grin.

Grandad faced the group. 'The losers often do think it's been unfair.'

There were stares and mutterings from the men.

'I hope there's not going to be any bother tonight. We've survived the Germans – don't let it be our lads who wreck the place, eh?'

'I'm sure it'll be a quiet night,' Grandad said, turning his back on the civilians.

We sat as far away from the contractors as possible, sipping. Well, I sipped, Grandad and Jonesy gulped their drinks. They had two pints before I was halfway down mine.

By eight o'clock, the place was packed. The sailors came into our side of the bar, other contract workers joining their mates in the other. I spent the evening listening to Grandad and his pals telling and retelling the events of the day. A few had bet on Grandad and were spending their cash freely. A steady stream of drunken sailors came to congratulate him, insisting they buy him a drink. Grandad accepted all offers.

As the evening became night, the place got rowdier and busier – more men, more beer, more noise and inevitably . . .

'Grandad.' I pulled at his shirt.

'What's up, H?' His words slurred.

What shall we do with a drunken sailor?

'I need the loo.'

'No problem,' said Jonesy. 'I need to pay a visit myself. Come with me.'

Grandad gestured with his thumb and I squeezed past the blokes around our table. The bogs were around the other side of the bar, where the contractors sat. As we passed them, one stuck his leg out, trying to trip us up, but he was so drunk that in his haste, he fell off his stool, only saved at the last moment by his mate grabbing him. We easily side-stepped the half-arsed ambush as catcalls and wolf whistles followed us into the gents.

The toilets reeked and there were puddles of pee all over the floor. Jonesy looked at me and shrugged.

'Welcome to my world,' he declared, then laughed himself silly as we used the urinals.

Someone else came in and we shuffled along to make room for the newcomer. But nobody joined us. There was plenty of space. They must be shy, waiting for us to finish . . .

Jonesy was singing some old Sinatra tune, holding the last note of each line way beyond his skill level until his lungs were empty. His good eye winked at me as we zipped up and turned. Three of the contractors were standing in front of the door.

Jonesy was straight in.

'The ladies' toilets are next door,' he said, ignoring the threat.

I could see Jonesy glancing in the mirror as we washed our hands. Considering that he was still sporting lumps and bruises from earlier that day, I thought that was brave. Some might say foolhardy.

'You should be on the telly,' said one man.

I recognised two of them from my first encounter with Sullivan. The newcomer looked like Sullivan, maybe his brother.

The door opened again. It was Grandad. He took in the scene.

'More trouble?' he asked.

'There's no trouble here, pal,' said sidekick one.

'Oh, you've got that one wrong,' said Grandad.

The sludge in their brains stirred. But before they could figure out his meaning, he was at them. He hit the first with a swinging right-hander, knocking him into a cubicle. The second made a run for the door as the third sent a left hook into Grandad's head. It had strength but no skill. Grandad dodged it and grabbed him by his lapels then nutted him. His nose exploded across his face. Grandad swung him round and sent him spinning towards his retreating mate, who was halfway through the door. They both flew out, sprawling into the bar, the bog door smashing into the seating, hitting somebody in the back and sending them flying across a table full of drinks, knocking glass and beer over everyone.

The entire pub had been waiting for a signal and this was it.

Before the noise of the smashing glass had stopped, everybody was fighting. The main scraps were between sailors and contractors, but there were even fights between each group. Some men just like fighting.

The two guys who Grandad had thrown through the door were still on the floor, struggling to get to their feet in the mayhem. Grandad jumped through the opening, landing with one foot on each of them. The guy face down dropped back to the floor, while the one on his back let out a loud whoosh as Grandad's foot squeezed the air from his lungs.

Jonesy grabbed me by the scruff of the neck and dragged me after him, pausing in the doorway as a pint pot smashed on the wall, showering us in glass and beer. He pushed me forwards, but bodies blocked our path. He lifted me off the floor by my belt and collar and threw me over the bar. I landed among a group of cowering employees. Chairs and tables were flying now, glasses and bottles sailing through the air or being smashed over heads, blood splatters spraying everywhere.

Untangling myself, I made my way behind the bar. The hinged countertop was down, but the gate underneath was open. I poked my *head up as much as I dared, catching brief glimpses of the action – a thump here, a kick in the balls there. Glass cascaded around me. Two pairs of legs were in front of me. I put my head forwards to get a better view – one pair belonged to Grandad. He took a scuffing blow to his ear, swinging back and landing a right hook into the other guy's body.*

Before the poor bloke had a chance to recover, Grandad stepped behind him and threw him to the floor, pouncing on him like the Wolf Man, holding him down by his throat, repeatedly hitting him in the face. Grandad's eyes were wide and wild. The guy was struggling hard, kicking at Grandad's back, but that just seemed to enrage Grandad even more. He paused the beating and looked at me. His mad eyes softened for a moment. He looked at his victim, then back at me. He smiled and gave me the thumbs up, still gripping the guy's throat. A pair of hands grabbed Grandad by the hair and pulled him backwards. He gave a comical 'Eeek!' and disappeared out of sight. His victim got up and dived after him.

A loud whistle blew. Was it half-time? Were they all going to stop fighting – like the soldiers did at Christmas in World War One – then restart after a pint and a singsong?

Coppers poured into the pub, truncheons ready, swinging at anybody within reach. As the cops progressed, the sailors and contractors forgot their differences and turned their anger on the bobbies. But the cops were better organised. Truncheons started cracking heads and it wouldn't take long for them to gain the upper hand.

Jonesy ran and dived over the bar, landing in a heap next to me. Grandad lifted the counter hatch, stepped through and looked down at him.

'Ouch,' Jonesy groaned as the smashed glass ground under him.

He got to his feet and twisted, trying to see his back. I helped him to pick out the shards to the tune of his occasional yelps.

Grandad interrupted. 'Shall we get out of here before the cops get their act together?' He pointed behind him to the back of the pub. 'Tradesman's entrance. Come on, H.'

We made our way through the bar into the back rooms. Dark figures loomed on the other side of the half-glass door at the end of the corridor. More cops. Grandad spun round and pushed me ahead of him.

'This way, Jonesy,' he shouted to his mate. Grandad grabbed my shoulder. 'In here, H.'

I looked left and right, but there was nowhere to go.

I shrugged. 'Where?' I asked, panic rising in my chest.

Grandad pointed to his feet.

What did that mean?

We were stood on a hatch. He lifted the metal handle that was set into the wood, pulled it open and gestured for us to go down. Jonesy led the way, flicking on the lights as we descended the steep wooden steps into the dank, stale underworld of the cellar.

Grandad moved quickly, closing the hatch behind him. A few moments later, large, flat feet thundered over the hatch as Bobbies ran above our heads. The narrow walkway was lined with barrels and we squeezed past until we stood at the bottom of another set of steps. This one ran up the side of a slide. I'd watched the draymen unload the lorries at the Legion and knew that this was where the barrels slid down. This was our way out. Hopefully, we wouldn't emerge by the side of a Black Maria.

Grandad cautiously slid back the bolts, lifting the heavy timber just enough to peek out. Gravel and dust fell on the battered steps.

'All clear,' he whispered.

He pushed the door open further and peered around, waving us forwards. We were at the side of the pub. Whichever way we went, we had to get past the cops.

Crouching low, we hurried across the car park, sticking close to a hedgerow that ran at its side, twigs and branches snagging our clothes as we made our way towards the front of the pub. A dozen or more police cars and vans stood abandoned on the street and pavement. There was no one around.

Jonesy was close behind me, puffing and panting. We reached the corner and jogged along the road, past the shattered buildings, until we came to the next structure the Germans had left intact. A figure stepped out from the doorway.

''ello, 'ello, 'ello,' said the man. 'What's all this, then?'

Grandad stepped forwards and pulled back his right arm to whack the bobby.

'Hold on, Jack, take it easy. Where's yer sense of humour?'

The figure grew another head.

'Hey-up, lads,' said Connie, stepping out from behind Digger and slapping Grandad on the arm. 'Another good night, eh, Jack?'

'How did you two get out?' Grandad asked.

'Through the bar and out the back door before the reinforcements arrived. We grabbed a bit of salvage on the way.'

Digger reached into his overcoat pockets and pulled a bottle of stout from each.

Connie chirped, 'I got a bottle of sherry.'

'Sherry?' said Digger.

'Who the bloody hell drinks sherry?' said Grandad.

Connie's enthusiasm deflated and he confessed. 'I panicked, Jack. It was all I could reach.'

Grandad spoke into the dark. 'Jonesy did a bit better, didn't yeh, Jonesy?'

'How did yeh know?' Jonesy sounded disappointed it wasn't going to be a surprise.

'I knew you wouldn't be able to miss a chance like that, yeh silly bugger. What did yeh get?'

Jonesy stepped out of the shadows with a cardboard box. 'Bingo,' he said with a grin.

Grandad lifted a bottle and held it up for us to see. The moonlight illuminated the label, a black girl in profile. Underneath, it said Rhum Negrita.

'Old Nick.' Digger looked admiringly at Jonesy. 'Well done, mate.'

Jonesy was basking in the glory, when Grandad suggested, 'Maybe we should put some more distance between us and the cops before we celebrate. What do yeh reckon?'

We looked back at the pub just as a stool flew through a window, smashing into one of the cop vans.

Without another word, we turned away from the mayhem. We walked past dark buildings, through the empty streets and through the dock gates. We shattered the reflection of the moon as we splashed through oil-topped puddles. Close to the ships, there was a sentry on duty. Grandad stopped abruptly and we concertinaed into him, Jonesy pushed Grandad forwards as our representative. We hung back, giggling.

'Go on, Jack, get him,' said Digger.

Grandad stumbled forwards and looked back at us.

'Why me?'

'You've got the gift of the gab, Jack,' Connie whispered.

Before Grandad could make further protest, a young voice rang out across the yard.

'Who goes there? Friend or foe?'

Grandad held up a hand to shield his eyes from the torch beam that singled him out. The Hood's *bulky silhouette overlooked the scene.*

Connie put his hand on my shoulder.

'Get ready to do a runner if it kicks off,' he whispered.

'What, and leave Grandad?' I said.

'That was a test,' he claimed, 'to see if you're good enough to be in our gang.'

I smiled as we watched Grandad approach the torch.

'Friend? Or foe?' the guard repeated.

'Well, if I was a foe, I wouldn't bloody tell you, would I, you daft sod,' Grandad shouted towards the light.

I admired his confidence in taking on the unknown voice.

'What would you say, then?' the guard asked.

'I'd engage you in friendly conversation as I made my way towards you,' he said as he made his way towards him. 'Then,' Grandad added, 'I'd grab my knife.'

'Have you got a knife?' the startled voice asked.

The bolt of the guard's rifle snapped a bullet in place.

'I haven't, but the foe would have. They've always got knives, the foe have.'

'You seem to be an expert on the foe.'

'Well, when you get to my age, you've learned a trick or two.'

'Hey, don't try any tricks,' the guard warned.

Grandad held up his hands.

'How do I know you're not the foe, then?' the guard asked.

'Cos I told yeh we weren't.'

'We?' The guard scanned his torch over us. He must be worse than me at maths, because although we were visible, he asked, 'How many of you are there?'

'Five, including me.'

'Another four, then,' confirmed the guard.

'Very good. I can understand why a bright lad like you got this job. You're doing well, by the way. But me and my mates just want to get back on the ship.' Grandad pointed towards the Hood.

'But you said you might try to trick me, and you might or might not have a knife.' He sounded uncertain.

'Do I sound German?'

'No.'

'Well, the Germans are the foes.'

'But you might have had specialist training. You might have had them . . . what do yeh call 'em? Elocution lessons.'

'Elo-bloody-cution lessons?' Grandad scoffed, incredulous. 'And the result of this elaborate training is that I sound like I'm from Yorkshire?'

'Your teacher might have learnt to speak English in Yorkshire.' He seemed pleased with this explanation.

'What do you think he, or she, was doing in Yorkshire?'

'I don't know. What is there to do in Yorkshire? Err . . . he could have been a miner.'

'So he or she was born in Germany, moved to Yorkshire to learn English and work down the pit, before going back to Hamburg to train crack SS troops in the art of espionage and killing?'

'Is that where you're from?'

'Yeah.'

'Hamburg!'

'No, Yorkshire.'

Grandad was getting closer. No need to shout now. We tiptoed up behind him.

'I can see yeh,' the guard shouted.

Grandad looked back at us. 'What the bloody hell are you doing?'

'Sneaking in,' said Jonesy.

'Shut up, you nutcase, and leave it to me. Err, where were we?'

'I was interrogating you to make sure you weren't German.'

'So you were,' said Grandad with more patience than I knew he had. 'Carry on.'

The guard changed tactics.

'You could be a Jap,' he suggested.

'Have you ever heard a Jap speak?'

'Er . . . no.'

'You're right, then. I might be,' Grandad said with brutal logic. 'Are yeh?'

'No, but I can do a ve-wee good Chinese accent. Whar you fink bout vaaart?'

'That's good, that,' the guard said, relaxing and lowering the torch, then realising his mistake and whipping it back up. The aggressive tone was back. 'Whose side are they on?' he demanded.

'Ours, but they're only fighting the Japs.'

'Yeh seem to know a lot about China,' the guard observed with suspicion. 'I mean, for a lad from Yorkshire, or possibly Hamburg. And that accent was good, really good.' He relaxed again.

We'd all shuffled forwards and now stood right in front of him.

'I never told you how the cunning plan with the chit-chat and the knife ended, did I?'

'Oh no! That's the knife you haven't got, right?'

'That's the one,' confirmed Grandad. 'So, having distracted you with idle chit-chat, I'd get close enough . . . say, er . . . yeah, about as close as I am now. Then I'd whip out my dagger and—'

'Dagger!' the guard shrieked. 'You said it wasn't a knife.'

'It's not a knife.'

'It's a dagger.'

'It's a non-existent dagger or a non-existent knife, what difference does it make?'

'Dagger sounds a lot more dangerous.'

'What, even if I haven't got one?'

'A lot more,' the guard said, ignoring Grandad's logic.

'Then I'd jump on you and slit your throat, from ear to ear.'

'From where to where?' the guard asked, puzzled.

Giggles erupted from our group. Grandad reached back and pushed Digger's face, shooing him away.

'From one ear to the other ear.' He drew his finger across his throat. 'Around the front, just in case that's not obvious.'

'Oh, from ear to ear. I always wondered what that meant. That's a good plan. A very good plan.' He straightened himself and pushed out his chest. 'Of course, yeh know it would never work.'

'Why not?' said Grandad, sighing.

'I'm too smart to fall for a trick like that,' said the sentry.

'I know that,' said Grandad, slapping him on the shoulder as we walked past, stifling our laughter as we delivered a salute.

'Outstanding work, young man,' said Digger, 'absolutely outstanding.'

Buoyed by the flattery, the guard dropped back into action stance.

'Who goes there?' he shouted into the night, ready to thrust his bayonet into the next intruder.

WHAT WAS THAT?

There it was again, a knock at the back door.

'Who goes there?' I asked Grandad.

The album was forgotten.

'Well, there's a standard procedure for situations like this,' he said, sarcasm dribbling down his chin.

'What? Wait for Gran to get it?' I said, wishing I'd meant it as a joke.

'It'll be you who's getting it if you're not careful.' He shook his bony fist at me.

'Harry?' Gran's voice pierced the stand-off. 'Your mates are here.'

'I didn't know you'd got any,' Grandad chuckled.

In the absence of a witty reply, I poked my tongue out at him. It was a feeble move, but it made my point.

'See yeh later,' he said. 'Don't do anything I wouldn't do.'

I reckoned that meant I could do anything I wanted, as long as the cops didn't catch me.

Keith and Mark stood at the back door looking suspicious. I glanced inside, knowing Gran would pick up on it, too, but she'd gone to check up on Grandad. I grabbed my coat and struggled to close the door as my arm got snagged in the sleeve. Keith was bursting to tell me something, but he contained his eagerness until we rounded the corner.

'We've got some paper and some matches.' He shook the box like a maraca. 'We're going to do the bull roar at the Legion.'

'Let's wait until it gets proper dark,' I said, looking up at the greying horizon.

We wandered round to the club steps. It was always a good place to find other kids. It gave you a clear view of the club car park and the street, so anyone other kids playing out would be spotted.

It didn't take long for more kids to turn up and organise a game of kick can. We took our place in the lower ranks, the older lads doing the organising. When we started there were about twenty of us and we were the youngest. A brother and sister sat on the club steps watching, clutching a bag of crisps each, two bottles of fizzy orange beside them. Their dad would no doubt be popping out from time to time to check they were okay. We gathered in an open space at the entrance to the garages, still illuminated by the sodium floodlights of the club car park.

We formed a circle and everyone put a foot in the centre, creating a tight formation. Nige Parkinson took on the responsibility of selector and knelt in the middle. His fingertip bounced from shoe to shoe in time with the rhyme.

'Dip, dip, dip, my blue ship . . .'

One by one, we were excluded until Glyn Redmond was declared 'it'. The limits of the game were set – no one was allowed to go beyond the club car park, the betting shop or the end of the garages. The can was set down and one of the bigger lads hoofed it into the gloom. Everyone scattered when Glyn found the can and set it down. The game was on.

I ran to the far end of the arena. The corrugated metal rattled all around as bodies banged into the ramshackle buildings. I turned sideways and shuffled between two garages, stumbling over bits of wood and brick as glass crunched under my feet. The smell of oil rose from the disturbed debris. I pushed myself against the wall as car headlights swept across the car park. Feeling my way, I shuffled into the darkness. Whispering voices brought me to a halt.

'Piss off, Manning. Don't come down here.'

Other voices giggled at the unnecessary aggression as I shuffled away from them. I crouched down at the exposed end of my hideout; if a car came now, I'd be done.

Glyn's lone figure walked towards me, checking each passageway, wary of leaving the can unattended. At any time, someone could emerge from the shadows, kick the can and reset the game.

He shouted out names and locations and the group of 'the got' grew as he worked his way in my direction. I was a sitting duck. Something spooked him and he ran back to the can. I made a move and ran out of my hiding spot to the outer edge of the garage complex, in full view of the procession of cars arriving for the Saturday night entertainment at the club. I crept round the backs of the garages as Glynn made his way down the centre towards the far end. I stuck my head round each garage, trying to see him.

There he was. We were moving in opposite directions. I was getting closer to the can.

As I approached the last garage, my heartbeat quickened as I ducked down and ran. Puddles flashed under my feet, reflecting the car park spotlights. I rounded the end of the last garage, increasing my speed as I passed the group in jail, swooping round the corner and kicking the can high in the air as I shouted, 'Kick can!'

The group in jail ran for cover and I continued on, finding a spot round the back of the betting shop. The game continued, kids joining and leaving. Escape and capture. Freedom and prison. I got tagged and stood in jail with Keith and some others.

There was a disturbance – angry voices multiplied. The game was abandoned as we all made our way to see what was happening. Two groups faced each other on the road to the car park. They were all in their twenties, shouting and swearing. A group of older men standing on the club steps looked on, powerless to prevent the conflict. The two young kids sat on the bottom step, gripped by the unexpected entertainment. They gaped open-mouthed, their pop and crisps forgotten in the excitement.

The shouting and cursing came to nothing, and the two groups headed in opposite directions. The last of the committeemen flicked a cigarette butt expertly. It flew across the road like a meteor, landing in the hedge, then he returned to his pint. Our group dissipated until it was just the three of us.

We hung around the club steps with the young brother and sister. Their dad popped out to check on them and deliver more fizzy orange and crisps. When the flow of people into the club slowed, we made our way to the car park where the tallest of the drainpipes were. We huddled around the grate. Mark opened his coat and pulled the newspaper from under his jumper. We pushed the sheets of paper up inside the cast iron drainpipe, careful not to compact it too much or it wouldn't light. The trick was to get enough paper up the pipe to make a fire that would burn long enough and fierce enough to create the bullroarer effect. Nobody knew how it worked, but we all knew it did.

Keith's first three attempts to strike a match failed, the ends breaking off and fizzling out in the grate. Mark and I tutted with disapproval and I looked around to make sure we hadn't attracted unwanted attention. The coast was clear as the fourth match did its job.

Instinct told us it was going to work and we stood up and backed away, our eyes glued to the roofline. Sure enough, the smoke emerged and the drone of the bullroarer started. Steady at first, it built quickly.

We ran to the back of the car park and into the fields beyond the reach of the floodlights. The roar filled the air as if it were coming from a low-flying aircraft. The curtains of the club were pulled aside and faces peered upwards. We stayed hidden long after the noise had stopped, then made our way across the playing fields, speculating on the cause of the conflict outside the club, happy with our night's work.

Some older lads sat on a bench drinking. We emerged from the dark to congratulations on our prank. We took the praise and a swig of cider, the sharp bitterness making me screw up my face. Keith refused the offer, but Mark guzzled it like a baby holding its bottle.

'Take it steady, young 'un,' said one of the lads. 'That's got to last us all night.'

We left them to it and wandered off. Laughter erupted in the darkness behind us when Mark let out an outrageous burp. Then he let out smaller aftershocks under each lamp post to mark our progress down the street. We parted outside the Legion, the sound of the band rising and falling into the night as the doors opened and closed.

I locked the front door and walked through the dark hallway. Canned laughter from the TV was a poor substitute for my mates' company. I hesitated outside the living room before shouting goodnight.

Once I was sure Gran wasn't coming out, I opened the sideboard door, reached past the bottles of sherry and advocaat, and grabbed the rum bottle, holding it as though it were an unexploded bomb. I took it up to my room, moving around in the dark, my eyes having grown accustomed to the night. The moonlight spilt in through the open curtains as I sat on the edge of the bed and ran my finger over the image of the woman's profile on the bottle.

There were murmurs of disapproval from Pickering as the screw cap gave way with gritty resistance and powder fell onto my hand.

'Do you think this is a good idea, Harry?'

The crystallised sugar reflected the moonlight on my skin.

He sniffed. 'Like the other drunken sailors, we'll find out what to do with you "early in the morning".'

Pleased with his joke, his sarcastic chuckle faded as I returned to the *Hood*.

I RESTED ON MY ELBOW and thumbed the caulking between the planks of the deck. Jonesy handed out a bottle of Old Nick to each man as I looked up at the gun barrels of Y turret high above me.

'What's Harry drinking, Jack?'

'He can have a nip if he wants.'

Each of us nursed a bottle as Connie asked, 'What's the toast?'

'To wives and girlfriends,' said Digger.

'Wives and girlfriends,' they all sang out, although I had neither.

'May they never meet,' concluded Jonesy.

He winked at me and I smiled at the old gag Grandad had told a thousand times. The sugar around the neck of the bottle was a false indication of what was to come as I took a swig. I managed to stifle the first wave of coughing, but the second escaped, along with the rum, in a fine spray that covered everyone.

'Oh, what a waste,' said Connie.

'Terrible, terrible waste,' said Grandad.

'Did yeh see him? He erupted like a depth charge,' Connie said in wonder, sending everyone into hysterics.

I'd regained my composure by the time they'd stopped laughing. The second sip was better, in as much as I was able to drink it. This actually turned out to be even worse; the searing heat from the rum burnt my mouth, throat and stomach. A few moments later, as the men laughed and joked about the brawl from earlier, I could feel the rum's heat spreading through my body.

The rum softened the hard timber deck as I gazed at the moon, high behind the clouds, each edged with its own rainbow glow. The huge gun barrels were silhouetted against the sky. The voices of the sailors mingled, as natural as the moon and clouds, rising and falling like the sea, the bonds between them as solid as the welded steel that made the ship. I played the day's events through in my mind, smiling to myself, my mind spinning off into oblivion.

Chapter 12

Sunday, 30 March 1975

I gripped the edge of the bed to steady myself as the waves rolled under the ship, lifting my head, my stomach and then my legs as my head fell into the next trough. The liquid in my belly sloshed around, hitting the sides and rebounding – a confused sea that washed into my throat. Sitting brought momentary relief, but as I closed my eyes, a wave of nausea threatened to smash me onto the rocks. My head pounded and my body shuddered as the throbbing of the engine reverberated around the room. Breathing in time with the flexing of the walls, I made my way downstairs, kicking the near-empty rum bottle across the deck.

LEANING ON THE LANDING windowsill, I rested my forehead on the cold glass and watched Dr Crowther sitting in his Rover for a long time. The V8 engine pulsated at just the wrong frequency for my head. A blip of throttle sent a cloud of fumes into the dull grey morning and the car pulled away. I'd always hated Sundays.

I went down to the bathroom. Leaning heavily on the sink, I splashed cold water on my face, turning away from the judgement of my reflection. Before I had a chance to escape back to my room the kitchen door slid open. A waft of burned toast escaped and my stomach churned in protest at the unwelcome intrusion.

'Harry, take this to your grandad, will you?'

I avoided her gaze and took the mug without speaking, unsure what noise might come out.

'Are you okay, love?'

'Yeah,' I croaked. 'I think I've got a cold,' I lied, turning away.

Grandad sat in bed looking at the photo album.

'Morning, shipmate. Is that for me?'

I put the mug on the bedside table, avoiding the bucket next to the bed that Gran had brought in to save him the trip to the loo.

He sniffed the tea. 'How about we make this "special tea", H?'

I went to get the bottle of rum from my room and handed it over. Grandad looked at the level of the liquid. The lady on the bottle turned away.

'Good night was it, H?'

I swallowed the sickness as it tried to escape.

'What about a bit of fresh air?' he suggested, pointing at the window.

I WALKED TO THE RAIL and looked over the stern. The sea was flat, the air still and cool. The flag hung limp at the stern. My stomach cramped, the sour taste of rum reactivated as my mouth filled with saliva, preparing the way for the inevitable. I vomited, the foul liquid splashing down the side of the ship. The pounding in my head increased as wave after wave of cramps swept through me until I was on my knees, but still it didn't stop. I thought I was going to pass out. I couldn't breathe, each wave of cramps lasting longer. My mouth hung open, saliva pouring out and dripping into the sea.

The retching continued long after my stomach was empty, my body determined to eject every scrap of its rotten contents.

It was over.

My head rested on the rail as I cried, spitting out the bile as Grandad stroked my back and head.

'Better out than in, H,' he said.

I stood up and looked around. The water, disturbed by a breeze, darkened. White horses galloped towards us. The ensign cracked in the freshening wind. I looked at Grandad as he gazed out to sea.

'Looks like there's a storm brewing.'

GRANDAD'S THIN ARM pulled me close, the bones of his chest sticking into my shoulder. He leaned on the windowsill next to me, his backbone visible through his pyjamas. The bottoms hung around his waist, his rounded shoulders blending with the curve of his spine. My head hung out through the open window, the breeze ruffling the curtains beside me.

'There's going to be a few jobs for you to do in the garden, H. Spring has sprung. Are you up for some weeding? And that lilac tree will need trimming next winter, or Ron next door will have something to say. There's some lettuce and spring onions to go in as well, and all the seedlings in the greenhouse to plant out.' He turned to me. 'Can you do all that, H?'

'I think so. You've shown me often enough.'

'Very good. You have been paying attention, haven't you,' he winked as he turned to sit on the bed.

I closed the window and helped him back into bed, lifting his legs as he lay back against the stack of pillows. His hand rested on the photo album like a witness swearing an oath in court.

'Why don't you make a start now? A bit of fresh air will do you the world of good.'

I emptied the sickly contents down the loo, rinsed the bucket clean of the foulness and stumbled into the garden. I spent an hour stabbing the weeds around the roses with the hoe. The sickness was lessening, each wave of nausea that swept through me less violent than the last.

The wooden handle slipped through my weak, sweaty grip. I could feel blisters forming at the base of each thumb, but I continued without taking precautions to stop them from worsening. Glancing at the living room window, I was unsure how to take Grandad's lack of interest. A bit of recognition for my heroics would have been appreciated, but at the same time, I didn't want there to be witnesses to my half-arsed efforts. Even Gran wasn't bothered. In the old world, I'd have been asked if I wanted anything to eat, two or three times. Did she know I wasn't feeling so good? Probably. Everyone knew more than me.

The smell in the moist, warm greenhouse didn't help my mood. Like those men in the movies, held prisoner by some despot, trapped in the fever-rich atmosphere of the Black Hole of Calcutta, I feared it would drive me mad. I checked if Grandad was watching before I opened the windows to increase the airflow. A little fresh air might do the plants good, too.

Soon after, fearful that I might have overdone it, I closed them, swearing at the seedlings as the temperature rose. It had been on the news – Prince Charles talked to his plants. I wondered what he'd make of my tirade of abuse at having to suffer the unreasonable heat that they enjoyed. Surely a plant didn't know what you were saying . . . Is it just the tone that soothes or upsets them? And what the bloody hell did a plant have to get upset about, anyway? What was it like for dogs? Did they understand the actual words? Or would anything that you said in a friendly voice be well received?

'Who's an ugly bugger, hey? You are. Yes, you are, you fat little sod!'

Too late, I looked over my shoulder. Gran offered me a mug and a plate of biscuits.

'Everything okay, love?'

'I'm fine, Gran, thanks.'

Please go.

She must have decided to let me off, as she returned to the house without giving me a lecture.

I took a sip of tea. Wow. I think it had four sugars in it. Maybe I did like it sweet, after all.

Not yet, but I could feel it building – it wasn't going to be long before I was starving.

I teased out the first of two dozen sprout plants with a lolly stick. The issue of the abundance of lolly sticks still needed to be raised with him. I was glad I'd got something to occupy my mind and body.

I checked on Grandad, keen to start a new adventure, but he was sleeping. Gran was dozing in the chair next to him, the TV playing to itself, the sound turned low.

Learning from previous mistakes, at last, I only half filled an oversize Pyrex bowl with stew and took it up to my room.

'Jesus Christ!' said Pickering. 'Are you going to eat all that?'

'This is just my starter,' I told him between slurps.

I closed my eyes after each mouthful. This could be the best stew in the world, ever. Lowering myself onto the pillow so as not to agitate my distended stomach, I let the top 20 drift over me as I fell into a deep sleep.

'Night night, you greedy bugger,' said Pickering.

Chapter 13

Monday, 31 March 1975

I peeped through the crack in the door. The curtains were closed and the dim glow of the bedside lamp only seemed to emphasise the gloom. Dr Crowther stood beside the bed watching as Grandad tried to push himself up against the pillows. My fists clenched and I willed him to find the strength. The doctor took his arm to help, but Grandad shrugged him off and continued to struggle. Gritting his teeth and swearing, he managed to sit up. Exhausted, his chest rose in sharp shallow breaths.

As I watched Grandad struggle, my heartbeat raced so loud I felt sure everyone in the house might hear it. I tried to calm my own breathing, but each time I held my breath, my gasps for air only undid any benefit.

The doctor wrapped the blood pressure cuff around Grandad's thin arm and pumped the small rubber sphere. He made notes in a small black book then moved his stethoscope around Grandad's chest as if unsure where to find his heartbeat. He used a small torch to look into Grandad's eyes, flashing it into and away from each eye, trying to catch it by surprise. With deliberate, unhurried action, the doctor placed the torch into his breast pocket before removing the stethoscope. He folded the rubber tube and placed it in his bag.

Gently clearing his throat, he said, 'You know I'm not here to mislead you, Jack. Your blood pressure is low and your lung capacity is well below what we'd expect at this stage.'

Grandad stared straight ahead, avoiding looking at him.

'You know what's happening, but I think things are moving faster than we'd expected.'

Grandad bit his lip. 'So what does that mean?' His harsh voice clashed with the doctor's calm tone.

'It means you've got to take it easy, and you've got to take these . . .' He tapped his finger on the cap of the pill bottle. 'You need to get plenty of rest, Jack,' he said, placing the bottle on the bedside table.

'There will be plenty of time for resting . . .' Grandad coughed, 'later on, won't there?'

'Jack, it's important not to get stressed.'

'Stressed!' Grandad snorted. He pointed his finger at the doctor. 'Don't tell me about stress.' He spat the words into the doctor's face, but another coughing fit interrupted him. 'I'll do what I bloody well want.' His hand dropped back to the bed and his body seemed to sink into the stack of pillows.

'This isn't helping, Jack.'

'What will help, eh?'

The doctor didn't answer but produced a small vial of liquid from his bag, loaded into a syringe. Grandad didn't protest or even acknowledge what the man was doing as Dr Crowther pushed the needle into him. I rubbed my forearm.

'That should make you more comfortable, Jack,' he said, packing his tools back into his battered bag. He stood up and snapped it shut. 'I'll pop in again tomorrow. Try to get some rest. I'll write another prescription, something to help you sleep.' He paused, but Grandad didn't look at him.

I backed away from the door and went upstairs. Dr Crowther joined Gran in the kitchen and I strained to listen to their muted conversation. I looked through the landing window as the Rover pulled away, watching the fumes from his exhaust evaporate, trying to focus on the last fragments long after the car had disappeared.

I sat on the lower steps and gripped the balustrade like a prisoner. Gran fussed around in the hall as she put on her coat. I looked past her into their improvised bedroom. Grandad was sat up, the effects of the injection already brightening his features.

'Jack,' said Gran, 'remember what the doctor told you about taking it easy.'

I stepped past her and hovered in the doorway between them.

'I'll be back as soon as I can,' she said.

'Don't rush, Lily, I'll be fine.' He winked at me. 'Won't we, H?'

I looked at Gran, but she was fumbling with her purse and handkerchief. She picked up her shopping bag and left, still muttering concern as she closed the door.

'Right,' said Grandad, 'give me a hand to get ready, H.'

'Where are we going?' I couldn't believe he intended to get up after all that with the doctor and then Gran.

'We're going to the allotment.' He struggled, pushing himself forwards.

'What about what the doctor said?'

He paused. 'Oh, you overheard that, did you.' His tone made it clear he disapproved of my snooping. His legs flopped out of bed. 'Well, like I've said before, they don't know what they're on about. Now, help me get my togs on. If we act sharpish, we'll be back before Gran gets home.'

After a struggle, I got him dressed. At least he was co-operating with me – I wouldn't want to have done it against his will.

We stood at the top of the drive, both wrapped up in our coats and thoughts. A thick layer of frost covered the world, the thin veneer helping to mask the ugly edges of the council estate.

'I can't stay cooped up, H.'

Grandad's tone had softened now he'd got his way, his grip tightening on my hand each time his stick slipped on the frosty pavement. My woollen gloves creaked under the pressure from his old leather ones. I scanned the pavement ahead for hazards as we weaved between frozen dog turds and the odd pile of fresh muck, still steaming. We'd never been dog owners and sights like that made it seem less likely we ever would be.

There were a few more people around as we passed the shops and our pace slowed to a stuttered crawl as Grandad stopped to chat with everyone he saw. I stomped around and flailed my arms, trying to keep warm as he chatted away, unaffected by his freezing surroundings. Kids shouted as they were released from class for morning break. My mates would be sliding up and down on the frozen paths. They knew why I wasn't there; I was going to have a few days off until Grandad got better. Others might be speculating about my absence and some wouldn't even notice. The shrieks from the playground would soon turn to groans. Mr Richardson, the caretaker, a man who took great pleasure in bringing any fun to a premature end, would be out throwing grit salt onto any patch of enjoyment before the dinner bell rang.

We crossed over the road and down 'the bumpy lane', a steep dirt track that twisted down to the allotments. Half-exposed boulders peppered the lane, their tops showing the battle scars of contact with the underbellies of cars driven by the careless or stupid. They were another favoured distraction when we were out riding our bikes, providing natural ramps to leap over. But caution was needed. Beyond the allotments, the neighbouring estate held unknown dangers and plenty of known ones.

The gate to the allotments was an old door, its paint peeling off in small brittle pieces, the kind that pierced the skin under your nail when the urge to pick at it overwhelmed you. I looked back at it, reluctant to leave any good edges unexplored as Grandad dragged me with him down the narrow path between tall wild hedges, bramble and elderberry, the occasional silver birch sapling poking through. A small gate led us through the hedge to Grandad's plot.

I held his gloves as he wrestled with the padlock on the shed. The hideaway was made from a collection of old doors and window frames, stretching the full width of the allotment. One end was a solid structure of brick, but as it had been extended, the quality of construction had deteriorated to a hotchpotch of scavenged material. The door creaked open and I followed him in.

Grandad wasted no time and started to gather newspapers to start a fire in the pot-bellied stove that was a focal point for the allotment holders nearby. Smoke would attract attention. Like Sitting Bull gathering his warriors, the crowd would assemble and wagons would circle.

The fire crackled into life and I shut the stove's sooty door. The airflow whistled gently through the vents and flames swirled behind the smoky glass. Grandad set about tidying things.

'Give me a hand, H. We need to get these pots ready for the seedlings in the greenhouse. That lot over there need cleaning...' He pointed at a huge stack of plastic pots and handed me a small brush. 'Stack them in that box over there when you've finished. At least if we make the mess in here, we won't get into trouble with Gran.'

'We?' I questioned. 'It's you who'll be getting into bother when Gran finds out you sneaked off.'

'I thought we were in this together.'

'Not if it means being put on short rations or short reins by Gran. What's that thing you say?'

'All for one and one for all?' he offered. 'Like the Musketeers?' He picked up his stick to parry my questioning.

'No, the other one. Er...'

'Every man for himself?'

'That's the one,' I exclaimed, pointing the brush at him.

A figure passed behind the cobwebs on the window. Moments later, the imposing figure of Joe Sefton stooped through the door, clutching his old canvas pit bag, continuing the habit of a lifetime by carrying his sandwiches in his snap tin.

'Now then! How are we?'

'Champion, Joe. Take a pew.'

Joe was halfway to sitting before the invitation was offered. No one seemed concerned about the order in which things were done. It was like a dustier version of Alice in Wonderland at the mad hatter's tea party. The wooden stool groaned under Joe's weight as he hitched it across the concrete floor to claim the next best spot near the fire. Grandad took out a thermos flask from his overcoat pocket. Joe did the same. The two men sat in silence, nursing their drinks as we all stared at the fire.

'What have you been up to, Joe?' Grandad asked.

Joe listed dozens of tiny jobs. It would have been easier and more accurate if he'd simply admitted he'd done nothing.

I left them to it and made a start on the pots, tapping each on the side of the barrow first to dislodge old compost and spiders before brushing them out and sticking them in the box beside me. The spiders took a while to figure out their only escape route was at the front of the barrow, where the gentler slope allowed them to gain purchase on the rusty metal, disappearing over the edge, abseiling down on their web to set up home elsewhere. I kept tuning in to the conversation back at the stove, but it was all gardeners' talk. When to plant out the peas, the best way to get rid of aphids.

'Burn the little bastards,' according to Joe.

We packed up to leave, then I lifted the box of pots and took it outside. As I placed the box on a bench, I found a fat spider staring at me from the back of my hand. I shook it onto the ground, but before it could find cover, a robin swooped down to claim it. The robin waited and cocked its head as if to ask, 'any more?'

I checked the bottom of the box and under the flaps that formed the lid, exposing two more that I tried to flick towards the robin, without success. The bird flitted around in excited anticipation before losing patience with me and flying into a hole in our shed. I made a mental note to check for a nest the next time I came down.

The sun was forcing its way through the cloud and patches of frost had melted where its rays had reached. Grandad locked up and we looked at the bare earth that he'd dug over in January – all plans for further action abandoned until he was better. Halfway up the bumpy lane, the trees on either side of us keeping the sun away, he was telling me about the plans for the seedlings, when his stick slipped and he fell. I heard something snapping and presumed it was his stick. It turned out to be worse. Much worse.

Grandad lay still on the ground. A low groan came from deep inside him. I shook his shoulder, 'Grandad,' but he didn't react. I looked around and shouted for help, but there was no one in sight. The damp seeped into me as I knelt on the cold dirt. I had to do something quickly to get Grandad off the ground.

'Help!' I screamed again.

I knew I should have put up a fight and stopped him from leaving the house. Now look what had happened.

I had to let Gran know. But first I had to help him.

I shouted down the empty lane, hoping that Joe Sefton would hear me, but there was no one around. I ran to the junction with the main road, but that was deserted, too. I ran back to him. I took off my parka and put it over him, the cold immediately biting into me. Freezing, I began to tremble and cry. But I knew that wasn't going to help.

'Young man.' A woman's voice pierced the air. 'What's the matter? Can I help?'

I looked towards the houses that bordered one side of the lane. A bobble hat disappeared from view. For a moment I panicked, fearing they might think it a prank of some kind. Kids playing truant, bothering the nearby residents.

'Please help me,' I cried after them, trying to trace where they might be behind the hedge.

A moment later, the latch on the garden gate clicked and an old lady, a bit younger than Gran, joined me in the lane. She was well wrapped against the cold and her large gloves held a pair of secateurs. She bustled towards me like an emergency Womble. She took one look at Grandad.

'I'll call an ambulance.' She turned away. 'Follow me, young man. I'll give you something to keep him warm.'

I followed the old lady into the house. As she put the receiver down, she threw two jackets at me.

'You take one and put the other over your grandad. I'll fetch some blankets.'

I stood paralysed.

'Go on.' She shooed me out. 'And keep talking to him; he can still hear you,' she said as she disappeared into a cupboard under the stairs.

I ran back to Grandad. Putting the coat over him, I told him what was happening, reassuring us both that everything was going to be okay.

She returned with blankets and I suggested we try to roll Grandad on top of them so he wasn't lying on the ground, but she warned me that if he'd hurt his back and we moved him, we might make it worse.

'I was taught that in my ATS training. Don't worry, I'll make sure the ambulance men look after him.'

Despite her warning, I tried to push the blankets under him with the flat of my hand, partially succeeding.

She asked our names and introduced herself as Mary Wilkinson. Then she told me about her time in the ATS and her husband, who'd died of a heart attack last winter, doing her best to keep my mind occupied. But she could tell she was losing the fight. Time slowed to a standstill.

'Why don't you go to the top of the lane and let them know where we are?'

Glad of something to do, I skidded up the dirt track.

'Careful, Harry, we don't want two casualties,' she shouted after me.

I slowed my pace, a little, and stood panting next to the road, the cold air burning my lungs, my eyes glued on the farthest point I could see in the direction of town. Some drivers looked at me as they passed, puzzled by my tearful stares, but nobody stopped to ask what was wrong. Would I stop if I were them? How busy were people if they didn't have time to help? My tears dried as I waited and my frustration turned to anger as I shouted at the passing vehicles.

'What are you looking at?'

After what seemed like hours, a blue light appeared round the corner, the siren's volume slowly rising until it filled the air around me. When it got closer I waved, pointing down the lane with my other hand, gesturing for them to slow down for fear of them smashing their suspension on the hump-backed obstacles. The deafening siren was muted as the driver made the turn, slowing to a crawl on the rough terrain. The blue light reflected on the foliage of the hedge despite the filtered sunlight.

I gave the ambulance crew the information they asked for and Mrs Wilkinson promised to ring Aunty Joyce to get a message to Gran.

They strapped Grandad onto the bed, the engine fired up and ambulance backed out onto the road. I felt queasy from the lurching motion as the ambulance wobbled over the rough lane. The ambulance man spotted my mood and told me to look out of the window. Not as easy as it sounds – the windows were a bit too high for me to see anything other than the trees whizzing past. If anything, it made me feel worse. I swallowed hard and shuffled up to the back door, bracing myself as my stomach took the corners a second later than my brain.

Grandad lurched around, the restraining straps biting into the red blanket. The oxygen mask steamed up with each breath. I looked around the ambulance, the frugal workman-like interior making no compromise to fashion or style. Like the *Hood*, everything was there for a reason.

I imagined cars pulling over to let the ambulance past before peeling back into the road in our wake as we sped through the town. After some short, sharp turns, we came to a stop. The ambulance doors opened from the outside. I was still regaining my senses as the nurse beckoned me out. Standing aside under the canopy, the large 'emergency' sign only added to my anxiety. The dull grey stone of the hospital exterior looked unable to contain the bright, sanitised interior.

I followed the trolley as the ambulance crew wheeled Grandad into accident and emergency. They lifted him onto another bed and the nurse raised the sides, locking them in place. I stood by his bed, gripping the metal guard rail. Moans from other emergency admissions filtered through the flimsy curtaining that separated the examination cubicles. I held his cold hand, willing him to fight, feeling the frailty of him, knowing it was a battle he could win.

Nurses and a doctor swarmed around him, pushing me aside as I struggled to keep hold of his hand. I looked at the wall of bodies between us. A warm hand took mine and I looked up at a friendly face.

'They're looking after him now. Come with me.'

The nurse took me away and asked me lots of questions. I was embarrassed when I didn't know Grandad's date of birth, but she assured me that people forget all sorts of things in stressful situations.

I sat in a seating area next to the intensive care ward, nursing a cup of tea until it was cold. There weren't any potted plants to pour it in, so I gulped it down. Grandad always told me to finish my drinks.

'If you don't finish it, they'll think you're not bothered and they might not ask you again.'

When Gran arrived, she bombarded me with more questions I didn't know the answers to. She soon realised 'I don't know' was the *only* thing I knew. The friendly nurse had shown me a kitchen we could use, so as tradition insisted, I made Gran a cup of tea. We sat together and watched the cup tremble on the saucer in her unsteady grip.

I looked around the waiting room. It reminded me of the hotel we'd stayed at in Falmouth in Cornwall. Chairs lined the wall with an inadequate number of coffee tables positioned just out of reach. Other families sat huddled together, speaking in anxious whispers, all hoping for the best and fearing the worst.

After hours of waiting, the ward sister arrived.

'If you could follow me,' she said in a brisk but not unfriendly tone. 'The consultant would like to see you in his office.'

She steered us down a twisting corridor, halting and knocking on an anonymous grey door. Gerald. H. Greaves, Consultant Neurologist, was engraved on a black plastic plaque. We stepped into a different world. The office looked like the library of a country manor. I looked down as we stepped in, surprised by the deep pile carpet. Wainscotting lined the walls and a large globe that looked suspiciously like it could be hiding a selection of booze sat in the corner. Shelves were filled with books, crammed into every space. Had he read all these? It seemed like a lifetime's work in itself.

The country manor décor was split open like a film set and one wall was dedicated to the practicalities of biology. It looked out of character with the rest of the room. The wall was painted white and medical equipment intruded into the oak oasis. A large frosted glass panel was framed with steel and the rest of the wall was made up of a collection of posters Alice Cooper himself would have been proud to own, illustrating body parts in various stages of dissection. A full-size skeleton stood in the corner.

I imagined a secret button, perhaps behind a book. At the flick of a switch, the wall would rotate, revealing the villain's lair behind. The wall would continue to rotate until the room was back to normal, the secret room hidden once again behind ancient portraits whose eyes followed you around the room.

The man sat behind the desk was busy writing. He wore a navy blue three-piece suit – now I was sure the globe contained the booze – with a pink tie and three pens stuck out of the breast pocket of his immaculate white shirt. He had a bald patch in the centre of his head.

'Mrs Manning to see you, sir.'

'Thank you, Sister,' he said without looking up.

I turned to watch the sister leave. A white coat that hung behind the door billowed out. Like a ghost whose timing was off, rushing to escape, it flopped back in disappointment as the door shut. Better luck next time.

He was still writing and hadn't acknowledged us yet, so Gran pointed to one of the chairs and sat in the other. The doctor looked up.

'Er . . . oh . . . sorry, yes, er, take a seat, please.' He scribbled a signature, sat back and looked at us. 'I need to discuss the treatment and prognosis for . . .' He picked up a file of papers. 'For Mr Manning, but I . . .' He paused and shuffled. 'I, er . . . I'm not sure it's appropriate to discuss it in front of the child.' He glanced my way.

Gran looked at me as if she wasn't sure if it was me he was talking about.

'Harry's been through quite a lot, Doctor, he'll be fine.' She glanced my way. 'He's tougher than he looks.'

The doctor looked as unconvinced as I was and was just about to say so, when Gran added, 'He's staying here with me.'

'Well, if you're sure . . .'

'I am,' Gran said, a little too quickly.

The doctor resigned himself to presenting his diagnosis to a kid and continued.

'I've been examining Mr Manning's X-rays.' He stood, a brown folder in his hands, and walked across to the frosted window, where he flicked a switch on the side. The neon tubes inside stuttered to life and he jammed the X-rays under metal clips. 'As you can see, Mr Manning has suffered a complicated fracture to his pelvis.'

We both followed his forefinger as he pointed out the gaps between bones.

'It will require extensive surgery.' He turned to face us. 'Unfortunately, he also sustained a head injury, which we are still assessing. We won't be able to operate until we've established the extent of the damage.' He paused, leaning forwards. 'Considering Mr Manning's existing condition, I think you need to prepare for . . .'

Jumping up, I ran, leaving the door open for the ghost to escape, too. I ran through corridors, bumping into staff and visitors, Gran's voice echoing after me. I ran to the only place I knew where she couldn't find me.

The small bolt slid easily into place. I lifted my feet and hugged my legs, so no one could see me under the door.

I'd seen Grandad fight – he could fight anybody. Nothing could stop him.

Someone came in. Tentative footsteps approached. Each cubical was opened, creaking in the echo chamber that was the toilets. The footsteps stopped when they reached the one I was hiding in.

'Harry?' the friendly nurse said.

I stayed silent, denying the obvious truth.

'Harry'—I could feel her touching the door—'you need to come out. We've . . . It's not long before you'll have to go home.'

I slid the lock and stepped out. She put her arm around my shoulder and we walked close together back to the waiting room and a more vigorous hug from Gran. We made our way to see Grandad, walking past all the other rooms, each playing out another family's nightmare.

He was lying flat on the bed, tubes and pipes going into his mouth and nose.

Standing next to the bed, I held the steel rail that ran along the side. There was a yellow stain on the back of his hand where the needle entered the vein, held in place by tape. I touched his arm; the skin was cool and clammy.

Gran sobbed. 'Oh, Jack,' was all she could say.

We sat beside his bed for hours in two vinyl chairs, low but comfortable. As I sank into the seat, I realised these weren't like the ones in the wards; these were meant for people who were staying for long periods, for families with loved ones they didn't want to leave alone. People like us. The tension and fatigue drained from my body as the day's events took their toll. As afternoon turned to evening, the more I tried to stay awake, the more I wanted to sleep. Eventually, I succumbed.

'WHERE ARE WE?' I ASKED Grandad.

The featureless grey sky hung heavy above the low land that surrounded us on all sides.

'Scapa Flow.' The words had a weight out of proportion to the number of letters. 'The Orkney Islands, just off the tip of Northern Scotland,' he confirmed.

There were ships of all shapes and sizes anchored around us. Auxiliary boats looked like toys as they scurried through the still water, the neat vee of their wakes expanding behind them, interlacing with others before they dissipated on the shore.

'It's like a lake,' I said.

Kicking myself for saying such nonsense, Grandad chuckled.

He explained its importance to the navy. It was the biggest and best natural harbour in the north. The place where the fleet rested and restocked the ships before heading out again to protect the Atlantic convoys bringing food and supplies from America.

He pointed to the north. 'The Bismarck *is out there somewhere. We're ready for a fight, but I'm not sure we're ready enough.'*

I felt the words fermenting inside me, bubbling up beyond my control to stop the foolishness that spilled out.

'What is enough, Grandad?' I said leaning on the rail, unable to look at him for embarrassment.

But the mickey-taking didn't come.

'Hmm,' he sighed.

I glanced at him, but he was focusing on something far away.

'What is enough?' He contemplated some more as a breeze whistled through the antenna of the Hood. *'That's the art of it, H, knowing what is enough.'*

We stood still in a space that was intimate and infinite at the same time.

'When something happens, and it's your job to deal with it, you have to decide what's enough.'

That seemed to make it easy. When I was fed up with doing my homework, I could just say I'd done enough and stop. Of course, he wasn't going to let me off so lightly.

'But . . .'

Ah! Here it comes.

'But you can't fool yourself, H. Although plenty try,' he said, huffing the last words with undisguised contempt. 'You can tell yourself you did enough, you can tell yourself there weren't any options left. But if you're going to do that, H, you'd better be sure you're right.' He turned towards me, leaning on his elbow. 'Because if you're wrong, it's going to stay with you forever. You'll be able to kid others, you'll be able to kid yourself, but at some point, probably when it's too late to do anything about it, you'll know.

'There was more I could have done, but I didn't.' He swallowed something hard. 'After your mum died and your dad started drinking too much, I didn't do enough.' He relaxed, the confession slipping into the water and lying like an oil slick, thick and hazardous. 'I always think about the way he told us your mum had died.' He was close to tears. 'My little girl, dying on her own in hospital, nobody there to hold her hand. I could have done more. I should have been there.' He composed himself, swallowing the bitter memories. 'I never forgave him and when he needed my help, well . . .' The confession went unsaid.

'What about Gran?'

'I don't think either of us did enough, but that's the other thing to be aware of, Harry.'

I always knew it was serious when he used my full name.

'Just worry about yourself – that'll give you plenty to go at. Whether or not other people did enough is not for you to decide. Other people work in different ways. What's easy for some is impossible for others. But that's what I'm saying. You know your own limit. You can't compare yourself to other people. You can't kid yourself and you can't hide from the truth.'

Again the words came out without thought. 'Did I do enough, Grandad? Could I have done more to help Dad?'

'I know this isn't what you want to hear, Harry.'

I'd always known I should have done something. I could have made a difference and now it was too late. Grandad bent on one knee and took *both of my hands. He looked me in the eye and I readied myself for the truth I'd always known.*

'You were just a kid, Harry. There was nothing you could have done.'

It couldn't be that simple. He read my mind.

'You've been through a lot, Harry, but you're still a kid. Don't wish it away. You'll grow up soon enough, then it'll be too late to be a kid any-more.'

More senseless questions poured out

'How will I know when I've grown up?'

'That's something else nobody can help you with. But don't worry, H, you'll know.' He stood up again. 'But this could be a good time for you to practice,' he said, pulling me close, 'just in case.'

The stillness of the sea added to my unease and I gripped the rail so hard my nails ached. The cold steel numbed my fingers, but the energy of the ship vibrated through me, reassuring, strong, like a sleeping beast. I looked up at him and reached for his hand. I could sense in him, like the Hood *and the sea, a power waiting to be unleashed. I shuddered at the thought.*

'Chilly, H?'

I was cold, but the chill that passed through me wasn't anything to do with that. I was glad he was on my side.

'Protected from the sea, but not from the wind, eh?' Grandad hugged himself, rubbing his arms. 'It's bloody freezing. Let's get inside and see if we can get a brew, shall we?'

Inside, the atmosphere was heavy with moisture and anticipation. Condensation ran down the walls, droplet connected to droplet until the momentum was unstoppable. We sat saturated in the nervous energy as the voice of Vera Lynn echoed around the mess. Men yawned in an over-ly casual way, making a show of their lack of concern. Others huddled in small groups playing strangely subdued card games while some wrote letters home.

A Military Police officer came up to the table.

'Are you Jack Manning?'

His manner wasn't unfriendly, but Grandad sensed a problem. The strain of waiting had everyone on edge.

'Yeah, what's up?' Grandad turned, scrutinising the man's face.

'The boss wants to see you.'

Grandad looked perplexed.

'What's the captain want to see me for?'

'It's not the captain, Jack, it's the admiral.'

Everyone in earshot turned their heads our way. The cogs turned in Grandad's head. He looked at the table and bit his lip. He was about to ask further questions, but the officer got there first.

'I've been told to escort you there.'

He waited a moment for us to comply. But Grandad stayed put.

'Now,' he said, his face hardening as his hand moved over his revolver, unclipping the retaining strap.

Grandad stood up. His chair scraped across the floor, like fingernails down a blackboard, as he pushed it back.

'And the boy,' said the MP.

Grandad realised the pointlessness of resisting.

'Lead the way,' he said.

'No, you lead the way, Jack. I'll make sure we all get there.'

Grandad huffed, took my hand and walked us to the Admiral's quarters. The grey steel walls of the Hood *continued until we stood outside the Admiral's cabin. Set into the steel wall was a wooden door. The MP knocked and stuck his head round the corner.*

'Jack Manning and his grandson are here, boss.'

Grandad looked at me.

I mouthed, 'Boss?'

Grandad shrugged his shoulders.

The MP stepped in and held the door open. We walked across the carpet and stood in front of the immense oak desk. The walls were lined with shelves of books and small lights with elaborate shades were dotted around, giving the place a warm, homely feel like a Victorian sitting room. The Admiral was writing in his journal. He blotted the ink and closed the red leather cover. He looked up.

'Take a seat,' he said in a casual, friendly voice.

Grandad did a smart salute. 'Yes, sir.'

The Admiral's thin lips smiled. His eyes were bright and sparkled with enthusiasm.

'There's no need for formality here, Jack. Sit down. Relax.'

We sat in the green leather chairs, but Grandad was anything but relaxed.

'Who's this young fellow then, Jack?' the Admiral asked as he held my gaze.

'It's my grandson, Harry.'

'Ah, yes.' He scratched his chin. 'Surname Manning?'

'Yes, sir.'

The Admiral looked at him.

'You can call me boss, or whatever it is lads call me when I'm not in earshot.' His smile broadened.

His attention dropped back to the journal on his desk. Opening it, he ran his finger over the pages. I looked at Grandad, but just received another shrug.

'No,' said the Admiral, 'there's no Harry Manning listed here.'

'He's with me, Adm . . . er, boss.'

Grandad wriggled uncomfortably at the informality.

'I know, Jack,' he said, 'but he's not supposed to be.' His smile faded. 'Is he?'

Grandad sat back and fidgeted with his beard. He rolled his top lip between his teeth. The gears in his mind were screaming now.

'Jack,' the Admiral said, 'do you know where you are?'

Grandad's mouth opened like he had the answer, but after several attempts, he gave up.

'This'—the Admiral's hand waved around—'this is what you wanted.' The Admiral sat back, happy that all was clear.

I looked for Grandad to explain, but he shook his head. His hands moved like he was playing with the pieces of a puzzle, trying to make the picture whole, unaware there were still bits missing. The Admiral stood and walked over to a large globe sat in a wooden frame, the surface of the world a rich umber, the antique varnish cracked and chipped. He beckoned us over. Spinning the globe absent-mindedly, it held us in a trance. He stopped it spinning and we jolted as the world stopped. The bookshelves loomed high above us.

'Where do you think we are, Jack?' asked the Admiral.

Grandad stepped forwards, rotating the globe to bring Britain into view. He placed his finger just above Scotland.

'Here,' he said, glad at being able to introduce some certainty.

The Admiral smiled again. It was getting annoying now.

'I don't mean where are you in space or time, Jack.'

Grandad was losing his patience with the game, but before he blew his top, the Admiral held up a finger.

'Allow me to explain.'

We both wanted answers. He removed a lock on the side of the globe and slid the top half open, like one of those illustrations in my geography textbooks, revealing not the Earth's molten core, but a control panel. He flicked a switch and the gigantic fireplace shuddered. The stone ground as it disappeared into the floor. Bright lights shone in from the other side of the wall. Another switch was activated and the wall split apart, sliding away to reveal an operating theatre, the green gowns of the staff the only colour in an otherwise white room. Someone lay on the operating table.

The Admiral moved forwards eagerly. We followed, coming to rest behind the surgeon. None of the theatre staff paid us any attention.

'Look,' said the Admiral. 'This man really knows what he's doing. Look at the work. Very neat. Very neat, indeed.'

Grandad leaned in, examining the patient. I tried to see what was happening through the wall of bodies. The steady pulse of the ventilator was punctuated as stainless steel instruments, glistening with blood, were dropped into a stainless steel bowl. I stood on tiptoe but still couldn't see anything.

'Can you see the problem, Jack?'

Grandad nodded.

'That clot is causing pressure here ...' The Admiral held his hand on the side of Grandad's head, just above his left ear. 'He's doing a sterling job, don't you think?'

Grandad didn't react.

'Of course, it's not going to help.'

I wriggled between them.

'The damage is already done, Jack.'

The patient was lying on his side, facing me, a tube in his mouth, tape over his eyes. A dribble of blood ran down from his scalp, through his grey hair and onto his grey beard. The old man lay completely still. I backed away.

'Do you see where you are now, Jack?' the Admiral asked.

Grandad nodded. Then almost whispered, 'I'll get him ashore before we set sail.'

I retreated into the Admiral's cabin. I ran to his desk and grabbed the leather-bound journal, spinning it round.

There were lists and lists of names. My fingers followed them. Each was marked with a date, but the dates were all the same: 06.00, 24 May 1941. Except for the last two. There was an entry for Midshipman William Dundas dated 1965. The last entry was for Able Seaman Jack Manning. The entry read 31 March 1975. I looked back at the theatre. Then I ran.

Grandad's voice echoed behind me, fading as I ran down the corridor. I went forward, to the place I knew I'd be able to hide. I sat still. There was always a hum from machinery inside the Hood, *generators, extraction and ventilation, workshops and winches. Despite the constant background noise, everyone was tuned to any changes. The rumble from the engines increased. They were getting ready to leave. It would still be a few hours yet, but this was the start of it. All I had to do was stay out of sight until we were out at sea, then it would be too late to put me ashore. The space was tight. I lifted my knees to my chin and waited.*

The ship shuddered. The Admiral had engaged the gears. We were on the move.

As the rumble of the engines increased, I imagined the ship moving between the islands that created our sanctuary. Grandad's voice came down the corridor, shouting my name. The door to the toilet block opened. I could hear him breathing heavily and I jumped as he kicked the cubicle doors open, getting closer with each crash.

'What the bloody hell's going on?' came a shout from close by.

Grandad moved towards the voice.

'Have you seen a young lad? He's thirteen.'

'I wouldn't tell you if I had. Now piss off.'

The door to the cubical was kicked off its hinges.

'What did you say?'

There was scuffling.

'Have you seen him?'

There was the smack of a fist and a cry, then more blows.

'Have you seen him or not?'

I peeped over the door as Grandad pulled the sailor out of the loo and threw him across the tiled floor. His head connected with a sink. I lost my balance as the boat rocked. That meant we were at sea.

Grandad kicked the sailor in the stomach. Then he grabbed his shirt, pulled him up, drew back his fist and landed another vicious blow, opening an ugly cut above his eye.

He roared into his face, 'Have you bloody seen him?'

But the sailor was already unconscious.

'I'm here,' I cried out, desperate to stop the beating.

Grandad spun round and came at me.

'What are you doing, you bloody idiot?'

Spittle flicked onto my face.

I tried to explain through the sobs.

'I wan-want . . . t-t-to b-be . . . w-with . . . you,' I sniffled.

He picked me up and hugged me, squeezing me tight, the muscles in his back and arms tense.

An alarm sounded, deafening in the confines of the Hood, *numbing my senses. Battle stations.*

I WOKE WITH A JOLT, Gran was already on her feet, looking out into the corridor for help. She didn't need to wait long. Nurses rushed past her and were soon joined by a doctor, who gave instructions to his team as other staff came to help. The alarm continued, disorientating me. I felt like I was in a dream. Or a nightmare. The heat of the room was overwhelming. Drugs were loaded into the syringe, Grandad's arm was gripped roughly and the injection was given. I hadn't realised at first that the man in charge was the consultant, the ghostly coat a cunning disguise.

'Let's get him to theatre,' he said.

We stood in the doorway as they rolled him down the long corridor and out of sight.

I reached out to hold the door frame as the world closed in, my vision narrowing, reducing until everything went black.

'COME, H, LET'S GO. We can tell the captain, get him to turn back.'

Grandad grabbed me.

We made our way aft, picking up waterproofs on the way. On the flag deck, we looked over the starboard side. The Hood *was heading into a full gale.*

'Jesus Christ!' said Grandad. 'It must be blowing 30 knots.'

Our escorts, unable to keep pace, had fallen back.

The Hood *was pounding her way straight into the wind at 27 knots, so the wind we were experiencing was around 60 knots. This is why she was nicknamed the navy's largest submarine.*

The foredeck was invisible. Waves were rolling over the bow and breaking on the forward gun turret. The spray was flying so high that it was almost clearing the spotting top. We hung on as the next wave was ripped apart by the bow and the spray lashed against the conning tower.

'How the bloody hell are they going to target anything in this?'

I followed Grandad's gaze. The guns of A and B turret were pointing full to port.

'To stop the barrels from filling with water,' Grandad said.

Behind us, off the starboard quarter, was another of our ships.

'That's the Prince of Wales.*' He pointed at her.*

The mood on the Hood *changed.*

'Something's up,' he said.

Men were running to their stations. Grandad stroked his beard and looked out to sea.

'They've spotted the Bismarck.*'*

The crew were released from the limbo of waiting. All the years of training and drills were distilled into the action of the next few hours.

Grandad looked out to sea. I followed his gaze, across the mountainous waves, the surface tortured by the wind, but saw nothing.

'When will we open fire?' I asked.

'Soon enough.'

The obvious reared its ugly, unwelcome head again.

'But so will they.'

We turned to watch the forward turrets follow the gun director as it attempted to find the range of the German ship. As we rose on the crest of a wave, I was just able to make out two grey smudges on the horizon. They disappeared as we dropped into the next trough.

'What's the other ship?' I asked.

'Prinz Eugen.'

I remembered it from the Airfix catalogue. I hadn't paid it much attention, but now its importance became clear. As the ships drew together, Grandad pointed out that they had a big advantage.

'Look at the angle they're closing at.'

How would that make a difference?

'Why does that matter?'

'Because they're coming in at a shallower angle than us. They can turn all four of their guns on the Hood. *We can only use the front guns. X and Y turret can't turn far enough to target them.'*

I looked at the aft gun turrets. They were turned full against their stops but still unable to point at the enemy.

'We need to go and tell the captain what's going to happen, Grandad. He can change course or something.'

'Come on, let's get up there,' he said, pulling me after him.

We climbed up the conning tower until we got to the compass platform. The voice pipes from all around the ship emerged here. As we entered the room, a voice came from one.

'Alarm starboard green 40.'

I was out of breath from the long climb. 'Captain!' I gulped in air. 'Captain.'

He held up his hand then replied into the pipe in a measured tone of voice.

'Pilot, make the enemy report.' Then into another pipe, he said, 'Twenty degrees to starboard.'

'Captain! Captain!'

I was determined to warn him of what was going to happen if he carried on, but he just ignored me. I moved forwards and pulled at his tunic.

'Captain, you've got to turn the ship before it's too late.'

He pushed me away and turned to Grandad.

'It's already too late. We all know how this turns out. You shouldn't have brought him with you, Jack. It's your fault he's here. There's nothing to be done about how this ends. It's your destiny to be here with your mates. But it's not his. I suggest you start to think about how you're going to get him out of it.' With that, he turned to one of the officers. 'If these men cause any trouble, throw them in the brig.'

The officer folded his arms and watched us as the captain continued his futile work.

We stood away from the action, separate and yet part of what was unfolding. This is what Grandad said was the best time of his life. What else had he said? He said it was like hea—

'All positions stand to.' The command came through the pipes.

This was the call to action. Everyone on the ship was at their stations. I looked at Grandad. He was watching the captain, willing him to make the right decisions. Another officer gave the instruction.

'Follow director.'

The huge gun turrets swung round as the rangefinder tracked the enemy on our new course.

'All guns load with armour-piercing and full charge.'

The gun crew responded without hesitation.

'Load, load, load!'

The rattles and bangs of the mechanisms delivering and loading the shells vibrated through our feet like the demonic music of a heavy metal orchestra. Then silence.

Moments stretched out as we held our breath, waiting.

The stillness was torn apart by the unmistakable roar of the 15-inch guns as they let loose their first salvo against the Prinz Eugen. *The* Prince of Wales *fired on the* Bismarck *a few seconds later.*

Relief swept through the ship. This was it – the waiting was over. She was going into battle for the first time.

After a few seconds, the Germans returned fire. The first shells from the Bismarck *fell short, the second went over us. We fired again, as did the* Prince of Wales. *We couldn't see how close our shells were landing, but we could theirs.*

The second salvo from the Bismarck *landed on both sides. Huge spouts of water shot up. The second salvo from* Prinz Eugen *found their target. One shell hit the* Hood *aft of us, somewhere on the boat deck.*

The shudder that swept through the ship knocked me to the floor and my ears rang as if in a giant bell. Feeling stupid and embarrassed, I stayed down to regain my senses, only then realising that everyone had been knocked off their feet. Grandad stood and helped me up. An officer went out onto the starboard wing as a voice came from the pipes.

'We've been hit at the base of the mainmast.'

'Grandad, do something,' I shouted.

'There's nothing to be done, H,' he said.

'You said you can make the world any shape you wanted it to be.'

He bent down.

'You said I could do anything I set my mind to,' I shouted in his face.

'Harry, you've got to understand. Most of the time you can do something.' He held my frightened gaze. 'And when you can, you must. It's your duty to do whatever you can to help.' He paused and shook his head. 'But sometimes the skill is in knowing when it's time to stop.'

Time slowed to a crawl as I looked at him, unable to bring myself to accept there was nothing we could do.

'Sometimes,' he added, 'the only thing you can do is save yourself.'

An officer returned to confirm the damage.

'She's hit us on the boat deck and there's a fire in the ready-use lockers.'

'That's where the 4-inch ammo and rockets are stored,' said Grandad, looking around to find a way out.

Before we moved, shells started to explode. The fire it caused poured out of the wound. Plumes of strange orange flames shot into the air, unlike any fire I'd ever seen. Fanned by the strong wind, the fire spread as rockets and ammo continued to detonate.

Another voice came through the pipes.

'The 4-inch ready-use ammunition is exploding.'

I could hear the screams of men from below decks filtering into the compass platform through the pipes. Then we heard the call feared by everyone on a ship.

'Fire! Fire!'

The screaming intensified as men shouted for help, crying out for the horror to stop. The moans of mortally wounded men filled my head. But it was only the start.

Grandad grabbed my arm and pushed me forwards. Pausing in the doorway, I looked back at the captain, who was still unperturbed by the surrounding horror.

I heard him give the command, 'Twenty degrees to port.'

The captain was trying to bring X and Y turrets into play.

Outside on the platform, I looked aft at the destruction as another salvo arrived. Shells whistled through the air, landing close by, shooting great geysers of water high into the air. The next hit the spotting top, sending debris and body parts raining down onto the boat deck.

We raced down an external staircase to join other men fleeing the firestorm. Almost immediately, another shell hit us at the base of the mainmast. The whole ship trembled. I'd just regained my footing, when there was an almighty explosion from within the hull. The deck opened up and a fireball shot into the air. The explosion engulfed the bridge in white flames and blew shrapnel across the ship.

We were protected by the armour around the 4-inch guns. A sailor next to me held his stomach. Blood seeped through his fingers, covering his hands. As he released the pressure to look at his wounds, his side opened up and his insides fell into his outstretched hands. I turned away and vomited.

Grandad shoved me forwards and we descended onto the flag deck. We headed to the port side, where the damage was least. The steel rail of the stairs onto the fo'c'sle deck was almost too hot to touch. Other sailors were heading the same way. We ran on as another explosion shot into the air behind us. Something hit me in the back, sending me sprawling on the deck. I was trapped. Something heavy lay across my legs. I looked over my shoulder at a man's shredded torso, screaming as I kicked myself free. Grandad grabbed me by the scruff of the neck and dragged me with him.

'Come on, H,' he said with grim determination.

I struggled to keep my footing as the ship listed to starboard. We stopped moving and waited. She heeled over about 20 degrees and we slid across the deck, coming to a stop when we came up against the superstructure.

'Hold on, H.'

She rested for a moment then slowly came back to an even keel.

'Thank Christ for that,' Grandad said, almost smiling.

But she didn't stop. She carried on rolling back the other way, on top of us.

We slid across the deck again, bracing ourselves by standing half on deck, half on the rail. She paused again at an angle of about 45 degrees, then more steadily, she continued to list further. I looked at Grandad, seeing the frustration on his face. For the first time in my life, I wondered if he knew what to do.

He thrust a lifejacket at me.

'Get that on.'

I fumbled with the last of the ties as he pushed me into the water. The cold shock paralysed me. Unable to breathe, I flailed my arms around, taking in mouthfuls of North Atlantic, the salty taste taking me by surprise.

'I'm in the sea, I'm in the sea.' I gasped in air and managed to regain some composure.

Grandad was shouting behind me. 'Swim away! Swim away!'

'Grandad!' I yelled, forcing myself to move, turning to see him. 'Grandad!'

Now screaming, I didn't recognise my own childish cries. I was just a kid, after all. Helpless again at the only time it mattered.

The Hood *loomed above Grandad, the main deck already awash, the towering superstructure, unstoppable, heading towards us. The conning tower was going to hit us if we didn't move fast.*

Grandad swam towards me, encouraging me on, willing me to move. There was nothing more he could do. I could swim faster on my own. Him helping me would only slow us both down.

The taste of fuel made me gag and the fumes stung my eyes. Whimpering at the thought of it catching fire, I redoubled my effort, but the work was too hard.

Exhausted, I stopped trying. I realised we weren't making progress, at least not fast enough. The spotting top was clear to see, its associated antenna and stays a tangled mess, large parts missing, the bare edges of torn steel 6-inches thick coming down on top of us. The devastation of the direct hit was clear to see.

I was swimming on my back, Grandad was behind me.

'Come on, Harry, faster!'

I slowed as his shouts continued, but he couldn't see what I could. That it was inevitable – the Hood *was going to take us down with her.*

Then there was another explosion inside the hull. The entire ship shuddered and the pace of her capsize sped up. There was nowhere left to go. We were going to be struck by the coning top.

I made one last feeble effort to swim away. But it was useless. Grandad raised his arm as the mast hit him and dragged him under. For a moment I was alone, treading water, unable to believe he'd gone.

An aerial hit me across my back. She rolled further and took me with her, dragged down under the water together. Explosions, the screams of men, the wind and waves, all stopped.

The grey-green water faded to black underneath me and the aerial flexed as I watched Grandad go down under the mast, looking up at me. As we continued down, the pressure in my ears sent stabbing pains through my head. Grandad was fighting to release himself.

I kicked and moved forwards. The aerial was now over the backs of my legs, but that was as far as I could move. Something else held me down.

I twisted and wriggled but I couldn't see which of the tangled mess of cables and rope was holding me. Each turn seemed to make it worse, no matter what I did. The bodies of sailors surrounded us, suspended in the opaque gloom, already succumbed to their fate. Soon we'd be with them on a slow journey to the ocean floor. The water was a peaceful cradle, rocking me to sleep.

Grandad wriggled free and swam to me then jerked to a halt, brought up short as another cable wrapped around him. He stopped struggling. For a few seconds, we just looked at each other, resigned to our watery end. He put his hand into his pocket, smiled and pulled out the flick knife from Malta. The blade, slowed by the water, opened, the faintest of clicks heard as it locked in position.

As he cut the wires that held me prisoner, I put my hand out to touch him. It must have been a trick of the light; I remembered something about things being bigger or at a different angle underwater, but he was too far away for me to reach. His knife sliced through the wires, one, two, three . . . how many more? He looked at the tangled mess, desperate to find what was keeping me there. Then I realised the wires weren't the problem. It was the suction from the bulk of the great ship that was dragging me down. This was it, then.

I looked at Grandad's face for the last time, his black hair swaying with the turbulence around us, the eternal blackness of the ocean his backdrop. We were done.

The void grew a little paler. A muffled explosion came from the Hood. *A brighter patch of sea rushed up to us.*

A giant cloud.

An explosion . . . in . . . a boiler?

A giant release below sent a huge plume of air towards the surface, past us, through us, taking us with it. We would be saved.

Up and up, faster and faster, like a cork from a champagne bottle, we rocketed upwards. I looked into the abyss but saw only bubbles.

I broke the surface, gasping for air. I looked around for Grandad, but the only thing I could see was the once-mighty Hood's *bow pointing skywards. A second later, it slipped away.*

I SAT UP IN THE CHAIR, my clothes soaked with sweat. It was over.

My confused mind took a moment to adjust to the dim light of the hospital room.

'We lost,' I said into the darkness.

Gran took my hand, 'I know love, I know.'

'Sometimes, H, all you can do is save yourself.' Grandad's words echoed inside me.

Alone in my bedroom I took the model of the *Hood* in both hands, raised it up high and brought it down on my knee, breaking it in half, pounding the pieces until the ship was unrecognisable, enjoying the pain in my hands as the plastic dug deep into the skin. I looked at the mess and wondered how it could ever be fixed.

Chapter 14

Wednesday, 9 April 1975

I stood at the top of the drive looking at the crowded scene. The street was lined with cars as far as I could see in both directions, except for the space immediately in front of the house. Couples walked from the Legion car park arm in arm. Wives picked fluff and hairs from the dark jackets of their husbands, brushing with unnecessary vigour, an outlet for their nervous energy. The curtains of all the neighbouring houses were closed, but nobody slept.

Groups of people congregated and broke apart, only to be absorbed into another cluster. Old friends who only met on days like these greeted each other with uncontrolled smiles before reigning in their happiness when the reality of the circumstances was remembered. Hands were shaken and held onto, clasped in both fists as if they were fearful of being released, some relishing the occasion, others desperate for it to be over, or at least for the bar to open. Like a tide, the movement was unhurried towards our house.

The men preferred it outside, keeping it all in, while the women went inside and let it all out.

Men nodded my way. Women looked at me with tight-lipped smiles and sad eyes, their heels clip-clopping on the steel manhole covers, trying to make it better by sheer willpower. Hushed tones turned to silence as two cars pulled up, gliding to a stop in imperceptible increments.

Men stepped out and straightened themselves before opening the rear door. Instructions were murmured before they raised Grandad onto their shoulders and walked towards me. Grandad would have nodded his approval at their immaculate suits and shoes polished 'so you could see your face in them'.

They passed me and I fell in behind them. People were moved aside by their bow wave as they ploughed cautiously through the crowded hall. I stood alone in the silent void created in their wake as they disappeared into the front room. The door closed and people talked again. After a few minutes, they emerged, leaving him alone. But not for long.

The lead bearer spoke to Gran in more muted tones and she walked towards me, took my hand.

'Shall we see him together?'

For the first time, I realised my gran was an old woman, slim and frail. The vitality she normally displayed had fallen away, revealing the truth of her ageing body, her spine already twisting, giving her a lopsided gait.

I looked around at the furniture, the carpet, the people, even the house itself. Everything seemed temporary, especially me. Her rheumatic fingers gripped my hand and we walked together. Aunty Joyce stopped dispensing drinks and looked on, wringing a tea towel around her hands, her red eyes willing things to be different, taking on more than her fair share of sadness, as a good friend will.

Every breath I took sounded like a sigh; it's not what he'd have wanted.

The door closed and the three of us were together again.

The coffin lid stood propped in the corner. I traced my finger over the engraved brass plaque: Jack Manning, 23 April 1902–31 March 1975. The room had been cleared of everything except a table holding a cluster of old photos of Grandad. His childhood, his marriage, his daughter, the war and me.

I looked at the figure lying in front of me. He was dressed in Grandad's suit, wore Grandad's shirt and tie, and was wearing his medals. He even had a beard just like Grandad's and I could smell the Brylcreem in his hair. His shoes were shiny like only a Grandad's can be.

Gran's tears smeared on my fingers as she wiped her face, still clutching my hand. She reached out and stroked his hair.

'Oh, Jack,' was all she said.

I stood with her and paid silent tribute to him, but inside I was screaming. '*That's not my grandad!*'

I remembered the dorado. I closed my eyes and held its supple body, struggling in my hands. I felt its rapid heartbeat weaken and watched its vibrant colours fade as it died, the flesh all that remained. I looked again at the shell that had once been my grandad. It was the only thing left of him here now. But I knew there must be somewhere that the rest of him was. It couldn't just be like the fish. I couldn't believe it just stopped.

Overwhelmed, I needed some fresh air. I made my way through the packed hall to the drive and leaned back on the workshop doors, breathing deeply, determined to avoid eye contact with anyone who might try to console me. Clouds of smoke rose from the groups of men gathered on the drive. Nervous fingers dislodged ash with an expert flick, the tiny grey cylinders falling to the ground in silent explosions. For the first time, I could see the benefit. Smoking gave you something to do when there was nothing to be done.

As soon as they arrived, they attracted attention. They were just different.

A ball of activity made its way up the street, weaving through the static groups, their energy building as they got closer. The men on the drive moved aside to let them through and three young men made their way towards me, one pushing another on the shoulder, the stumbling victim reacting with a slap from his chip bag hat, the third shaking his head in disbelief at the unruly behaviour. Their uniforms were like white wave crests in a black sea. Bell-bottomed trousers danced over their shining black shoes. They looked like they'd arrived straight from a night on the town, but as they got closer, the movement slowed and white clothes faded to dark blue and grey. Their faces, once flushed with youth, became the wrinkled reality of their old bodies. They came to rest in front of me, three old sailors. Their youthful features still occasionally washed across their faces like waves on a beach.

In the hall, Jonesy took off his gloves and offered me his warm grip. Enclosing my hand in both of his, he held my gaze, assessing me. Satisfied, he patted my arm as Joyce took their overcoats. They stood in their navy blazers, a modest collection of medals on display, the humble chain-entwined anchor shining on the blue berets. Connie discarded a bag and patted the colourful folds of the Union flag.

'For the coffin,' he said.

'Can we see him?' asked Digger.

I led them into the front room. Glasses chinked behind me as we passed the sideboard. Holding open the door, I let them pass, turning to leave.

'Harry.' Jonesy held out a glass. 'Come and join us.'

We stood in a small circle beside the coffin. Jonesy put his arm around me.

'Here, look.'

The men still enjoyed a conspiracy and we huddled together. Jonesy reached into his pocket and pulled out a bottle, holding it out for us all to see. The label had a picture of a black girl wearing a headband above the words Rhum Negrita.

'Old Nick,' I whispered.

We all stared at the bottle until Connie broke the spell.

'Come on, serve it up.' He nudged his old shipmate into action.

Jonesy distributed the drink in generous glugs. We stepped apart, faced Grandad and raised our glasses.

'To Jack,' declared Jonesy.

'To Jack,' we all repeated.

We clinked glasses. The liquor's heat and the company of the old sailors transported me back to the night out in Portsmouth. Envious of the bonds between them, I thought about my future. Would friends like this be there for me?

Jonesy looked at Connie.

'Where there's life, there's hope.'

'Where there's washing, there's soap,' Connie said to Digger.

Digger smiled at me. 'What can't speak, can't lie.'

'What can't walk,' I concluded, 'wheel it home in a barrow.'

They all looked at me and smiled.

'He's as daft as Jack,' said Connie.

Jonesy looked at me. 'No,' he said, looking serious. 'I think he could be dafter.'

The three men had a laugh at my expense, but that was fine with me. Even if I wasn't one of them, they'd allowed me close enough to warm myself in the glow of their friendship.

'Come on, lads, let's get him ready for action,' said Digger.

Connie unfolded the Union Jack. The other two picked up the coffin lid and fixed it in place with the brass screws. Digger stroked the oak, admiring the workmanship. I took one end of the flag from Connie and we draped it over the coffin. The funeral director's head appeared round the door and nodded. The four of us lifted Grandad onto our shoulders, manoeuvring him through the door with care. There were lots of sobs as we passed through the hall and onto the drive. Gran walked behind as we crossed the street to the Legion. There'd be no visit to church today.

Johnny Cash's 'I Walk the Line' faded as I stepped onstage and told the world about my grandad. Others told of the Jack Manning they'd known, in the navy, the Allotment Society, at work and from the club. To conclude, we sang the sailors' hymn, 'Eternal Father, Strong to Save', sung with gusto by the three sailors behind us.

The luxurious interior of the limousine seemed irrelevant. As the cortège pulled away, I looked back at our house. A figure was at the window. It must have been Aunty Joyce, who had stayed to clean up.

I held Gran's hand as the thick straps slid through the expert grip of the Co-op's men as they lowered the coffin into the neatly dug grave. Close by, mounds of earth were disguised with fake grass.

'That's the stuff the veg man on the market uses to trim his stall with,' said Grandad.

I concentrated on removing the smile he'd brought to my face.

Connie stepped forwards to throw a handful of dirt onto the coffin, timing his throws to perfection as Jonesy declared, 'Earth to earth, ashes to ashes, dust to dust.'

As we turned from the grave, the reality of a life without Grandad hit me and I cried for the first time.

'Come on, H,' said Grandad as I walked away from the grave. 'How did you think it was going to end?'

Chapter 15

06.30, Thursday, 24 April 1975

Spring was in full bloom. Gardens burst with colour and veg patches were soaking up the early morning April sunshine with their vibrant green foliage. The scene wasn't spoilt by the occasional garden piled with car parts or overgrown with nettles and brambles. Even the privet hedges looked good.

I increased the length of each step, warming up, the routine having helped my mind and body.

Smiling at myself, I realised this was the first day I'd felt happy since Grandad's funeral. The undertaker who had make the arrangements had stressed how important it was to do the right thing. He'd warned us that to make do, just to get it out of the way, was a mistake.

'It needs to be right,' he'd said, 'because if you look back at it and think you should have done more, it will live with you forever. Don't settle for anything less than what you know is right for him.' He'd looked at me. 'A lifetime is a long time to live with regret, lad.'

So we'd done the right thing. The music. The speeches. The rum-fuelled party in the Legion. And no church. Everything was as good as it could be. Even Frank Watson was involved, bringing the congregation to order for the toast – nobody was going to argue – before handing over to Jonesy for the traditional toast with a shot of Old Nick. I even downed it without coughing. Everyone had had a part to play as supporting actors in the Jack Manning show.

Mr Waddington, the undertaker, was right. When I look back at it now, I wouldn't do anything different. We did our best. We did enough. When it was all over, the undertaker came over to me.

'You've done him proud, lad. I'll be telling people about this'—he gestured to the throng—'for the rest of my career.'

It was as though Mr Waddington was channelling Grandad's words from . . . well, from who knows where. He didn't believe in God; he wasn't just doubtful, he was certain. His explanation was that different cultures believed different things at different times. 'If any are "the true faith", what are the chances of it being ours?' When he laid it out like that, it was hard to disagree. But for Gran, it was simple. It was real. She didn't need to question it. For me, I like the idea that he'll spend eternity on the *Hood* with his mates, sailing through 'the happiest time of his life'. If that's not heaven, I don't know what is.

I stretched out my stride and picked up speed, registering the moment when walking fast becomes running. I've got to the stage already where I can get myself going and put my mind elsewhere. Often with Grandad, or Jane Fellowes!

To say I thought a lot of him or about him would be an understatement beyond compare. The house felt empty. Gran didn't even try to compensate for his absence. How could she? She misses him just like I do. Gran did her best, looking after me, providing all that I required. Grandad hadn't just given me what I wanted – he made sure I got what I needed, even when I didn't know I needed it. Not by buying me things. Gran fed my body, he fed my imagination.

My breathing settled into the hypnotic rhythm that I can keep up for an hour, so far.

Grandad was a beggar for mixing fact and fiction. I'd spent endless hours going through his photo album, remembering the stories. I'd found some more photos in the bottom of the strongbox, among them a photo of Jonesy sat on the same horse, in the same pose as Grandad's picture. On the back, it read: Montevideo 1940. The horse and I were both stuffed.

A couple of days later, I was talking to Gran and I asked if she'd known him when he had the Jag. She looked at me and shook her head.

'You're as daft as him.'

Turns out, for the first ten years of their marriage, he'd only had a pushbike. The Daimler-powered Yorkshire Traction buses were as close as he got to a Jag. But then there was the swimming medal, never mentioned before those final few days. Just like the *Hood*, it was a story he needed to tell. Unlike many men who fought in the war, the unimaginable horror couldn't stay locked inside him. The stories were too good. Irresistible.

He had a knack, the ability to blend the truth with fiction. I don't know how he learnt it, or where. Maybe it was a gift from the god he didn't believe in. Whatever it was, it worked. When he told a story, I was there with him. In the moment, on the *Hood*, or in the Jag. He could bring the story to life like a master.

They did what they thought was best, shielding me from the diagnosis until the truth couldn't be hidden any longer. The cancer was aggressive and had spread. The decline, so quick and so brutal, was horrendous. Dr Crowther was fantastic, visiting every day, doing all that he could to make the inevitable a little easier to bear. He gave us some time with Grandad that we wouldn't have had if he'd gone into hospital. My school was understanding, too, giving me whatever time off I needed. We all did our best. Including him.

I left the estate and ran into the countryside. It was a meditation and keep fit-routine . . . well, more of a get-fit routine. The revelation that physical exercise could have such a beneficial effect on my state of mind still made me smile.

I'd decided I was going to try for the marines. Digger had told me they made the officers run everywhere during their training, so that's where I thought I'd start. Not that I thought I'd get a commission; it was just something to latch on to.

A mallard mother quacked at her brood, encouraging them away from the threat as I turned onto the towpath and into the shade of the muck stack. She relaxed in a flurry of wings on the far bank as I splashed my way through the puddles that never dried up.

Grandad's memory hadn't faded, but the sadness had, a little. He'd reassured me many times that 'everything will be alright in the end, and if it's not alright, it's not the end'. I'd got a plan and felt as though I were on my way.

The collie sheepdog emerged from under the bridge, the owner still out of sight. Racing at full pelt, ears flat, he circled me, banking at an impossible angle. Getting closer with each lap, he brushed against my leg, forcing me to slow. Fearful of stepping on him, I stuttered to a halt. His pale blue eyes held my gaze as I stroked his face and his rough tongue licked my fingers as he nuzzled into my hand. He squirmed around my legs as I scratched his ears and tickled his ribs. This was the first time I'd been this close to a dog, and it was thrilling. It was the same breed as the one . . .

'He's not usually that friendly with strangers.'

The owner's voice echoed off the stonework as he walked from under the bridge, but there was still no mistaking who it belonged to. I looked around, anxious, hoping to find someone else, but we were alone. I stood and faced him, but Watson seemed oblivious to my fear. I could sense the dog's confusion at my sudden lack of interest. He changed sides and sat next to his owner. Watson's hand dropped to the dog's head and played with his ears.

'I heard about your grandad,' he said, looking at the dog.

The dog's eyes narrowed.

He lifted his head. 'My dad said he was a good bloke.'

I nodded. 'He was.' I held his gaze for a moment, then turned to walk away.

'I was jealous of you when I found out your dad had died.'

The words hit my back. Unable to penetrate, they fell into the dirt.

'What?' I turned, my curiosity overwhelming my desire to leave.

'I was jealous.'

'What *are* you on about? Why?'

'I wish my dad would die so I could live with my grandad.'

'You never know what goes behind closed doors,' whispered Grandad.

The dog cocked his head to one side, sensing the mood change.

'What's his name?' I asked.

'Wilf Newman,' he said with a half-smile.

'Not your grandad, the . . .'

I heard Grandad groan.

'I know,' he said. 'He's called Hitler.'

'Hitler,' I repeated, helpless as the trapdoor opened.

'Manning,' said Watson, 'how daft are you?'

'Dafter than me.' Grandad finally conceded defeat.

'What kind of nutter would call his dog Hitler?' Watson asked.

It was tempting to point out that he was that kind of nutter, but I came to my senses before I signed my death warrant.

'He's called Rommel,' he said.

I wasn't going to fall for it a third time.

'No,' Grandad agreed, 'being made to look like a pillock twice in less than a minute is more than enough.'

I looked at Watson for clues to the truth.

'He's called Rommel,' he repeated, not a sign of emotion to work with.

'After the German tank commander, Field Marshal Erwin—'

'Rommel,' he confirmed. 'The Desert Fox.'

I looked at Rommel. He looked like a Rommel.

'It's a good name.'

The dog yawned then lay down, chin on paws, bored with the conversation. Maybe he'd heard it all before.

'It would be if he was a German shepherd, or a fox, you plonker. His name's Monty.'

'I'm glad you decided not to be duped again, H,' Grandad said.

Monty's eyes lit up at the sound of his name.

'Where are you going?' asked Watson.

I pointed in the direction he'd come from, still wary of a trap.

'Come on,' he said, bending to pick up a stick and throwing it for Monty.

Calmed by Monty's presence in a way I didn't understand, I followed.

As we walked along the towpath, Watson told me about his grandad's time as one of Field Marshal Montgomery's Desert Rats. The sky was clear but we walked in the shade. I let my hand run through the long grass until I spotted a choice stalk, gripping it and plucking it out. The grass squeaked as I extracted the pale inner stem from its green sheath. Monty gambled around us, fetching the stick that Watson repeatedly threw for him.

'How long does it take to train a dog?'

'It depends on the breed and its personality. Some dogs are a lot brighter than others.'

I thought only a person could have a personality, but he seemed to know what he was talking about.

'Monty's five and I'm still training him. The brighter they are, the longer it can take.'

'How come?' Maybe it was just his excuse to explain away his shortcomings as a dog trainer.

'Because there's more stuff they can learn,' he said, not pointing out that it was obvious, but I knew that's what he meant.

'What's his best trick?' I asked.

'It's not about doing tricks,' he said. 'It's about training him to obey commands, getting him to stay when he wants to be up and about. They're really smart. That's why farmers use them as sheep-dogs.'

I could see the intelligence in his eyes, but I was still disappoint-ed to hear it wasn't about doing tricks.

'He's not a pure Collie, but that's the main bit. Watch this,' he said as we paused.

Watson made a high-pitched whistle, just like the farmers did on *One Man and His Dog*. It was impressive. I could only whistle us-ing my fingers. Monty stopped, dropping his stick. Watson whistled again and Monty lay down. Then Watson issued a guttural, 'Ear-ba.' Monty came running towards us at full pelt. At the last moment, he jumped. Watson turned his shoulder to him as Monty launched him-self. Watson's strength was clear to see as the dog sprang off his back, pushing against the dog's weight. Before he landed, it seemed Monty was jumping again, this time into Watson's arms.

'Okay,' he said, 'some of it is about tricks.'

The narrow canal opened up into 'the cut', the dead-end of the waterway. The top of the pit's muck stack was silhouetted against the rising sun. Conveyor belts from the mine head dribbled more spoils onto the pile. The mine's winding gear looked down on us, the re-flection on the water ruined by the wind playing across the surface. Once, this was a bustling port. The old, rusted iron mooring rings still hung from the quay wall. Now it was just a place to fish. We walked on.

'What are you going to do when you leave?' asked Watson. Be-fore I had a chance to reply, he added, 'I can't wait to get out of here.'

'Where are you going?' I laughed.

His expression set to concrete. I'd misjudged him.

'I'm going in the army,' he said, as if I were an idiot for asking. 'I'm going to join the paras.'

Shamefaced by my stupidity, I fell silent. Why was I surprised that Watson had ambitions I didn't know about? Why not go in the army? If I could do anything, maybe he could, too.

As an offering, I gave him the chance to ridicule me by confessing, 'Grandad wanted me to go in the marines.'

'Do it, Manning,' he said without hesitation. 'Is that why you've started running?'

'Yeah.' I looked away, embarrassed, but not knowing why.

'Even the navy's got to be better than this shithole,' he winked and I relaxed.

The cut was deserted. At the weekend, it would be busy with fishermen and kids trying to catch sticklebacks with the net they got on the club trip, taking them home in a jam jar. The shadow of a dozen ghostly barges passed across the water's surface. I bet the men thought they'd work on them forever. I looked up at the winding gear. How long would the pits stay open? What would it be like to live here all of your life? When Grandad had shown me so much more . . .

'Come on,' said Watson, 'it's time to move on.'

He was right, it was.

Monty ran ahead, splashing through the muddy puddles. Surprised at my lack of discomfort in Watson and Monty's company, I smiled as I bent to pick up a stick, almost knocking heads with Watson as he had the same idea. Monty turned to see what was happening then backed away, his front feet bouncing, keen to start the stick game again.

The three of us followed its arc as Watson launched it high in the air. Monty's eyes locked on the target. The stick landed and cartwheeled. His head bobbed in synch with its erratic movement, ready to pounce. The stick did one final somersault, high and to the left. Monty jumped, twisting in mid-air, grabbing the stick. But his momentum took him off the path and into the water. We sprinted forwards to see him swimming around, the stick still held in his mouth.

'He's good at the doggy-paddle,' I said as the dog swam around at the bottom of the sheer stone wall.

Watson looked around, unimpressed by my joke.

'He can't get out,' he whispered.

I raised my arm and I was about to point to the far corner of the old harbour. My jaw opened but stayed there as Watson jumped in. He resurfaced, flicking his head around. He seemed surprised to find himself in the water. Monty was still playing, swimming around Watson with his prize. I crouched and smiled as they splashed around. Monty broke off and headed for the broken wall on the opposite bank. Watson seemed to make a big deal of treading water.

'Follow Monty,' I said.

I pointed to the other side, but the gurgled reply from Watson was simply, 'can't swim.'

The dark green water discoloured his skin as he sank. I looked around for help, my gaze lingering on a post where a lifebuoy had once hung.

'Bollocks.'

For a moment I was motionless, unable to rid my brain of the thought that if I did nothing, the 'Watson problem' would end. All I had to do was nothing. Easy.

'Mmm . . .' Grandad stared into the still water with me. 'Not an easy thing to live with, H,' he said.

I thought through my options.

'Oh,' Grandad said, 'you think you've got options?'

I kicked my trainers onto the grass and jumped. As I fell through the air, I registered Watson's head, just visible through the murk, his face turned upwards.

The freezing water gave me an instant headache. I fought the tightness in my chest and took several deep breaths before diving. But Watson had vanished.

The pain in my ears built. I held my nose and blew to equalise the pressure. Twisting round as I went down, I looked for any sign of him. The disturbed sediment rushed at my eyeballs like snowflakes in headlights. I was running out of breath and he wasn't here.

'He definitely is here, H.' Grandad's sarcastic tone was undiluted by the water.

I widened the arc of my circles, like a dog chasing an increasingly long tail. There was a dull recognition that I wasn't cold any more.

'That's probably not a good thing, H.'

My search took me deeper into the gloom. I saw a lighter patch of water and made my way over. Watson sat slumped in the mud, like a puppet with its strings cut. I grabbed him by the scruff of the neck and kicked off the bottom. We didn't move.

My feet sank into the mud and I panicked, releasing a series of undignified aquatic whimpers. Kicking out, I wriggled, desperate to free myself from the sludge, sending up clouds of muck. I felt the grip of the mud loosen and we headed up. We broke the surface and I grabbed Watson around the neck, swimming on my back, holding his head clear of the water.

'What sort of chuffing idiot jumps into the water when he can't chuffing swim?' I cursed into his ear. 'You thick pillock!'

A gurgling sound came from deep inside him.

Swimming through the water with Watson was easier than I expected. I couldn't imagine what it would be like if he were putting up a struggle.

'I should have just let you drowned,' I told him.

Relief swept over me as the stones from the collapsed wall dug into my back. Scrambling from under him, Monty's warm panting breath on my neck, I wedged my stockinged feet between the stones, ignoring the pain of unseen debris digging into my skin. I pulled Watson's still body over the slime-covered boulders. Clear of the water, I turned him face down, pressing on his back.

'It's not a cartoon,' said Grandad. 'You'll not be able to pump the water out of him.'

I rolled him onto his back, hitting his chest in frustration.

'It's not Stan Laurel. He's not going to spurt it out like a whale. You're going to have to give him the kiss of life.'

'Bugger that,' I said, thumping his chest for punctuation.

He coughed, turned over and puked. The warm, repulsive contents of his guts spilled over my lap.

'Oh, you dirty bastard.' I pushed him off me.

The sick ran down the side of his face. He coughed again and opened his eyes.

'There's no need to swear,' he said.

As the sun cleared the top of the muck stack, we sat together, shivering. Monty sat between us, no longer interested in his stick. Like us, he knew the game was over.

Chapter 16

Monday, 26 June 1978

I unfolded the paper, sat at the table and waited. The *Chronicle* had nothing newsworthy. I looked at Grandad's wristwatch: eight forty. I folded the paper and sipped my tea. The watch was a constant reminder of him. I remembered the headlines from three years earlier: *Hood* Survivor Loses Final Battle. The paper had told the story of Grandad's survival of the *Hood's* sinking in 1941 and his fight against cancer. The fight he couldn't win.

My training preparation had got more serious when I started training with Watson. We pushed each other. Well, the truth was, in the beginning, it was him pushing me. In the summer of my fifteenth year, I hit a growth spurt and made up some of the difference between us. Now, at sixteen, the work we'd put in was hopefully going to pay off.

Watson had left school at Easter, foregoing the embarrassment of failing his exams. He was halfway through his basic training with the paras by now. I should have done the same, but Gran persuaded me to stay on at school until the summer results finally confirmed my lack of academic ability. I cringed at the thought of handing over my CSE certificates, a feeble collection of grade 3s and 4s, to the recruitment officer. But hopefully, if the information I'd collected was true, I was in the right place to extract any worth that may be latent within me. I hoped so.

I looked at my watch: eight fifty-two. I didn't expect I'd become a killing machine – I'd leave that to Watson. But maybe there was a place for me. Despite Grandad's encouragement, the tedious bullying from Watson hadn't ignited the desire to fight back. It didn't make me want to retaliate; it made me want to help.

My skill seemed to be a capacity to connect with people, whoever they were. Maybe that would be useful somewhere. My other interest seemed a little obscure and I was nervous even thinking about mentioning it. I opened the booklet again and stared at the picture that had finally shown me what I wanted to aim for. The pair stared back at me.

I looked at the second hand as it swept towards nine o'clock. As the hand struck the hour, I glanced at the shopfront across the street. The closed sign flipped to open. I drained the last of my tea, gathered my things and headed across the road.

I paused, my hand on the handle.

'Second thoughts, H?'

'No.'

'I'm proud of yeh, you know.'

'You too,' I told him as I pushed the door and stepped inside.

'Hey, look after my watch, H. There's some rough buggers in there, you know.'

I closed the door and looked around. The images showed the best on offer. Ships, helicopters, and tanks competed for my attention. I walked over to the desk. The officer looked up.

'How do I become one of those?' I held out the photograph of the Royal Marine commando kneeling beside the Alsatian. The officer started to speak, but I cut in, anticipating the gag. 'That one . . .' I pointed at the soldier.

He smiled and opened a drawer. He took out a form and clicked the top of his pen.

'Well, let's start with a few details, shall we. What's your name?'

I held out my hand. 'The name's Manning, Harry Manning.'

Epilogue

'DAD! DAD!'

I turned to the voice. Emily is halfway through the hatch, delivering a mug of tea. She waves a KitKat at me and sits in the loft, her legs dangling through the hatch.

'Are we sharing?' she asks.

I crawl over to join her and watch her struggle with the new plastic wrapper.

'Some things just aren't as good as they used to be.' I point at the packaging.

'Some things are better, though,' she claims, arms outstretched, smiling, offering herself up as evidence.

She snaps the KitKat in two. I know she's right. I take my share and watch in horror as she dunks her half into my tea. She stares at me, going cross-eyed, holding it there for the chocolate to melt.

She takes a bite. 'By the way,' she says, slurping up the molten chocolate but still getting it down her chin, 'that's twenty pence you owe me!'

HMS Hood

06:03, 24 MAY 1941

The final blow from the German battleship, *Bismarck*, was delivered and the *Hood* was sunk. Of the 1,418 men on board, only three survived. Able Seaman Robert Tilburn (1921–1995), Midshipman William John Dundas (1923–1965) and Ordinary Signalman Ted Briggs (1923–2008).

The method, by which Harry Manning is saved, reflects the experience of Ted Briggs.

Ordinary Seaman Jack Manning was my fictitious fourth survivor.

For more information about the *Hood*, including links to resources, please visit chrispearsall.co.uk or find me on social media, chrispearsallwriter.

Acknowledgements

IT HAS TAKEN A LONG time, nearly four years, to get this book into the world. Throughout that time I've had fantastic support from family and friends, including my daughters Emmaline and Rosie, along with my partner Allison who have patiently suffered the outpouring of ideas and have consistently encouraged me to continue when I was sure I'd had enough. My best mates Digger and Mark were also subjected to more than their fair share of my ramblings. Their friendship is testament to their belief in me and my story. I would also like to thank William Taylor for his tolerant, measured and wise words, and for providing me with employment to allow the project to continue. My thanks also to James Lovett for his inspirational encouragement and for introducing me to my editor, Claire Dean. Lastly, Tim Allen whose judicious counsel I am always keen to seek.

Printed in Great Britain
by Amazon